BATTLE OF QUANG TRI, 1972

UNDAUNTED VALOR
BOOK 4

MATT JACKSON

MATT JACKSON BOOKS

"Will give the reader insight into one of the pivotal battles of the Vietnam War. Matt's work putting this together was prodigious. I don't know how he did it. As a historical novel, I think it is great."

— GENERAL WALTER E. BOOMER
UNITED STATES MARINE CORPS, (RET)

INTRODUCTION

This historical novel is based on actions, discussions and events that occurred during the spring, summer and fall of 1972, when North Vietnamese forces attacked into South Vietnam on four fronts. This became known as the Easter Offensive of 1972. This novel focuses only on the northern-most battle, the battle for Quang Tri.

Some have stated that this was the last American battle of the Vietnam War. I disagree. There were no major US ground forces left in South Vietnam at the time. South Vietnamese ground forces were not under the command of US officers, and the leadership and the decision-making were all on the South Vietnamese generals. American involvement consisted of providing US Marine Corps advisors to the Vietnamese Marine Corps battalions and brigades. The US Army provided advisors to the South Vietnamese Army at brigade and higher levels, but not at the battalion level except in the Vietnamese Airborne and Ranger units. The US also provided limited helicopter support from both the US Army and US Marine Corps. Extensive close-air support and B-52 support was provided and was a major factor in preventing the North

Vietnam Army from being more successful. Naval gunfire was employed where it could be used along the coast.

I have written his novel as a small tribute to those American servicemen, officer and enlisted, that gave so much to come to the aid of this fledgling democracy. The determination, courage, loyalty and discipline of these service members should be recognized. Therefore, in many cases I have used the real names of those that participated, extracting their names from public, noncopyrighted sources. In some cases, I was able to contact several and discuss the events of those days. Unfortunately, time is taking its toll on many of us that served in the Southeast Asian theater back then. I hope that I have achieved my goal and honored them.

Created by Matt Jackson through Infidun,LLC
(www.infidiun.net)

1

POLITBURO

1 MAY 1971
Politburo
Hanoi, North Vietnam

The 19th Plenum of the Central Committee of the Vietnam Workers Party had been scheduled weeks in advance. Originally founded in 1930, the Communist Party of Vietnam had been the sole political party in the Democratic Republic of Vietnam since 1954. Over the years, the Communist Party of Laos and Cambodia had been folded into the Communist Party of Vietnam, only for the latter to be split into three parties in the late 1950s, but with Hanoi retaining the right to override the activities of the other two parties. Today, throughout the communist world, it was International Workers Day, so everyone had the day off. The cold winter was coming rapidly to a close and people were out enjoying the warm sun and clear skies. Absent since 1968 were the white contrails high above of the American B-52 bombers unloading their cargo of 750-pound bombs. For the most part, things were relatively quiet for a city choked with motor scooters, three-wheeled taxis, and bicycles. To this group of men, a day off didn't register. Important matters had to be discussed. Le Duan,[1] General Secretary of the Central Committee of Communist Party of Vietnam, had assumed the leadership with the death of Ho Chi Minh and even before his death had been running the show. Born in Quang Tri Province of what would become South Vietnam, he had become enthralled with communism while working as a railway clerk in the 1920s. He had been a founding member of the Indochina Communist Party in 1930. When Duan called for a meeting, no one questioned why; they just came. Other members that were seated around the large conference room table were Pham Van Dong, Prime Minister of North Vietnam; Ton Duc Thang, President of North Vietnam but in actuality a figurehead at most; Nguyen Van Lin, General Secretary of Vietnam; and Truro'ng Chinh, the number-three man in the Politburo. Military officers also present were General Hoang Van Thai, general staff member; General Van Tien Dung, Chief of Staff, PAVN; General Hoan Minh Thao, Commander PAVN Forces; and General Vo Nguyen Giap.

Once everyone was settled, Duan surveyed the room. Satisfied that everyone was present, he began. "Comrades, the ARVN advance into Laos has been stopped and their forces rooted out. Little damage was done to our supply sites around Tchepone. Some damage was done to the Ho Chi Minh Trail, but nothing that cannot be quickly repaired, which is happening as we speak. The Americans are continuing to withdraw their forces, which will continue as their presidential election draws near in November of next year. The South Vietnamese forces did not acquit themselves very well in the Lam Son 719 offensive. But they did prove their heavy reliance on American airpower," Duan said, scanning the room as he spoke. Blank stares were returned.

"I believe, as does General Giap," Duan continued, acknowledging the general with a nod, "that we may have destroyed or seriously hurt the best of the ARVN forces in the Lam Son 719 operation. With the American drawdown, the ARVN forces may be stretched very thin," Duan indicated as he picked up a piece of paper and paused as if reading it. "I have a communication from Le Duc Tho.[2] He is concerned that the Americans and the South Vietnamese will take a hard position at the next round of talks because of the outcome of Lam Son 719. He and I have some other concerns as well. This protracted campaign has not produced the results that we had hoped for. Small-unit operations are not giving us significant military gains or curbing the pacification program. The strength of the National Liberation Front is declining and will require a greater effort on our part.[3] The South Vietnamese forces are finding and destroying their cache sites, their headquarters, their hospitals. The local populations are turning more to the central governments than the National Liberation Front. The situation in Cambodia with the loss of the Port of Sihanoukville is creating serious logistical problems in that arena. As the Americans continue to withdraw from the theater, we are being deprived of political and strategic leverage. America is making progress in enhancing their relationships with the Soviet Union and China, which could easily threaten our sources for military supplies. We have got to reverse these trends. Le Duc Tho is asking if we could do something to discourage their enthusiasm. What are your recommendations?" Duan asked.

Silence hung in the air, but only for a moment before Truro'ng Chinh spoke up. "I believe we should continue on the path that we have been following and rebuild here in the north. Since the American bombing campaign stopped two years ago, we have had time to improve our infrastructure, rebuild our bridges and our roads. We have committed enough of our sons to assist the south and it is time for them to shoulder the burden of this campaign."

"That course of action does nothing to move us closer to achieving our goal of reunification," General Giap said hotly. General Giap was the mastermind behind the Tet Offensive of 1968. "We are committing our forces without achieving our goals. Guerrilla warfare is appropriate when one does not have strength but does have time. We have had time, but the longer we wait, the more I fear that the South will grow stronger as they have realized their weakness as well and will be seeking more in the way of aircraft for themselves. Lam Son 719 demonstrated that the ARVN soldier is as good as our soldiers and has equipment comparable to ours. Their junior officers and noncommissioned officers are good leaders. Their weakness is in their senior officers. They showed their inability to work together, their political alliances, and their incompetence. Right now, we have an opportunity, as the opinion of the American public will not allow for American ground forces to be reintroduced to the region. To do so would be political suicide for the American President when he has an election year approaching," General Giap outlined. There was a moment of silence again as each member digested Giap's comments.

Giap had been the military strategist for the North for many years. He lacked formal military training but had been a history teacher at a private French school. He had studied the military leaders of the past and put that knowledge to use. He had fought against the Japanese when they'd occupied Southeast Asia in World War II, rising quickly in the ranks of the Viet Minh. At the war's end, he had been the military leader of the Viet Minh and close to Ho Chi Minh. As the French returned to Southeast Asia and attempted to reestablish their dominance in the region, Giap led the forces of Vietnam and soundly defeated the French forces at Dien Bien Phu. The next day, France announced the withdrawal of all forces from Southeast Asia. However, his campaign in Tet of 1968 had not achieved the military victory that had been expected. It was a psychological victory, especially when the renowned American journalist Walter Cronkite had declared on a nightly TV news broadcast that the only rational way for the United States to end the war in Vietnam was "to negotiate, not as victors, but as an honorable people who lived up to their pledge to defend democracy, and did the best they could."[4] Giap and others had been expecting the 1968 Tet Offensive to lead to the over-throw of the South Vietnam government. As a result, Giap had lost some of his political power.

"What do you propose, General?" Truro'ng Chinh challenged Giap, already having a good idea that Giap was going to take the same position he had for the past three years.

"I propose an all-out invasion of the South. We have considerable forces that have never been committed. We have tanks from the Soviets and Chinese as well as long-range artillery. They could be committed under an air-defense umbrella that would easily challenge any air support the ARVN may receive. In our recent meeting with the Chinese delegation at the end of March, Yeh Chien-ying, Deputy Chairman, Central Committee's Military Commission, along with Chiu Hui-tso, their chief of staff for rear services, departed with a list of additional equipment we would like to have. They expressed optimism that much of what we requested would be delivered, and it is flowing to us now as we speak. Although the American President went to China between 21 February and 27 February of this year, China views our struggle as their struggle against imperialism in Southeast Asia. They see us as the front lines and themselves as the supplier. Of course, they are competing with the Soviets, who also want to gain our favor and support. I propose that we take whatever equipment we can get and launch a major offensive next year against the South that will end this conflict," Giap said with emphasis on the last three words spoken.

"Why next year?" Duan asked. "Why not wait until 1973, when all American forces will be out of Vietnam?"

"We could wait, but there are several advantages to launching sooner. First, waiting will provide the leadership in the South time to become more proficient in controlling operations. They proved incompetent in Lam Son 719. Second, it will give the South time to enhance their equipment and train on the new equipment that the Americans are leaving and providing. Third, a defeat at this time will embarrass the Americans as they will be associated with this defeat. They have removed most of their ground forces and will be an even smaller force of maybe one hundred thousand if they continue their withdrawal. Those will be mostly, as the Americans say, cooks, bakers and candlestick makers and not combat-hardened troops. Fourth, it will strengthen our position at the Paris talks," Giap explained.

Truro'ng Chinh retorted, "This is a war that should be waged by the People's Liberation Front of Vietnam and not by our forces. Since the failure of Tet in 1968, we have carried the fight. We have lost almost one hundred thousand young men in maintaining something that the People's Liberation Front should be doing but has not been able to due to the losses they suffered in Tet in 1968. They have now had two, almost three years to recover from that debacle and should be able to resume. We have no need to cast our young men into this effort." Chinh was attempting to control his emotions.

Not voiced was the fact that Giap had already discussed this subject with Duan prior to the meeting and right after the Chinese delegation had departed. The Chinese offer of equipment was just too good to pass up and would provide the capability to face the ARVN forces with overwhelming force.

No one was eager to speak. Finally, Duan broke the ice. "General Giap, please develop a plan of action on how you believe that an invasion to the south could be achieved. Please provide as much detail as you can and the reasons you feel success would be in our favor as well as what weaknesses we will face. Can you have that by December for us to review?" Duan expressed.

"I can do that," General Giap said, nodding slightly to Duan.

"Does anyone object to exploring this course of action?" Duan asked, knowing full well no one would. "Good, let us table the matter until General Giap enlightens us on it."

On that note, everyone stood and began leaving the room. Chinh's supporters, although few in number, gathered around him as he departed. Giap eased up to General Van Tien Dung and motioned for him to stay behind. Once they were alone, Giap motioned for them to sit.

"I have asked you to stay behind as I want to discuss this with you before we get too far along," Giap started.

"Certainly, General. I look forward to many discussions with you on this subject. I suspect you feel strongly about this Soviet type of action versus the guerrilla actions that have been the Chinese way," Dung responded.

"I think if we continue to expect the People's Liberation Army to conclude this war, we will be here until—how do the Americans say? Until hell freezes over. This slow prodding is slowly draining our resources and does not give us any strength at the peace negotiations, and the next time the People's Liberation Army gets mutilated as they did in 1968, they will drag us right back into doing the fighting for them. A powerful conventional invasion is the way to end this," Giap stated.

"I agree with you, and you will have my full support," Dung indicated with a smile.

"I was hoping you would say that. I do have one thing I would like you to do," Giap said as he moved to the front of his chair. "I will gladly plan the operation, but I would like you to command and lead the operation. I lost a great deal of status with the failure of the Tet Offensive, and Chinh's supporters will not support this plan at all if I'm in command. If you command the operation, that will remove this obstacle," Giap explained. Dung thought about it for a minute.

"If you plan it, I will command it, and together we will end this," Dung stated as he stood and extended his hand to Giap.

2

DISSATISFACTION

1 MAY 1971
Oval Office, White House
Washington, D.C.

The Washington, D.C., weather was delightful. Spring had brought pleasant temperatures and just the right amount of rain. The cherry blossoms had appeared right on schedule along with the beginning of the tourist season. A few demonstrators prowled the Mall, but not like last year with the riots on college campuses. Even the mood in Washington was pleasant. The drawdowns announced and continuing in Vietnam were the reason. The public wanted the United States out of Vietnam, and that was occurring. Increased pressure to end the draft was being applied, although it had not happened yet.

President Richard Nixon had implemented a policy of Vietnamization, turning the fighting over to the South Vietnamese Army with US air and naval support as well as military advisors. The 1st Air Cavalry Division had already left Vietnam for the most part, leaving one brigade behind in the

III Corps area north of Saigon. The 101st Airborne Division was located in the north and scheduled to depart along with the one brigade of the 1st Air Cavalry Division in the first quarter of 1972. The last unit, the 196th Light Infantry Brigade, would leave in the second quarter of the year. Some Army Aviation units would remain a bit longer in-country, flying lift and resupply as well as air cavalry reconnaissance and fire support. Overall, total US strength had been reduced from a high of 550,000 to 240,000 by May 1, 1971.

Secretly, the Nixon administration continued the talks with North Vietnam in Paris and even had Henry Kissinger, the National Security Advisor, travel to North Vietnam to discuss a possible peace treaty. Today Kissinger was seated with Secretary of Defense Melvin Laird, Ron Ziegler, the White House Press Secretary, General Earle Wheeler, Chairman of the Joint Chiefs of Staff, and the President.

"Mr. President, I met with Le Duc Tho and we discussed the possibilities before us," Kissinger stated.

"Did you ask him about his cache sites around Tchepone in Laos and the supplies and equipment he's pouring into Vietnam?" the President snapped.

"We spoke of that operation that the South Vietnamese government calls Lam Son 719. He was displeased that the South Vietnamese forces launched such an attack. But he was more disappointed at his army's poor performance, even when they had intelligence telling them that an attack was imminent," Kissinger acknowledged.

"Well, the South Vietnamese performance was no better. The press photos of South Vietnamese soldiers running away from the battle, hanging from the helicopters in fear for their lives, tossing their weapons down and running from the fight —pure cowards!" the President fumed.

"Mr. President," Secretary Laird interrupted, "let's be fair about this. Soldiers under constant pressure will break at some point. Those soldiers had been in direct combat for almost forty days when they began to withdraw, and not by helicopter. They started walking out of Tchepone to LZ Sophie. Only when they were surrounded, low on ammunition, without any fire support, did they begin to panic. You will recall even our own soldiers in the initial days of the Battle of the Bulge left the battlefield in a panic. The difference is that the press wasn't there in those opening days of the Bulge to instantly report what was happening, unlike today, when it makes the nightly news."

"Well, dammit, Ron, why can't we keep the press out of the operational areas?" the President asked, his frustration level still running high.

Ron Ziegler was caught off guard by the question. "Mr. President, the South Vietnamese government would have to place restrictions on the press's movement in Vietnam. If it had been a US action, then General Abrams could have limited access to the press, but Lam Son 719 was a Vietnamese operation," Ron confessed.

"Everything that happens in that country militarily is a US action. Abrams should have gotten with the Vietnamese and looked into this operation better. His headquarters approved the plan, did it not?" the President asked.

"Yes, sir, it did, and it was the same plan that General Abrams briefed us on last December," Laird said.

"So, what went wrong?" Everyone could see the President was not going to let this bone go. "I'm starting to believe that Abrams has been there too long, and we should pull him out of there." Kissinger and Laird shot each other a concerned look.

"Mr. President," Laird said, "General Abrams has done a great job since coming into that position. He's playing a military role, a peacekeeper role, and a political role. Aside from Lam Son 719, he's been doing a great job."

"If he's been doing such a great job, what happened with Lam Son 719? Did we not give him enough support? He had almost every helicopter in Vietnam in that operation," Nixon complained.

"Sir, it appears a number of factors contributed to this operational failure. First, we believe that a Vietnamese captain provided the plans to the North, which allowed them to move considerable forces to the objective area. Second, the intelligence was bad on the number of enemy troops in the area, the condition of Highway QL9, and the air-defense threat. Third, there was a lack of leadership at the Vietnamese senior commander level. The young officers fought well, but senior leaders, colonels, and generals were incompetent, it appears. Fourth, the jealousy between senior officers greatly affected the cooperation between commands. Lastly, there was a reluctance on the part of Vietnamese officers to employ artillery closer than one thousand meters to their positions as they didn't trust the artillery to be able to shoot the missions," Laird explained.

"Why was that?" the President asked, leaning forward in his chair.

"The Vietnamese artillery units were brought up from the south. There the terrain is flat, so they never shoot high-angle trajectories. The ground commanders had no faith that the artillery could shoot high-angle trajectories, and so they limited the artillery to no closer than one thousand meters."

"Couldn't the advisors call the artillery support?" Nixon asked, reaching for another cup of coffee.

"You will recall, sir, that no advisors were allowed to go into Laos with the Vietnamese. Only US helicopters and Air Force assets were authorized to participate in the operation," Laird said.

"Damn congressional amendments," Nixon mumbled. "The Cooper-Church Amendment killed any chance we had to get advisors into Laos with the Vietnamese and look at the result. Disaster. All we've done is strengthened the hand of the communists at the Paris summit."[1]

"Mr. President, it's water under the bridge," Kissinger said. "We need to consider those things that we can influence now. Rehashing the last battle will do us no good. We need to look to the future and what we can do to influence the outcome."

"You're right, Henry," the President agreed. "Okay, what is our current strength in Vietnam, Melvin?"

"Sir, we currently have two hundred and forty thousand US ground personnel in Vietnam. Our plan is to continue the reduction to one hundred and thirty-nine thousand by January first. Some of this can be achieved by moving some Air Force assets to Thailand, Guam, Okinawa, and the Philippines," Laird said, checking his notes.

"Has Abrams agreed to this reduction?" Nixon asked.

"He has, sir. He will be reorganizing some headquarters and consolidating some aviation units that remain. He has specifically asked that Army Aviation units be the last of the units to be withdrawn," Laird explained.

"Why?" the President asked, looking troubled.

"Sir, he feels that the aviation units can best support the Vietnamese forces with transportation, fire support, resupply and medevac—much better than the Vietnamese units can. In addition, it provides him with a means to remove advisors from the battlefield if the need should arise. He is still, however, along with McCain, asking for more authority to conduct an air campaign along the DMZ. He even has the Joint Chiefs voicing a similar opinion. They want more authority to launch tactical air and B-52s against air-defense and logistical targets in the DMZ and in North Vietnam along the southern border."

"What did you tell them?" Nixon asked in an irritated tone.

"I reminded them that the key to the military situation in the Republic of Vietnam is the complex of will, desire, and determination of the South Vietnamese people, not expanding air operations in North Vietnam.[2] I told them the existing authorities were adequate, and we have no indications that the threat has increased sufficiently to justify this increased bombing. Besides, the political fallout would be detrimental to our position in future peace talks," Laird explained.

"Well, I don't see that need arising. The ground combat is about over, isn't it? Lam Son 719 will probably be the last battle of this war, at least while we're there," Nixon said, pausing for a moment. "How effective has Vietnamization been?" The question caught everyone off guard.

"I'm not sure what you're asking, Mr. President. We think it's been very effective in preparing the Vietnamese forces to take over," the SecDef said.

"We think it's been effective, but has it? Based on what we just said with this Lam Son mess, I'm not so sure. Commanders write nice reports saying all is well, but Lam Son didn't bear that out, at least not with the press. We need some independent eyes on this program. Some eyes not associated with the commands. Mel, let's get an independent team over there to look things over and send us back an impartial estimate. Keep it small, and place it under the DoD IG's office. Can we do that? I want something that we can hand the press after this is all over with that will show we did a good job of getting the Vietnamese ready to assume the responsibility," Nixon said as he stood to indicate that this meeting was over.

3

SITUATIONAL UPDATE

30 December 1971
MACV Headquarters
Saigon, South Vietnam

The six-month update brief had been planned for a couple of weeks, mainly to bring everyone up to speed on what had happened across Vietnam in the last month and what might be expected in the first quarter of the new year. The briefing covered a wide range of subjects, to include intelligence updates, ground combat actions, and logistics. With Vietnamization in full swing, redeployment and redistribution of equipment was also high on the list of discussion topics. This six-month review generally took all day. The update brief was being held for a selected group of officers assigned to MACV —Military Assistance Command, Vietnam—and a couple of civilians. General Abrams had been the commander of MACV for three years, replacing General William Westmoreland, a West Point classmate of Abrams. Abrams had been Westmoreland's deputy for the previous year. Since the Lam

Son 719 debacle, Abrams was questioning everything presented by the intelligence community after getting burned over the Tet '68 battle and the intelligence failures with Lam Son 719.

Also present were a couple of gentlemen in civilian attire. William Colby from the CIA was present as he headed up the Civil Operations and Revolutionary Development Support program, or CORDS as it was known. They were tasked with "winning the hearts and minds" of the rural villages. Another was Félix Rodríguez. Everyone assumed he worked for Colby. Also present was Mr. John Paul Vann, a key advisor to MACV for ARVN I Corps or the MR-1 and MR-2 regions. Several military members were also present, to include Brigadier General James F. Hollingsworth, Rear Admiral Robert Salzer Jr., Commander US Naval Forces Vietnam, and Major General Robert N. MacKinnon, Commander 1st Aviation Brigade. Major General Frederick Kroesen Jr. was also present as he commanded the XXIV Corps, which covered MR-1 and MR-2. The headquarters for XXIV Corps was being reorganized into the Regional Assistance Command, as most ground forces would be gone in the next six months and logistic support to the South Vietnamese would be the primary function once that happened. Seated in the back of the room were the Inspector General for MACV, General Standish Oscar Brooks, and four majors that had not been present before.

At one end of the room stood a podium for the various briefers as well as a projection screen and a VGT projector. The windowless interior room had been selected for its security and the inability of an NVA sympathizer to fire an RPG round through a window at the meeting audience. Once everyone was seated, Major General John Carley, MACV J-3, stepped to the podium. General Carley. A graduate of West Point in 1945, he had seen action in Korea as an infantry platoon leader and had come away as a captain and infantry company commander. Returning, he had attended the nine-month Infantry Officer Advanced Course at Fort Benning. Being an infantry officer, he had several assignments at the home of the Infantry, Fort Benning, Georgia. When not at Fort Benning, he cherished his time in the 82nd Airborne Division at Fort Bragg, NC, serving as division G-2, G-3, Deputy Battle Group Commander, Chief of Staff and Commander of the 2nd Brigade. Although not an aviator, he helped develop the tactics used by helicopter forces in Vietnam as a member of the Howze Board. Like all rising stars, he served as a strategic planner in the Army War Plans Division, the Pentagon. In the Vietnam War, he commanded the 2nd Brigade First Infantry Division for one year (1968-69) and returned to Vietnam in 1971 as J-3 MACV. The nod from Abrams told him to get the show on the road.

"Good morning, sir. Today's briefing will recap the past six months, cover the current intelligence picture and offer some opinions on what the People's Army of North Vietnam may be contemplating," Carley said as a slide of appeared on the screen. "Sir the J-1 could not be here today but he asked me to cover these next two slides as you had requested some information from him about past draw downs" Carley stated pausing for the slide to come up. Abrams surveyed the slide before Carley began to speak. "As you can see sir, our troops strength for US forces has come down to the desired levels as mandated by Washington. As US strength has decreased so has foreign military forces strength been dropping. South Vietnamese end strength has also decreased leaving an overall shortfall of twelve thousand in the Vietnamese ranks."

Table 1

Actual Strength of Military Forces in Vietnam 1971

	US	FWMAF	RVNAF
January 31	334,850	67,433	1,054,125
February 28	323,797	67,791	1,049,163
March 31	302,097	67,513	1,057,676
April 30	272,073	66,563	1,058,237
May 31	252,210	66,586	1,060,597
June 30	239,528	66,842	1,060,129
July 31	225,106	64,762	1,057,924
August 31	216,528	61,256	1,052,353
September 30	212,596	60,538	1,047,890
October 31	198,683	58,813	1,043,232
November 30	178,266	58,526	1,040,640
December 31	158,119	54,497	1,046,254

Source: COMUSMACV Command History, 1971, Annex J

"Planned incremental reductions for last year are depicted on this slide," Carley said as the slide came up. Abrams studied it without comment for a moment.

US Redeployments in 1971

Period	Ceiling	Space Reduced	CBt MVR BN	ATY Bn.	ATK/FTR SQD*
1/1–30/4	284,000	60,000	15	8	0
1/5–30/6	254,700	29,300	6	2	2
1/7–31/8	226,000	28,700	6	5	5
1/9–30/11	184,000	42,000	8	10	2
1/12–31/1/72	139,000	45,000	6	5	2

*Includes both USAF and USMC Squadrons.

Source: COMUSMACV Command History, 1971, F-1-

"What maneuver battalions are going to be left in-country after January of '72?" Abrams asked.

"Sir, the last two will be the Garry Owen Brigade just north of Saigon and the 196th Light Infantry Brigade guarding Da Nang."

"Okay" was all Abrams said, indicating he was satisfied with the information and to move it along.

"Next slide, please," Carley called, and it appeared on the screen. It was a map of Vietnam, Cambodia and Laos.

"Since the conclusion of Lam Son 719, we've monitored a buildup of North Vietnamese forces along the DMZ in the southern portion of North Vietnam. In the last three months, North Vietnamese units have been moving down the Ho Chi Minh Trail to Tchepone in southern Laos and Snuol in Cambodia." A pointer appeared on the screen, indicating both towns on the map. "They have built up their supply bases in the area of Snuol again as well as base camps 604 and 611 in Tchepone. Our air campaigns in both Cambodia and Laos have hampered their efforts but have not stopped their flow south," Carley stated. Another slide appeared of the Mekong Delta, Military Region IV.

"Sir, in the Mekong Delta, Military Region IV, activity has been consistent with past military operations. Small-unit attacks of squad size against fixed ARVN compounds by night and active patrolling by ARVN squads and platoons by day. There've been no indications of a large military buildup," Carley concluded, looking at his notes and waiting for a question. When none came, he looked up and another slide replaced the slide of the Mekong Delta. This new slide was of Military Region III, with Saigon in the center.

"Sir, Military Region III has had indications of a major buildup, with the 5th NVA Division as well as a second division and a combined NVA/VC division all located around Snuol. The main avenue of approach would be down Highway 13 from Snuol to Loc Ninh, An Loc, Lai Khe and Saigon," Carley explained as a pointer indicated each of the towns identified.

"Do we have advisors with the Vietnamese units in that area?" Abrams asked.

"Yes, sir. Advisors are located with each of the Vietnamese units in Loc Ninh and An Loc, and Brigadier General Hollingsworth commands those advisor groups," Carley indicated. Abrams appeared satisfied, so Carley continued. "In Military Region II, Pleiku is centrally located. The enemy could launch from Base Area 601 down towards Dak To, to Kontum to Pleiku, and cut the country in half if they reached Highway 1 on the coast."

"Sir, if I may," Mr. John Paul Vann interrupted. Vann was a civilian advisor on the MACV staff. He had spent many years in Vietnam as an Army officer, retiring as a lieutenant colonel and immediately returning to government service as an advisor on Vietnam and Vietnamization. As such, he had become the civilian overseeing MR-2 and MR-1, with the military advisors for both regions reporting to him. His arrogance grated on many senior officers who had worked their way up through the ranks while Mr. Vann acquired his rank as a state department appointee and now was the equivalent to a major general.

"Mr. Vann," Abrams acknowledged.

"Sir, I think that we're going to see a major thrust by the NVA through MR-2 in an attempt to cut the country in half. I think this is where the main attack will come," Vann stated.

"And just when do you expect this operation to commence?" Abrams asked with some concern.

"Sir, I think we're looking at TET. We're seeing NVA units that were operating in Cambodia in support of the Khmer

Rouge moving back to the border area. They're also moving their T-54 tanks and PT-76 amphib vehicles closer to the area bordering MR-1 and MR-2. The reconnaissance teams that we've sent into the Mu Gia and Ban Karai Pass regions have reported large buildups in both areas of men, armor and logistics," Vann explained.

"General Carley, do we know what units he has moved to the border regions?" Abrams asked.

"At this time we're tracking the 304th and 308th NVA Divisions. The 308th is located just north of the DMZ on the eastern and central portions. The 304th is in Laos, just west and south of the DMZ. We estimate they have about one hundred tanks. The 312th Division is located in the vicinity of Tchepone along with two independent regiments, we think. The 324B Division has operated in the A Shau Valley for years and is still active there," General Carley indicated.

"When are we looking at the monsoon starting in MR-1 and MR-2?" General MacKinnon asked.

"Sir, the weather folks tell me the monsoon season up north will begin around mid-March or early April," General Carley stated, referring to his notes.

"If that's the case, then I predict the North Vietnamese offensive will start around the end of March," Mr. Vann stated.

"Why's that?" Abrams asked.

"Sir, our close-air support can't be matched by the North. Their air force is just no match for ours or the South Vietnamese. They know that as soon as they start something, our aircraft will be all over them. They need crappy weather to negate the effectiveness of our close-air support. I say the end of March," Vann concluded. Abrams said nothing but considered what he had heard and thought for a moment.

Finally, he asked, "What units does South Vietnam have up in the MR-1 area?"

It took Carley a moment to shuffle through his notes to find the answer. *Why didn't he save that question for the Vietnamese briefer?* He thought as he flipped through papers.

"Currently in MR-1, there's the 1st ARVN Infantry Division, the 2nd ARVN Infantry Division, and the 3rd ARVN Infantry Division, along with the 147th and 258th Vietnamese Marine Brigades and the 1st ARVN Armor Brigade, which has a newly formed tank battalion with M48 tanks. They're supplemented by the 51st Infantry Regiment, the 1st Ranger Group and regional and popular forces, about thirty thousand personnel all told. The 2nd Division is in the southern portion of MR-1. The 3rd Infantry Division is on the southwest side of the DMZ. The 1st Infantry Division is headquartered at Camp Eagle," Carley outlined.

"How are the forces arrayed up there?" Abrams asked.

"Sir, if you'll give me a second, I have a slide that can show you that. Sergeant?" Carley said, indicating to the sergeant to find the slide and get it up. It went up almost immediately. The sergeant had anticipated that it was going to be needed and had it handy.

"As you can see, sir, the positions starting along the DMZ are as indicated. Along the Cam Lo/Cua Viet River, there are five firebases with Alpha 1 in the east and Fuller on the far west. Charlie 3 and Charlie 1 are in depth behind these forward bases. Between the Cam Lo River and the Thach Han River, there are seven firebases, all oriented against approaches from Laos. Between the Thach Han River and the My Chanh River, there are four firebases west of QL1. These firebases form a semicircle around Quang Tri."

"Sir, if I may," Vann interrupted. Without waiting for acknowledgment, he continued, "Sir, these firebases have been in those locations since 1965. The enemy knows exactly where they are and every detail about them. They have supporting artillery fire, but that's it. The ARVNs run daily patrols out of each of these places, but they don't have any integrated defensive belts as we would think of them in a conventional fight. They're set up for guerrilla warfare, not a conventional fight if it comes to that." Vann's interruption annoyed General Carley, but for now he let it go. Abrams simply nodded in acknowledgment.

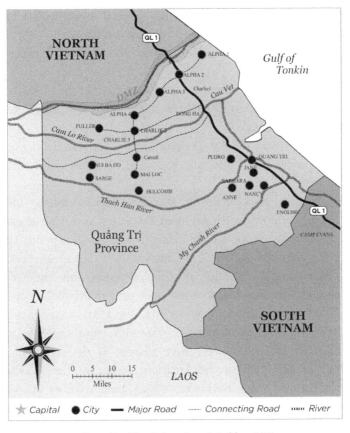

Created by Matt Jackson through Infidun, LLC

"Who's commanding the 3rd now? They just had a

change of command, did they not?" Abrams asked, looking at General Kroesen.

"Sir, currently the 3rd Infantry Division is under the command of Brigadier General Vu Van Giai. He was previously the deputy commander of the 1st Infantry Division. Tough as nails, I'm told. Unfortunately, the ARVN I Corps commander is still Lieutenant General Hoang Xuan Lam, the poster child for indecision and ineffectiveness, which he demonstrated in Lam Son 719," Kroesen explained.

"Can we get him moved to some admin job in Saigon?" Abrams asked.

"Sir, he's in tight with the President. I doubt the President would move him as it would be a slap in the face if he did," Kroesen indicated.

"How does the 3rd Division look? They just stood that division up in October, did they not?" Abrams asked with concern.

Kroesen responded, "Sir, they did. They moved the 2nd Regiment and the 11th Armored Cav from Corps reserve and placed them under the 3rd. They're both good, experienced units that performed well in Lam Son 719. They created two new regiments consisting of misfits, deserters, and criminals, all under the command of piss-poor performing officers and NCOs. The misfits are from the MR-3 and MR-4 regions and have no idea of the terrain or connection with the people up there in MR-1. We only have advisors at the regimental, brigade and division headquarters, except in the ARVN Ranger and Airborne units, which have advisors at the battalion level. The Marine brigades also have advisors at the battalion level."

"Let's have the regimental advisors keep us posted on those two regiments in the 3rd. How is the 20th Tank training going?" Abrams asked, looking at Vann.

Before Vann could answer, General Carley broke in. "The

20th Tank was understrength but has received the M48A1 tanks and is undergoing gunner training at this time," he stated, reviewing his notes.

"How is that going?" Abrams asked, turning to Mr. Vann.

"Sir, it's going. The Vietnamese are having difficulty with the integrated range finder and ballistic computer. The old M41 tanks had no range finder, so the Vietnamese are reluctant to use them. In addition, the M88 tank retriever vehicles didn't show up until just before training started and the M548 tracked cargo vehicles haven't shown up yet. There were also a lot of maintenance issues with the tanks received that needed to be corrected before we could send them downrange," Vann outlined.

"Keep me posted. We want them well trained and to the same standard as our own crews must meet," Abrams directed.

"Sir, if I may...," Mr. Colby requested.

"Please do," Abrams acknowledged as Colby looked at General Carley.

"General, do you think the North would be stupid enough to attack across the DMZ?" Mr. Colby asked. "That would be a violation of the 1957 treaty. They can't do that."

"Sir, Washington doubts that they would cross the DMZ, but I anticipate the attack will come from the west out of Laos to cut the country in half," Vann injected.

"What US units do we have in the regions?" Abrams asked.

Again, Carley had to dig in his notes. *I hope these figures are correct*, he was thinking as his blood pressure rose. Finding what he was looking for, he replied,

"Sir, this picture is changing rapidly. As you know, all US ground forces have received redeployment orders out of country. All armored and air cavalry squadrons are to redeploy by April thirtieth. The last ground units will be Troop F, 17th Cavalry, which will depart Da Nang in the first week of April, and the 1st Squadron, 1st Cav, which will depart right after that, leaving its Air Cav troop, redesignated Troop D, 17th Cavalry, in Da Nang for security. There will be an Air Cav troop remaining in MR-1 at Marble Mountain—Troop C, 16th Cavalry. The 7th of the 17th Cav will leave two troops, redesignated Troop H, 10th Cavalry, and Troop H, 17th Cavalry, and they'll be in MR-2 at Camp Holloway. F Troop, 4th Cav, was supporting the last brigade of the 25th but has since been moved to the 1st Cav, or what's left of the 1st Cav, in MR-3," Carley outlined.

"The 1st and 3rd Brigades of the 101st Airborne are clearing country today, with the last plane leaving in a few hours. That will leave one brigade from the 1st Cavalry Division in MR-3, and one brigade of the 101st in MR-2. The 196th is at Da Nang providing security. There are twenty-five Army Aviation units currently in-country, providing lift, resupply, medevac and reconnaissance operations, and General MacKinnon will cover aviation next. We also have the two Republic of Korea divisions, the ROK Capital Division and the ROK 9th Division, both operating in MR-2. The 2nd ROK Marine Brigade has been redeploying back to Korea and will be out of country by February first."

"What is Washington saying about this coming year?" Abrams asked. He knew the answer but wanted those present to hear it as well so everyone would be on the same sheet of music.

"Sir, Washington agrees that a major offensive along the lines of TET '68 is coming and probably over TET as well. It'll be an offensive to stir up public opinion back home. They don't feel that there will be a major push from the Laos-Cambodian regions nor an attack across the DMZ. They believe that the threat of enemy armor is negligible even though the NVA inventory is about three hundred tanks at this time, of which two regiments are in Cambodia," Carley replied.

Abrams noticed John Paul Vann shaking his head. "You do not agree, Mr. Vann."

"No, sir, I don't. As I stated before, they're going to conduct a major campaign and it's going to come at us from Laos and Cambodia. Those tanks are going to be leading the charge. I think he's going to come right at Ben Het and Dak To and make a beeline for Kontum and the coast, cutting the country in half. And I think it'll be sometime after TET. He knows we're expecting something around then. He'll wait and then come at us when we relax from TET," Vann reiterated.

After a moment of silence as Abrams sat in thought, he finally looked around the room. "Gentlemen, the one thing it appears we all agree upon is the fact that we're in for a major campaign by the North. We need to provide all the support we can to the South Vietnamese as they go into this campaign. We need more intelligence on this situation. Let's see if we can expedite turning over some equipment to the South Vietnamese, especially the M88 and M548 tracks for the 20th Tank. Okay, General Hollingsworth, what are we looking at in the MR-3 area?"

General Hollingsworth came to the podium, but he carried no notes. "Sir, traditionally when the NVA have attacked out of Cambodia, they've come by way of Tay Ninh, seizing populations versus ground. However, I have some suspicions at this point. Just across the border around Tay Ninh Province there are three or four major base camps for him. Base Camp 708, which is right against both Tay Ninh Province and Binh Long Province; base camps 363 and 354, which are on the west side to Tay Ninh Province; and 713, which is adjacent to Tay Ninh Province in the south and west of Hau Nghia Province. We know his forces in that are adjacent to Tay Ninh Province consist of the 24th NVA Regiment, the 271st NVA Regiment and the 7th NVA Division. We expect this to be the main attack. We also have the 9th VC Division and 5th VC Division operating in Cambodia north of the Tay Ninh Province. Are there any questions?" Hollingsworth asked. Abrams indicated he had none.

"General MacKinnon, you're up," Hollingsworth said as he stepped down.

General MacKinnon took the podium and called for the first slide.

Reduction in Force, 1st Aviation Brigade

Increment VIII: July–August 1971, completed
Increment IX: September–November 1971, completed
  One group, one battalion, 11 companies reduction
  2837 personnel
  363 aircraft
Increment X: December 71–Jan 72, currently ongoing
  One group, three battalions, 14 companies, 12 detachments.
  4501 personnel
  297 aircraft
Increment XI: February–April 1972
Thirteen battalions, 37 companies, 28 detachments
  10,603 personnel
  422 aircraft
Increment XII: May–June 72
  Two detachments
  147 personnel

"Sir, we started with a peak of three thousand, two hundred rotary and fixed-wing aircraft assigned to the 1st Aviation Brigade in July of '71. At the conclusion of increment XII on July first of '72, we will be down to nine hundred and eighty-four aircraft. We have completed increments VIII and IX. We are currently into increment X and it appears to be moving with some extensive personnel turmoil due to the early release for the Christmas holidays. Some critical shortages, especially for LOH pilots, standardization pilots and test pilots, were excluded from the early release. As you can imagine, this has caused some morale problems. Some others were only one day short of meeting the early release dates and therefore were retained in-country, which has also contributed to morale issues," MacKinnon explained. "Any questions, sir?"

Abrams simply shook his head no.

"Next slide, please," MacKinnon called.

Accelerated Transfer of Equipment

Project 981
November 71-June 72
284 UH-1H   500-1500 hours
22 CH-47   1966 A Models
101 O-1G
Criteria, Like New condition for UH-1H.
VNAF Capability
Four UH-1H Squadrons
One CH-47 Squadron
Project 982

November 71-June 72
Transfer of aircraft repair parts providing a 385 day requisition period. Cost: $13.7 million
Retrograde
Jan-Jun 72
1200 aircraft
OH-6 & OH-58 Sealand Van, 2 per.
Seatrain for all others. 130 aircraft per ship.
MSTS responsible.
Schedule: Jan 184; Feb 434; Mar 404; April 76; May 114; Jun 114.

"Sir, this slide shows the transfer of equipment to the ARVN Air Force. The transfer is going relatively smoothly with no major problems in the case of Project 981 and 982. The completion of Project 981 will allow for the increase of four UH-1H squadrons and one CH-47 squadron in the Vietnamese Air Force. We will continue to retrograde aircraft back to the States with the amounts indicated for the period January through June of the coming year. Seatrain has five ships and they're all committed to supporting this effort. Do you have any questions, sir?" MacKinnon was not about to read the slide.

"I don't see any transfer of the AH-1G to the Vietnamese," Abrams observed.

"No, sir. All AH-1G gunships are being retrograded back to the States. I don't believe the South Vietnamese have any pilots training in the AH-1G aircraft, sir." After a brief pause, MacKinnon announced, "Sir, that concludes my portion of today's briefing. I will be followed by General Brooks."

General Standish Oscar Brooks was small in stature at five foot six inches but known to be a bundle of energy. He was considered one of the most intelligent members of the MACV staff and knew the workings of MACV extensively. He generally made Abrams uncomfortable as he frequently raised complaints that were sent to him from throughout the MACV organization but filtered up only those that required Abrams's attention. *What is the complaint this time?* Abrams wondered as General Brooks approached the podium.

"Morning, sir," Brooks started off. "I'm happy to say that my topic today will not be a complaint filed against the command. Today, sir, we have been directed to support an element from the DoD IG's office. The President has directed an independent assessment of the Vietnamization program and has sent four majors to examine Vietnamese forces and prepare that assessment."

General Abrams's eyebrows rose slightly. He turned to look at the four majors in the back of the room.

"Gentlemen, would you please stand?" All four majors did as requested. "From left to right are Major Jack Turner, USMC, and Major Hank Sabine, Major Josh Steinhauer and Major Derrick Perez. The last three are US Army officers. These gentlemen have extensive service in Vietnam in both advisor roles and as conventional forces. They will be responsible for preparing the assessments and filing the report back to

Washington. Per the DoD IG, their reports will not be screened by my office or any office at MAC," Brooks added.

"Why not?" Abrams asked, visibly upset that a report would be submitted without him having an opportunity to see it before it was forwarded to his higher headquarters.

"Sir," Brooks said, "the President wants to be able to present to the Congress a completely objective report. It was felt that our examination of their report before it was sent to Washington would subject the report to criticism of white-washing if the report was glowingly favorable. We will have an opportunity to respond to their report after it's received by the President," Brooks said. "Our interaction with them is to provide whatever support they require, and my office has provided the necessary documents for that. Initially each officer will be assigned to one of the four military regions to make their initial assessments. Major Jack Turner will be going to MR-1, Major Hank Sabine to MR-3, Major Josh Stein-hauer to MR-2, and Major Derrick Perez to MR-4. Sit, gentlemen," Brooks directed. "If you have no questions, General, that concludes my portion of the brief. I will be followed by the logisticians, who will continue the briefing right after lunch."

Standing and stretching his back, Abrams turned to the assembled officers. "Gentlemen, good brief. We need to stay on top of the intel picture. It's obvious that he's going to launch a major offensive. We just need to track when and where. Understood?"

A unanimous "Yes, sir" was heard as Abrams left the room.

General Brooks turned to the four majors, "Gentlemen if you will accompany me to my office for a brief discussion," he asked as a general "asks" majors. Once in Brook's office, he motioned for the majors to have a seat around the conference table.

"Before you all take off to the four winds, I just want to cover a few points that should have been covered in the brief and would have if I had given General Abrams a heads up that you were there. Let me just review what has taken place since General Abrams has taken over MACV. I think you will find it helpful as background information. First when General Abrams took over the South Vietnamese forces had about eight hundred and fifty thousand soldiers. That number now sits at about a little over a million. Most, if not all of the weapon's systems from pistols to tanks have been upgraded to current US standards. Under General Abrams guidance the South Vietnamese armed forces have transitioned to a modern up to date fighting force," Brooks said pausing for a moment to access any reactions. There were none so he continued. "The South Vietnamese forces have reorganized their division to mirror the force structure of American units down to platoon and squad level. General Abrams has been a champion of getting South Vietnamese officers to our training course in the states such as the captains advance courses, Command and General Staff College, flight school as well as increasing the number of advisor training teams in country to work hands on with the local forces. General Abrams considers the advisors as key players working with the South Vietnamese forces giving them hands on training, logistical support and coordination for close air support," Brooks said. He paused again. "Okay, I just wanted you to know that for background information. The man has done a lot to support the Presidents Vietnamization program. I guess you gentlemen can now go see how well it has been done. Good luck. Let me know if you need anything," Books said as he stood and indicated the meeting was over.

1

4

THE PLAN

5 JANUARY 1972
   PAVN Headquarters
   Hanoi, North Vietnam

Seated in the large auditorium on the outskirts of Hanoi and under camouflage nets hopefully concealing it from American reconnaissance aircraft were the fourteen division commanders for the People's Army of North Vietnam and twenty-six separate regimental commanders for artillery and tanks. Each had brought one member of their staff as well, and the atmosphere was electrified as they had never all been together in the past five years. They felt it in their bones that something big was coming. They each had been handed a packet when they'd entered but were ordered not to open it until told to do so. In front of the assembled chairs was a podium with a large screen and a viewgraph projector. A soldier sat next to the projector with a stack of slides.

A voice from the back of the room called out, "*Chu y*," and everyone stood to attention. General Van Tien Dung,

Chief of Staff, PAVN, General Hoan Minh Thao, Commander PAVN Forces, B-3 Front, General Le Trong Tan, Commander MR-1, General Tran Van Tra, Commander B-2 Front, and General Vo Nguyen Giap as well as Lieutenant General Tran Van Quang walked down the center aisle and took seats that were reserved for them in the front row, except General Dung, who moved to the podium and picked up a pointer.

"First slide," he called, and a slide of Southeast Asia, to include North and South Vietnam and a portion of Cambodia and Laos, appeared. The DMZ between North and South Vietnam was clearly marked with arrows projecting from North Vietnam, Laos and Cambodia. Dung moved to the picture and with his pointer began, "Along the DMZ there are several outposts, as well as along the western border with Laos. They are, as the South Vietnamese say, a ring of steel protecting Quang Tri and Hue."

Moving his pointer lower on the slide, he went on, "In the center is the central base at Kontum with Dak To protecting the approach to Kontum, and in the south are Loc Ninh, An Loc, and Lai Khe along Highway 13 to Saigon." Dung called for the next slide but moved back to the podium. "Our mission is the destruction of the South Vietnamese Army, the capture of Quang Tri Province, Kontum, and control of Binh Phuoc, Binh Long and Tay Ninh Provinces in the south. This will be executed as a conventional force operation," Dung said. The response was immediate. Hushed voices and shocked looks were heard and seen. "Next slide." A picture appeared of Quang Tri Province with the respective firebases and unit designations.

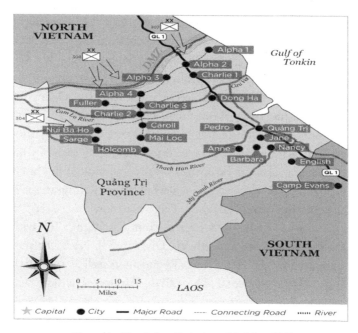

Created by Matt Jackson Books through Infidun, LLC

"Phase 1. In Quang Tri Province we will be opposed by the 3rd ARVN Infantry Division, the 1st ARVN Infantry Division and the 2nd ARVN Infantry Division to the south, as well as the 147th and 258th ARVN Marine Brigades. The 51st Infantry Regiment is also present, along with the 1st Ranger Group and some regional and popular forces. They are all in static positions with little mobility. The 3rd Division was newly formed and consists of deserters and released criminals. Their leadership is inferior. The 1st Division, however, fought well in Lam Son 719 and could be formidable. Their Marine brigades and Ranger group are also well trained but, again, have limited mobility. Under the command of Lieutenant General Tran Van Quang"—the speaker paused to acknowledge the general—"the 304th and 308th Infantry Divisions will attack with two tank regiments across the DMZ and destroy the firebases north of the Cam Lo River along with the 312 Infantry Division attacking from the west side of the DMZ along Highway 9 from Khe Sanh to Dong Ha. On order, the 324B will attack from the A Shau Valley against Fire Base Bastogne. The final objective is the seizure of Quang Tri City and Hue. But you must seize and hold Quang Tri. There are more details, to include movement times, assembly areas, and fire coordination and phase lines, outlined in each of your respective packets, to be opened at the conclusion of this briefing." The general picked up a glass of water, waiting to see if any questions would be raised. There were none.

"Phase 2. On order we attack from Base Camp 708 with the B-2 Front's 5th and 9th VC Division, 7th NVA Division supported by the 203rd Tank Regiment as well as the 205th and 101st Regiments. The 609th Artillery Division will provide fire support and anti-aircraft coverage. They will attack along Highway 13 to seize the border outpost of Loc Ninh. Elements of the 9th ARVN Regiment and a battalion of Rangers are located there, so it should be an easy seizure. They will continue the attack to seize the airfield at Quan Loi and the town of An Loc. Simultaneously, the B-2 Front will send two regiments to attack Tay Ninh and dominate ARVN forces, preventing them from reinforcing Loc Ninh or An Loc.

VIETNAM
III CORPS AREA OF OPERATIONS

CAMBODIA

Snoul

Bu Gia Map

Bu Dop

Song Be

Loc Ninh

An Loc

SOUTH VIETNAM

Chon Thanh

Tay Ninh

13

Phuoc Vinh

Lai Khe

Bein Hoa

Saigon

N

····· *Highway* —— *Road* ⋆ *Capital* ● *City*

Created by Matt Jackson Books through Infidun, LLC

"Phase 3 is the seizure of Kontum and Pleiku. On order, the B-3 Front attacks to seize Kontum and Pleiku, thus splitting South Vietnam in half. The attack will include the 320th and 2nd Infantry Divisions in the advance on Kontum along with the 203rd Tank Regiment. The 3rd Infantry Division attacks in the lowlands along the coast to disrupt the possibility of the ARVNs reinforcing Kontum or Pleiku. The opposition in the Central Highlands will be the 22nd and 23rd Divisions along with the 2nd Airborne Brigade.

"Phase 4 of the operation will be in the Mekong Delta region. The 101D Regiment of the 1st Division will attack the ARVN 42nd Ranger Group outpost in Kompong Trach, Cambodia. The 18th B, 95B, D1 and D2 Regiments will initiate actions in the Chu'ong Thien Province against elements of the ARVN 21st Division. On order the 52D and 101D Regiments will attack Kien Luong," the briefer concluded and stepped back behind the podium. As if on cue, General Van Tien Dung stood and moved to center stage. The slide of Quang Tri Province came back up.

"South Vietnamese forces or ARVNs as they are referred to by the Americans have established positions along the demilitarized zone that have been in place for the past five years. Daily they run patrols out of each of those firebases as indicated on this slide," the briefer stated, pointing to each firebase starting in the east.

"Between the Cam Lo River and the Thach Han River is Highway 9 from Tchepone in Laos to Khe Sanh to Dong Ha as well as firebases at Nui Ba Ho, Khe Gio, and Mai Loc, and former American firebases Sarge, Camp Carroll, Holcomb, and Pedro." Again Dung paused. "South of the Thach Han River and north of the My Chanh River are firebases Anne, Jane, Barbara, and Nancy. All these firebases ring Quang Tri City," Dung said as the audience exchanged looks.

"They are Alpha 1, Alpha 2, Alpha 3, and Alpha 4 right along the DMZ. Backing them are Charlie 1 and Charlie 2, FSB Fuller and the Rock Pile. All are north of the Cam Lo River. Highway QL1 runs through Alpha 2 and Charlie 1 and crosses the Cam Lo River at Dong Ha, where there is the only bridge across the Cam Lo River," the Dung indicated, pausing to allow the audience to study the map for a moment. "The objective for you gentlemen is the seizure of Quang Tri and Hue.

"We have waited long enough to bring this war to a conclusion and now is the time to do so. The long, slow war of attrition has not succeeded in attaining our goals but has only damaged our nation and taken the lives of so many young men. It is time to hand the enemy a crushing blow so we will be in a position of strength at the Paris Peace talks instead of a position of weakness. This is a conventional attack, which the forces of South Vietnam have not seen or trained against. The American ground forces are gone or will be when we launch our attack. American advisors will be with ARVN battalions and brigades, but there will be little that they can do. The biggest threat the Americans pose to our operation is their airpower, and we will negate that with our air-defense systems and the weather. Soon the monsoon season will start and we will utilize that to minimize the American capability to mass forces against our positions. Speed is of the essence in this operation. We must move quickly to cross the Cam Lo River and seize Quang Tri. The main effort is to seize Quang Tri Province with second priority of seizing Kontum. Exploitation of our success in Binh Long and Tay Ninh provinces will be evaluated and may be followed up. I cannot stress enough the importance of seizing Quang Tri and holding it," Dung said.

"Each of you have your orders and the details of your assignments. Study them, and if you have questions, ask before we launch this offensive. I will meet with the corps commanders over the coming weeks to finalize any details that are not understood or require modification. You have your orders—let us go forth and be victorious."

5

ROUGH MONTH

For the past month, General Abrams had been attempting to get some cooperation out of Washington on expanding the bombing campaign north of the DMZ. Unfortunately, the White House was not cooperating nor listening. In addition, things had not gone well in Cambodia and the intelligence indicators weren't favorable.

As Abrams entered the briefing room, those present stood.

"Keep your seats. This jumping up and down is worse than Sunday church services," Abrams said as he walked to his chair and then noticed the MACV chaplain sitting off to the side. "No offense, padre," he added.

"None taken, my son," the chaplain responded. He and Abrams had this thing going that the staff got a kick out of.

Taking his seat and accepting a cup of coffee from his aide,

Abrams got comfortable for a long update. "Let's get started," he directed, and the briefing officer, Colonel Hartsell, an assistant operations officer, called for the first slide. It listed several events by dates for the month of January.

"Sir, the first item of interest is that the last remaining road link between Cambodia and South Vietnam has been abandoned. The Cambodian Khmer National Army withdrew from Ponhea Kraek near the Fishhook on January tenth. In addition, the ARVN forces commenced Operation Prek TA in the Parrot's Beak region in Cambodia. The purpose of the operation is to disrupt the North Vietnamese in their attempt to conduct an offense come TET next month."

Interrupting, Abrams asked, "When does TET kick off?"

"Sir, February fifteenth is the start day for TET this year," Colonel Hartsell responded. Abrams acknowledged the information with a nod and motioned to continue.

"There are believed to be two regiments of North Vietnamese tanks in Cambodia, but Pacific Command believes, as we do, that there's little chance that they would be employed due to the terrain, logistics and the threat of our airpower. It's felt that any attempt to use a force larger than a company would require a major logistic buildup that would be easily identified and destroyed.

"In MR-2, along the Laotian border, we continue to see intelligence indicating a buildup of NVA forces in the vicinity of Ben Het. Engagements continue around Firebases Five and Six along what has been referred to as Rocket Ridge. These two firebases change hands frequently between ARVN and North Vietnamese forces. There have been unconfirmed reports of North Vietnamese PT-76 armored vehicles operating in the area.

"In MR-1 in the vicinity of Tchepone, the NVA base camps at 604 and 611 continue to receive supplies moving down the Ho Chi Minh Trail. The ARVN's attempt to destroy these supply bases in 1971 appear to have done little damage," Colonel Hartsell indicated. Abrams just shook his head. "As in MR-2, we're getting unconfirmed reports of armored vehicles operating in the vicinity of the base camps in Laos.

"Along the DMZ we've identified several new anti-aircraft positions of SA-2 and SA-3 missiles as well as radar-controlled guns. We haven't seen a buildup of ground forces north of the DMZ, and signals intelligence hasn't seen an increase in activity," Colonel Hartsell said.

"What's the assessment of the objective of TET this year?" Abrams asked.

"Sir, it's believed that the objective of TET will be to embarrass the South Vietnamese government and show that the Vietnamization program is a failure. As opposed to the 1968 TET Offensive, which went after the major cities, we believe that this year it will focus on smaller, more rural villages," Colonel Hartsell stated. A grunt from John Paul Vann got General Abrams's attention.

"You disagree with that assessment, Mr. Vann?" Abrams asked.

"I do, sir. I believe he's going to hit and hit hard with everything he has, to include his armor," Vann said.

"Why is that?" Abrams asked.

"Sir, he's going back into the peace talks and wants to go into them from a position of strength. Right now he's in a stalemate with no real gains for the past four years and really only losses. We're leaving and the South Vietnamese are the strongest they've ever been—with our air support, of course. We're talking to his two principal suppliers, China and the Soviets. He can't afford to have us build relations with those two, especially if they reduce the flow of logistics to him. To go into the peace talks with a position of strength, he's going to need a decisive victory as well to show China and the Soviets that he has the capability of winning this conflict," Vann explained.

"Interesting theory at this point" was all Abrams said before returning his attention to Colonel Hartsell. "Colonel, I'm pressed for time today, so let's cut to the things I need to know before I have the SecDef on the line. What's the status of ARVN forces along the DMZ?"

"Sir, the ARVN have eight firebases north of the Cam Lo River. Those eight have been there for the past year if not longer and are well established. Daily patrols are run out of those firebases. Between the Cam Lo and Thach Han Rivers there are nine firebases, with only one bridge over the Cam Lo, and it's located at Dong Ha. Since our last update he hasn't changed his force structure in MR-1 or MR-2," General Carley pointed out.

"Okay, I'm sure you're all aware that for the past two years, Mr. Kissinger has been holding peace talks with the North in Paris. More troublesome is the fact that those peace talks don't call for the withdrawal of North Vietnamese forces from South Vietnam when we depart. That's probably going to be a nonstarter for the South Vietnamese. I suspect that if that's the case, then the North is going to make a major push soon to gain as much ground in South Vietnam as they can get if and when a cease-fire is declared," Abrams indicated. Turning to his operations officer, General Carley, he asked, "John, have we sent that request for additional authority to use airpower against the southern side of North Vietnam to counter his buildup of surface-to-air missiles?"

"Yes, sir, we have, and word from D.C. is that the President is going to approve the request. It should be approved by early next week. It'll also include the border region with Laos," Carley replied.

"Good," Abrams responded. Turning, he spotted General Brooks. "Stan, where are our four majors?"

"Sir, they've deployed to the various regions and are talking with and observing the Vietnamese units and advisors. I've heard nothing back from them," Brooks said.

"Well, if you do, let me know," Abrams instructed.

6

ARRIVE IN MR-1

1 February 1972
I Corps Headquarters
Da Nang, South Vietnam

Major Jack Turner had spent the past month in Saigon receiving briefings by the various staff members of MACV headquarters. General Abrams decided that the group should be fully knowledgeable on the background of the Vietnamization program. Abrams wasn't supposed to pressure them, but he could certainly inform them. Jack was just glad to finally get away from the head shed and get into the field to do what he was most comfortable doing, acting like a Marine.

Jack had been an infantry grunt his entire military career, following in the footsteps of his dad, whom he had never known. His father had left for the Pacific when World War II started and had been posthumously awarded the Navy Cross for his actions on Guadalcanal. Born in 1938, Jack had only shadowy memories of his father. As soon as Jack turned seventeen, he enlisted in the US Marines for the infantry. It was quickly noted in his initial testing that he had an aptitude for languages, and the Marine Corps sent him to language school. Vietnamese was the language the Corps chose. Jack had to look on a map to find Vietnam.

His first assignment was as a radio operator/assistant for an advisor team in the Quang Tri Province of Vietnam in 1957. He had also been promoted to buck sergeant. After a year, he found himself at Marine Corps Base Camp Pendleton and applied for officer candidate school. Upon commissioning, he was assigned as a platoon leader for an infantry platoon in the 1st Marine Division and served there until he finished his company command time. Jack was quickly noted for his ability and leadership as well as his physical fitness. At five foot eleven inches and two hundred pounds, he was as solid as a rock and always excelled in the physical training. His superiors noted this and sent him to Fort Benning to attend the Infantry Officer Advanced Course, followed by the US Army Ranger Qualification Course. However, he would not be using those newly acquired skills as he was sent back to Vietnam.

HMM-362, a medium-lift helicopter unit under the command of Lieutenant Colonel Archie Clapp, was sent to Vietnam in 1962 to assist the Vietnamese Army. Jack was tagged to join the unit and serve as a trainer/advisor for the Vietnamese soldiers in the use of helicopters by the ground forces in 1964. His skill with the language and his infantry knowledge made him the perfect candidate. Although there was no official Marine advisor unit in Vietnam at the time, Jack was serving in that capacity. After a year, it was back to the States and then a stint at the Pentagon, where few others had been to Vietnam and most didn't know it existed. He was saved from this duty for a year when orders arrived assigning him to the 3rd Marine Division and placing him in Da Nang as an infantry battalion operations officer. For the next five years, he would find himself in repeated assignments in Vietnam. Now he was a senior major looking at the next lieutenant colonel's promotion board.

Jack had learned in his many tours in Vietnam that some things never change. The weather was the same, hot and humid with monsoons arriving on time every year. The smell of crap burning in diesel fuel constantly hung in the air each morning and well into the afternoon. The dust along the unpaved roads, a red clay that got into every pore of the human body and didn't wash out in only cold showers. Jack remembered it all and loved it. He was single, never having found the time or put the effort into a lasting relationship. His love was the Corps. Prior to departing Saigon, he stopped at the Marine Advisory Unit at the Bo Tu Linh compound, which was headquarters for the Vietnamese Marines and where the Marine Advisory Unit was located. Entering, he saw a familiar face right away.

"Jack Turner, what the hell are you doing here?" Lieutenant Colonel Jim Portland asked, approaching Jack as he moved down the hall. They had served together several times.

"Sir, how are you doing?" Jack replied.

"Fine, fine. Are you assigned here now?" Jim asked, curious that he'd not heard of Jack's assignment.

"No, sir, I'm here on a special assignment for the DoD IG," Jack responded.

"Oh, so you're one of those guys we've heard about," Jim said with raised eyebrows.

"Afraid so," Jack chuckled.

"Well, what do you need?"

"Sir, I'd like to see the Senior Advisor's Journal," Jack stated. The Senior Advisor's Journal was a journal started by the very first Marine advisor, Lieutenant Colonel Vic Croizat, in 1954. Each of the following advisors had made entries that highlighted events during their tours as well as opinions.

"Colonel Dorsey, the current senior advisor, has it. I think we can get it for you to read. Can you have it back here say the day after tomorrow?" Jim asked.

"Yes, sir. That shouldn't be a problem," Jack said, knowing he was going to be doing a lot of reading for the next two days.

"I wish I could give you more time with it, but our new deputy senior advisor is coming in tomorrow. Lieutenant Colonel Gerald Turley—ever serve with him before?" Jim asked, opening the door to Colonel Dorsey's office.

"Can't say that I have, sir," Jack responded.

"Well, you'll probably run into him as he'll be touring our units and advisors up north while you're there. He's a good guy. We served together before. Ah, there's the journal," Jim said, reaching across Colonel Dorsey's desk. Handing the journal to Jack, he added, "Enjoy."

At Da Nang, Jack went to FRAC headquarters and introduced himself. General Kroesen had been present at the December meeting, so he'd already given his staff a heads-up that Jack would be coming. To Jack's surprise, he was welcomed.

"Major Turner," said General Bowen, the deputy FRAC commander, standing and extending his hand as Jack entered his office. "We've been expecting you and want to extend every service you require."

"How do you do, sir?" Jack replied, accepting the extended hand. "Sir, your staff has been most helpful. Got me a set of quarters over at the BOQ, a jeep with driver and all the combat equipment I could possibly hope not to have to carry," he added with a smile.

Motioning to one of the two overstuffed chairs in the office, General Bowen asked, "So what's your game plan?

Where do you want to start and how do you want to proceed?"

"Well, sir, I thought I'd start at the lower levels first and see for myself what the Vietnamese are doing and how they're doing it before I start talking to the Vietnamese brass. In my previous tours here, I found that what the private is saying and what the brass is saying didn't really match up," Jack said.

"That's an understatement," Bowen remarked. "General Lam is the I Corps commander, and he for one does not like to pass bad news up the chain to the JCS. General Giai is the 3rd Division commander and operates in a similar fashion. We have a separate advisor radio net where the advisors pass information up through their chain, notifying us if things aren't right. Sometimes, this pisses off the Vietnamese chain of command because General Kroesen will confront Lam with news that he didn't know about or knew and didn't want reported," Bowen explained. "At the 3rd ARVN Division, we have Military Advisor Team 155 with Colonel Metcalf in command. Each of the ARVN regiments has two advisors. There are no US advisors at the ARVN battalion levels, only the regimental level. The Marine brigades, however, have advisors at the brigade level and two at the battalion level."

"How's that working?" Jack asked.

"I have my opinion on that but will let you form your own opinion and then we can compare notes. I was told not to influence you," Bowen added with a smile.

"Okay, sir," Jack responded, chuckling.

"Under the 3rd ARVN Division, there are two Marine brigades, the 147th and the 258th, along with the 56th, 57th and 2nd ARVN Regiments," Bowen offered.

"That's a sizable division considering all the support elements as well," Jack commented.

"We think so, but General Lam has it that way," Bowen replied. After pausing a moment, he added, "Well, you have a lot to see, so I won't hold you up. Just want you to know if you need anything—a vehicle, an aircraft, or access to someone or someplace—and aren't getting the cooperation you need, call me. I'll let Colonel Metcalf know you'll be in his AO." Bowen stood and extended his hand. "I mean it when I say call me if you need anything."

After Jack left the general's office, Bowen picked up the phone. "Please get me Colonel Metcalf." A few minutes later, his phone rang. "Colonel Metcalf, Bowen here."

"Yes, sir," Metcalf responded. *You called me—of course I know it's you*, he was thinking.

"There's a Major Jack Turner, Marine, here conducting an assessment for the DoD IG. He has carte blanche to see anything and speak to anyone. Give him all the cooperation he requests. Understood?" Bowen emphasized.

"Certainly, sir. What's he assessing?" Metcalf asked.

"Vietnamization program and how well the Vietnamese are doing taking over. In other words, he's evaluating how the advisory team program has worked," Bowen added. "Another thing, stay out of his way. If he asks for something, don't hesitate to give it to him, but don't attempt in any way to influence what he's doing or seeing," Bowen added.

"Well, sir, I should at least have input to his report, especially as it's an evaluation of my team and—"

"Colonel, stop right there. I repeat, you provide whatever he asks for but do not interject yourself into his assessment. Do I make myself clear on this?" Bowen said slowly and clearly.

"Yes, sir," Metcalf responded almost dejectedly.

"Good. Keep me posted on how Giai is doing. Have a good day—oh, you know the new deputy for the Marine Advisor Group is going to be in your AO visiting the Marine advisors, don't you?"

"Yes, sir, a Lieutenant Colonel Turley, I believe. I know

he's coming up sometime this month, just not sure when," Metcalf replied.

"Well, same goes for him. Extend every courtesy to him that you can. We can't afford to have the Marines pull their advisors," Bowen directed and placed the phone back in the cradle.

7

VISIT FORWARD OUTPOSTS

1 MARCH 1972
3rd ARVN Division AO
Ai Tu, South Vietnam

Jack wanted to spend the first week of March visiting the numerous outposts and firebases south of the My Chanh River. However, out of courtesy, he hopped a ride with an aircraft from the 48th Assault Helicopter Company, the Blue Stars, going up to Ai Tu. He felt he should introduce himself to Colonel Metcalf before going to any of the firebases. He told his driver to take the jeep and his gear and meet him at Camp Evans. Arriving at Ai Tu, which was the forward command post for the 3rd ARVN Division, he was directed to the advisory team bunker, which he noted was not collocated with the 3rd ARVN Division command post. Entering the team bunker, he was taken aback by the spit and polish of the interior. *How long has this palace been here?* He wondered.

"Can I help you, sir?" a young Marine sergeant asked.

"Yes, I'm Major Jack Turner. I would like to speak to Colonel Metcalf," Jack said.

"Sir, do you have an appointment?" Sergeant Swift asked.

"An appointment?" Jack stammered.

"Sir, Colonel Metcalf requires that appointments be made for all visitors below the rank of colonel," Swift said. "I can make you one for thirteen hundred today, right after chow."

"Now, Sergeant Swift, you wouldn't be jerking my chain, would you?" Jack asked, not believing what he was hearing.

"No, sir—you're a Marine, so no, sir," Swift replied as he wrote Jack's name down in an appointment book. "I'm heading over to the mess hall now, sir, if you care to join me. Maybe some of the other Marine advisors will be over there, although I think most are out on the firebases now. Been having a bit of activity of late," Swift added. "Just leave your gear here. It'll be safe."

With that, Jack placed his M16 rifle and load-bearing equipment next to Swift's desk.

Arriving at the mess hall, Jack accepted a tray from Swift and moved along the steam line. Vietnamese servers placed the chow, which did appear appetizing, as an Army sergeant first class supervised. Jack was a bit surprised at the quality of the food as he started on the steak.

"So, Sergeant Swift, how did you wind up as the colonel's clerk?" Jack asked.

"Oh, I'm not, sir. I'm with the ANGLICO team that provides naval gunfire and tac air support up at Alpha 2. We rotate from up there to back here in our support cell. Colonel Metcalf insisted that everyone pulls duty, and one of those duties is clerk for a day. He has a clerk assigned, but that broke-dick spends his time as the colonel's choji boy.[1] I get stuck once a month sitting at that desk, if I'm not out at Alpha 2. Sir, even the cook there has to pull one day a month over there. We eat peanut butter sandwiches on that day," Swift joked, or so Jack hoped. As Jack ate, he noted that the only people in the mess hall were Army personnel, and all appeared to be support types—mechanics, communications, supply personnel. Once they were done eating, Swift and Jack returned to the advisor headquarters.

"I'll see if he's free now, sir," Swift said, moving straight to Metcalf's office. When he came out, he motioned that Jack could go in. Metcalf was standing with his back to the door, looking at a map. He didn't turn for a moment. Jack just stood in the frame of the door. *Power play*, he thought. Finally, Metcalf turned and motioned for Jack to have a seat.

"I've been told to provide whatever support you require, Major," Metcalf started. "So what do you need?" *Oh, wow, let's get right to the point, why don't we?* Jack immediately thought. *Okay, if that's the way you want to play, Colonel.*

"Sir, I require access to all personnel in your command as well as access to each of the firebases in the 3rd ARVN Division area of operations. In addition, I will select certain Vietnamese officers that I would like to speak with once I've conducted a tour of the area of operations. FRAC provided me a vehicle and driver, but I may require air support at some point and will coordinate that request through your command. Once I'm finished, I'll return to sit down with you with some questions and an exit interview. My final report is confidential, and you are not privileged to read it, but neither is General Abrams, so don't feel bad," Jack said, hoping his last comment would cut off any discussion or bitching by Metcalf.

Metcalf didn't say anything for a few moments but toyed with a pencil, doodling on a scratch pad. Finally, he looked up and the daggers in his eyes were obvious. Slowly, he said, "Major, you will be provided with whatever you require. Coordinate with the folks in operations. I ask that you keep me informed on a daily basis of where you are and where you're going."

"Sir, I can do that, except I won't know where I'm going until I get there. But I'll keep you informed of where I am," Jack replied, knowing he was digging his spurs into Metcalf. He didn't want Metcalf calling ahead of his arrival to give people a heads-up.

Surrendering, Metcalf said, "Very well, good day, Major." Jack knew this interview was over, so he stood and walked out.

"Sergeant Swift, you have a good day," Jack said as he picked up his gear.

"You too, sir...and if you need anything, you can call me," Swift added. Jack got the message. Walking out the door, Jack headed towards the UH-1H helicopter that was waiting for him. Almost immediately, the crew began getting the aircraft ready for departure. As Jack climbed into the back, the aircraft commander turned around. "Where to now, sir?"

"Can you take me over to Alpha 2 and then follow QL1 back to Camp Evans?" Jack asked.

"Can do, sir." And with that, the engine slowly came to life.

Jack pulled out his map, which Sergeant Swift had updated for him with the locations of the various firebases and outposts while Jack was in with Metcalf. Lifting off, Jack followed the flight path and compared what he was seeing with what the map was showing. As they passed over Alpha 2 at one thousand feet, Jack noted the position of the artillery and the layout of the outpost. He also noted that the DMZ was only about fifteen hundred meters north of Alpha 2 and was only five thousand meters wide. Jack could easily see into North Vietnam. The large North Vietnamese flag positioned where QL1 entered the DMZ in the north was clearly visible. Turning south, the aircraft followed QL1 back to Camp Evans. Time to start his assessment from the ground.

Camp Evans had been a major firebase for many years and had been occupied by various units over the years. The 1st Air

Cavalry Division had been there in 1967 when a lucky NVA round had hit the ammo dump and it had continued to explode for several hours. When the 1st Air Cav had moved south, the 101st Airborne Division had moved in and occupied it until they'd departed back to the States. Now it was occupied by the Vietnamese Army. As Jack moved around the firebase, it was obvious it wasn't being maintained to the same standards as before. Weeds had grown up in the rows of concertina wire surrounding the perimeter. Some of the wire was sagging badly. Bunkers were in need of repair and maintenance. Some families of the ARVN soldiers were living inside the wire. Jack didn't divulge that he was fluent in Vietnamese and therefore was able to eavesdrop on many conversations. It quickly became evident that morale was not very high. He observed daily patrols departing the firebase each day, but always returning before dark and with no one venturing out after sunset.

The next morning, Turner and his driver, Lance Corporal Ed Hanner, started up QL1. Corporal Hanner was from Tennessee and assigned to the Marine Advisory Group. He knew the lay of the land well, and Dorsey wanted an American traveling with Turner. The plan was to swing by those firebases that were closest to QL1 for a quick orientation look but to move up to the northernmost locations before the end of the day. Traffic on QL1 was moderate and moving along nicely considering it was a mix of military vehicles, civilian vehicles, motorcycles, bikes, oxcarts, overloaded buses, and pedestrians. Little girls lined the roads selling Cokes as they had done for years, but there were no longer any US Gis to buy them. Boom-boom girls were also looking a bit hungry now that business had dried up. Some things had changed. Driving north, they made a quick stop at FSB Nancy. As Turner rolled through the main gate, a Vietnamese Marine halted his vehicle and smartly saluted. In Vietnamese, Turner asked for directions to the command bunker, which the young Marine pointed out and saluted again. As he pulled up in front of the command post, a US Marine officer walked out.

"I hope you're my replacement," he half joked.

"Afraid not, I'm Jack Turner and am up here—"

"On an inspection tour," the officer said, extending his hand. "Easley, senior advisor to the 258th Vietnamese Marine Brigade. Dorsey called all of us and gave us a heads-up that you would be in the area and said to give you anything and everything you wanted. Let's get you settled in for the night. You are spending the night with us, aren't you?" Easley asked.

"If you're inviting, then, yes, we are," Jack replied.

Placing his stuff in the advisor bunker, Easley explained that when the advisors in the field with the battalions came in, they stayed with him. There were several cots in the advisor bunker. His invitation extended to Hanner as well. Once settled, Easley and Jack walked around the firebase. It was in a lot better condition than what Jack had witnessed at Camp Evans. The concertina wire was taut, with no weeds but plenty of claymore mines, trip flares and fougasse barrels positioned around the perimeter.[2] As they walked, Easley briefed Jack on the brigade's operations.

"The 258th is oriented to the west with our battalions occupying Barbara, Jane, Anne and Pedro. The 147th Brigade is north of us and also oriented to the west, but I'll let Major Joy tell you his story. The battalions run patrols and usually stay out for two to three days. I have eight advisors right now, with two advisors with each battalion," Easley explained.

"How's the brigade commander?" Jack asked.

"Colonel Ngo Van Dinh is good. He'll make a decision and he accepts advice. Doesn't always follow it but listens and considers what I have to say. We get along pretty good," Easley said.

Jack spent the rest of the day observing the Vietnamese

Marines in the execution of their duties. He noted the 105-millimeter howitzers oriented to the west and the condition of the guns. All were well maintained, with ammo properly stored. The night was quiet, with an occasional call for fire from one of the units in the field. People quickly became accustomed to the sound of outgoing artillery and most slept through it.

In the morning, Jack and Hanner resumed their trip north. This time he avoided Ai Tu, figuring he'd left enough of an impression with Metcalf for now. At Charlie 1, across the Dong Ha Bridge, which spanned the Cam Lo River, Turner stopped at the headquarters for the 57th ARVN Regiment. As he got out of his jeep, "Can I help you?" was called out in a Midwest accent. Turning, he saw an Army lieutenant colonel approaching.

"Yes, sir, I'm Major Turner. I'm looking for the advisor here," Jack said as he smartly saluted.

Returning the salute and extending his hand, the man replied, "Well, you found him, Major. What can I do for you?"

Jack noticed the name tag on the lieutenant colonel's uniform—Twitchell. "Sir, I'm here on an evaluation assignment for the DoD IG, assessing the Vietnamization program," Jack said.

Twitchell smiled and placed his hand on Jack's shoulder. "So you're the guy that got under Metcalf's skin. Took him down a notch, I understand, and did it tactfully," Twitchell added. Jack wasn't sure how to respond to that comment. "How about a cold soda and we can talk in my bunker?" Twitchell offered. Turning to Lance Corporal Hanner, he said, "The advisor CP is that bunker. Make yourself comfortable and grab something from the fridge."

"Thank you, sir," Hanner replied and moved off in the appropriate direction.

Inside his bunker, which measured ten feet by ten feet,

Twitchell pointed at a cot for Jack to have a seat. Retrieving two cold sodas from a small refrigerator, he handed one to Jack and took a seat in a lawn chair. "So, what do you want to know?" Twitchell asked.

"First, what's your assessment of the 57th Regiment?" Jack asked.

"No attribution, correct?" Twitchell replied.

"No names," was Jack's response.

"The 57th is an okay unit."

The two officers talked for an hour before Jack wanted to get moving north to Alpha 2. He didn't want to be running the road at night, and Twitchell approved of that plan. He assured Twitchell that he would be back and for a longer stay.

The drive from Charlie 1 to Alpha 2 was only ten kilometers, but in the monsoon rain it felt a lot longer. The northern monsoon season was still in full swing and would remain so for the rest of the month and into early April. Pulling into the compound, Jack entered the command post, which appeared to be an old French fortification with a tower on top.

"Sir, you must be Major Turner. Welcome to our home," Lieutenant Johnson said, standing up. Jack looked around. The CP was also doubling for their quarters. All five members were present and Johnson made the introductions. Once Jack was settled, the lieutenant took him up to the observation post they had on the tower.

"How did you know who I was, Lieutenant?" Jack asked.

"Sergeant Swift gave us a heads-up that you'd be visiting. Told us that Colonel Metcalf wasn't happy when you left his office."

"Seems that story has gotten around to a lot of folks," Jack said.

"Sir, we're a small community. News travels fast," Johnson said, handing Jack a starlight scope. "Sir, if you'll look north towards the North Vietnamese flag and to the left, you'll see some activity," Johnson pointed out. Jack accepted the night vision scope and proceeded to look towards the DMZ. The lighted North Vietnamese flag he'd seen on the fly-by was still there. What caught his interest, however, were the numerous lights to the west of the flag that appeared to be in the DMZ.

"Lieutenant, are they in the DMZ?" Jack asked.

"Appears that way, sir. Every night for the past month, we've seen activity up there. Nothing in the daylight, and we can't see where they've been doing anything as, whatever it is, they're covering it up pretty well. We've been reporting it but no one has done anything about it, at least not that I can see," Johnson stated.

"What infantry unit is providing security up here?"

"They rotate, but right now it's a battalion from the 57th Regiment."

"What have you got for fire support up here?" Jack asked, handing the night vision scope back.

"Besides the 155 howitzers, there are two ships about a mile off the coast. They rotate in for fifteen days at a time and are very responsive to our calls. I send the fire mission to our cell in Ai Tu and they forward the initial call to the ship. The ship contacts me and I adjust the fire. Works fairly well and fast. The cell in Ai Tu will sometimes forward the call to a FAC if one is overhead, which hasn't happened much since December, when the northern monsoons started," Johnson pointed out.

Leaving the tower, they returned to the CP and continued their discussion late into the night.

The next morning, Jack said farewell. "Lieutenant, thank you for a very informative evening. I'll be back to talk to you some more."

"Sorry, sir, I won't be here. I'm rotating back to the fleet and Lieutenant Bruggeman will be coming up to replace me."

"Well, in that case, Take care," Jack said and climbed into the jeep.

Johnson watched the jeep roll out of the compound and onto Route 558 towards Alpha 3 and 4 as well as Charlie 2. *I wonder if he'll ever get back here*, Johnson thought as he watched them leave.

8

DISBELIEF

30 March 1972
3rd ARVN Infantry Division TOC
Ai Tu, South Vietnam

Colonel Donald Metcalf, commander of the US Advisory Team 155, had a busy day ahead of him.[1] First order of business was to speak with Lieutenant Colonel Gerald Turley. He wanted to get some insight into what Turley had seen and heard. It appeared that Turley was avoiding coming to Ai Tu but had spoken with the team operations officer, Major Wilson, and mentioned he would be in today. The Marine Advisory Unit provided all the advisors to the Vietnamese Marine units down to battalion level. Usually, two Marine officers were assigned to each Vietnamese Marine battalion and regiment. The unit had fifty-eight officers and nine enlisted men along with one Navy corpsman that treated the Vietnamese Marines as well. After that, it was off to Saigon to catch a flight to the Philippines to visit his family. General Giai was accompanying him to Saigon for the Easter weekend.

Having concluded with Lieutenant Colonel Turley, who had divulged nothing, he went to the 3rd Division TOC, looking for General Giai, the 3rd Division commander. Seeing him in the rear of the TOC, looking at a map, Metcalf approached.

"Good morning, General, you ready to depart?" Metcalf asked, trying to tone down his frustration with Turley.

"Yes, in minute. You have plane for us?" Giai asked, holding a sheet of paper in his hand.

"All gassed up and ready to go. We should be down in Saigon in about two hours. I'm going to stop over at MACV headquarters and discuss a few matters with those people. I want to see if we can get some Army advisors to push down to the battalion levels in the 56th and 57th and an advisor for the 2nd Regiment. The Marines have advisors at their Marine battalions and I think we should have Army advisors as well at the battalion level."

"Good. I review message from General Lam. He say NVA launching an invasion. I think intel weenies, as you say, got it wrong. We continue the relief of the 2nd Regiment by the 56th and 57th Regiments. There no need to hold that up since supposed invasion not happen," General Giai said. Giai was an experienced, tough warrior. He had been fighting ever since he'd left his home in Hanoi in 1954, when the communists had taken over. "JCS in Saigon say attack commence yesterday. Think it may launch across DMZ. General Lam does not believe that. He say it would violate the 1954 Geneva Accords. He think if they do attack, it will be in Central Highlands in Military Region II."[2] Turning to his division G-3 operations officer, Giai gave some final guidance and departed with Colonel Metcalf.

Lieutenant Colonel Turley was being escorted by Major Jim Joy, USMC, who was the senior advisor to the 147th Marine Regiment. Both the 147th and the 258th Marine

Regiments were attached to the 3rd ARVN Infantry Division. Joy had arranged for Turley to visit both regimental headquarters after a tour of the 3rd Division Headquarters. Standing in the 3rd Division TOC, Major Wilson, the teams G-3 Ops advisor, briefed Turley on the disposition of the 3rd Division and the Marine regiments. Joy stood off to the side and listened.

"The 3rd Division has the 147th Marine Regiment located at Mai Loc," Wilson said, pointing at the map. "The 258th Marine Regiment is located at Firebase Nancy, located here." He pointed about ten miles south of Quang Tri City. "Both regiments are at full strength and well equipped. Their logistic system is functioning okay, making the regiments combat effective. Truth be told, they're probably the strongest regiments of the 3rd Division," Wilson added.

"If they're the strongest regiments, why are they positioned back and to the west of the other regiments?" Turley asked.

"General Giai feels that the most dangerous avenue of approach is from the west into his flanks, down QL9 from Khe Sanh, so he's positioned them to block that approach," Joy explained as Turley studied the map. Joy added, "The 1st of the 5th Infantry Brigade was stationed along this route until they were rotated back to the States a couple of months ago. They were also at our northernmost firebase, Alpha 2, about a mile south of the DMZ. The only US unit in the area now is the 196th Light Infantry Brigade and it's pulling guard duty in Da Nang until it rotates home in a few weeks."

"Does the 3rd Division have any tanks?" Turley asked Wilson.

"Yes, sir. They have the 20th Tank Battalion, which has just recently been activated and is in final training south of Quang Tri. They have M48 tanks, fifty-one I believe. They have an Army advisor assigned. Also, but not under the command of 3rd ARVN, is the 1st Armored Brigade, which is operating in the AO."

"What's the disposition of our battalions and who are the advisors at each?" Turley asked, taking out a notebook and pencil. His question was directed at Joy.

"Well, sir, the 147th, as I said earlier, is at Mai Loc. I have Captain Murray as my assistant senior advisor. The 4th Battalion is split between Firebase Sarge and Nui Ba Ho Mountain, with Bravo Company at Nui Ba Ho. Major Boomer and Captain Smith are the two advisors, and Smith is up on Nui Ba Ho with the Bravo Company commander,"[3] Joy said.

"Wait one, they split their force? Any special reason for doing that?" Turner asked.

"Sir, they do that frequently. The battalion commander takes two companies and the battalion executive officer takes the other two. Not an uncommon practice, although we discourage it," Joy responded. Turner didn't say anything but had a confused look on his face as he wrote a note. "The 8th Marine is at Firebase Holcomb with Major Huff and Captain Embrey," Joy continued. "It has two companies there. At Pedro is the 1st Marine with Major Cockell and Captain Livingston." Joy pointed out each location as he spoke. "We had some contact the other night outside of Pedro. They sent out an ambush patrol, squad size, and just after they set up, an NVA squad walked into it. More remarkable was that one of the NVA had a map that showed every firebase location and the units on each firebase."

"You said it was a squad and they had that kind of information?" Turley asked with some surprise.

"Oh, it gets better. The next night, they have contact and bag two guys with B-40 rocket launchers." Pausing, he continued. "The 258th Regiment has three battalions, with Major Easley at the regimental headquarters. The 6th Battalion is at

Firebase Barbara. The 7th Battalion is at Da Nang with Major DeBona and Captain Rice. There's also an ANGLICO team at Alpha 2 with Lieutenant Bruggeman, Staff Sergeant Newton, and Corporals Grounds, Worth and Beougher," Joy said and began to look around. "Excuse me, sir, there's someone I want you to meet." And Joy stepped around a partition and returned with another Marine officer.

"Sir, this is First Lieutenant Joel Eisenstein. He's the commander of the ANGLICO team. Joel, this is Lieutenant Colonel Turley." Before Joel could raise his hand to salute, Turley extended his hand. "Glad to meet you, Lieutenant Eisenstein."

"Welcome aboard, sir," Eisenstein said, accepting the extended hand.

"Sir, it's about lunchtime and the advisor mess hall here does a pretty good job. You ready for some chow?" Joy asked. "Lieutenant, would you like to join us?"

"Thank you, sir, but I have some things to take care of right now," Joel responded.

"Right behind you, Major," Turley said as they departed the TOC to walk over to the mess hall. As they did so, Turley noticed the helicopter they'd arrived in, with the crew relaxing around the bird.

"Who provides aviation support up here?" Turley asked.

"Well, the Army provides most of our support. They have an assault helicopter company at Marble Mountain, the 48th, call sign Blue Stars. There's also two Air Cav units up here. One is from the 196th Light Infantry Brigade, which conducts reconnaissance missions for the 3rd Division. It's Delta Troop, 1st of the 1st, and their call sign is Sabre. The other is F Troop, 8th Cav, and their call sign is Blue Ghosts. However, call signs are frequently changed up here, so it may be one thing today and totally different the next. It's supposed to confuse the NVA, but I think all it does is confuse us. We get heavy lift support as well out of Marble Mountain and when available from the fleet. HMM-164 is coming on station soon from aboard the USS *Okinawa*."

"Colonel Metcalf commands the 155 Advisor Team and they're all located here, correct?" Turley asked.

"Yes, sir. He wanted this compound as his headquarters and believes in keeping everything in military order. You noted his starched jungle fatigues and spit-shined boots. I think if he had the soldiers, he'd have them painting the rocks," Major Joy said, adding, "Just my opinion, sir."

"What's his background?" Turley asked.

"Sir, I think he was an advisor on a previous assignment in the late fifties, early sixties, in the Pleiku area. I know his wife and family were over here with him back then as most advisors had their families here until early 1964, when they were all evacuated out. Then he was in Europe for a while and the Pentagon."

"How do you know he had his family over here?" Turley asked, a bit confused.

"His wife told me. She was here about two months ago. Spent almost a week up here," Joy replied.

"His wife was up here?" Turley responded, almost in shock. "Is she military too?"

"No, she isn't military, but she came up and visited him. She lives in the Philippines, Clark Air Force Base, I think." Turley just shook his head at that piece of information.

Entering the mess hall or dining facility as some said, Turley noticed several service members from the different services scattered about the room. Absent were any Vietnamese officers. Fixing a tray of food, Turley and Joy moved to an officer-designated seating area where a lone Army officer was seated.

"Mind if we join you?" Joy asked, approaching.

"Nah, how you doing today, Jim?" the Army major asked.

"Good. Hey, I want you to meet Lieutenant Colonel Turley. He's the new deputy senior Marine advisor," Joy said, setting his tray down. "Sir, Major Smock is the advisor for the newly formed 20th Tank Battalion." As Joy made the introduction, Turley placed his tray down and Smock rose, accepting Turley's hand.

"How do you do, sir?" Smock said.

"Glad to meet you, Major. Please, be seated," Turley responded and they both sat.

"Sir, have you met Major Jack Turner?" Joy asked.

"No, I haven't, although Colonel Dorsey has and explained it all to me. Is he up here now?"

"Yes, sir, has been for a month now. He's made multiple trips to almost all the firebases. Asks a lot of questions."

"Where is he now?"

"He wanted to watch the relief between the 56th Regiment and the 2nd Regiment, so he's somewhere out on Route 558. He'll duck into one of the firebases and spend the night," Joy said. "He won't tell Metcalf where he's going as he doesn't want him to be calling ahead of him and giving people a heads-up," Joy added.

"For what he has to do, can't say I blame him," Turley said, taking a sip of his coffee.

* * *

Warrant Officer Mike Williams was assigned to Delta Troop and would fly anything, anytime he could. After high school graduation, he attended the US Naval Academy as a cadet, but it was mutually agreed that he should pursue other interests. He signed up the next day for the Army Warrant Officer Rotary Wing flight program. Initially arriving in Vietnam, he was assigned to the 101st Airborne Division, where he was flying AH-1G Cobra gunships. Due to the drawdowns, he had been bounced from the 101st Airborne Division to the 196th. This happened to a lot of pilots that had less than six months in-country when their unit was sent home. Mike was Cobra-qualified, but today he jumped into a UH-1H to fly as a copilot. He wanted to build flight time and wasn't getting it as the unit was overstrength on Cobra pilots. The morning's mission was a VIP run flying a news team around the area. They had finished the tour and dropped the news crew off and were told to shut down and wait at Ai Tu.

"Okay, I'm going to wander up to the TOC and see what Metcalf has for us today. Actually, I think I'll see if I can piss him off again," Captain Mike Keenan, the aircraft commander, said. Days before, Mike had been flying the command-and-control or C&C aircraft for a pink team.[4] Mike's commander had put the word out that no aircraft were to fly over the terrain marked as the DMZ, which was about five kilometers wide. On the mission, the LOH reported seeing tank tracks on the DMZ and reported that he had seen the tank. When Metcalf received the report, he ordered Mike to have his team engage. Mike refused the order. Metcalf was visibly upset and had a confrontation with Captain Keenan when he returned to the TOC for a debrief. Mike's commander backed him up. Metcalf was not happy.

"Okay, I guess we'll just get comfortable, then," Mr. Williams said, taking a supine position on the floor of the helicopter. The crew chief assumed the position under the tail boom in his hammock and the gunner took the bench seat. Everyone was down for some sleep.

* * *

Lunch was satisfying and took about an hour. As Turley and Joy were finishing up, Turley's ears perked up. Silence fell over the entire mess hall. The distant sounds of artillery could be heard and almost immediately thereafter the unforgettable sound of a freight train approaching. "*Incoming!*" someone yelled, followed by a mad dash for the door and the nearest bunker as incoming artillery rounds impacted on the runway and compound. As he ran, Turley glanced back to see the helicopter crew scrambling to get into the air. The crew already had the blades turning and was beginning to lift off. *Funny, the pilot isn't wearing a helmet*, Turley thought as he dove into the nearest bunker.

Mr. Williams had been dreaming about home when a pounding noise woke him. Looking up, he saw the crew chief standing in front of him and the gunner as well. Both were looking away from the aircraft when the next artillery round impacted five hundred meters away, followed by a second round maybe four hundred meters away. A flight of Vietnamese helicopters immediately started their engines and were departing like a covey of quail that had just been flushed.

"Untie the blades, we're getting out of here," Williams yelled and didn't need to repeat himself. While the crew chief retrieved his hammock off the tail stinger, the gunner untied the main rotor and Mike scrambled into the copilot seat. *Where's the captain?* he was thinking, then decided, *Why wait for him? He's in a nice bunker.*

"Clear!" Mike yelled, notifying the crew he was starting the engine. Mike didn't bother to follow the normal starting procedures. Instead, he went right to the battery switch, on, the main fuel switch, on, and throttle set. He pressed the start button and the turbine engine began to turn. Another round impacted only three hundred meters away. Mike's eyes were glued to the N1 gauge, watching the turbine speed increase. At forty percent, he rolled the throttle on and watched as the power increased. Another round impacted one hundred and fifty meters away. When Mike felt that he had sufficient power to move the aircraft, he picked up to a hover and started. As he did so, the tail boom suddenly pitched the nose down and a loud explosion could be heard, along with "Son of a bitch!" from the crew chief.

"What?" Mike yelled, but he heard nothing except the loudness of the engine, the whopping of the blades and the wind. That was when he realized that he hadn't put on his helmet, or his seat belt and shoulder harness. But they were flying, and that was what mattered at that moment.

* * *

Lieutenant Colonel Camper, an Army advisor, was on his second tour as an advisor. He had recently been posted to the 56th ARVN Regiment, 3rd ARVN Infantry Division, a newly formed regiment with less-than-stellar officers, noncommissioned officers and soldiers. The regiment was made up of officers that had been relieved for a variety of reasons in other units. The soldiers were a mixture of deserters, slackers and ex-convicts. To say the least, Camper and Major Brown had a leadership challenge to go along with a training problem. Major Brown was also Army and on his second tour, his first as an advisor. Standing next to their jeep, they had a map spread out on the hood and were going over the day's activities.

"Okay, the 56th and the 2nd Regiments are going to conduct a relief in place. The 56th will move southwest from Charlie 2 to Camp Carroll. The 2nd Regiment will come north and occupy the vacated positions. First Battalion will move to FSB Fuller and relieve a battalion of the 2nd," Camper outlined as he pointed at the map that he and Brown were reviewing.

"Do you think they're going to run into any trouble?" Brown asked.

"Well, the guys in the Army sensor readout bunker say

there's been a lot of indications of heavy vehicle movement west of FSB Sarge along Highway 9. Truck movements in the DMZ are also increasing over the past three weeks. They claim there's been a lot of truck movement across the DMZ," Camper explained.

"Well, last night's rain should slow any movement down. I just hope it doesn't impede the 56th," Major Brown surmised.

"I'll move with the regimental headquarters, which is following behind First Battalion. Why don't you travel with the logistic elements and bring up the rear?" Camper suggested as he started to fold the map.

"Sounds good, sir, I'll see you at Carroll," Major Brown responded before he exchanged a salute with Camper and moved back to his vehicle.

As the column passed Firebase Charlie 2, the First Battalion peeled off and took the first right turn that would take them to Firebase Fuller. The regimental headquarters continued to move towards Charlie 3 and Firebase Carroll. Around noon came the sounds of artillery being fired in the distance, and it was all coming from the north.

As the rounds began to fall on the First Battalion, panic broke out. ARVN soldiers had never been engaged with 130mm artillery in such quantity or quality. It quickly became obvious that this was adjusted artillery due to the accuracy of the impacting rounds. Key command-and-control vehicles were destroyed in the first fifteen minutes, cutting off communications with the outside world. In one hour, over two hundred rounds had engaged the First Battalion, with almost no response in return. The NVA howitzers were positioned beyond the range of the 175mm howitzers at Carroll. There was little relief for the 56th Regiment's First Battalion, and it dissolved.

* * *

As the radio traffic increased with initial calls for artillery support and any air support that could be launched, the mood wasn't excited, until reports of probes on the firebases south of the DMZ began coming in. Air support was out of the question due to the low ceilings and cloud cover. When the sound of incoming artillery could be heard outside the command bunker serving as the 3rd Division's tactical operations center, the activity in the TOC kicked into high gear. Unfortunately, the antenna farm for the Divisional TOC was also one of the targets, and communications with forward elements were sporadic at best.

During a lull in the artillery that was slamming the compound, Turley and Joy made their way back to the TOC. Joy was concerned about the 147th Regiment and wanted to get back to Mai Loc. Calling the Sabre aircraft, he requested they return and pick him up for the flight back.

"Sir, I'm going to head back to Mai Loc. I'll give you a call when I assess the situation up there if that's alright," Joy said. "I'll leave Captain Murray here with you and Lieutenant Eisenstein."

"Sure, I'll get an aircraft through the advisor unit and get back to Saigon. Be safe," Turley said as they exchanged handshakes. Once Joy departed, Turley turned to the G-3 advisor, Major Wilson. "If there's anything you want me to do, just ask." Wilson was an Army officer and a stranger to physical fitness as he appeared to be fifty pounds overweight.

"Thank you, sir. Could you monitor the advisor net? We have two nets here, the Vietnamese command net and the advisor net. Depending on the traffic, we compare what the Vietnamese commanders are reporting to what's confirmed by the advisors on a separate net," Wilson explained.

"Can do," Turley responded, expecting to be in Saigon that evening.

9

INVASION

  48th Assault Helicopter Company
  Marble Mountain, South Vietnam

"Alright, listen up," Major Kingman said with an elevated voice over the pilots' conversations. "Here's the situation as of right now. The NVA are pounding the forward outposts as well as Carroll and Ai Tu with adjusted artillery, mortars and rockets. They're hitting everything north of Quang Tri. They caught the 56th Regiment and the 2nd Regiment with their pants down doing a relief in place. 2nd Regiment was moving up to Alpha 1, 2, 3 and 4 with 56th Regiment coming back to Camp Carroll and FSB Fuller. The 57th Regiment at Charlie 1 and Alpha 1, 2, and 3 has been getting the crap pounded out of them but have no radio comms with anyone, so they couldn't get the word out. Simultaneously, FSB Mai Loc and FB Holcomb and Dong Ha are also being pounded. T-54, T-55 and PT-76 tanks are reported in the area of FSB Fuller and FSB Con Thien, Alpha 1 and Alpha 2."

As Major Kingman outlined the enemy situation, pilots exchanged concerned looks. Older pilots who had flown in Lam Son 719 the previous year were having flashbacks to the intense fire in that operation.

"It appears that the 304th and 308th Divisions are making the attack with a total of nine regiments, to include tanks, PT-76s, and artillery. MACV is scrambling to figure this mess out. I've heard that the Saigon Warriors don't believe this is a major invasion," Major Kingman explained with some disgust.

"The weather is the shits and is going to be worse tomorrow, I understand, so we're on standby to launch when it does break. Get out and check your aircraft. If anything needs to be fixed, get it to maintenance ASAP," Major Kingman directed.

Looking around, he spotted his next target. "Captain Cole, do you have contact with the people back at 1st Aviation Brigade?"

Captain Tom Cole had previously been the maintenance officer for the 48th during the Lam Son 719 operation. He was currently serving on the 1st Aviation Brigade staff and looking into aircraft availability in Military Region 1. He had stopped at the 48th to visit with old friends.

"Yes, sir, almost daily I talk to General Belew about the conditions up here," Cole responded. "Last time I spoke with his staff, they were concerned about the small number of aircraft that are here in I Corps."

"What are the numbers? Kingman asked, concerned as the 48th was the only combat aviation company in the region besides the Air Cav troops.

"Sir, there are a total of thirty-nine UH-1H aircraft, of which eighteen are in our unit, twenty OH-6 aircraft, mostly with the cav units, eighteen AH-1G gunships, and six CH-47s. There are also the Vietnamese Air Force helicopters, but I don't have any numbers on them," Cole finished.

"Good, get on the horn and tell him what's going on. It

appears that the intel weenies in Saigon don't believe this is an invasion. We need more Cobra gunships up here and gunships that can knock out a tank—birds with a twenty mike-mike."[1]

"Yes, sir—" Cole said before he was interrupted.

"Or better yet, some of those 2.75 rockets, HEAT I believe they're called, with the shaped charge to use against tanks, and lots of them. Also see if any gunships are in-country with the SS-11 antitank missiles."

* * *

Jack wanted to witness the relief in place being conducted by the 56th Regiment and the 2nd Regiment. From what Jack had observed, he wasn't impressed with the 56th Regiment. The level of professionalism was dismal and the officers' leadership wasn't much better. The 56th Regiment was supposed to assume responsibility for the area previously occupied by the 2nd Regiment, to include Camp Carroll, FSB Khe Gio and FSB Fuller. The 2nd Regiment would assume responsibility for Alpha 3, Alpha 4 and Charlie 2. He was sitting at the intersection of Route 558 and the road out to Fuller. What he was watching could only be described as a clusterfuck. The vehicles from both regiments were mixed together with no obvious traffic plan and apparently no plan for when units were to move. Jack remembered from his days at the Benning School for Boys, as the US Army Infantry School was called, that a relief in place was one of the most difficult military maneuvers to perform. It had to be precisely timed, organized and supervised, and none of that was happening. Jack hadn't seen one advisor or senior leader. *This is not good*, he was thinking when he heard a distinct sound in the distance to the west.

"*Incoming!*" Hanner yelled as the first round slammed into the roadbed, immediately followed by several other rounds that began to walk up the road. Jack was lying on the ground close to his vehicle, observing this. *Shit, that's observed and adjusted fire. There has to be a forward observer around here adjusting this shit.* As he continued to lie there, he observed the panic set in amongst the Vietnamese soldiers. Rather than driving their vehicles out of the danger zone, many jumped from the cabs and ran down the road to the south. The abandoned vehicles blocked the road and prevented others from moving to their respective locations.

"Hanner, are you okay?" Jack yelled as another round slammed into the road to the south.

"Sir, I'll be a lot better when we get out of here," Hanner yelled back.

"Well, let's go, then. I've seen enough," Jack said and pushed up to run to his jeep. Hanner won that foot race and had the vehicle in gear and moving even before Jack was seated.

"Head for Carroll. I've got to call Ai Tu," Jack said.

"Yes, sir." And Hanner floored the accelerator.

10

ANGLICO

155th Advisor Team TOC
Ai Tu, South Vietnam

The 155th Advisor team was collocated with the 3rd ARVN Division Headquarters and consisted of about fifty-five people, but most were support personnel and not advisors. Two Army majors were with two of the regiments of the division, the 56th and 57th Regiments. The 2nd Regiment was considered a squared-away unit and no American advisor was located with them. The elements collocated with the 3rd ARVN Headquarters were mostly cooks, bakers and candlestick makers and not frontline soldiers. They were commanded by an Army colonel, Colonel Donald Metcalf. Ai Tu was previously home to a US Marine division but had been abandoned or at least downsized and appeared mostly abandoned when Colonel Metcalf and his team had arrived in August 1971. Since then, they had made it a comfortable place with a PX, an officers' club, an NCO club and a mess hall that worked wonders.

Captain Bob Wells was the team adjutant responsible for the administrative duties for the team. On a previous tour, he had been an infantry advisor in the southern part of Vietnam, referred to as the Delta. Hoping not to pull another tour in Vietnam, he branch transferred to the Adjutant General Corps and wore the "shield of shame" as infantry officers referred to the Adjutant General's Corps insignia. He was also in the headquarters TOC when the first 130mm artillery round screamed into the compound and landed two hundred yards away. Simultaneously over the radio he heard, "Enemy tanks, trucks, troops in the open, coming through the DMZ... my God...as far as I can see."[1]

"Who made that call?" Wells asked, hoping someone had gotten the call sign. No one responded as everyone was moving to the covered bunkers next to the TOC. Wells immediately notified Colonel Metcalf, who was in the process of departing to go on Easter leave in the Philippines to see his family. Major Wells began to count the rounds and counted over one hundred in the first hour. *It's going to be a long night*, he thought.

* * *

3rd Battalion, 57th Regiment
Firebase Alpha 2

Alpha 2 was located just east of Highway 1, the main road from Saigon to Hanoi. The surrounding terrain was low scrub brush covering the gently rolling landscape. The base was nothing special but laid out like a typical firebase. Positioned on a small ridge with a steep north-facing slope, the firebase was in close proximity to the town of Gio Linh, where many of the soldiers' families lived. On the north side of the base were six 155-millimeter howitzers oriented north and northwest. The center of the firebase was dominated by a building left over from the French occupation days that had a lower level where the ANGLICO team resided. An observation post on the roof stood about thirty feet. Defensive positions for infantry soldiers were oriented around the artillery tubes. Several Quonset huts were located to the south side of the firebase and used for storage and ammunition holding.

"Well, sir, what do you think of this place?" asked Staff Sergeant Newton, USMC. Sergeant Newton and his ANGLICO fire control team had arrived the previous month, but Lieutenant Bruggeman was fairly new. He served as the team chief.

"I think this is going to work just fine, Sergeant," First Lieutenant Dave Bruggeman replied as he scanned the surrounding terrain with his field glasses. Lieutenant Bruggeman was a Marine Corps artillery officer. "After they finish eating lunch, have Corporal Worth and Lance Corporal Beougher start loading some sandbags up here on the roof and let's build up this position some. Keep Lance Corporal Grounds on the radios," Bruggeman directed. Corporal Worth was a senior radio operator and had proven his ability to make radios function as intended even under dire circumstances on more than one occasion. He was from Chicago, Illinois, and had an Irish background. Being a ladies' man, he had the nickname Diamond Jim. He'd volunteered to be here, turning down a desk job back in Saigon. This was his second tour in Vietnam.

"Yes, sir, I'll get them right on it—" Sergeant Newton said before he was interrupted.

"*Incoming!*" someone yelled as the first rounds of incoming artillery began slamming into the compound.

Bruggeman and Newton were scanning the distant terrain, looking to see if they could spot the gun positions or targets of opportunity.

"I can't tell where this fire is coming from," Bruggeman said as he maintained a low crouch on the rooftop behind a wall of sandbags.

"Wherever it's coming from, it's awfully accurate," Newton said as someone bumped into him. Startled, he started to swing his weapon at whoever it was, only stopping short of clubbing Corporal Worth.

"Sarge, where is this mortar fire coming from?" Grounds asked with wide eyes.

"This ain't mortar rounds, Grounds. This is long-range artillery fire," Newton said as four more rounds exploded in the area of the Quonset huts. "Mortar rounds don't come screaming in like this. You don't hear them coming," Newton explained, ducking again as four more rounds announced their arrival and impacted in the area of the Quonset huts. The origin of the incoming rounds wasn't visible, but by the sound, they were coming out of North Vietnam across the DMZ. Bruggeman quickly decided to begin looking closer for targets of opportunity. It didn't take long before he saw those targets.

Moving through the low brush, small groups of infantry soldiers in the traditional green uniforms with pit helmets were moving south across the DMZ.

"Sarge, get on the radio and notify the 3rd Division TOC what's going on here. Tell Lieutenant Eisenstein we're receiving long-range artillery fire and it appears we have some probes approaching," Bruggeman ordered as four more rounds impacted forward of the artillery position on the lower slope. Cranking the field telephone, Bruggeman called the fire-base fire direction center with the intention of adjusting the fire from the 155mm howitzers.

"Fire mission, troops in open, TRP 21, HE with VT."
And he completed his call for fire to the English-speaking Vietnamese officer he'd been working with since arriving. The Vietnamese officer repeated the call back to be sure he had it right. He and Bruggeman had plotted out target reference points, TRPs, days earlier so the artillery could adjust quickly from one target to another. Bruggeman waited and waited. The only sound he was hearing was the screaming of incoming artillery and no announcements of outgoing artillery. Frustration finally overcame him and he stood and leaned over the sandbag wall to see the 155 artillery position.

"Oh, shit," he mumbled and ducked back down.

"What is it, Lieutenant?" Newton asked. "Did they hit the howitzers?"

"No. The gun crews abandoned the tubes!" Bruggeman said.

"They've never been on the receiving end of artillery fire like this. Let me go down and see if I can kick some ass," Newton said and quickly departed.

Picking up the field phone handset, Bruggeman called Eisenstein. "Joel, the gun crews have abandoned the guns. We have no counterbattery fire. Newton is down in the trenches kicking ass to get them on the guns, but they're not moving from what I can tell. Over."

"Dave, we have two destroyers offshore that I've requested they move in and support. It's the USS *Buchanan* and the USS *Joseph Strauss* and they're standing by for fire missions. They'll be contacting you soon. I'll try to get some air over you, but the weather has everyone grounded right now. Over."

"Roger, standing by," Bruggeman said. Almost immediately, the FM radio squelch indicated a call was coming.

"Custom House Five, Sharp Note, over."[2]

"Who's Sharp Note?" Worth asked.

"The *Buchanan*," Bruggeman said as he glanced at Worth

and keyed the handset. "Sharp Note, Custom House Five, fire mission, over."

"Custom House Five, send it." The USS *Buchanan* was on station about a mile offshore. It had two five-inch guns, each with a single tube. The .54-caliber shells were capable of firing about fourteen miles and well within range of Alpha 2. Bruggeman quickly passed the fire mission to the ship, which commenced firing. Bruggeman turned to watch enemy troops moving through the brush. Small-arms fire was beginning to increase along the forward perimeter. *Damn the Vietnamese gunners*, he was thinking when the distinct sound of a naval shell increased in intensity before the shell impacted forward of the slope. The probing enemy faltered as the second round followed the first, followed by several others. *This is going to hold off the assault, but without counterbattery fire, we're not going to be able to hold out here. We've got to get some counter-battery fire*, Bruggeman thought as he continued to adjust naval gunfire.

* * *

FSB Mai Loc

While Bruggeman was frustrated by the lack of initiative on the part of the Vietnamese artillery gunners, the situation on the far western flank was no better. "Hey, Chief, can you land at the firebase?" Major Joy asked Captain Keenan. Keenan was able to get Mike Williams to return to Ai Tu once Williams got his helmet on and started answering the radios.

"Sir, I can land at the Huong Hoa District Headquarters airfield but not the firebase," Keenan responded, noticing the impacting artillery rounds on the Mai Loc firebase. "I can drop you and go refuel. You call when you want me to come back for you," he added.

"Roger, that'll work, just put me down," Joy agreed as Keenan started a steep-turning rapid descent towards the small runway at the district headquarters, barely touching the ground. Joy was out of the aircraft and running for the road leading to the firebase. A military truck from the 147th Vietnamese Marines was hauling ass up the road towards the firebase. Joy managed to flag it down and ride the short distance to the firebase between incoming artillery.

When he entered the underground command bunker for the 147th Regiment, the first person he saw was Major Tom Gnibus, USMC, advisor for the 2nd Battalion. "Tom, what's the situation?" he asked.

"Not good. We can't get any artillery support in a counter-battery roll or any support for Sarge."

"Why not?" Joy asked, surprised and concerned.

"One, our communications are spotty at best. One of the first things they hit—" Tom didn't finish his sentence before both Marines heard the incoming round and hit the floor just before it went off next to the bunker. The shock wave was bad enough and the dust it raised was choking, but at least that was the extent of the damage. "—was the antenna farm. We're jury-rigging some antennas to restore comms. Second, whenever the gun bunnies begin to get incoming, they leave the guns and hide in the bunkers. We can't get them back on the guns unless we practically threaten to shoot them."

"We've got to do something, or this could get real bad. What about air support?" Joy asked, already having an idea what the answer was going to be.

"The weather has just about everything grounded. Surprised you got in here. We can't get any tac air support or gunships. We've sent a request for B-52 strikes, but that won't happen until tomorrow morning. We're on our own until then, I'm afraid," Gnibus admitted.

"Well, who's providing some fire support?" Joy asked, looking at the map board.

"Carroll's providing some support to us, but when they're not supporting us, they're doing counterbattery fire. The one-seven-fives are all at Carroll with the range to reach the one-hundred-thirties that are hitting Sarge and Nui Ba Ho. The one-five-fives here, however, can't reach that far and are supporting almost every firebase up here when we can get the gun bunnies out of the bunkers. The one-five-fives just don't have the range of the one-hundred-thirties the NVA are using."

Joy responded by just shaking his head.

* * *

FSB Sarge

Since noontime, FSB Sarge was receiving incoming artillery that was intense and accurate at times. There was no doubt that the North Vietnamese had a spotter adjusting the fire. Collocated on Sarge was a listening post manned by two soldiers that were listening to the chatter on the North Vietnamese frequencies. Although they were located at Sarge, they did not work for the advisors at Sarge. In fact, the advisors were not allowed to ask them about their work. They weren't allowed to tell the advisors what they were hearing either. As they were all Americans, the advisors did look out for their well-being.

"Specialist Westcout, this is Major Boomer. You two doing okay?" Boomer asked as another artillery round slammed into the base. "Are you and Crosley doin' okay?"

Boomer repeated himself as he wasn't sure Westcout had heard him.

"Yes, sir. Our bunker had a couple of close ones, but we're good."

"Good, keep me posted that you're okay," Boomer said, hanging up the TA 312 field phone.

"Yes, sir," Westcout replied and hung up the field phone. Specialist Crosley was listening intently on the radio frequency that the North Vietnamese were using. They had identified other frequencies that the North Vietnamese were using, but this particular one was an immediate concern to them. The other frequencies that they monitored, they passed on to higher headquarters.

Westcout grabbed a cup of coffee from their in-house percolator coffeepot, then handed the cup to Crosley. "Any more traffic?" he asked.

"No, he's quiet right now. He must be moving to a new location, the little bastard," Crosley said, accepting the cup. As it was just the two of them at this listening post and they had a bunker to themselves, they had all the comforts of home, such as they were in Vietnam. Their individual sleeping areas were along two of the walls, with their makeshift kitchen along the third wall and the work area on the fourth wall. The dirt floor was covered with flattened, discarded C ration cardboard cases to keep the mud and dust on the floor to a minimum. Each wall had an opening for a window approximately twelve inches by twenty-four inches to allow for a cross breeze supplemented by their individual fans. A doorway was at the corner of two of the walls on the north side.

As Westcout poured another cup of coffee for himself, he noticed Crosley setting his cup down and pressing his hands to his earphones. Crosley's face took on a look of intensity as he slowly turned towards Westcout, who started to reach for the field phone.

"*Fire mission!*" Crosley yelled. Westcout immediately cranked the field phone to warn Major Boomer.

"*Incoming!*" Westcout yelled. His warning was immediately followed by the increasingly loud sound of a freight train approaching.

The impacting artillery round sent a shock wave through the bunker and threw everyone to the floor in Boomer's bunker. As more rounds impacted around the bunker, everyone remained on the floor. Many attempted to get under desks and tables, which in hindsight wouldn't have offered much protection if the ceiling had collapsed. As Major Boomer lay on the floor, more rounds continued to slam into the firebase. Some of the Vietnamese staff were attempting to call regimental headquarters to get counterbattery fire. The engine roar of a rocket was suddenly heard as the roof of the bunker was penetrated. Prior to exploding, the 122mm rocket buried its nose in the dirt floor of the bunker. The explosion was deafening to those inside. Boomer lay on the floor wondering what the next life was like when he realized that he was still alive. Slowly looking around, he saw others doing the same through the dust and smoke. He heard nothing, only silence, but could see some movement. When he looked up, sunlight poured through a hole in the roof about a foot across.

This went on for thirty minutes, with almost a constant barrage of 130mm artillery laying in ten rounds to fifteen rounds a minute.

As Boomer's hearing returned and incoming rounds stopped, he slowly stood, coughing on the dust that had been raised during the barrage.

"Everyone okay?" Boomer asked, looking around. A few Vietnamese that understood English gave him a thumbs-up. Looking at the center of the bunker where the round hit was a hole two feet wide and three feet deep. The rocket had penetrated the roof of the bunker and buried itself three feet into the ground inside the bunker before it exploded. Rather than spreading out, the blast had gone straight back up through the hole in the roof. Silent prayers of thanks initially occupied all thoughts.[3]

"Were you counting rounds?" Boomer asked his Vietnamese counterpart.

"Yeah, about ten to fifteen a minute. What about you?" Major Quang, the 4th Battalion commander, asked.

"I got the same number," Boomer responded.

"They must have three tubes devoted just to us, I suspect. Rate of fire on a one-thirty is what? Five rounds a minute?" Boomer stated.

Boomer picked up the field phone and cranked the handle to check on Westcout. The line was dead. "The wires must have been cut. Let me run over there and get us reconnected," Boomer said, placing the receiver back in the cradle and heading for the doorway. As he emerged from the damaged bunker, he was appalled at the destruction of the firebase. It seemed like he was looking across the surface of the moon covered with trash as there were so many craters from impacting shells. Anything that had been above ground was destroyed and unusable. Anything flammable was burning. Amazingly, some people were moving around and very few people appeared to be injured. The ARVN Marines were already moving from their bunkers back into their fighting positions on the perimeter. Many hadn't left the safety of the perimeter bunkers, knowing the primary targets at this point would be the larger structures in the center of the firebase.

As Boomer followed the exposed TA-1 field wire towards Westcout and Crosley's position, he couldn't find a break in the wire. Looking up, he saw the crater where the wire was cut. *Good, found it and can fix this quick*, he thought. Then it struck him. The crater was where Westcout and Crosley's bunker had been. Peering into the hole, Smith quickly realized that the explosion wasn't an external explosion—from the scattered debris, the round must have come through the open doorway and exploded inside the bunker. There was no sign of either men.

Throughout the rest of the day, the pattern repeated itself. Short, intense artillery barrages followed by a lull of thirty minutes to an hour. As night closed in, the North Vietnamese forces began to probe the perimeter, attempting to identify fighting positions that were still occupied. The disciplined South Vietnamese Marines didn't take the bait but only engaged when they had a clear target to shoot, and when they did, fire discipline was exercised as they engaged with minimal fire.

"Sarge, this is Spectre, over," came over the advisor net radio. Boomer looked up with a sign of hope registered on his face.

Grabbing the hand mike, Major Boomer replied, "Spectre, this is Sarge, over."

"Sarge, this is Spectre. Understand you could use a bit of help. I believe I'm over your location, but I have a solid overcast below me. Is there any way you can mark your position? Over."

Spectre was a US Air Force C-130 cargo plane specially equipped with multiple Gatling guns mounted inside and pointing outward through the existing windows. In a banked turn to the left, Spectre could put one round in every square inch of a football field in one pass, and these were 25mm rounds. It also mounted a 105-millimeter howitzer in the left-side doorway that was extremely accurate at engaging targets. Other classified equipment made the aircraft extremely accurate in engaging targets at night.

"Spectre, I'm activating our electronic positioning device. Wait one," Boomer said as he grabbed it out of a container and went outside to position it on top of the bunker. A few minutes later, he returned.

"Spectre, this is Sarge. Device is set. Over," Boomer stated and waited...and waited.

"Sarge, this is Spectre. We're not receiving a signal. What else have you got?"

Looking around, Boomer spied the next best thing. "Spectre, I have an IR strobe. Give me a minute to go outside and initiate the strobe. Over," Boomer said, heading out the door with the infrared strobe light. After a few minutes, he heard, "Sarge, this is Spectre, negative contact. This cloud cover is just too thick. Over."

"Spectre, that's all we have. Over," Boomer said in a dejected voice.

"Sarge, I have some flares on board. I'm going to drop them and you tell me where they are in relation to you, over."

"Roger, we'll be looking for them." And Boomer moved outside the bunker and stood outside, turning to look in different directions to see the flares. An airplane could be heard, and from the sound it was obvious he was either very high or a long ways off or possibly both. Boomer was holding the AN/PRC-77 FM radio.

"Sarge, we've dropped the flares. Where are they in relation to you?" Spectre asked.

"Spectre, this is Sarge. We don't see any flares, over." Spectre could tell that Sarge was dejected at this point.

"Roger, Sarge, I'm sorry. This weather is just too thick. Spectre breaking station. Good luck," were Spectre's departing words. Major Boomer suddenly felt very alone.

* * *

It was getting dark when Jack and Hanner rolled through the gate at Camp Carroll. At first the Vietnamese guards wouldn't allow Jack to pass until he broke into Vietnamese and explained what bodily harm he would do to them if they didn't get out of his way. Arriving at the command post, Jack entered and viewed the chaos for a moment. He couldn't tell who was in charge or who was doing what. Finally a Vietnamese lieutenant colonel approached him. He didn't look happy.

Mustering up his Vietnamese, Jack was about to speak when the lieutenant colonel spoke first in broken English. "You go, you go!"

"Sir, I'm—"

"I say you go. Advisor bunker over there. You go." And then he turned and walked off, mumbling under his breath. *What's this all about?* Jack was thinking as he walked out and started in the direction the colonel had indicated. Finally he saw a light from a doorway of a bunker and entered. Two American officers were seated, drinking coffee.

"And who might you be, Major?" one asked as they both looked up.

"Sir, I'm Major Jack Tuner and I was looking for the senior advisor."

"Ah, the illustrious Major Turner who pissed off Metcalf. Hi, I'm Lieutenant Colonel Camper and this is Major Brown. Sorry we weren't here when you stopped by the last time. Have a seat. We have a couple of spare cots if you're going to spend the night," Camper offered.

"Thank you. We will. What's going on?" Jack asked to the sound of outgoing artillery. Carroll was a major fire support base with over twenty artillery tubes, and four of those were the long-range 175mm artillery howitzers.

"It appears that the North Vietnamese have decided it was time to shake things up a bit. They're hitting every firebase with long-range artillery. We've had reports of ground attacks supported by tanks but no confirmations of that," Camper indicated.

"Were either of you with the relief operation today?" Jack asked.

"You mean with that clusterfuck? Yeah, I was with Colonel Dinh. The plan was for the regimental command post to follow the lead battalion. Another battalion was to provide flank security and flow into Fuller while 1st Battalion got to Khe Gio. When the battalion got to Fuller, it was hit by a ground attack supported by tanks and artillery. We've heard nothing from them for the past four hours," Camper replied.

"Who's the angry Vietnamese lieutenant colonel in the command post?" Jack asked.

"That would be the regimental executive officer, chief of staff. He no likey American GI. Guy's a real ass. Tries to keep us from talking to Colonel Dinh. He toss you out of the CP?"

"Yup" was all Jack said.

"They're trying to figure things out and he doesn't want any advice on how to do that. We'll look at it in the morning and get it changed. Might as well get some sleep. I suspect it's going to be a while before we do," Camper said, stretching out on his cot.

11

NAVAL GUNFIRE

31 MARCH 1972
USS *Buchanan*
Gulf of Tonkin

Sitting off the north coast of South Vietnam, the US Navy had several ships in the area. Over the years, US aircraft carriers had been standing by, providing close-air support, MiG suppression, and bombing missions in both North and South Vietnam in support of the US Forces but also the South Vietnamese forces. Aircraft carriers generally held position at one point in the Gulf of Tonkin commonly referred to as Yankee Station, which was about one hundred miles off the coast. Smaller ships such as destroyers were much closer to the shore, sometimes well within the artillery range of North Vietnamese shore batteries.

The USS *Buchanan* (DDG-14) had been sailing off the coast of Quang Tri since the March 17. She was accompanied by the USS *Joseph Strauss* (DDG-16). Both ships were Charles Adams–class destroyers and both had been commissioned in

1962. They were significant upgrades over the old destroyers of the great war in the Pacific and Atlantic. Both carried two Mark 42 5/57in (127mm) autoloader guns capable of firing forty rounds a minute with a range of fourteen miles in support of ground forces. The USS *New Jersey*, the only battleship commissioned during the Vietnam War, had already returned to the United States and had been decommissioned.

"Excuse me, sir," Lieutenant Murdock said, approaching Commander William J. Thearle on the bridge. Thearle was sitting in the captain's chair, holding a cup of coffee and enjoying the late-afternoon cruise. Seas were calm and the lush green coastline was inviting for someone seeking some shore leave.

"What's up, Mr. Murdock?"

"Sir, we have a flash message. Operation Freedom Train has been initiated. Appears that the North Vietnamese have begun shelling the firebases along the DMZ. I would expect that we'll be getting calls for fire shortly."

Standing, Thearle said, "Okay, let's take a look at the map and move in closer to the shore to extend the range of our support. The water depth here should let us get about a mile off the coast. Have you got a plot on each of the firebases up here?"

"Yes, sir. We received that when we arrived as well as a target reference point with each firebase."

"Good. Let's move so we can support the bases the farthest north. Which ones would those be?"

"Sir, Alpha 2 is in range, and there's a bridge at Dong Ha that we received as a target reference point."

"What else is within range?"

"That's about it, sir. They have a lot of artillery on those firebases that should protect them."

"Okay, let's move to a firing position and notify Strauss of our intentions."

"Aye-aye, sir," Murdock said, and he left the bridge and returned to the Combat Information Center or CIC.

Engine vibrations throughout the ship notified the three hundred and fifty-four crew members that something was happening as *Buchanan* increased speed to reach the point where she could maximize the range of her guns. With the increase in speed came a familiar refrain.

"General quarters, general quarters, this is not a drill," came over the ship's loudspeaker, accented by a clanging bell. Crewmembers moved rapidly to their assigned positions, dogging hatches and breaking out equipment that was unique to the command of general quarters. As each department was fully manned and ready, each reported to the CIC. When all departments had reported fully manned and ready, CIC notified the captain. Almost immediately, the radio traffic commenced.

"Sharp Note, Sharp Note, Custom House Six, over."

"Custom House Six, Sharp Note, over."

"Sharp Note, contact Custom House Five for fire mission. He is standing by, over."

"Roger, break. Custom House Five, Sharp Note, over."

"Sharp Note, Sharp Note, Custom House Five, fire mission," crackled over the radio.

"Custom House Five, send it."

"Sharp Note, troops in the open, indirect, grid location..." And Bruggeman provided the coordinates of the hilltop north of Alpha 2. "Fragmentation, variable time, will adjust. Over."

Almost immediately the call for fire was read back to Custom House Five, who confirmed the ship had gotten it right. Within a minute, five-inch rounds were in flight.

12

ONLY GETS WORSE

It had been a long night, and from the sound of things, the day was going to be just as long. Radio traffic from all the firebases along the DMZ was the same—heavy and continuous artillery bombardment and concentrated ground assaults by NVA soldiers. The weather was supporting the NVA, preventing any close-air support from tactical fighter aircraft or attack helicopters. Attack helicopters of F Troop and Delta Troop sat on the ground at Marble Mountain outside Da Nang, waiting for an opportunity to get in the air. The 48th with their attack platoon, the Jokers, sat at Marble Mountain as well. The Charlie-model UH-1C gunships that had flown the previous year in Lam Son 719 had all been replaced as all but one had been shot down and destroyed in that engagement. Reports had been coming into the TOC all night from each of the firebases along the DMZ and in Quang Tri Province for heavy artillery barrages and probing infantry assaults. The news was so bad, Colonel Metcalf cut his trip to the Philippines and walked into the TOC, approaching Lieutenant Colonel Turley.

"Gerald, what's the status?" he asked, almost as if he thought Turley worked for him, which he didn't.

Why the hell doesn't he ask his Ops officer? Turley was thinking, but he responded, "Sir, every firebase is under pressure. One battalion of the 56th that was going to FSB Fuller has just disappeared. Sarge and Nui Ba Ho are under a lot of pressure, and I doubt if Nui Ba Ho will hold out much longer. Alpha 1, 2, 3 and 4 are all receiving incoming artillery. The problem is no air support and minimal artillery support," Turley explained.

"What's the problem with the artillery?"

"Sir, the gunners are abandoning the tubes as soon as incoming rounds land and won't leave the bunkers until someone threatens to shoot them."

After a long pause, Metcalf said, "Okay, I've talked to General Giai and we're moving the 3rd Division TOC back to Quang Tri, the Citadel." This was the first Turley had heard about a movement, but he suddenly knew the reason for the absence of personnel in the TOC. Metcalf had already talked to the members of Advisory Team 155 before coming to the command post. "Everyone is packing their shit right now and loading up. I want you to stay and man the forward TOC until we get established and then move everyone back to Quang Tri."

"Sir, I'm not in your chain of command and am only here as a visitor to the Marine regiments. I have no authority here," Turley stated with a bit of annoyance at being put in this position.

"I know, but I'm shorthanded right now and need your professional assistance. I'll get this cleared with Saigon. Once we're operational, I'll have the trucks come back and pick you up and I'll have an Army field grade come replace you," Metcalf said, quickly gathering material up from his desk and work area.

What kind of shit sandwich have I got myself into? Turley was thinking when Eisenstein came up to him. "Sir, I'll stay here with you. I have my team out on Alpha 2 and I'm not bugging out with them sitting out there," Eisenstein said. Turning to Metcalf, he added, "Sir, I'd like to extract that ANGLICO team as soon as possible."

"Hell no! They need to stay there and keep us posted on what's going on," Metcalf replied as he quickly stuffed papers into a briefcase and grabbed his hat. Turley just exchanged looks with Eisenstein.

"Lieutenant, how are they doing out there?" Turley asked as Metcalf brushed past him, heading for the door. If looks could kill, Metcalf would be dead from the look of disgust that Turley and Eisenstein threw his way.

"They're all okay, but under a lot of artillery fire and ground probes," Eisenstein said.

"Sir," a voice from behind them said, getting their attention. Turning, Turley saw Captain Murray standing behind him.

"Yes?" Turley responded, expecting bad news.

"We'll stay and help you. We'll work out a shift schedule," Captain Murray responded. Turley nodded in acknowledgment.

"Where's Major Wilson?" Turley asked.

"Sir, he's been medevacked out for combat fatigue," Captain Murray responded.

Combat fatigue my ass, Turley thought. *The fat son of a bitch is plainly too incompetent to deal with this intensity and gave up.* Keeping his thoughts to himself, he replied, "Okay, we'll manage without him." He paused. "First things first, let's get a good update from each of the firebases on their status, personnel, equipment, and supply status." Pointing at Captain Murray, he said, "You start a consolidated log and start putting together an intelligence picture of where the main attack is coming from. Who's the intel officer for this outfit?" Turley asked.

"Sir, Captain Howard." A young officer raised his hand. "I'm the intel officer, but I just arrived in Vietnam last week."

"Well, welcome, Captain. Get with Captain Murray and start painting that picture," Turley directed.

"Eisenstein, how far can the destroyers' gunfire cover?"

"Sir, they're good for about ten miles depending on the terrain. Naval gunfire is a flat trajectory, so once it gets into the hills, the reverse slopes are difficult to hit. Right now they're concentration of Alpha 2," Eisenstein explained. Sergeant Swift, Eisenstein's senior NCO, nodded in agreement.

"Sir," Major David Brookbank, USAF, interrupted. "Excuse me, sir, my team and I will be staying with you. We can get some B-52 support and start requesting close-air support for tomorrow morning. Not sure what the weather is going to be like or how much we can get with the weather constraints. I have a FAC coming up now and we'll see what he can find and hit. This new storm front that's over us now is going to make things difficult," Brookbank went on to explain. Brookbank's team consisted of himself, a captain and two noncommissioned officers.

"Thank you, Major," Turley said, turning to the assembled group. "Okay, let's get some updates and sit down in an hour and go over the situation of the last twenty-four hours."

The group broke up and began collecting the data. Turley, now in charge, felt it necessary to have a good picture of what had happened and where they currently stood before they could direct actions to salvage what was happening.

"Sir, I just made a fresh pot of coffee. Would you like a cup?" Sergeant Swift asked as Turley studied the map mounted on the wall.

"Sergeant, that sounds pretty good right now. Thank you. Oh, what time is it? Forgot to wind my watch."

"Sir, it's 1015 hours," Swift responded. "I'll get that coffee. You take cream or black?"

"Black is good," Turley answered as Captain Murray stepped up. His expression wasn't hopeful.

"What is it, Murray?" Turley asked.

"Sir, it's Alpha 4. They're calling being overrun and abandoning the outpost. The ARVNs are pulling out for the most part or surrendering. I already ran this by Colonel Metcalf," Murray added.

"Are there any advisors up there?"

"Not that I'm aware of, sir."

"Okay, then get F Troop on the horn and see if we can get some eyes up there."

"Yes, sir," Murray said and went off to start the ball rolling on the reconnaissance of Alpha 4. Turley was starting to feel the lack of sleep, but the first sergeant coffee was certainly helping him at this point. He closed his eyes for a moment as the caffeine worked its way through his system.

"Excuse me, sir," a voice said. Turley opened his eyes to a major, Army type, standing in front of him.

"Yes, Major."

"Sir, we've not been introduced. I'm Major Nearly, communications officer."

"Glad to meet you. How are our comms?" Turley asked. He had assumed that they were all functioning okay.

"Sir, comms are working fine. I'm staying here along with my lieutenant and nine enlisted soldiers, all volunteers, to keep the comms functioning. Our biggest problem is the antenna farm keeps getting hit and we lose a coax cable or a 292 antenna. Aside from that, we is good."

"Major, I appreciate you and your team staying. Once the 3rd ARVN move to the Citadel, we're the only people giving support to those out on the firebases. Comms with them are going to become critical."

"Well, sir, we'll do our best to keep the comms working," Nearly said and departed. Turley attempted to close his eyes again until the next interruption.

An hour later, the group reassembled in the G-3 area, which was mostly devoid of people as everyone had packed up and moved back to Quang Tri. The 3rd Division's abandoned TOC was the only command-and-control headquarters north of Quang Tri City now.

"Okay, Captain Murray, give us a rundown of the current situation," Turley directed.

"Sir, in the past twenty-four hours, the situation has not been good. It appears that every firebase is under heavy long-range artillery throughout the night. They're being hit with 130mm artillery that's beyond the range of the one-five-five howitzers. The one-seven-fives at Carroll are the only guns within range of those 130mm guns, and Carroll is on the receiving end as well. In addition to hitting the firebases, they're pounding the villages, driving the people to flow south, and then they're hitting road intersections. The people are in a panic, clogging roads," Murray said and checked his notes.

"As for the firebases themselves, Alpha 1 and 2 currently have ground probes attempting to breach the wires, as well as at Charlie 1 and 2. We have no word from Fuller, and Alpha 4 is being overrun as we speak. Firebases Sarge and Nui Ba Ho have elements of the 308th NVA Division launching ground attacks and it's doubtful that either location will hold out much longer. Both are in need of resupply. Seventy-five percent of Sarge's northern perimeter bunkers have been destroyed according to Major Boomer. Firebase Holcomb is under pressure as well from elements of the 304th NVA Division." He paused and checked his notes again.

"On the positive side, Marine Brigade 258 has reported that they're now at Dong Ha, completing their night convoy move. As soon as the last element closed, the 3rd Battalion, they were hit with artillery fire. This was confirmed by Captain Ripley. He said he and Captain Johnson were doing okay and closed in as well. The 7th Marine Battalion made the move from Da Nang to Dong Ha and closed in at 0200 this morning. At 0430, the 7th moved to Throm Truong Chi and is currently moving out west along Highway 9 to keep it open. It's the main supply route for Camp Carroll and Mai Loc. We lose it and helicopter resupply is it for those places. Sir, that's all I have right now," Captain Murray concluded.

"Okay, good update. Everyone now understand the situation?" Turley asked. Affirmative nods were the response.

"Major Brookbank, what is our Air Force support?" Turley asked.

"Sir, there's currently a FAC up, but this overcast isn't revealing much for him. He did spot three suspected gun emplacements and adjusted artillery fire on them using the one-oh-five artillery out of Mai Loc. He has a couple of fast-movers on standby if he gets an opening, but for right now there's not much support coming. We did request B-52 strikes for this morning along the DMZ in previously identified assembly areas and air-defense sites. They're in the air. I'll get an update in about thirty minutes," Brookbank said.

"Good, keep us all posted. Lieutenant Eisenstein, what's the naval situation?"

"Sir, we have two destroyers off the coast providing naval gunfire to Alpha 1 and Alpha 2. Lieutenant Bruggeman has been keeping them busy attempting to stop the flow around his position. He has indicated that they're currently surrounded, having been bypassed by elements moving down Highway 1," Eisenstein explained.

"Do we need to get them out of there?" Turley asked with concern.

"Sir, I would recommend that we get some helicopters on standby for all the advisors' extractions," Captain Murray interjected.

"Contact Regional and request choppers on standby to extract. It's going to take time for them to get up here in this weather," Turley directed. Murray departed to get a request sent.

"What's the logistical situation?" Turley asked.

"Sir, the artillery has been firing for twenty-four hours and is probably getting low on ammo. I'll get a call out to the artillery advisors and see what the status is," Eisenstein said.

"Okay, gentlemen, we all understand the situation. Let's see what we can do about increasing the artillery support, getting some attack helicopter support, and bringing up logistics. As things progress, let's keep each other informed." The group dispersed except two Marine captains that Turley hadn't noticed as they stood off to the side and behind him.

"Colonel Turley, sir," one said, getting his attention. Turley turned around and surprise registered on his face.

"Captain O'Toole, what are you doing here?" Turley said, extending his hand.

Accepting the handshake, he replied, "Sir, this is Captain John Theisen and he's my replacement as I rotate home in two weeks," O'Toole began to explain. "I brought him up to see the lay of the land and visit our Marine intel advisors in the field. We were with Major Easley at the 258th when they got the word to come north, so we moved with them. This morning Easley recommended that we get our butts over here to see if we could help or get a ride back to Saigon. Can we help?" O'Toole asked.

"Captain Theisen, welcome to Vietnam and you belong to me here now. Yes, you can help. Find the intel captain, Howard, and develop the intel picture. I am not sure he is tracking too well. That would be a big help," Turley said.

"Sir, we will find him and get right on it," Theisen said and they moved off.

* * *

Nui Ba Ho

As the day wore on, the reports didn't improve. Pressure continued on each of the firebases with intense artillery fire and ground assaults. By 1700 hours, the perimeter around Nui Ba Ho was a wall of dead North Vietnamese bodies hanging in the wire. This was attributed in part to the tenacious stand by the South Vietnamese Marines and artillery support that Major Hoa, the battalion executive officer, had been able to secure. As Captain Smith and Major Hoa sat together in a bunker overlooking the steep downslope, movement caught Smith's eye.

"Shit, Chinh, do you see what I'm looking at?" Smith asked, using the Vietnamese term for major.

Raising his field glasses, Major Hoa scanned the slope. Finally, he responded, "Yes, I see it. It appears to be a large artillery tube they are trying to haul up here."

"Christ, they get that thing in position, they're going to blow our perimeter to pieces. Let me see if I can get the artillery guys on this." Smith moved back to the command bunker. As he entered, he heard a voice from heaven.

"Arrow Two-One, High Eye Three, over." High Eye Three was an aerial FAC in an OV-10 aircraft.

"High Eye Three, Arrow Two-One," Smith responded, grabbing the hand mike from the Vietnamese soldier that was on radio watch.

"Arrow Two-One, I understand you have a target for me. I have two fast-movers with me and need a target. Over."

"High Eye, do you have eyes on our location? Over."

"Arrow Two-One, just barely. Over."

"Roger, I have a target at..." And Smith read off the coordinates to the artillery piece that was being dragged up the hill.

"Roger, good copy. Wait one." Smith hung his head in anticipation of a negative response. "Arrow Two-One, I have your target in sight and will be delivering shortly, over."

"Roger, standing by," Smith said, tossing the handset back to the Vietnamese soldier and running out of the TOC. Major Hoa looked at him as he jumped into the trench line beside him.

"Just wait and see," Smith said. Major Hoa raised his field glasses again. As nothing happened right away, he started to become disappointed until he heard the unmistakable sound of a jet engine screaming past his location. Almost in slow motion, he watched as the two napalm canisters dropped from under the wing of the F-4 Phantom jet. As the first two canisters impacted, two more canisters were released from the second aircraft. The artillery piece and everyone around it were immediately engulfed in flames. That was one artillery piece that would not bother them this evening.

* * *

Pedro

. . .

Pedro lacked the amenities that most firebases had, like overhead cover. It wasn't really built for battle but more as a way station and patrol base. All day, artillery had been landing around or on the base, but not at the level of intensity that Sarge and Mai Loc were receiving. Major Nguyen Dang Tong, the 1st VNMC Battalion commander, in consultation with Major Cockell, had pushed all but one company off the firebase to the surrounding hills. Two companies had been engaging a large NVA force.

"Major Cockell, the companies have been engaging all day those enemy forces. The enemy knows their position well. What you think?" Major Tong asked.

"Major, I think they'll wait out the night, then hit our positions hard come first light. Probably shoot harassment artillery all night to keep our guys awake," Cockell said as he scanned the friendly position with his field glasses.

"We think same-oh same-oh, Cockell. After dark, we pull off hilltop; in morning, hit hilltop with artillery when they attack. What you think?" Hoa said.

"Sounds good to me. Might be a nice present for them," Cockell agreed with a grin.

Once the sun set and ground contact had all but ceased, Tung gave the order directed his forces to vacate as quietly as possible the position they were sitting in. As they'd predicted, throughout the night, the NVA hit the location with an occasional artillery round, just frequently enough to deny everyone some sleep. As the sun eased over the eastern horizon, the ground attack commenced with a human wave typical of NVA ground assaults. Fire-and-maneuver tactics were foreign to the NVA attack formations.

"Cockell, they are attacking in typical fashion," Tung said, handing his field glasses to Cockell to take a look.

Cockell watched as the NVA advanced towards and over the previously held Marine positions. As the NVA came to realize that no one was there, the first barrage of artillery began to fall on them. Cockell had arranged earlier to have artillery on standby, so when the call for fire was sent, it was quickly executed. Cockell could see the toll it was taking on the NVA.

When the last round impacted and the smoke and dust cleared, Cockell looked over at Major Tung. "We had some real fine kills there."[1]

* * *

Jack woke up to the sound of outgoing artillery. From the sound of it, every gun on the firebase must have been firing. Camper was sitting next to the advisor radio, listening to the traffic.

"How's it going, sir?" Jack asked.

"Right now every firebase is receiving incoming. When there's incoming here, the gun bunnies run into the bunkers, abandoning the tubes, so no one's getting fire support. We have a battery of Marine artillery here and they're the only ones standing by their guns. The Alpha outposts all have ground attacks and are calling for extraction. Alpha 4 expects to be overrun in the next twelve hours. Ai Tu is getting some choppers together to get up and pull people out that are up there. These firebases were built to handle small-unit unconventional fights, not conventional combined-arms assaults. If the NVA press this with conventional tactics, infantry, armor and artillery working in a combined-arms formation, they'll overrun these places. Pray the weather breaks so we can get some air support to go after their long-range artillery. That's what's hurting us right now," Camper explained.

"Sir, where do you think I could do some good? I can't just sit here and take notes. Must be something I can do?" Jack asked, pulling his boots on.

"The road to Ai Tu is still open, I believe. I would recommend you get back to Ai Tu and pop that question to Colonel Metcalf. I'm sure he'll use you. Take Highway 9 to Cam Lo and Dong Ha. It runs along the south side of the river," Camper recommended.

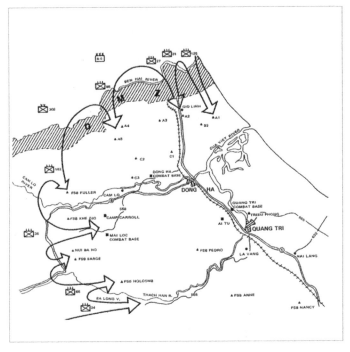

Created by Matt Jackson Books through Infidun, LLC

2

13

WHO'S IN COMMAND?

31 MARCH 1972
3rd ARVN Division TOC Forward
Ai Tu, South Vietnam

Colonel Metcalf and General Giai along with thirty personnel, mostly American members of the 155th Advisor Assistance Team, had departed for Quang Tri to establish a new command post. Lieutenant Colonel Turley was the senior officer present but had no command authority. He was a visitor, helping Metcalf out until he could get a chopper in to extract him as well.

"Colonel, you have a call from Colonel Metcalf on the landline," the watch officer said, handing Turley the phone.

"Turley here, sir."

"Turley, Metcalf. How are things up there?"

"Well, sir, Nui Ba Ho and Sarge are under intense fire. Charlie 2 is in trouble and I suspect before morning some of the others will fall as well. Alpha 4 is barely holding on as they have T-54 and PT-76 tanks on their perimeter. They've called requesting an extraction. Mai Loc is holding but in need of a resupply of ammo, food and water, but the weather won't allow it right now. We're still getting incoming around our position, but they haven't hit us yet," Turley went on to explain.

"How bad is it really at Alpha 4? General Giai is considering pulling out of Alpha 1, 2, 3, and 4."

"Sir, they've been hit heavily with 122 rockets and 130 artillery. They have enemy in the wire and now the tanks are moving forward. They have artillery support but no air support due to the weather," Turley reported.

"Okay, I won't get back there tonight, so do what you can. I spoke with General Bowen, the deputy FRAC commander. He may be giving you a call later as well. Keep me posted on the situation. I'll talk to you in the morning. Good night." And the line went dead. Turley just looked at the receiver for a moment, almost in shock at the extent of the conversation. *Son of a bitch* crossed his mind.

"Get me Major Joy on the radio," Turley told the watch officer. A few moments later, he said, "Joy, what's your situation up there?"

"We're getting hit with artillery and probes. Boomer reported that the NVA are in formation, sling arms, walking down QL9 towards his position, and he can't get any artillery support," Joy explained.

"Roger, how is your supply situation?" Turley asked.

"We're low on artillery ammo, food, and water. If we don't get a resupply soon, we may not be able to hold out here much longer," Joy said with some concern in his voice.

"Roger, I'll see what I can do to get you a resupply. Good luck, and keep me posted. If we can get some tac air in, we'll send it your way. We're laying on B-52 strikes and those will go in around you. I need to talk to the folks at FRAC on that," Turley said, hoping to raise Joy's spirits.

"That would certainly help. I'll keep you posted. How about keeping Captain Murray there to help you? Getting back here may be tricky. He'll be more of an asset with you than back here. Anything else?" Joy asked.

"No, I'll let you know on the B-52s when we have a schedule. I'll hold Murray here. He's already doing a great job. That's all. You take care."

Turley hung up and walked over to the map to examine the marked positions of the enemy. "Has anyone heard from the 56th Regiment at Camp Carroll?"

Several "No, sirs" could be heard.

Turning to the watch officer, Turley said, "Get me Lieutenant Colonel Camper on the landline, please." A few moments later, he said, "Camper, this is Turley. Metcalf has displaced with the 3rd Division TOC. What's your situation up there?"

"Welcome aboard. Hope you're having fun. I'm not," Camper said. From the sound of his voice, Turley could tell the man was dead tired. "I'm having trouble getting a clear picture of what's going on. First, we have no advisors below the brigade level, so I have no direct communications with anyone there. Second, the Vietnamese have the 'face-saving' attitude, so only good news gets reported and there's not a lot of that. We're getting a lot of false reports as to who's where and who's holding or falling back. One minute they're fine and the next they're screaming for reinforcements, which we don't have," Camper explained. "Third, this outfit is a bunch of misfits, convicts and deserters. These guys were from the 1st Infantry Division and sent here as punishment as they couldn't run away easily along the DMZ. Holcomb is getting some probing and incoming artillery. Khe Gio is under pressure from ground attacks and not sure if he's going to hold much longer. None have advisors. I understand that Sarge and

Nui Ba Ho are in danger of falling. Is that correct?" Camper asked.

"That's about right," Turley said, looking at the map. "That makes you, Mai Loc and Holcomb the main defensive line if that happens. Can you hold?"

"We certainly have the artillery here to do some damage, if I can keep the damn gunners on the guns. As soon as incoming rounds land, the gun bunnies are in their bunker. Battery B, 1st Vietnamese Marine Artillery Battalion are the only ones that don't bug on the sound of incoming. We have to literally go in and kick everyone else's asses out," Camper said in exasperation.

"Okay, let's keep each other informed and coordinate our actions. We're requesting B-52 strikes. I'll get you a schedule and target list. Any questions?"

"Yeah, one. How did you get stuck with this shitty job?" Camper asked. "Have you heard from Major Turner? He left here this morning and is heading your way. Said he wants to do more than just take notes."

"Haven't heard from him, but I have heard about him. Still trying to figure out how I got this shit sandwich job. Talk later."

As Turley hung the phone up, the watch officer was handing him another phone. "General Bowen, for you, sir."

"Sir, Lieutenant Colonel Turley."

"Turley, why is Metcalf back in Quang Tri with the division staff and you're up there?" Bowen did not sound happy.

"Sir, I came up to visit my advisors with the 147th and the 258th. When the shit hit the fan, I couldn't get out and told Metcalf I would be willing to help out. He left me here while he displaced with General Giai and the division staff back to Quang Tri. I have about thirty guys, mostly American advisors, up here with me," Turley explained.

"Why isn't his XO, Lieutenant Colonel Norm Heon, up there?" Bowen asked.

"Sir, I have no idea. I've never met the man," Turley explained.

"Is Major Turner with you?" Bowen asked.

"No, sir. He was at Carroll this morning and left there heading this way, I'm told, but I've had no contact with him," Turley stated.

"Well, thank you for stepping up to the plate. What's your situation up there? MACV has sent out a message to the Puzzle Palace in Washington saying this isn't critical. What's your opinion?" Bowen asked.

"Sir, if we don't get some air support and quick, we're going to lose every firebase north of the Cam Lo and Thach Han Rivers. We have two major attacks on each side of QL1 and a major force moving east on QL9 towards Dong Ha, all with tanks. The weather is preventing any close-air support or attack helicopters. Firebases are running low on ammunition, especially artillery ammo. As the Army didn't put advisors at the battalion level, I'm not sure what the situation is with the 56th, 57th or 2nd ARVN Regiments. The 56th and 57th were in the process of conducting a relief in place when the attack started. I know we lost the first battalion of the 56th attempting to move to Fuller when they were hit by artillery fire.

"Alpha 2 was able to hold out thanks to naval gunfire from the USS *Buchanan* and the USS *Joseph Strauss*, initially. Two more destroyers joined them today for four ships now providing naval gunfire. Unfortunately, naval gunfire can only reach ten miles inland, so the western firebases have to rely on ARVN artillery, which are receiving counterbattery fire effectively. The enemy's 130mm guns are just outside the range of the 155s and the 175s, so our counterbattery fire has been less than effective."

"Was there any ground action against them?"

"Just intense artillery fire for the most part. Some ground probes. Alpha 4 may have been overrun as we have no comms with them. Sarge and Alpha 2 have had limited assaults so far," Turley said.

"Damn," Bowen said, taking a pause. "Okay, what do you need?"

"Sir, I need any B-52s that you can send our way. We've been plotting targets and suspected locations that we can feed them," Turley explained with some hope in his voice.

"Colonel, sit tight. You'll be getting those aircraft." And Bowen hung up.

14

MARINES

31 March 1972
Highway 9
Dong Ha, South Vietnam

Between incoming artillery fire, Jack and Hanner got in their jeep and hightailed it out the gate at Camp Carroll. Jack was surprised to see only a few shrapnel holes in the vehicle and none in the tires. *Somebody up there must like me*, he was thinking as they slowly moved along Highway 9. The road was filling fast with civilians carrying their meager belongings on oxcarts and overloaded ancient buses, all moving east towards Dong Ha. Artillery rounds would impact in close proximity, but not on the road, sparing the civilian population.

"Sir, that looks like ARVN soldiers up ahead," Hanner said, slowing the vehicle even more. They were just coming up on the town of Cam Lo, which had a bridge across the Mieu Giang River, or the Cam Lo River as the advisors called it.

Pulling up alongside an NCO who was standing in the middle of the road with his arm raised, Jack told Hanner,

"Keep your eye on these jokers. They may be thinking of hijacking the jeep."

Hanner immediately picked up his M16. Jack stepped out of the vehicle and with all the military bearing he could muster approached the NCO and group.

"What unit are you and where are your officers?" Jack asked in Vietnamese. That Jack had a command of the language caught the NCO off guard. He looked confused and suddenly unsure of what to do next.

"Don't you salute senior officers in your unit?" Jack said in a stern voice. "Well!"

The NCO and the soldiers came to attention and saluted. Jack really didn't want a salute as a sniper would love to see him identified as an officer, but he needed to take charge of this group before they decided to take him and Hanner. Jack returned the salute and told them to stand at ease. He again asked what unit.

"We are from the 3rd Battalion, 2nd Regiment. We were at Alpha 4 when we were hit with a ground attack. We were ordered to make our way south of the river and stay at the bridge at Cam Lo until relieved," the NCO said.

"Well, why are you not at the bridge putting in a defensive position, and where are your officers?" Jack asked, looking about.

"Our lieutenant said he was going to Dong Ha to get engineer equipment. He left this morning and has not returned."

He probably won't be back either, Jack was thinking. "Alright, come with me," he said and motioned for them to follow him. Going to the south end of the bridge, Jack started pointing at places for two-man foxholes to be dug. As he walked the riverbank, more soldiers were coming south across the bridge.

"Sergeant, round up these soldiers when they cross and put them to work preparing fighting positions. If they don't have a weapon, let them dig—with their hands and helmet if they have to. Understood?" Jack directed. The NCO acknowledged the order and took charge of establishing a defense. Jack went back to his jeep and climbed in.

"Do you think they'll hold the bridge, sir?" Hanner asked.

"No, I think as soon as we pull away, they'll pull out, but they won't be eyeing our jeep anymore. Let's go," Jack said as he pointed down Highway 9.

Moving down the road, they saw more and more ARVN soldiers mixed in with the civilians moving east. Most didn't have a weapon or any combat equipment. From the looks on their faces, Jack could see they were demoralized soldiers. *I'll bet the first guys retreating before the Germans at the Battle of the Bulge looked like these guys. Ill-trained, low-discipline soldiers break so easily*, he was thinking when Hanner slammed on the brakes.

"What the hell, Hanner!" Jack yelled as the vehicle came to an abrupt stop. He looked over at Hanner, who just pointed ahead. A well-fortified roadblock was on the west side of Dong Ha and manned by Vietnamese Marines.

"Damn, maybe the cavalry has arrived. Let's go," Jacked exclaimed as Hanner accelerated the jeep forward. On closer examination, Jack saw a Vietnamese crew grinning at him and pointing towards the town and bridge. "Head over there," Jack ordered.

Turning a corner, Jack found a command post set up and occupied by what appeared to be a Marine battalion. Stopping the vehicle, a US Marine captain approached.

"Don't salute, please," Jack said, "I have no desire to be identified as a target for a sniper."

"Sir, I'm Captain Ripley, advisor for the 3rd Battalion, 258th Regiment." Captain John Ripley was about the same height as Turner and solid muscle. Jack suspected right away that one should not challenge Ripley to a push-up contest.

"Hi, Jack Turner. I've been at Camp Carroll last night and was told I might be of use back at Ai Tu. I thought the 258th was back at Nancy," Jack stated.

"We were, sir, but noon yesterday us and the 3rd Artillery Battalion were ordered up here. Got here late last night and told to hold the bridges at Dong Ha. The 6th Battalion left Nancy and got here about 0300 this morning and is on its way to push out to cover the bridge at Cam Lo," Ripley added.

"I just came through there. Left a group of ARVNs from the 2nd Regiment guarding the bridge. I doubt if they'll be there when the 6th arrives." Jack pointed towards Highway 9. "Most of those ARVNs are from the 2nd, I suspect. They're pretty well demoralized," Jack stated, accepting a warm soda from Ripley. "Where's the regimental CP?"

"Our battalion CP is back up this road, over at Dong Ha Base, an old, abandoned airstrip. Regiment is there as well," Ripley said.

"Sir, I need to go back and coordinate a few things with them. Want to come along?" Ripley asked, finishing his soda. "You should be able to speak with Major Easley as he is there."

"Yeah, hop in and we'll take my jeep," Jack offered.

The Dong Ha Base as it was referred to was an abandoned dirt strip airfield. At the height of the war and before the drawdown of American troops, it had been used extensively. Abandoned in 1969, it had come back to life in 1971 as a major stage field for helicopters supporting Operation Lam Son 719, then it had returned to its abandoned state.

Arriving at the 258th Regiment Command Post, Jack entered the command post, a concrete bunker left over from the days of the French occupation. Jack had to take a moment to let his eyesight adjust as the lighting was provided by propane lanterns. When his eyes adjusted, he spotted Easley right away.

"John, how you doing?" Jack asked, approaching Easley.

"Damn, you do get around, now don't you?" Easley responded.

"I wanted to see the Vietnamese and how well they were doing, but I didn't expect to see them in a major operation like this. I hope you didn't arrange this all for my viewing pleasure," Jack said.

"Well, stick around. The 20th Tank Battalion might be on its way to reinforce us. They were in tank qualifications with the M48 tanks and it was cut short for them to get up here. You'll get a firsthand look at how well the training and Vietnamization program is working," Easley replied.

"Well, if what I've seen so far is any indication, I'd say it's lacking in several areas."

"Oh, how's that?" Easley asked.

"It seems that the artillery folks don't like being on the receiving end of incoming and run to the bunkers when it starts. The northern outposts are screaming for fire support and getting none from Carroll. The 2nd Regiment is disintegrating along the DMZ as the outposts are being overrun. The 56th at Carroll is a bunch of criminals and misfits according to Camper, and he expects them to bolt sooner or later. I wasn't impressed with the command and staff at the 56th either. Not a good relationship with Camper and the deputy there," Jack summarized.

"Well, you may come away with a different impression about these guys," Easley said, meaning the Vietnamese Marines.

"I already have from what I saw in town."

"Why don't you hang here for a while and observe what we're doing and what 20th Tank will be doing if they get here? Might help your assessment," Easley offered.

"Okay, I'll do that."

Turning to Hanner, Jack yelled, "Hey, Hanner, we're

staying for a while. Let's get our gear out of the jeep." And he moved off.

When he returned, Ripley and Easley were going over some items, so Jack stayed out of the way. When Ripley was done talking to Easley, he turned to Jack. "Sir, let me show you our distribution on the map," Ripley offered and guided Jack to a map hanging from the wall.

"Right now our battalion occupies the town, with one company on the west side of town, here. That's the one you drove through. One company is overwatching the railroad bridge, with another on the south end of the road bridge and one in reserve here. The 6th Battalion is moving up and going to Cam Lo to secure that bridge and the 7th Battalion is pulling palace guard at Ai Tu, in reserve. The artillery battalion is on the far side of the airfield," Easley briefed him.

"I understand you may have a tank battalion coming up. Where are you going to put them?" Jack asked.

"I don't know what the plan is there," Easley said. "Colonel Dinh wants to discuss the disposition with the tank battalion commander before making a decision on that. He's looking over the bridge as we speak. If the 20th gets here, he'll have figured out where he wants them and where best to employ them. It's also going to depend on how well they're trained and how proficient they are. We shall see," Easley added. "We shall see."

"One question, why is this position so damn important?" Jack asked, studying the map. "I see that QL1 comes right through here and Route 9 from the west out of Laos intersects just south of here."

"Sir, that bridge is the only bridge that has the capability of supporting tanks over the river. It's a sixty-ton bridge. None of the others except the railroad bridge have that capability, and the railroad bridge has been damaged for years," Ripley explained.

As they studied the maps and discussed the tactical situation, impacting and exploding artillery could be heard outside the concrete bunker. *Thank God the French knew how to build concrete bunkers*, Jack was thinking when another round slammed into the ground adjacent to the thick reinforced concrete walls. That one made everyone squat down and look upward.

"Getting a bit frosty around here," Easley commented, standing back up.

Moments later, Colonel Dinh entered the command post. "Major Easley, we go," were his first words. Then he looked at Jack and unleashed his second string of words: "Who you?"

"Sir, this is Major Jack Tuner. He's on a special assignment from Washington and not an advisor. Just a visitor today," Easley said. Dinh looked Jack over for a moment.

"You may be visitor today, you will be an advisor by tomorrow," Dinh said to Jack and then turned back to Easley. "General Giai wants us to move back to Ai Tu. We leave 6th Battalion by Cam Lo and 3rd Battalion at Dong Ha to hold the bridge. Headquarters and artillery move to Ai Tu. Leave now," Dinh explained. The staff must have been listening as they immediately started gathering up their materials and heading for their vehicles, which had been back some distance from the command bunker.

"Jack, you going back with us?" Easley asked.

"If it's okay with Colonel Dinh, I'd like to stay and observe 3rd Battalion at the bridge," Jack said, turning to Colonel Dinh.

"See, I was wrong. You no advisor tomorrow. You advisor today," Dinh said with a smile.

15

MOVEMENT

First Lieutenant Ken Mick had just returned to Vietnam the previous day after a two-week leave. He had been home in Columbus, Ohio, and the long flight back had worn him out. With his unit short on pilots, he was immediately on the board to fly and punched eight hours of flight time in his logbook at the end of the day's flight. As he and his copilot climbed out of the AH-1G Cobra gunship, his thoughts were focused on a cold beer and the dedication party the unit was having for its new officers' club. The month prior, the Centaurs, as they were called, had left their home base of Lai Khe, where they had a great club built by Company A, 227th Assault Helicopter Company, the Chickenmen, who had occupied the base before them. Since arriving in Long Binh, they hadn't had a club for the officers. That would all change tonight.

The party started with little coaxing to get everyone over

to the new club. Beer was flowing and war stories were dominating the conversation. That was all about to change.

"Hey, listen up...quiet!" Captain Haynie announced. Captain Haynie was the Cobra Platoon leader. When he was sure he had everyone's attention, he continued. "Alright, listen up. It seems that the NVA have launched a major offensive up north across the DMZ." Looks were exchanged, but disbelief dominated the expressions.

"Hey, sir, April Fools' Day to you too," one of the warrants yelled out.

"This ain't no April Fools' joke, gentlemen. They're coming across the DMZ with what appears to be two divisions of infantry supported by tanks. We've been ordered to haul ass up to Da Nang and set up operations there. The 48th Assault Helicopter Company is up there now with their gunships and there may be another cav unit there as well. Now you know as much as I do. Get your shit packed tonight and stand by for the mission brief at 0700 tomorrow morning. I doubt if we're coming back here, so pack accordingly."

"Sir, who are we supporting up there?" Ken asked.

"Right now it appears we're supporting the South Vietnamese as there are no US ground forces up that way, I don't think. The Vietnamese units have US advisors with them, and I suspect we'll be talking to them," Haynie offered. "I'll see you ladies in the morning." Almost immediately, the dedication party ended as individuals headed to their quarters to start packing.

The next morning, the troop commander, Major Spencer, gave the mission brief. "Gentlemen, we will depart here at 0800 hours with three flights. The little birds will lead off, followed by the Cobras, and lastly will be the slicks. Our first refuel point is Phan Thiet, then Cam Ranh Bay, Tuy Hoa, Chu Lai, and lastly Marble Mountain outside of Da Nang. We've coordinated with the folks at Marble Mountain in Da

Nang. We'll spend the night there and fly the next day to our final destination, the former Navy base at Phu Bai. It's a four-hundred-mile trip, so plan on logging about eight hours to get up to Da Nang. I suspect we'll be receiving missions right away, so when we get to Marble Mountain, get some sleep. Are there any questions?" he asked. There were none. "Let's start them up and get going, then."

Ken and his copilot, Mike Woods, headed out to their aircraft and conducted the preflight. "Mike, I'll take the head and you take down below," Ken directed as the two began. Ken always inspected the main rotor head. Almost anything else could break or be damaged and the aircraft would fly. The rotor head was a different story. Anything up there broke and the aircraft would be in serious trouble. The sound of the LOH aircraft departing got everyone's attention. Everyone knew they would have a very tiresome flight as several of those aircraft had only one pilot on board with the gunner/crew chief occupying the other seat. Many of those gunner/crew chiefs had been taught how to handle the aircraft in flight, but it was still going to tax the pilots to the fullest.

The flight was over new terrain, which made the flight somewhat interesting. The ground around Lai Khe and Long Binh was flat, with dense rubber tree plantations and thick jungle. At Phan Thiet, the flight picked up the coast and followed it north. Everyone thought how beautiful it was, with crystal-clear emerald water, white sand beaches, lush green rice paddies inland for a mile or so and then the jungle-covered hills. As Ken flew, he thought, *We shouldn't be fighting here. We should be looking at resorts and golf courses.* Finally, five refueling stops later, Ken shut down the aircraft. As Ken and Mike climbed out, they noticed several pilots standing by a hangar.

"Let's see what accommodations we have for tonight," Ken said as they approached the group.

"Ken, how is your aircraft? Any maintenance issues?" Captain Haynie asked.

"No, sir, she's good. Where are we sleeping tonight, sir?" Mike asked.

"There's a mess hall over at the 48th that you can get chow at. As for sleeping, pick a spot on the floor of this hangar and make yourself comfortable," Haynie exclaimed.

"Thank you, sir, I think I'll skip chow and just get some sleep. Mike, you coming?" Ken asked. He shouldered his kit bag and headed into the hangar, with Mike right behind him. Finding what appeared to be a quiet area away from the maintenance folks, Mike and Ken started to lay out their sleep pads.

"You know, it's cool up here. Never thought I'd need my flight jacket in Nam, but damn. I hope a poncho liner is going to be warm enough tonight," Mike lamented as Ken sat down and started digging through his kit bag.

"Mike, I have a Danish salami that I brought back from the States. Want some?" Ken offered, pulling out the salami and his survival knife.

"Yeah, I'm too tired to walk to a mess hall, but I'll take some of that," Mike accepted. The Danish salami was good and a welcome relief from C rations if one didn't want to walk to the mess hall. After they finished and washed the salami down with sodas, both pilots stretched out and quickly dropped off to sleep, as did most of the others when they returned from the mess hall.

The next morning was overcast with some rain in the forecast. Off in the distance, rumbling sounds could be heard, too much and too long to be thunder. Everyone was anxious to get to their final destination and new home base, so the first aircraft launched right at daybreak. Their new home was a former CH-47 unit's base camp, so the accommodations should be satisfactory.

As it turned out, they were anything but satisfactory. It

appeared that the CH-47 unit, the Lift Masters, had left sometime before and the base had been turned over to the ARVNs. The Quonset hut shells were present, but the windows and doors were gone. For that matter, anything of value was missing, to include toilets and sinks. Finally, a truck arrived and cots were issued to everyone. The process of building a new home started all over again.

16

ALPHA 2

"Turley. Metcalf here. I have a bird inbound to your location to take out Major Wells and some of my people and get them back here. They've moved to the helipad and should be gone in a minute or so. Just wanted to be sure and close the loop with you on that," Metcalf said.

It took every bit of control for Turley to keep his emotions in check. He'd been wondering why so few Army personnel were in the TOC. Now he knew.

"Thank you for informing us of this, Colonel," Turley said, spitting the word *colonel* down the receiver in the hope it would reach Metcalf. He hung the phone up without another word. As he did so, he could hear the pulsating sound of the UH-1H helicopter's rotor blades as it came to a hover on the helipad and set down. Turley walked to the door of the TOC and looked out. Major Wells was putting people on board wherever they would fit. With the crew of four, the aircraft could only take seven, so some people were told another aircraft would come back for them. They could only hope.

Warrant Officers Ben Nielsen and John Frink along with their door gunner and crew chief had been flying in bad weather all morning, resupplying firebases. They had been confronted with low clouds and rain squalls moving through the area as well as dodging .51 anti-aircraft fire for the past nine hours. The rain was still coming down when Major Kennedy approached Nielsen while he was sitting in the refuel point in Quang Tri.

"Ben, how's your aircraft?" the major asked.

"Good, sir, why?"

"We have some Americans up at Alpha 2 that may need to be extracted. They may be about to get overrun and we want to get them out," Kennedy said.

"Sir, I used to fly a lot in that area when I was with the 101st," Nielsen replied.

"Can you take this one?"

"Yes, sir, we'll try to get out there, but the weather is the shits."

"Thanks, and be careful," Kennedy ordered. He walked back and climbed back into his aircraft as Specialist Jim Lowe finished refueling Nielsen's aircraft. Once everyone was aboard, Nielsen started to explain the mission.

"Guys, we have some Americans stranded at Alpha 2 that may need to be extracted. Let's see if we can get up there through this weather and get them out." Frink rolled the throttle up to 6600 rpm and requested tower clearance as Nielsen plotted a flight route on the map. Lowe loaded his twin M60 machine gun while Matt Vickers did the same with his .50-cal M2 machine gun. Lowe had been an AH-1G Cobra crew chief but wanted to fly. When the powers that be had approved moving him to a door gunner position on the UH-

1H aircraft, he'd redesigned and built a mount for the M60 machine-gun pedestal that would allow him to mount two guns instead of just one, doubling the firepower on that side of the aircraft.

Departing Quang Tri, Frink took a northwest heading but quickly started running into inclement weather. Over the next hour, they attempted to find a way through the weather, with no success.

"Underground Three, Underground Three, Blue Ghost Three-Four, over," Nielsen transmitted.

"Blue Ghost Three-Four, Underground Three, over," Captain Murray responded.

"Underground Three, Three-Four, the weather is just too bad to get to Alpha 2. We're coming back to Quang Tri and will wait for it to improve. When that's going to be, I don't know. Over."

"Roger, Three-Four. We have some extra beds that you're welcome to, and the mess hall is still open for chow when you get in. Over," Murray told them. Calling Alpha 2 was not going to be easy.

* * *

ANGLICO Team
   Alpha 2

Alpha 2 had been under fire for the past forty-eight hours. Naval gunfire was the only thing keeping the NVA from over-running the firebase, but now the firebase was surrounded, with more NVA streaming past the firebase down QL1.

"Sergeant Newton, I don't think we're going to hold out much longer. I'm calling for an extraction bird."

"Roger, sir," was all Newton said. Moving off the tower,

Bruggeman made his way to the radio room. Picking up the handset from Worth, he made the call.

"Custom House Six, Custom House Five, over," Bruggeman called on the ANGLICO net.

A moment later, he heard, "Custom House Five, Custom House Six, over." It was Lieutenant Eisenstein.

"Six, requesting extraction be laid on. Alpha 2 is receiving heavy artillery fire from across the DMZ and we have troops probing the perimeter. The ARVNs are basically cowering in the bunkers."

"Custom House Five, roger, wait one," Eisenstein responded. *Why is it whenever the heat is on and you request something, the response is "wait one"?* Bruggeman was thinking.

Turning to Lieutenant Colonel Turley, Eisenstein said, "Sir, Alpha 2 is requesting an extraction. I doubt they can hold out for another hour. Colonel Metcalf turned down a request yesterday afternoon to plan for their extraction, but I know Bruggeman. He wouldn't request it if he thought he could stay longer. We have five Marines up there. There's an aircraft in Quang Tri that will go get them if I give them the word."

"Eisenstein, I don't have the authority to authorize an extraction. Get Metcalf on the horn and see if he'll authorize it," Turley said with some frustration.

Grabbing up a phone, Eisenstein placed the call to the 3rd Division TOC at Quang Tri and asked to speak to Metcalf.

"Sir, this is Lieutenant Eisenstein. Alpha 2 called and is requesting extraction. They have NVA approaching on all three sides. The Vietnamese have abandoned their guns. His only support is naval gunfire as the weather is still overcast. We have five Marines up there, sir, and I would like to get them out. There's an aircraft in Quang Tri that can take them."

After a long pause, Metcalf directed, "Okay, you can plan and coordinate the extraction, but do not execute until I authorize it. Understood? Contact F Troop, 8th Cav. They're in direct support. Any questions?"

"No, sir. I'll get right on it," Eisenstein quickly said, not wishing to waste any time with Metcalf. He turned to Turley. "Sir, we're running out of time. Metcalf said I could plan but not execute. Sir, Bruggeman wouldn't be calling for an extraction if he thought they could hang on longer. Please let me launch the mission," Eisenstein pleaded.

"Lieutenant, I have no authority to authorize that extraction. You've got to talk to Metcalf and get the approval. I'm sorry, but I have no authority here," Turley said with some disappointment.

Eisenstein turned to Sergeant Smith once Turley's attention was taken over by another crisis. "Call the cav and see if they can get a bird here. I'm going to see if any aircraft are outside that can do it. Keep bugging Colonel Turley to authorize the extraction." With that, Smith picked up a receiver and started making calls while Eisenstein ran out to the TOC, looking for an aircraft. There was one, a CH-47. Approaching the aircraft, Eisenstein recognized the pilot.

"Bob, I need your help," Eisenstein said. Bob Gedzun was a CH-47 pilot on his second tour. He had been flying with Company A, 228th Assault Support Helicopter Battalion, until it had stood down in the beginning of 1972. He along with others had been transferred to the 2nd Squadron, 241st Vietnamese Air Force, where all Vietnamese helicopters were located.

"What you need, Joel?" Gedzun asked.

"I need an aircraft to get up to Alpha 2 and extract an ANGLICO team, now. They're about to be overrun," Eisenstein explained.

"We have an emergency resupply to get out to Mai Loc, but let me get on the radio and find you an aircraft," Gedzun said as he climbed up into the aircraft and started calling on the radio.

* * *

Nielsen and company had spent the night at Quang Tri airfield waiting to get the call to launch to Alpha 2. When the phone rang, he was given a new mission to fly to Ai Tu and pick up seven pax to take to the Citadel in Quang Tri. When he arrived at Ai Tu, a major and six cooks, bakers and candlestick makers loaded the aircraft with personal gear, to include a TV. Nielsen could barely get off the ground with the load. Just after lifting off, he got a call.

"Blue Ghost Three-Four, Blue Ghost Three, over."

"Blue Ghost Three, Three-Four, over."

"What is your location? Over."

"We just left Ai Tu with seven pax and are heading to the Citadel. Over."

"Roger, change of mission. Drop those pax at the first available place and proceed back to VIP pad at Ai Tu for a briefing. You're to proceed to Alpha 2 for an immediate extraction."

Warrant Officer Ben Nielsen and First Lieutenant Robert Sheridan exchanged looks of concern. Switching over to intercom, Nielsen looked over his shoulder while Sheridan started a descending turn.

"Hey, Major," Nielsen said, catching Major Wells's attention.

"Yeah, Chief?" Wells responded.

"Sir, we got a change of mission. We're dropping you off at that artillery position down there. We'll come back and get you after this mission is done, or send another aircraft," Nielsen explained. He could tell the major was not a happy camper after receiving this news.

As the aircraft approached, Nielsen determined that the only place to land was on the other side of a small knoll from the artillery position. He touched down, and the seven passengers jumped out of the aircraft with their personal equipment and bags. They all had weapons and four magazines.

"Sir, I'll be back for you as soon as I can. You have your FM radio and I'll be on 40.55, which is our unit FM frequency. Blue Ghost Three-Four is my call sign. Back in an hour," Nielsen said above the sound of the aircraft, and he lifted off, leaving the major standing in a swirl of dust.

"Okay, let's get our gear and move down to the artillery position. Be safer with some security around us," Wells ordered. Everyone immediately complied, not wishing to be outside of the ring of security provided by the artillery soldiers. As they moved over the crest of the knoll, Wells immediately knew something was wrong. Fifty yards away sat three 105mm howitzers, but no soldiers could be seen. As they approached the artillery tubes, it became evident that they had been abandoned by the Vietnamese soldiers. Wells and company were alone.

Thirty minutes later, the two pilots landed at Ai Tu and were met by Eisenstein.

"Sir, I'm Mr. Nielsen and this is Lieutenant Sheridan. We were told you have an extraction mission for us at Alpha 2. Is that correct?" Nielsen asked Lieutenant Eisenstein, who was standing on the pad. Both were experienced pilots, with Nielsen the more experienced of the two, having graduated six months from flight school before Sheridan. Initially he had been assigned to the 158th Aviation Battalion, 101st Airborne Division, but he'd transferred to F Troop, 8th Cav, when the 158th had stood down to redeploy back to the States. Sheridan had gone straight to F Troop when he'd arrived in-country. As they shut the aircraft down and climbed out of their seats, Eisenstein started his briefing.

"That's correct. I've worked out a flight route and naval gunfire support along the route. I'll be going with you and am in contact with the ships that will be firing for us," Eisenstein explained.

"Sir, I would feel a lot better about this if we had gunship support. Let me contact our flight ops and see if we can get some," Nielsen requested.

"Fine by me, but time is becoming a factor. I still need to get approval for the launch. Let's get in TOC and start making some phone calls." As they walked to the TOC, Eisenstein explained the situation at Alpha 2.

"Chief, you can use that phone," Eisenstein said, pointing at a landline. "Let me know when you hear something."

"Yes, sir," Nielsen replied as Eisenstein grabbed another phone to call Metcalf.

* * *

"Son of a bitch," Newton said as he lay on the floor of their observation post with 130mm artillery and mortars impacting on the firebase. Suddenly it was quiet as the incoming rounds stopped. Rising up slowly, Newton and Bruggeman looked over the edge of the sandbag wall. About one thousand meters to their front and sides, it appeared that the bushes were all moving in the same direction as the enemy had covered themselves with branches as camouflage.

Newton looked quickly to the south. "The damn Vietnamese have abandoned the guns again," he exclaimed with a bit of disgust in his voice. Bruggeman turned to confirm the fact for the record. The 105 howitzers were silent, and crews were nowhere to be seen. Suddenly a helmet appeared, coming up to the tower. It was an American helmet, a steel pot in Marine jargon. Everyone but Bruggeman was wearing one. The night before, Corporal Grounds had realized that his steel pot had been stolen by a Vietnamese and Bruggeman had given his to the young man.

"Worth, what's wrong?" Newton asked. Worth was normally down below, working the radios.

"Sir, the Vietnamese are beating feet out the south perimeter. A couple of Vietnamese officers are attempting to stop them, with little luck," Worth explained.

"Alright," Newton said. In the distance, the sound of mortar rounds leaving the tubes could be heard. No one doubted where they were going to land.

"Stay down. I'm going to call Eisenstein again," Bruggeman said before going down below with Worth. As they reached the M151 jeep that supported the unit, he said, "Worth, when I'm done, I want you to disable the jeep. Get Grounds to help you. Where's Beougher?"

"Sir, he's over by the pad," Worth responded.

"Okay, get as much of the radio equipment together and be prepared to destroy it. Got it?"

"Yes, sir."

* * *

Damn, it must be bad out there if he's calling for an immediate extraction, Eisenstein was thinking as he laid the handset down and Mr. Nielsen approached.

"Sir, I have two Cobra gunships inbound to provide escort for us," Nielsen said. "They'll be here in five mikes and we're ready to go."

"I still haven't gotten us clearance to execute. The colonel is off with General Giai and the deputy can't be found," Eisenstein said in frustration. "Wait one, let me talk to Colonel Turley." Eisenstein moved over to where Turley was looking at a map. "Excuse me, sir, but the shit is getting serious at Alpha 2. They're asking for an immediate extraction of the

ANGLICO team. It's five Marines with equipment. I've tried to contact Colonel Metcalf, but he's out with General Giai and the executive officer can't be found. Sir, I need an execute order or we're going to lose that team," Eisenstein pleaded.

Turley absorbed what the young officer was telling him. *Damn, where's Metcalf? I don't have the authority to authorize this. That's his decision or the executive officer's. But if we don't do something damn fast, those Marines aren't going to make it. Okay, I'm here and the senior officer on the scene...*

"Do it" was all Lieutenant Colonel Turley said.

Einstein immediately grabbed his hand mike. "Custom House Five" finally crackled over the radio.

"Six, go ahead." Small-arms fire along with the chatter of an M60 machine gun could be heard in the background.

"Custom House, extraction approved. Call sign is Blue Ghost Three-Four. Will contact you on this freq. How copy?"

"Roger, understand Blue Ghost Three-Four. What's his Echo Tango Alpha?"

"ETA is one-five mikes. Over."

"Roger, standing by. Out."

Ten minutes later, Bruggeman entered the radio room where Worth was monitoring the radios.

"Get Lieutenant Eisenstein on the horn," Bruggeman directed.

"Custom House Six, Custom House Five, over," Worth said and passed the handset to Bruggeman.

"Custom House Five, Custom House Six, over," came the reply.

"Six, what's the status of an extraction? This place is going to fall soon. Over," Bruggeman said. Silence was heard over the radio.

"Roger, Five," was finally heard. "Five mikes out, get to the pad. How copy? Over."

"Roger, I'll keep one radio. The rest is history. Out,"

Bruggeman said, turning to Worth. "Get some thermite grenades. Keep one PRC-77 and stack the rest. Burn them all."

* * *

The crew chief handed Lieutenant Eisenstein a headset so he could talk to the pilots as he climbed into the cargo bay on the UH-1H.

"Can you hear me?" came over Nielsen's helmet. *Everyone initially asks that same question*, Nielsen was thinking when he pressed his intercom switch.

"Yes, sir, I have you fine."

Eisenstein looked to the side and slightly behind to see a Cobra gunship on each side of the Huey. Nielsen was talking to the lead Cobra as Sheridan guided the aircraft at treetop level. The gunships were slightly higher and covering the Huey as it followed the folds of the terrain, which was fairly flat. As they approached the area of Alpha 2, two destroyers could be seen off to the left about a mile offshore, their main guns firing towards Alpha 2. Alpha 2 was easy to identify, with eruptions covering the firebase from incoming artillery and mortar fire.

"Sir," Nielsen said, getting Eisenstein's attention, "we're about five minutes from there. You want to call them now?" FM Radio 1 was set to Alpha 2's frequency. Eisenstein made the call. "Custom House Five, Custom House Six, over." He didn't get an immediate response. "Custom House Five, Custom House Six, over."

"Custom House Six, Custom House Five, we need an immediate extraction. We're at the pad in two bunkers on each side of the pad. We have five pax. How copy?" In the background, the pilots could hear the sounds of automatic weapons fire as well as the sounds of impacting mortars. Worth and Bruggeman were in an open bunker on one side of the pad, Newton and the others on the other side in a covered bunker.

"Ben, I think we're in for a hot extraction," Sheridan said, looking ahead at the smoke and dust swirling around Alpha 2. Red and green tracers crisscrossed the firebase. The artillery howitzers on the south side of the firebase were silent.

"Blue Ghost Two-One, Blue Ghost Three-Four, over," Nielsen said, calling the lead Cobra gunship.

"Blue Ghost Three-Four, Two-One."

"Two-One, as we go in, can you lay down suppressive fire in front of us and circle back to cover our departure? Over."

"Three-Four, roger. That's the plan."

"Six, Five. I have you in sight. Do you want smoke?"

"Negative, Five, we have the pad, two minutes out," Nielsen transmitted before Eisenstein could answer. Nielsen didn't want the enemy to know he was landing as it would only attract additional indirect fire. Turning to Sheridan, he said, "I have the aircraft."

"You have the aircraft," Sheridan replied, removing his hands and feet from the controls and indicating positive control of the aircraft being transferred. The two Cobra gunships remained alongside Nielsen and began launching 2.75-inch rockets along the flight path towards the landing pad. Some rockets exploded on impact; others were antipersonnel flechette rockets that separated in flight, spraying the area with two thousand one-inch nails with fins—absolutely deadly for troops in the open with no cover.

"Guns up," came over the intercom system for the gunner and crew chief. As they approached the firebase, Nielsen went into a rapid deceleration towards the designated helipad.

"Taking fire!" the crew chief announced and began expending ammo from his M2 .50-cal machine gun. Lowe added his two M60 machine guns to the mix of automatic fire. As Nielsen touched down, Newton and Grounds began moving to the aircraft along with Beougher. Almost immediately, a mortar round impacted on one side of the helipad— the side with Bruggeman and Worth. Initially, everyone that wasn't in the aircraft hit the ground. Eisenstein looked up to see a body on the ground.

"Bruggeman's been hit," Eisenstein screamed. Newton looked back at the young officer lying on the ground. The back of his shirt was developing a wet area below the collar.

Eisenstein jumped out of the aircraft along with the crew chief and ran to the fallen Marine. Newton and the others also saw the lieutenant was down and came to assist in getting him to the aircraft.

"Come on, run," Sheridan and Lowe were yelling as Eisenstein half dragged and half carried the wounded Marine.

"Where's Worth?" Eisenstein asked as he grabbed one of Bruggeman's arms. Both he and Newton looked first at the aircraft and then behind them. Worth had last been spotted in the bunker with Bruggeman. Now he was nowhere to be seen.

"I'll go look for him. He may have gone down the hill or be unconscious in one of the bunkers," Newton said and took off in a low crouch-run, shouting Worth's name. Grounds and Beougher each grabbed one of Bruggeman's arms or legs and helped Eisenstein get him to the aircraft.

Nielsen didn't roll the aircraft back to flight idle but kept the engine rpm at 6600 to make a quick departure. Silently praying, he looked over his left shoulder and could see four wounded Vietnamese soldiers standing on the edge of the helipad. He motioned for them to quickly get aboard. They didn't need a second invitation. He also noticed another stream of minigun fire from Blue Ghost Two-One, who was making another pass along the perimeter of the firebase. The crew chief was back in the aircraft, moving the wounded Vietnamese to make room for Bruggeman. Newton was climbing back in when a mortar round landed next to the pad, showering the aircraft in dirt and shrapnel.

"Sir, I couldn't find him. Gooks are through the wire and coming up the hill," Newton said with some dismay in his voice.

"Go, go!" yelled Lowe when everyone was aboard or standing on the skids.

Nielsen wasted no time in pulling up the collective and easing the cyclic forward to execute a rapid departure. As he did so, Newton and Beougher were pulling first aid kits from the bulkhead of the cargo area and tearing Bruggeman's uniform to see the wound. Grounds scanned the firebase, attempting to spot Worth. Eisenstein turned and looked at one Vietnamese soldier who had been pushed back and remained on the helipad. He was holding an M79 grenade launcher, and the look in his eyes was not the least bit friendly. *My God, that son of a bitch is going to blow us out of the sky*, Eisenstein thought as the helicopter continued to gain altitude.

"Blue Ghost Two-One, coming up" was heard on the radio as two streams of minigun fire were laid down in front of the departing Huey, followed by the expenditure of all the remaining rockets.

"Chief, he needs to get to a medical facility fast. We have a medic at Ai Tu and I can have him meet us on the pad. Let's head there," Lieutenant Eisenstein directed.

Nielsen turned to Sheridan. "You got it, and head for Ai Tu."

"I have the aircraft" was all Sheridan said. They could see that everyone in the back was working to save Bruggeman. As Ai Tu came into view, Sheridan started his approach to the VIP pad, where an individual with a bag was standing. As soon as they'd landed, the corpsman, Doc Williamson, ran over to the aircraft and took a quick look at Bruggeman. The Vietnamese soldiers were getting out.

"We need to get him to the hospital in Da Nang, *now!*" the corpsman exclaimed as a medevac helicopter landed next to Nielsen. Bruggeman was placed on a stretcher and carried over to the medevac aircraft, where an IV was immediately started. Doc Williamson climbed aboard as well. The medevac executed an immediate and hasty takeoff and headed for Da Nang.

As Da Nang came into view, Doc Williamson tapped the pilot on the shoulder and shook his head. Lieutenant Bruggeman had died of his wounds before they could land.

* * *

Quang Tri Combat Base was getting another pounding of incoming artillery at 1615. First Lieutenant John Thoens lay on the floor of the command bunker along with everyone else. Suddenly the radio squelch cracked.

"Wolfman Six, Wolfman Five Bravo." Thoens couldn't believe his ears until the call was repeated. He attempted to reach up and grab a hand mike when a second round impacted. He recognized the voice. It was Corporal Worth.

"Custom House Six, Custom House Five Bravo, I...Dong Ha. Current position...Dong Ha" was all he heard. An hour later, after the artillery had ceased, an attempt to contact Worth was made, with negative results.[1]

* * *

It had been three hours since Major Wells and the small group of seven had set up a perimeter around the abandoned artillery tubes. Things had been quiet except for the sounds of a battle to the north. Major Wells was on the radio attempting to contact anyone and wasn't having much luck. Calls to Blue Ghost weren't answered. They were beginning to feel lonely when the first bullet pinged off the side of one of the artillery tubes. They were no longer alone, unfortunately.

"Major, we have company," a supply sergeant yelled and opened fire with his M16 in the "spray and pray" mode.

"Cease fire, dammit!" Wells yelled. "Don't waste your ammo shooting at nothing. Stay down." These weren't combat infantry soldiers but supply, cooks, clerks, typists, mailmen and motor pool mechanics.

"Sir, there's artillery ammo with the tubes. Can we shoot back with that?" the mechanic asked.

"Do you know how to operate that gun?" the major asked.

"No, sir" was the sheepish response. "I thought maybe you knew how to do it."

"Well, I don't. I was infantry, not artillery. Let me see if I can get someone on the radio," Wells said and picked up the hand receiver on the AN/PRC-77. "Mayday, mayday. Any aircraft, mayday." This went on for five minutes before an artillery round impacted about one hundred yards away. The artillery tubes were now attracting the attention of an NVA spotter.

"Sir, what do we do?" the former cook, now an infantry soldier, asked as he pressed lower into the ground.

"Pray I get someone on the radio," Major Wells responded and made another call. "Mayday, mayday, any aircraft," he repeated as another artillery round impacted a bit closer. *If we don't get someone soon, we're moving away from these tubes*, Major Wells was thinking.

"Station calling mayday, Blue Ghost Three-Four" suddenly came over the radio. Every head snapped to look as if they would see the speaker.

"Blue Ghost Three-Four, we need to be picked up. We're receiving incoming artillery. Over," Wells transmitted.

"Roger, I have you in sight but need you to move back to the spot where I dropped you. I can't land next to the artillery position. How copy?"

"Blue Ghost, we're moving," Wells said, and no one needed any further instructions. Everyone immediately stood and grabbed their gear, rapidly moving to the previous landing zone. Halfway to the landing zone, another artillery round impacted, this time on the artillery tubes they had just vacated. Suddenly the pace picked up from a rapid walk to a labored dash as the seven attempted to run with their baggage. At about the time they reached the clearing, Blue Ghost Three-Four touched down, much to the pleasure of Major Wells and his band of soldiers.

17

FIRST TO FALL

1 April 1972
Team Bravo
Nui Ba Ho, South Vietnam

Team Bravo, part of the 4th Vietnamese Marine Battalion on Firebase Sarge, had been receiving artillery fire all night, and the longer the night went on, the more accurate the fire became. Captain Raymond Smith spent the night moving from bunker to bunker, checking the perimeter, and encouraging the Vietnamese Marines holding those positions.[1] As the first rays of light appeared on the eastern horizon, his concern for their situation increased with the first large assault on the perimeter. Grabbing a radio, he called Major Boomer on Sarge, which was located slightly below Nui Ba Ho, on a lower pinnacle from Sarge.

"Mike Six, Mike Six, Mike Six-One, over," Smith called, hoping Major Boomer was available.

"Mike Six-One, Mike Six, over."

"Mike Six, we have an assault on the north perimeter.

Appears to be company-size. We need some artillery support up here. The incoming rounds are pretty damn accurate to the point that it's not recommended to move outside a bunker at this time. We have our 106 recoilless with flechette rounds and it's doing a number on them, but artillery's what we really need. Over," Smith explained.

"Mike Six-One, I wish I could help you. Let me get with the artillery people here and see what I can do. We have a FAC operating in your area, but with this weather, he's having difficulty seeing you, or anything else for that matter. Over," Major Boomer responded.

Throughout the rest of the day, Team Bravo faced three more human wave attacks. The NVA might finally take the hill, but it was costing him dearly. At 1730, Captain Smith left the command bunker to look over the perimeter.

"What the...?" Smith mumbled as the entire hillside was moving upward. NVA soldiers covered in brush for camouflage were closing on three sides of the perimeter. Returning to the command bunker, Smith got on the radio to Boomer.

"Mike Six, I need some artillery support or we're going to be overrun. Over," Smith said, attempting to maintain a calm voice.

Throughout the evening hours, the situation at Nui Ba Ho deteriorated. Finally, Major Ho gave the order to clear out. Grabbing his M16 and a PRC-25 radio, Smith exited the bunker and ran into three NVA soldiers just outside the door. They had their backs to the door and didn't see him. He plowed right through them without a shot being fired. Reaching the wire, he found a group of South Vietnamese Marines.

"Let's get through the wire," Smith directed. No one moved.

"Booby traps in wire," one of the ARVN Marines said, pointing to where two booby trap explosives lay.

"If we don't move, we'll be captured," Smith started to say when a burst of AK-47 fire passed over their heads. One Marine raised his weapon to return fire, but Smith stopped him. "No shoot. Only give our position away. Then more come." *I've got to do something other than just sit here.* Looking to his left and right, he realized the answer was easy. As with most American advisors, they had forty to sixty pounds more weight and six inches of height on the South Vietnamese Marines. Smith grabbed the closest kid on the right and tossed him onto the wire. Before anyone could react, he grabbed the kid on the left and tossed him as well. No booby traps went off and everyone scurried over these two and then helped get them out of the wire. One more wire to go. Now the Vietnamese soldiers were more afraid of Smith than the enemy and none would stand near him. *Shit, these kids aren't going to move through the wire. I'm going to have to open this breach,* Smith was thinking when he stood, took a running start and in John Wayne fashion threw himself across the barbwire fence. Quickly the South Vietnamese Marines followed, using Smith for a walkway over the wire. It took Smith a few moments to get himself out of the wire, shredding his uniform and his skin in the process, but they were through and heading down the mountain to FSB Sarge. Smith still had his PRC-25 radio and began calling for artillery fire as his small party moved down the hill.

* * *

2140 Hours
FSB Sarge

"Mike Six-One, Mike Six, over." Major Boomer on Sarge was trying to contact Captain Smith, to no avail. At this point

Major Boomer was convinced that Captain Smith had been captured or worse.

"Chinh Quang," Boomer called across the TOC to Major Quang, "it appears that Team B is no longer."

"Major Boomer, I no comms with Team B. You may be right," Chinh Quang, who was the battalion commander for the 4th VNMC Battalion, responded.

"Chinh, I think we should consider evacuation of Sarge considering the loss of Nui Ba Ho," Boomer recommended.

"Let me consider the possibility. I walk the perimeter one more time before I make decision. Do you wish to join me?" Quang offered.

"Yes, sir, after you."

Quang and Boomer left the TOC and began an inspection of the firebase. Morale was good considering they had been getting pounded with artillery and ground attacks for the past twenty-four hours. Coming upon the battalion mortar platoon, they found that every member had been wounded, but they still continued to support the line dogs. Returning to the command TOC, Quang made the decision just after midnight.

"Boomer, I think not prudent to fight to the last man and all die here. We should evacuate and live to fight another day," Quang said with some regret. He glanced at his watch. It was 0340 in the morning, April 1.

"Chinh, I think that's a wise decision. I'll notify division," Boomer said meaning he would notify the senior advisor at division. Moving over to the advisor command net, Boomer made the call. "Uniform Three, Uniform Three, this is Mike Six, over."

"Mike Six, go ahead."

"Uniform, this is Mike Six. Situation is untenable, we're moving out. How copy?"

"Roger, understand moving out of Sarge."

"Affirmative, out."

Lieutenant Colonel Turley had monitored the conversation. *God, I hope Boomer and Smith are alright*, he prayed. At 0345 hours, those in 4th VNMC Battalion, 147th Marine Brigade, passed east through the wire with Mai Loc as their objective.

18

ESCAPE AND EVADE

1 APRIL 1972
4th Battalion, 147th VMC Brigade
Nui Ba Ho, South Vietnam

The weather had not improved during the night, nor had there been a decrease in the amount of artillery and mortars that were hitting the firebase. Major Joy was informed that morning that the 155 howitzers were out of ammo and could no longer provide fire support to Nui Ba Ho or Sarge. Things were rolling downhill fast.

"Is Lieutenant Colonel Turley there?" Joy asked over the phone line.

"Wait one, sir, and I'll get him" was the response he got. A few minutes later, he heard, "Lieutenant Colonel Turley here."

"Sir, Major Joy. Is there any way you can get some 155 ammo up to us? We're out of it. Small-arms ammo is low, and we haven't eaten in two days," Joy said as Turley rolled his eyes towards heaven.

"Major, let me see what I can do. I might be able to get the 56th Regiment to send you something, or the 3rd Division. How are you doing up there?" Turley asked.

"Sir, we're getting the crap pounded out of us, but we're still here. Carroll isn't providing much support as I think they're shooting counterbattery fire up north. Colonel Bao, the 147th commander, is madder than a water buffalo in a pen and is calling everyone and anyone that will listen to him at 3rd ARVN. Boomer contacted me at 0345 and told me they were abandoning Sarge. I've got no word on Smith. I think they've abandoned Nui Ba Ho. If not, I'm sure they won't be holding out much longer," Joy indicated.

The weather offered some relief for Captain Smith and his small group as the moon was covered by the overcast. The night was so dark it was difficult to see the man in front as the group walked single file.

Outside the wire, Smith asked, "Major Hoa, how many men are with us?"

"Dai'uy, I am not sure.[1] We had three hundred to start with. Last count one hundred maybe left," the Bravo Company commander said. Smith could tell the man was exhausted after so many days of hard fighting and a lack of sleep and food.

"Major, we should form up single file and move as quietly as possible," Smith suggested, then followed up with an order. "Pass the word, Major," Smith instructed, taking command of the situation. Major Hoa didn't object. The element formed and started down the hill. The downpour was almost welcomed as it covered their noise but reduced visibility to only a few meters. Their movement was cautious as the voices of NVA soldiers were all around them. Smith raised his hand and everyone took a knee, facing outward and prayed an enemy patrol didn't stumble into them.

"Major Hoa, check your map, sir. I want to let Mai Loc

know where we are so we don't walk into a B-52 strike or our own artillery," he whispered to the Bravo Company commander. Major Hoa pulled out his poncho and placed it over his head. Underneath, Hoa and Smith turned on a flashlight and with map and compass estimated their position. Smith attempted to contact Boomer and pass the coordinates to him, but no one answered his call. He attempted to contact Joy but had the same results. The short whip antenna on the PRC-25 radios just did not have the range.

"Major, I have no contact with Sarge or Mai Loc. I think we should head for Mai Loc and hope for the best," Smith said, attempting to encourage Major Hoa, who only nodded in reply. Turning off the flashlight, they removed the poncho. With hand signals, everyone resumed the march. Rather than taking the easy trail along the ridge to Mai Loc, Smith chose to move midway between the crest of the ridge and the valley floor. In both locations, he could hear the chatter of NVA soldiers as well as the grinding of gears on track vehicles. *Shit, these guys are moving some heavy stuff up on Route 9*, Smith thought as they moved along.

"Hold up," Smith said, and again everyone took a knee.

"What?" asked Major Hoa, who was reaching the point of exhaustion.

"Do you hear that?" Smith asked in a whisper. Major Hoa listened for a moment. Using hand signals, Major Hoa indicated that someone was walking in the stream in front of them.

Smith nodded his head and mouthed, "Affirmative." He then motioned for everyone to lie flat on the ground. The signal was passed down the line. Right now, Smith didn't want to get into a firefight, being surrounded. He turned his radio off, so no one would call him at this point. Thirty minutes later, things appeared to be quiet. Smith looked at Hoa, who was asleep. A gentle nudge made him open his eyes and he silently acknowledged that they needed to move out. Smith again took the point position. As the overcast sky began to lighten, Smith had managed to avoid the NVA units moving on both sides of him. They had been moving all night, and he and the Vietnamese Marines were dragging ass tired. *If we get in contact, I don't know if they have the strength to put up a fight*, Smith feared. He checked his compass now that he didn't need a flashlight to read it. *Good, still on heading.*

Major Hoa came up behind him. "Dai'uy, how much further?" he asked. Smith could tell the major was on his last legs.

"Sir, we have about four more hours to reach E-45, which is three klicks west of Mai Loc." Smith could see the stamina drain from the major.

"Do you think anyone will be at E-45?" the major asked, hoping the answer would be yes, and trucks too. E-45 was a small hamlet just west of Mai Loc and a road intersection.

"I don't know, sir. I have had negative contact with anyone" was Smith's answer.

The group continued to move cautiously eastward, reaching E-45 three hours later, only to find it abandoned. They still had another three thousand meters to travel. Major Hoa was exhausted.

"Sir, let's take a break here. You need some rest and I think we all could use some," Smith said, feeling the strain of the past few days catching up to him. As Smith sat, he started to take a head count. There were only sixty-nine soldiers present. He also noticed that Major Hoa was starting to shake from exposure and lack of water. That was when he heard what sounded like a small-arms firefight in the distance, but not in the direction of Mai Loc. That made his decision for him. "Sir, we need to get moving. It's only another three klicks to Mai Loc," Smith said with some enthusiasm.

"Dai'uy, you go and leave me here. I will only slow you

down and I cannot go any further," Major Hoa said with a shaky voice.

"No, Major! You're coming with me if I have to carry you," Smith said none too gently. The major just lay there. He was physically done. Reaching down, Smith grabbed the major's load-bearing equipment and pulled him to his feet. Turning, Smith squatted, and a Vietnamese soldier helped the major climb on Smith's back. As they moved out, Smith and the Vietnamese soldier would switch off carrying Major Hoa into Mai Loc firebase.

Within sight of Mai Loc, they came across a small hamlet. Mai Loc was on the receiving end of intense artillery and Smith laid Major Hoa down and dispersed the column. No one objected. As most soldiers do, some went scrounging and found some food, which they quickly turned into a soup and began passing out bowls. Spoons were not a requirement for hungry men.

"Dai'uy, Dai'uy, soldiers come," an excited young Marine said and pointed west. Other Marines began taking up fighting positions as they anticipated the fight they had avoided was about to begin. Smith moved to the western side of their hasty fighting positions, attempting to determine how they would meet the new threat. As he studied the approaching group, a smile crept across his face. The advancing soldiers were being led by none other than Major Boomer.

"Damn, I'm glad to see you, sir," Smith said as Boomer approached him. They exchanged a back-slapping hug.

"You too," Boomer said as young Vietnamese Marines streamed past him, following the scent of soup. As hungry as they were, they were disciplined in lining up to get some. Those that had already had some passed their empty bowls to the new arrivals that didn't have a canteen cup or shared their canteen cup. A young Vietnamese Marine approached

Boomer, holding out a bowl of soup. Sitting down for the first time, Boomer relaxed for a moment.

"So, sir, what happened at Sarge?" Smith asked.

"We realized before midnight that we couldn't hold and we pulled out at around 0330 hours. We were out of mortar ammo, low on small arms and hadn't eaten since Friday. The pullout went fairly smooth and I think we got almost everyone out, to include some wounded. Somewhere along the way, the kid carrying my radio lost it, so I've had no comms with anyone. I was about to beat his ass when we heard voices off to our left. About two hours ago, we had an enemy patrol come up behind us and the shooting started. At first we held, but then everything just broke down and they started running. I was yelling for them to stand and withdraw when the gooks heard me and started calling for me to surrender. I recognized that they were now focused on capturing me, so I did the only thing left to do—emptied my magazine in spray and pray and ran like I was on fire. About an hour later I was in the lead of those running and stopped to regroup everyone. Then we came in here. Damn, it's good seeing you," Boomer said as he heard a commotion and looked towards the cause. More Vietnamese Marines from the 4th Battalion were approaching the perimeter, having found their way towards Mai Loc.

19

SHIFT CHANGE

2330 Hours
1 April 1972
3rd ARVN Division TOC
Ai Tu, South Vietnam

It had been two and a half days of constant shelling and confusion. Misinformation was noted that only added to the confusion, partly because people didn't know what was happening and partly because of the reluctance of the Vietnamese to report the conditions as they were. Turley and his small staff of thirty volunteers were all that remained at Ai Tu after Metcalf and the others from the 155th had bugged out. Earlier in the evening, Lieutenant Colonel Norm Heon, Metcalf's deputy, had told Turley that all US personnel were evacuating Ai Tu. When asked about the advisors out with the units, he had no answer. Heon left with all the others, which were mostly personnel that worked in administration and supply for the team. Operations, communications, intelligence and fire support personnel in the TOC all volunteered to stay. Turley was running the show now with no tactical guidance from higher headquarters or Metcalf.

Gathering the staff around, Turley said, "Okay, let's review the last twenty-four hours and see where we're at. Captain Murray, do you want to go first?"

"Sir, we've lost all the firebases above the Cam Lo River except Charlie 3. As I understand it, Major Boomer and Captain Smith are E and E to Mai Loc, which is under artillery fire and some ground probes. We've just not had any contact with them. If Mai Loc has to be abandoned, they intend to fall back to Carroll. Charlie 1 and Charlie 2 have fallen as well as we've had no contact with those units since about 1700 hours. The 258th Brigade completed its move to Dong Ha and secured the south side of the river. They report that QL9 and QL1 are clogged with refugees, all moving south. The brigade headquarters and artillery battalion have repositioned and are now collocated with us here. Carroll is still in operation and providing fire support but is also on the receiving end of counterbattery fire," Captain Murray concluded.

"What's the enemy situation as we understand it now?" Turley asked.

"Sir, as best we can tell, the B5 Corps is running the show in the east with one division on the east side of QL1 and one division on the west side, which is the 308th Division. In the west, the 304th Division is going against Nui Ba Ho, Khe Gio and Sarge. The 324B Division is moving on Holcomb. He's using his tanks, T-54s and PT-76s. The tanks are on QL9 and the PT76s for the most part are in the vicinity of Charlie 4 on the coast," Murray went on to explain.

"What are we looking at if Mai Loc, Holcomb and Carroll fall?" Turley asked.

"In that case, sir, we have two battalions from the 258th at Dong Ha, Firebase Pedro, Ann and Barbara, for a second line of defense. The 20th Tank is in reserve on the outskirts of

Quang Tri and ready to move to Dong Ha if necessary," Murray said, pointing to each location as he spoke.

"Well, let's hope they don't become the second line of defense," Turley responded, attempting to keep everyone's spirits up. "Major Brookhaven, air support?"

"Sir, we will continue to have marginal weather for tac air support or attack helicopters. We've been processing requests for B-52s, and they're flowing. We had six drops today and more planned for tomorrow in suspected assembly areas, supply locations, and locations of identified frontline troops," Major Brookhaven stated.

"Right now, the B-52s are saving our asses, so let's keep them busy," Turley pointed out. "Lieutenant Eisenstein?"

"Yes, sir. Alpha 2 was abandoned today with the loss of Lieutenant Bruggeman. We have four destroyers off the coast now responding to calls for fire for an area within ten miles of the coast. We have naval gunfire supporting Carroll, but that's the extent of their range," Eisenstein stated.

"How are the rest of the folks from Alpha 2?" Turley asked.

"Sir, they're fine and I put them in a bunker here until I can get them out tomorrow."

"Good," Turley answered. "Captain Murray, what's the status of the advisors with the 56th and the 57th?"

No one spoke up. Finally, Murray said, "Sir, there's been little word from them. We have reports of men from both regiments coming into Carroll or moving down QL1, but organized defense, especially in the case of the 56th, is nonexistent at this point. We've had no word from the advisor there."

"Any word from Boomer?" Turley asked. Again no one answered.

20

EASTER SUNDAY

2 APRIL 1972
147th VNMC Brigade
Mai Loc, South Vietnam

"Sir, we're out of 105 ammo, small arms is very low and food is scarce," Major Joy informed Turley. "On top of that we're starting to have probes on the perimeter." The day was starting off no better than the previous night had ended. The overcast skies were still hanging low over the entire area and the tops of some hills to the west were hiding in clouds, with valleys concealed in fog. All night, the sound of artillery fire could be heard, both outgoing and incoming. Contact with several firebases had been lost, to include Alpha 1 through 4, Charlie 1 and 2, and FSBs Sarge and Holcomb. Charlie 3 was the only firebase north of the Cam Lo River and it was a matter of time before it fell as enemy tanks were moving down QL1. Intelligence reports were still confused and contradictory. And it was only 0700 hours. *How much worse can this day get?* thought Turley.

"I'll see if we can get 3rd ARVN to get a resupply to you. Carroll is reporting probes as well. What about stragglers?" Turley asked.

"Sir, we're getting a mixed bag of people from Sarge."

"How's the artillery support from Carroll?" Turley asked.

"Critical. That support is about all that's holding them at this time. Without it we would be in very serious trouble, and I doubt we could hold out here."

"Have you got an exit plan in case you need to beat feet?" Turley asked and silently prayed they had worked out a plan.

"Yes, sir, and everyone has been briefed on it. We'll make for Carroll or Holcomb," Joy responded.

"Forget Holcomb. Make it to Carroll or Pedro or here. Okay, let me work on getting you a resupply. Keep me posted. Have you heard from Boomer or Smith?" Turley asked.

"Heard from Boomer this morning just before I called you. He called and is sitting just outside the wire after outrunning and outgunning the NVA. Boomer covered the Vietnamese with him while they ran to the perimeter. The battalion commander, Major Quang, came in with one group and said they only made it because of Boomer's actions. Boomer has eight other Vietnamese with him."

"Is Boomer okay?"

"Yes, sir, just a little beat up. He'll be fine."

"What about Smith?"

"He's with Boomer now. They linked up coming down from Sarge."

"What's the status of 4th Battalion?"

"Sir, 4th Battalion had six hundred and thirty-two when they went to Sarge. We now have two hundred and eighty-five back and accounted for. We're rearming those that need it and distributing ammo to them. Boomer said the NVA attack on Sarge was classic and flawless. Coordinated artillery supporting the ground assault that exercised fire-and-maneuver. Not what we're used to seeing."

Communications between Mai Loc and the outside world had been difficult. The antenna farm on Mai Loc was under constant artillery fire. The AN/RC-292 antennas had to be set back in place several times by Captain Earl Kruger or one of the other captains on Joy's team. When not working on the antennas, Captains Dave Randall and Clark Embrey would be moving across the firebase, checking on the defensive positions and battalion command posts and offering guidance and encouragement. Communications with Carroll was critical to keep the artillery support from its twenty-two howitzers, of which four were 175mm guns.

* * *

0745 Hours
Ai Tu, South Vietnam

The limited staff of volunteers had been working for the past ninety-six hours. Everyone was tired and nerves were frayed. The good point, however, was that dead wood was no longer present in the TOC and those present were the cream of the crop as soldiers, airmen and Marines. Maintaining communications was the key for this headquarters to receive information, coordinate actions, request resupply, and inform higher headquarters of the deteriorating situation.

"Captain Murray, see if we can get 3rd ARVN to get a CH-47 load up to Mai Loc with small arms, artillery, and food. And get me the status of the ammo at Carroll. I suspect they're running low with all the support they're giving to Mai Loc," Turley said, reaching for another cup of coffee from the TOC pot.

"Sir, Carroll is fine with ammo. They have a huge stockpile up there. This morning's report indicated they had over a thousand rounds," Murray said. Turley let out a small sigh of relief.

His thoughts were interrupted by Sergeant Smith. "Excuse me, sir, you have a call on the landline from Colonel Metcalf."

"Thanks," Turley said, taking the receiver. *Wonder what he could want now. He ought to have his ass up here.* "Turley here."

"Turley, this is Colonel Metcalf." *Oh boy, now we're playing "who has the bigger dick?"*

"Yes, sir. What do you need?"

"Turley, you are directed to take over as senior American advisor to the 3rd ARVN Division Forward, by order of the Commanding General, FRAC. Understood."[1] At first Turley just stared straight ahead. *This cannot be happening to me. I'm just here to visit my advisors. I'm not even of the same branch of service as these people.*

"Sir, has this been cleared with my superiors in Saigon?" *Surely they wouldn't hang my ass out like this*, Turley was thinking.

"That's not your concern, Colonel. You are in charge up there until further notice," Metcalf stated with a bit of fluster in his voice.

"Sir, before I take charge up here, I want that in writing," Turley said. *I smell a rat*, he was thinking.

"We don't have time for that. Just do the job and get on with it," Metcalf directed.

"Then, sir, I want your Social Security number," Turley responded. After a moment, he added, "I'm ready to copy when you give it, sir."

Metcalf hesitated but finally responded with the nine digits. "Now you understand your orders?"

"Well, sir," Turley responded, almost spitting *sir* through the receiver, "if I'm to be the senior advisor for the 3rd ARVN Division Forward, and since the entirety of what's left of the 3rd ARVN Division is forward, what are you advising?" Metcalf didn't answer—the line went dead. Turley stood still for a few minutes, contemplating the situation, when one of the radios broke squelch. Sergeant Swift picked up the receiver.

"Station calling Underground, go ahead," Smith said. He gazed at Turley with a look that said, *I didn't catch their call sign.*

"Underground, this is..." Again the caller's identification was garbled. "Enemy armor on QL1, vicinity of Charlie 1. Approximately twenty, I say again, twenty Papa Tango Seven-Six and Tango Five-Four vehicles moving south. 57th cannot hold. Withdrawing. How copy? Over."

"Who is that?" Captain Murray asked, stepping up next to Smith, who shook his head.

"Station calling Underground, identify yourself, over," Smith requested. Again squelch broke and the caller's call sign was garbled.

"Sir, I think that might be Lieutenant Colonel Twitchell. He's the advisor for the 57th, which abandoned Charlie 1 about twenty-four hours ago," Smith said.

"Ask him if they can stop those tanks north of the Cam Lo River," Turley said.

"Station calling Underground, can you stop those tanks north of the Cam Lo River? Over," Smith asked.

"That's a negative" was the response.

"Ask if they can adjust fire on them," Eisenstein said as the tanks were within naval gunfire range.

"Station calling Underground, can you adjust naval gunfire? Over," Smith relayed. There was no response after multiple attempts to establish communications. Turley walked over to the map with Murray and Eisenstein.

"Gentlemen, there's nothing to stop them from reaching Dong Ha and the bridge. Sergeant Swift, find me Colonel Dinh and ask him to come here now," Turley requested. Swift was out the door in a flash. A few minutes later, he returned with Colonel Dinh in tow.

"Colonel Dinh, here's the situation. We have about twenty armor vehicles moving down QL1 towards Dong Ha. We must try and stop them from crossing the Cam Lo River. I see that the 3rd Battalion is located south of the bridge. Can they stop them?" Turley asked.

Dinh took a moment to study the map. "I order them to move and establish a defensive line on the south bank of the river and defend with two companies. I retain two companies in reserve. I move four 106mm recoilless rifle jeeps from the 6th Battalion to reinforce them. Major Binh is the battalion commander and a good officer. He will stop them," Dinh said. "I call. Make sure all is good to go." And he departed the TOC to return to his headquarters.

"Captain Murray, who's the advisor with the 3rd Battalion?"

"Sir, that would be Captain John Ripley," Murray replied.

"And with 20th Tank?"

"That would be Major Smock, an Army armor officer."

"Okay, get Major Easley on the horn and tell him what's going down. Easley is the advisor to the 258th Brigade, correct?" Turley asked.

"Yes, sir," Murray responded.

"Tell Easley that if things don't happen as we expect Major Dinh to do them, let me know right away. I'm going to inform Metcalf of what's happening...and call Major Smock and tell him to move 20th Tank to Dong Ha...and put that in Vietnamese command channels too."

Metcalf wasn't present at the 3rd Division TOC, but his deputy was present and took the information. Turley could only hope that it got passed to the appropriate people so some support would be forthcoming. As Turley was reaching for another cup of coffee, Major Brookbank approached him.

"Hey, sir, need to hear some good news?" Brookbank asked.

"Right now I could use some. What is it?"

"The weather is definitely clearing. This stuff will be out of here by this afternoon most likely."

"Hot damn. Finally, we're getting a break. Let me find that Vietnamese Air Force liaison officer and get his working on some air support," Turley said with some hope in his voice.

"Sir, you best move quick. I saw him packing his stuff along with his team. I think they're leaving."

"What the—" Turley didn't finish but headed to the Vietnamese Air Force area, where he found the Vietnamese Air Force officer stuffing his kit bag in a panic. Turley grabbed his shoulder and spun the smaller man around.

"Where do you think you're going?" Turley said, towering over the Vietnamese.

"We go. We go. What's the use? We go. Go now." And he pushed past and departed the TOC.

* * *

1030 Hours
3rd Battalion, 258th Brigade
Dong Ha Bridge

"Ripper Two, Ripper Six, over," Major Easley called on the FM radio.

"Ripper Six, Ripper Two, over," Captain Ripley

responded. Ripley was considered by many as an exceptional officer. He had commanded a rifle company in Vietnam on a previous tour and had attended the US Army Ranger Qualification Course, where he'd received extensive training in demolitions, followed by a tour with the Royal British Marines.

"Ripper Two, how you doin'? Over."

"Ripper Six, I understand from talking to my counterpart that we're to move up to the south bank of the Cam Lo River and hold the bridge at Dong Ha, over," Easley said.

"Ripper Two, that's affirmative. Two companies are to remain as the reserve, but two move forward. There are four 106 recoilless jeeps heading your way for reinforcement. Over."

"Roger, understand. My counterpart just sent a message to his higher that as long as the Marines draw a breath of life, Dong Ha will belong to us. Over,"[2] Easley said, flashing a look at Jack, who had remained with the 3rd Battalion, observing their actions in preparing for the coming fight.

"Cocky SOB, but I'll give him respect. We have no radio contact with the 57th. Refugees are clogging the QL1, so that may slow down the armor headed your way. The 20th Tank is heading your way to reinforce you, but I need a confirmation on that and will get back to you. What time do you expect to have elements on the bridge? Over," Major Easley asked.

"Ripper Six, first elements are there now. Second Company is moving into position as we speak. Sort of anticipated this order, over," Ripley replied.

"Roger, I'll get a confirmation on 20th Tank and get back to you. Ripper Six out."

Captain Ripley continued shadowing Major Binh as they moved up towards the bridge at Dong Ha. Jack was observing and liked what he saw in Major Binh. Refugees were indeed clogging the road as they moved south ahead of the North Vietnamese onslaught. Artillery rounds were still impacting on road intersections, indiscriminately killing civilians. In some cases, wounded civilians received assistance from others, but many were left on the side of the road. Motorbikes, some cars, and carts pulled by water buffalo clogged the road along with people moving on foot, carrying what few possessions they could.

As they moved, Captain Ripley heard a sound that gave him some hope. It was a track vehicle moving up the road behind and towards his position.

"Dai'uy," Binh said, getting Ripley's attention. "Look." He pointed south. The lead M48 of the 20th Tank Battalion was coming into view. It was followed by four more tanks and a M113 armored personnel carrier, which stopped next to Ripley, Binh and Jack. The back ramp dropped and Lieutenant Colonel Ton Ta Ly, commander of the 20th Tank Battalion, stepped out with Major James Smock, US Army advisor.

"Major Binh," Ly said as Binh, Ripley and Jack came to attention and saluted. Ly and Smock returned the salutes, and handshakes were exchanged as well as introductions.

"Major Binh, I taking command of all forces here as I senior officer," Ly said in broken English so the advisors would understand who was in charge. Binh had no objections, nor did Ripley. It was refreshing for someone else to take overall responsibility after ninety-six hours in the fight. Ripley pulled out his map, and he and Smock started going over the situation at the Dong Ha bridges. A large North Vietnamese flag was flying from one of the girders on the partially destroyed railroad bridge west of the main highway bridge supporting QL1. As they looked over the map, a group of ARVN soldiers in almost a military formation walked south past them, away from the fighting. Few had weapons and even fewer acknowledged the presence of the two American officers.

"Stop," Major Binh screamed as he stepped in front of one of the soldiers. "Where do you think you are going?"

At first, the soldier looked at him with a blank stare. "It is no use, no use," the soldier said emotionlessly as others continued to walk past him and Major Binh. The soldier attempted to push his way past. Major Binh immediately drew his pistol and shot the soldier dead. Still the others walked past, not even acknowledging that anything had happened.

Ly was unfazed by Major Binh executing the soldier and motioned for the others to gather around his map as he spread it out on the hood of a jeep. "We have two bridges here at Dong Ha, the main bridge supporting QL1 and the railroad bridge. The railroad bridge can support troops and light vehicle, but the main road bridge can support tanks. The road bridge is clogged with refugees at this time and the railroad bridge appears to have enemy troops on it," Ly reiterated as he looked around to see if everyone was following. "Major Binh, move two companies to the west side of Dong Ha and take up defensive positions blocking QL9 and the railroad bridge. Leave one company on the QL1 road bridge and I will cover with one company of tanks. They are going to be exposed to the enemy on the north side. Understood?"

"Understood, sir," Major Binh responded. Ly looked at Ripley and Smock, who just nodded in agreement.

"Question, sir," Ripley asked. "Do we have an idea of what's coming down QL1?"

"It appears to be reinforced division, four artillery regiments, a rocket regiment, and an air-defense regiment. A target-rich environment as you say, Dai'uy," Ly said with a smile. "For now we will hold 20th Tank in reserve to see where they will attempt to make their main attack." With that, Major Binh and Ripley departed to get the units moving.

"Major Turner, we have NVA infantry on the south side

of the railroad bridge. Can we get artillery fire to clear them?" Ly asked.

"Sir, I'm just an observer of this operation and have no tactical authority but I'll see what I can do," Turner replied. He had monitored the calls for fire from the day before, and now he tuned his FM radio to the appropriate frequency and called Eisenstein.

"Custom House Six, Raven Two, over," Turner called, using Ripley's call sign.

"Raven Two, Custom House Six, over," was heard with a question in his voice.

"Custom House Six, Raven Two Actual is forward and I'm assisting. We met at your location a few weeks ago, Over," Turner transmitted to establish his credibility.

"Roger, Raven Two, understood, over."

"Custom House Six, fire mission..." And Turner passed the mission to Ai Tu, who relayed it to the USS *Buchanan*. Moments later, the welcome sound of naval gunfire could be heard, and the results seen as the north side of the railroad bridge was enveloped in smoke, dust and explosions. For the next hour, four destroyers provided deadly naval gunfire. Under this cover, two companies of Marines along with the 3rd Troop, 20th Tank, moved into Dong Ha and set up defensive positions on QL9. As the command group consisting of Ripley, Smock, Binh and Ly as well as Turner watched from some high ground south of the main bridge, Ripley spotted four PT-76 amphibious tanks moving south along QL1.

"Custom House Six, Raven Two, over."

"Raven Two, Custom House Six, go ahead."

"Roger, Custom House Six, four Papa Tango Seven-Six, east of main bridge on north bank. Shift fires one thousand meters east. Over."

"Roger, shift fires." The naval gunfire was so responsive that, moments later, the four PT-76 tanks were burning hulks.

For the moment, friendly forces were in control of the bridges, mostly.

* * *

1200 Hours

"Dai'uy, we have tanks approaching," Major Binh said, tapping Ripley on the shoulder and pointing north over the QL1 bridge. Looking up, Ripley could see four tanks about one thousand meters north of the bridge moving south on QL1. *Oh, now it's going to get interesting*, he was thinking when a strange sound, not heard since the offensive had started, captured his thoughts. Seconds later, Ripley knew exactly what was making the sound and looked skyward at the broken cloud cover. He spotted the four A-1 Skyraiders flown by the South Vietnamese Air Force loitering overhead above the broken clouds. Moments later, the first of the four, followed by the remaining three, executed a half barrel roll and dropped its nose, diving straight for the four tanks. As each aircraft pulled out of its respective dive, two tiny silver objects fell from the underside of the aircraft. One exploded and the other became a fireball of burning napalm all over the tanks. Ripley and Binh were so happy they were cheering and hugging each other. Their joy ended, however, as one of the Skyraiders began to trail black smoke and an object was seen falling from the aircraft, quickly followed by a parachute. They watched as the lone pilot drifted down into the waiting hands of the enemy.

As Ripley and Binh watched the air show, Smock and Ly were hunkered over Ly's command radio, monitoring a call from 1st Troop, which was west of the railroad and QL1 bridge. The troop was observing the road from Charlie 1 to

Dong Ha. Smock wasn't fluent in Vietnamese. Turner was serving as a translator for him to some extent.

"1st Troop has sighted enemy tanks on the road from Charlie 1. Ly has given him permission to engage. He wants to go observe," Jack said as Ly stood and moved towards his track vehicle. They all boarded Ly's command vehicle for a run to a place where they could observe the action. 1st Troop was in a hull defilade position with only the turrets and main guns visible above the round, just as they had been taught when they'd received the M48 tanks. At first, Smock couldn't see the enemy vehicles and thought they were just across the river, approaching the bridges. Ly tapped his shoulder and pointed twenty-five hundred meters further up the road. *Oh crap, they'll never hit them at that range*, Smock thought, remembering that the Vietnamese hadn't demonstrated any faith in the M48 range finder. Smock counted eleven T-54 tanks moving on the road.

Smock heard a .50-caliber suddenly open fire from the troop commander's tank, but just one round. He observed the round as it ricocheted off one of the T-54 tanks across the river. Right away, all the main guns on the M48 tanks opened fire. Across the river, six NVA tanks immediately exploded and commenced burning. The remaining five tanks instantly reversed their engines and hightailed it back up the road and out of sight. Smock looked at Ly with amazement.

"That was some damn fine tank gunnery," Jack observed, looking at Smock.

"Sir, how did they do that? And at that range? We've got to talk to the troop commander. Can you get him over here?" Smock asked Ly.

"No, we go him," Ly said and gave the order for this track to join the troop commander. Arriving at the troop commander's position, the major jumped down from his tank and walked over to Ly's vehicle, smiling from ear to ear. He saluted smartly and began a conversation with Ly. Smock was picking up bits and pieces, but Jack was filling in the pieces.

"Appears that the gunners didn't trust the range finders but have no doubt now. He fired his .50-cal first and watched through range finder. When round ping off tank, he knew he could trust it and he told everyone the range and they fired together. Trust the range finder now. He is telling everyone," Turner indicated as Ly surveyed the group with a broad smile. Smock just shook the company commander's hand, but their victory didn't last long.

* * *

1215 Hours
QL1 Bridge

Refugees continued to stream south across the Dong Ha Bridge on foot and by car, truck, motorcycle, and oxcart. More troublesome to Jack, however, was the number of ARVN soldiers from the 57th Infantry Regiment that were streaming south as well, some with weapons but most having lost them or tossed them away. Most were uninjured, but all were demoralized and demonstrating a total lack of discipline. But this wasn't the worst of it. As they crested a small hill where the burning tanks from the air strike were sitting, more tanks appeared, coming down QL1. Word was now reaching Turley that the rearguard battalion of the 2nd Regiment was almost encircled and cut off from reaching the Cam Lo River.

"Underground Six, Raven Six, over." Major Easley, the 258th's advisor, was on the radio.

"Raven Six, Underground Six, go ahead."

"Underground Six, large enemy tank and infantry force sighted twenty-five hundred meters north of Dong Ha Bridge on QL1. We need reinforcements, tac air and artillery support. Over. Request permission to blow the bridge. Over."

"Raven Six, understood. Do not, repeat, do not blow the bridge. Rig it but do not blow. How copy?" Turley directed.

"Roger, understood. What about reinforcements? Over."

"Raven Six, I'll work on that. Underground out." Turley hung up the radio receiver and picked up the phone, placing a call to the 3rd ARVN Division TOC in the Quang Tri Citadel.

"Colonel Chung speaking." Colonel Chung was the division chief of staff.

"Colonel, Turley here. Is Colonel Metcalf around?"

"General Giai and Metcalf not present in TOC. What have you?" Chung asked.

"Colonel, we have a large force moving on the Dong Ha Bridge. We need to commit a reserve and blow the bridge," Turley explained.

After a long pause, Chung replied, "I do not have authority to authorize those things. You must wait General Giai comes back and he decides."

"When do you expect him?" Turley asked, his frustration level increasing.

"I do not know, but I cannot authorize those measures," Chung reiterated. Turley was learning that indecision among senior officers in the South Vietnamese Army was rampant— unlike among American leaders and decision-makers, where the commander's intent was known and junior leaders could make decisions that accomplished the commander's intent in the absence of orders. Turley set the phone back in the cradle. *More than one way to skin this cat. Where is Colonel Dinh?*

Turley started prowling through the TOC. He spotted Colonel Dinh over by the 1:50,000 scale map. Colonel Dinh commanded the 258th Marine Brigade.

"Colonel Dinh, you understand the situation at the Dong Ha Bridge, don't you, sir?" Turley asked.

"Yes, it is bad."

"Yes, sir, it is, and it could get worse. Sir, we have this enemy tank column coming south right now. We really have no one defending the bridge. 3rd Battalion has two companies to the west of Dong Ha blocking QL9 and two companies in reserve. We need to commit those two companies to the defense of the bridge," Turley explained. Dinh turned to study the map.

Finally, Dinh said, "Yes, I see your point, Colonel."

Hope springs eternal, Turley thought. "Then, sir, let's order those two companies to the south end of the bridge and set up a defense."

"No, I cannot do that. I must get authorization from Saigon to move the reserve. We must wait," Dinh said. Turley was in a state of shock.

"Sir, if we don't do this and don't blow that bridge, those forces have a clear path to the Citadel and Hue," Turley pleaded. "There will be no stopping them. We must do this and now."

"I cannot," Dinh said and looked away.

Turley just stared at the map and visualized the enemy tanks rolling over the bridge as if it was a slow-motion picture in his mind's eye. He was exhausted, tired, hungry, and now totally depressed. He took a chair and placed his head in his hands as he leaned forward. In all his years in the military, he had never come across officers that couldn't make timely decisions in the absence of orders. He was watching the fall of a nation and none of the senior leaders were willing to make a decision. At the gentle touch of a hand on his shoulder, he looked up into the eyes of Colonel Dinh.

"I will issue the order to move the two companies to the bridge and move the two companies on QL9 along with elements of 20th Tank back to the bridge. Let your advisors know. We do now." Miracles happen all the time.

* * *

1230 Hours
Ai Tu TOC

"Raven Six, Underground Six, good news. What's the situation now? Over."

"Underground Six, more tanks are approaching but not moving onto the bridge. Taking up overwatch positions. Reserve companies are moving to positions on the south side. Request permission to blow the bridge. We cannot hold if a determined effort is made. Over," Major Easley said.

"Raven Six, understood, but I cannot authorize that. Let me go to higher and get permission. Over."

"Roger, but don't take too long. This river and one battalion of infantry and tanks is all that stands between them and Quang Tri. Over."

"Understood, Underground Six. Out." Turley was faced with a hard decision. *How the hell did I get into this mess? If this whole thing goes to hell in a handbasket, I'm the one getting the blame. Son of a bitch Melcalf dumped this mess in my lap and has washed his hands of it*, he thought as he placed the receiver on the desk.

"Murray, get FRAC on the landline for me, please," Turley requested. He had to get to higher on this one. A few minutes later, Murray handed him the receiver. "It's the FRAC operations officer, sir."

"This is Lieutenant Colonel Turley at Ai Tu. Whom am I talking to?"

"This is Lieutenant Colonel Harrison, FRAC assistant operations officer."

"Here's the situation. Enemy tanks are moving on QL9 from Charlie 2 to Dong Ha. Enemy tanks in force are moving on QL1 and are holding in overwatch of the Dong Ha Bridge. We have one battalion of Marines and one battalion of tanks covering both the railroad bridge and the main highway bridge. If they make a push, we can't hold, and they have a clear path to Quang Tri. Request permission to blow the Dong Ha Bridge," Turley requested. There was silence, but only for a moment.

"What are you talking about? We've heard none of this here. We're hearing that there's some artillery fire and some ground probes, but nothing about tanks or firebases being overrun," Harrison said with some surprise.

"Hasn't Metcalf and 3rd ARVN informed you of what's going on up here?"

"Yeah, but only that it was as I described. Are you nuts? Do not blow that bridge. That needs to be intact if a counterattack needs to be executed," Harrison said.

"What counterattack? Between Dong Ha and Quang Tri there's nothing to counterattack. Who's blowing smoke up your ass?" Turley said as his blood pressure started to rise.

"Who do you think you are?" Harrison responded.

"I think I'm now senior advisor to the 3rd ARVN Infantry Division Forward and the senior officer present on the scene. Now get me someone who can make a damn decision, which had better be someone who outranks me."

"Wait one" was Harrison's response. A few minutes later, he came back. "We're going to have to run this up to Saigon, MACV headquarters, to authorize this, so you're just going to have to wait," Harrison said with an attitude.

"Well, someone better tell the damn North Vietnamese to wait while you people make a decision. I'll wait until the first tank steps on that bridge and then I'm going to blow that damn bridge," Turley said with anger dripping from every word. He slammed the phone down and immediately picked up the FM hand mike.

"Raven Six, Underground Six. Over."

"Underground Six, Raven Six. Over."

"Raven Six, rig the bridge but do not, repeat, do not blow the bridge. How copy?"

"Underground Six, understood rig but do not blow at this time. Over."

"Roger, keep me posted. Underground Six out."

* * *

1300 Hours
MACV Headquarters

While Ripley and Smock were moving to prepare the bridge, Colonel Dorsey, Turley's boss at MACV headquarters, was attempting to explain things to General Abrams.

"Does this Lieutenant Colonel Turley work for you or not?" Abrams asked. The MACV G-3 was standing next to a Marine colonel.

"Yes, sir, he does. He arrived in-country a week or two ago and went up to Quang Tri to visit the Marine advisors up there," Dorsey replied.

"So why is he requesting to blow the bridge on QL1?" Abrams asked, looking at the G-3, Major General Carley.

"Sir, we're not sure. There's some activity being reported north of the Cam Lo River, but 3rd ARVN hasn't reported anything of the magnitude that would warrant the destruction of the bridge," the general stated.

"Well, this lieutenant colonel is reporting something. And

where's the senior advisor for the 155th Advisor team? Why isn't he filtering this stuff, or at least requesting it? Something isn't right here, gentlemen. What's the Vietnamese staff saying?" Abrams asked.

"Sir, they're saying that there's some activity up north as reported by the 3rd ARVN Division but nothing of major importance."

"Well, blowing the bridge is a Vietnamese decision, so tell the lieutenant colonel we cannot give him the authority to blow that bridge. That's going to have to come from the Vietnamese command...and let's get a clear picture as to what's going on up there," Abrams said.

* * *

Major Binh received the order to move his two reserve companies forward to the bridge and move his two companies on the west side of Dong Ha as well along with elements of 20th Tank. At the same time, Ripley and Smock were receiving the same orders. 1st Company moved and assumed a defensive position on the south side of the QL1 bridge. 2nd Company took up a position facing west along QL9 on the west side of 1st Company. Once in position, both companies waited.

As smoke continued to rise from the burning tanks north of the bridge, others bypassed and moved south towards the bridge. Turner, Ripley and Smock were discussing the optimal way to blow the bridge when movement on the southern approach to the bridge got their attention.

"What is that sergeant doing?" Smock asked, observing some soldiers leaving their foxhole on the southern end. His question was quickly answered.

"There's a damn tank coming across the bridge," Jack said, pointing to the north end of the bridge.

Sergeant Huynh Van Luom was a section sergeant responsible for six Vietnamese Marines and occupied one of the positions on the south end of the bridge. As they occupied their foxholes, Sergeant Luom heard the clanking of tank treads approaching.

"Sergeant, there's a tank approaching the north end of the bridge," a young Marine pointed out. Sergeant Luom had been attempting to get some sleep and wasn't happy that it had been disturbed. He looked over the brim of his fighting position, confirming what he had just been disturbed about. He had had enough of this and decided to take action. Picking up two M72 light antitank weapons, commonly referred to as LAWs, he walked out onto the bridge and took up a kneeling position. The members of his squad crouched low in their fighting positions and watched as Sergeant Van Luom placed the weapon on his shoulder and fired.

* * *

"Underground Three, Underground Three, Raven Six, over," Major Easley radioed.

"Raven Six, Underground Six," Turley responded. *This cannot be good*, he was thinking.

"Underground Six, Raven Six. Update, over."

"Roger, send it."

"Underground Six, six tanks destroyed by tank fire on QL9, vicinity..." And he read off the coordinates, which Captain Murray immediately plotted. "Four tanks destroyed by air, vicinity..." Again, he read off the coordinates. "And one tank damaged and retreated at QL1 bridge. How copy?" Turley and Murray exchanged looks.

"Raven Six, understood one tank damaged and retreated at QL1 bridge. Explain, over."

"Underground Six, that is correct. Tank ventured on

bridge. Vietnamese sergeant moved out on the bridge with two M72 LAWs. Took up a kneeling position about two hundred meters in front of the tank. He fired the first LAW and missed. Engaged with second and hit, disabling the turret. Tank retreated, as did the ones following. Our troops now realize that they can defeat the tanks with the M72s. Best damn thing to happen today. Over."[3]

"Raven Six, glad to hear that. How is Ripley doing in rigging the bridge for demolition?"

"Underground Six, he's working on it. Smock and Turner are assisting. Over."

"Ask Turner to come back here as soon as he can. I could use him at this location. Over."

"Roger, I'll pass that along."

* * *

The two advisors and Jack rode on Smock's tank, which was accompanied by a second tank. When they reached the intersection of QL1 and Route 9, Ripley and Smock dismounted. The bridge was over five hundred feet long, supported by steel girders on concrete pilings.

As they dismounted, the open ground to the base of the bridge was under small-arms fire and indirect artillery and mortars, but not of the intensity that had been seen frequently on the firebases.

"Why don't you stay here and cover us? When we get down there, I'll call you and tell you what we need so you can go back to Dong Ha Base and get it, sir," Ripley said, looking at Turner.

"Are you sure?" Jack asked, looking at Smock.

"Sounds like the captain has the plan, and you speak Vietnamese and I don't. You'll be able to explain to the tankers what we need a whole lot better than me," Smock pointed out.

"Okay, if that's the way you guys want to play it. I'll cover you and just tell me what you need," Jack replied.

When a lull appeared, Smock and Ripley made a broken field run for the base of the bridge.

Reaching the base, Ripley and Smock were surprised to find a squad of ARVN engineers sitting under the bridge. They had five hundred pounds of explosives, a mix of TNT and C-4, as well as fuses. Everything you needed to blow a bridge. It quickly became obvious to Ripley that they didn't know how to blow a bridge, however. They were in the process of placing the charges just under the bridge's planking, which would only have torn a hole in the roadbed that could be easily repaired. Ripley made a quick assessment of what had to be done and how to do it. He called back to Turner, who was outside on the tank.

"Hey, Major," Ripley yelled.

"Whatcha need?" Jack responded.

"Nothing. There's a Vietnamese engineer squad down here with everything we need. Me and Major Smock have this, so I'm sending these guys back up. Don't shoot them."

"Okay, I promise I won't. Send them up." The Vietnamese engineers began scrambling up the embankment to Jack's location.

"Hey, Captain, why don't I take these guys over to the railroad bridge and rig it for demolitions?" Jack asked.

"Sounds good to me, sir. Don't bother with the rail line but go for the bridge supports," Ripley yelled back.

As Jack and the Vietnamese engineers departed, Ripley made an assessment of the resources available to him and the layout of the bridge structure.

"Major, I'll climb over this fence, and you pass the demo over the fence to me. I'll go out and place the charges. They must be placed in a staggered alignment under the girders. Okay?" Ripley asked.

"Captain, you're in charge here. I know nothing about blowing a bridge. Just tell me what you want done," Smock responded. The C-4 explosives were arranged in thirty satchel charge bags, each weighing approximately forty pounds. The TNT was in boxes and weighed seventy-five pounds each. Access to the bridge was over a chain-link fence topped with steel tape concertina wire. Ripley started up the fence and worked his way through the concertina wire. Dropping to the ground, he started receiving the first of the satchel charges. His uniform appeared to be rags as the concertina had torn it in several places. Smock lifted the forty-pound charges over his head to pass them to Ripley as well as the seventy-five-pound boxes of TNT. It did not take long for this exercise in weight lifting to wear Smock out. When Smock took his first break, Ripley picked up the first satchel charge, draping the sling over his shoulders, and moved to the first I beam steel girder. Hand over hand, he worked his way out over the water to the inter-section of the I beam and the first concrete piling.[4] To get up on the I beam, he had to swing his legs up and hook his feet over the beam to pull himself up. On the third attempt, he made it. *Got to drop this damn flack jacket, 782 gear and my CAR-15.*[5] *Sure as hell not going to need them here*, he was thinking as he stopped for a moment to rest. *Why couldn't I have just shown the Vietnamese engineers how to do this. Why me, Lord?* He thought he heard a voice say, *Because you are dumb enough to do it!*

He started placing the charges. Several times he had to return to the fence, get another satchel charge or a box of TNT and move under and over an I beam girder to place the next charge and connect it to the previous one. He slide the TNT boxes along the I beams and into place. Occasionally he would have to take a break as his arm and shoulder muscles were screaming at him. Major Smock wasn't faring any better. This was all being done over the course of an hour under the sights of the North Vietnamese forces on the north bank of the Cam Lo River. When the charges were set, Ripley began placing the primer cord and percussion caps. Ideally, he would have been using an electrical blasting cap and wire, but they hadn't found any. They also did not find any crimps for the percussion caps. Looking like a pair of pliers almost, they was specially designed to crimp the percussion cap to the primer cord. *Well, do what they taught me in Ranger School. I just hope they knew what they were talking about,* he was thinking when he placed the percussion cap with the attached primer cord in his mouth and bit down. He felt the cap compress but not detonate. *I guess the Rangers did know what they were talking about.*

Placing the last cap in position, he began moving back to the south side of the river and Major Smock's position.

"Hey, Captain, I found the electrical blasting caps and wire," Smock yelled out.

"Great, now you tell me, sir," Ripley responded. *Always have a backup.* Ripley retrieved the electrical blasting caps and a roll of TA-1 wire and moved back out to set the charges again. The percussion fuses and primer cord he left in place as a backup for the electrical blasting caps. Once it was completed, he moved back up to Smock's position.

The moment of truth was at hand. There was an abandoned jeep next to the bridge. Opening the hood, Ripley held the two TA-1 wires, placed them on the battery terminals and ducked. Nothing. He repeated the process and still no detonation. The destruction of the bridge was now dependent on the time fuse, which Ripley could see was burning from the smoke trail. They were set for approximately forty-five minutes.

Moments later, there was an explosion at the railroad bridge, but Ripley didn't hear any spans hitting the water. Turner returned to the tank moments later.

"Did you drop it, sir?" Ripley asked.

"No, but nothing is going to cross it. I guess that'll be good enough for now," Turner responded. Suddenly and unexpectedly, a UH-1H helicopter passed over their heads at fifty feet, flying northwest at high speed. He was immediately followed by an AH-1G Cobra gunship.

"Wonder where those two are off to in such a hurry," Smock commented. The three watched as the aircraft raced low over the Cam Lo River and disappeared behind the trees.

"Two helicopters going into harm's way," Turner mumbled.

* * *

1630 Hours
1st ARVN Armored Brigade

"Colonel Luat, there is the bridge," Lieutenant Colonel Wagner, advisor for the 1st ARVN Armored Brigade, pointed out. Colonel Luat commanded the 1st ARVN Armored Brigade and had been ordered to move north, cross the Dong Ha Bridge and destroy the enemy advance. He was told it was sporadic small-arms fire and mortars, with friendly air and naval gunfire in support.

As they were talking, Ripley, Smock and Turner approached. "Sir I hope you aren't planning on crossing the bridge," Ripley said. "It's set to blow."

"No blow bridge," Luat yelled. "We attack over bridge. I in command and order you not to blow the bridge. We move lead elements immediately across and secure the far side, pushing —" Luat didn't finish his statement as the bridge suddenly rose from the riverbed in a cloud of smoke and flying debris, highlighted with an overpowered explosion. When the smoke cleared, the girders lay in the river with the wood planking burning and scattered. The Dong Ha Bridge would not be supporting any crossings.

"Underground Six, Raven Two, over," Ripley transmitted.

"Raven Two, Underground Six, go ahead."

"Underground Six, Raven Two, Dong Ha Bridge and railroad bridge destroyed. Nothing will cross them, over."

Turley heaved a sigh of relief.

21

BAT 21

2 APRIL 1972
  30,000 feet
  DMZ

The Douglas EB-66 jet cruised through a smooth, clear sky at thirty thousand feet. Below were low scattered clouds and some rain showers over a carpet of green crossed by the northernmost river of South Vietnam. The aircraft was twelve miles south of the demilitarized zone separating North and South Vietnam. Originally designed to be a bomber, this aircraft had been modified. The mission for today was the same as every other mission the aircraft had been modified to perform— radar surveillance. Once it found an enemy radar site, it would jam the radar, clearing a path for the flight of B-52 bombers and fighters that were following. Another EB-66 was accompanying Bat 21 and had the call sign of Bat 22. The aircraft had a crew of six: a pilot, Major Wayne Bolte; First Lieutenant Robin F. Gatewood, the copilot; Lieutenant Colonel Iceal "Gene" Hambleton, navigator; and three electronic weapons officers, Major Henry Serex as well as Lieutenant Colonels Anthony Giannangeli and Charles A. Levis. The aircraft cruised at 528 miles per hour. Although the bomber version had defensive tail guns, the EB-66 did not.

"Hey, Henry, how are we looking?" Major Bolte asked.

"We good. As long as we stay south of the DMZ, we shouldn't have to worry about a SAM threat," Major Serex responded over the intercom. "We're south of the DMZ, aren't we?"

"Are you doubting my navigation?" Lieutenant Colonel Hambleton asked. Hambleton was the senior officer on board. At fifty-three years old, he had flown in World War II, Korea and now Vietnam. He had a break in service between Korea and World War II, and when he'd returned, he'd done a stint in missiles. He was married and an avid golfer with dreams of playing professionally in the senior circuit after he retired from the Air Force.

"No, sir, just checking," the EWO said.

"Well, we're ten minutes out from the target area," Hambleton answered and turned his attention to the electronic monitoring console, which replicated what the four in the back were looking at as well. As the system came online, Hambleton's mind was drifting to another time and place as well as contemplating the stupidity of the politicians and military strategy for this war. His thoughts were interrupted. "SAM on scope!"

He was immediately thrust back into the present. No missiles showed up on his scope. Almost immediately, the aircraft pilot executed a violent left diving turn. The next thing Hambleton did see was the nose of a SAM missile pointed right at the aircraft. The aircraft was violently tossed as the missile exploded in the compartment with the EWO officers. Next came the sound of the bailout bell and the explosive kick in the ass from the ejection seat leaving the aircraft. As the ejection seat reached the apex of its launch, Hambleton began to separate from the seat. At thirty thousand feet, air was difficult to breathe, and even though he was over Southeast Asia, it was cold. In training, they had been taught when ejecting from altitude, remain stable and flat, skydiving to fourteen thousand feet, when your chute would automatically open. Hambleton found himself in anything but a stable position as he was spinning, his eyesight beginning to blur. He knew that he was about to pass out unless he stopped the spin, so he activated his chute manually. His spin stopped and the chute fully deployed.

At any altitude above fourteen thousand feet, breathing would be difficult, and again he noticed his vision blurring. Reaching into his survival gear, he located a small oxygen bottle and breathed from it. As he drifted down, he was almost enjoying the descent. Occasionally he would pass through a cloud. Recognizing that he was south of the DMZ but aware of the offensive being conducted by the North Vietnamese, he thought it best to activate his emergency radio.

"Mayday, mayday, Bat Two-One Bravo," he transmitted and waited for a response.

* * *

Blue Ghost Three-Nine was a UH-1H flown by First Lieutenant Byron K. Kulland. Byron was from a small town in Nebraska. His copilot was WO1 John Laughlin from Albuquerque, New Mexico. The crew chief was Sergeant Ronald Paschall from Alderwood, Washington, and the gunner was Specialist Four Jose M. Astorga from Oakland, California. The mission that day was to fly a United Press International reporter, Stu Kellerman, around for a tour of the area around Dong Ha. The day had been uneventful as far as flying was concerned, and on the return to Da Nang, they were instructed to stop at Hue/Phu Bai to change copilots. Upon landing, Laughlin exchanged seats with WO1 John Frink. Laughlin was due to rotate back to Marble Mountain, their home base, for a couple of welcome down days of rest. Along with the change for copilots, Captain Thomas White, operations officer for F Troop, hopped aboard for a ride back as well.

"Hey, Captain White, did you just hear that emergency call on Guard?" Kulland asked as they had just lifted off Hue.

"Yeah, I did. Wait one," White directed. After a few minutes deep in thought, he said, "Byron, tell you what. Take me and Mr. Kellerman back to Hue/Phu Bai. I want you to refuel and stand by in case I need to send you up there for a pickup."

"Roger, sir. John, you have the aircraft, and let's get back to the refuel point. I'll get us clearance back into the airfield," Byron ordered. Laughlin immediately took the controls and executed the return to the refuel point.

"Byron, drop me and Kellerman off at the TOC," White requested. "I'm going to monitor the situation in the TOC and may launch you up there to see if we can help."

"Roger that, sir."

"I'll hop out here too," Laughlin said, departing the aircraft with Mr. Kellerman.

As the aircraft was being refueled after dropping the passengers off, another Blue Ghost UH-1H aircraft came in to refuel. Two Blue Ghost AH-1G aircraft were already in the refuel point as well.

"Blue Ghost Two-Eight, Blue Ghost Three, over," Captain White transmitted from the TOC. Blue Ghost Two-Eight was flown by Captain Mike Rosebeary.

"Blue Ghost Three, Blue Ghost Two-Eight, over."

"Blue Ghost Two-Eight, we have a situation of a downed pilot up north. Take Blue Ghost Two-Four and Blue Ghost

Three-Nine and head up there. Stand by for a possible rescue attempt. I want you and Two-Four to provide gun cover for Three-Nine. How copy?"

"Roger, Blue Ghost Three, we're on the go. Break, Blue Ghost Three-Nine, did you monitor?"

"Blue Ghost Two-Eight, roger. I'll get us clearance for a flight of three." A few moments later, Three-Nine transmitted, "Blue Ghost Three-Nine is on the go." The three choppers, two Cobra gunships and one Huey, lifted off and headed north. As the three aircraft climbed out, White contacted Blue Ghost Two-Eight with further instructions.

"Blue Ghost Two-Eight, Blue Ghost Three, over."

"Blue Ghost Three, Two-Eight, over."

"Blue Ghost Two-Eight, Contact Bilk Three-Four for additional information on the location and enemy situation in the vicinity of the downed pilot. How copy?"

"Blue Ghost Three, roger, contact Bilk Three-Four for additional information."

"Blue Ghost Two-Eight, be advised the enemy situation is not clear, but do not, repeat, do not take your flight north of Dong Ha River without fast-mover support."

"Blue Ghost Three, roger, understood." Switching frequencies, Rosebeary attempted to contact Blue Ghost Three-Nine but never received a reply.

"Blue Ghost Two-Four, Two-Eight, over." Blue Ghost Two-Four was the other Cobra and flown by Warrant Officer George Ezell.

"Two-Eight, Two-Four, go ahead."

"Two-Four, did you monitor Three's last transmission?"

"Two-Eight, roger."

"Okay, let's drop back and take up positions on either side of Three-Nine and a bit higher. We should be up at Dong Ha in about twenty minutes. I'll contact Bilk Three-Four."

"Roger, Two-Eight." Rosebeary was a man of few words.

Back in the TOC, Captain White was monitoring the situation with Bilk Three-Four. What he was hearing was not comforting. *Maybe I best get another bird up there*, White was thinking when he picked up the radio handset. Checking his tasking order for the day, he noticed that another aircraft was up at Quang Tri, standing by for missions.

"Blue Ghost Three-Oh, Blue Ghost Three, over." Blue Ghost Three-Oh was flown by Warrant Officer Ben Nielsen. Ben had been monitoring the radios and understood what was going on. He had flown extensively in the area for the past several months and knew it well. Mentally he was mapping the operation out in vivid detail and didn't like what he was seeing.

"Blue Ghost Three, Blue Ghost Three-Oh, over."

"Three-Oh, have you been monitoring the situation with the down pilot? Over."

"Three, I have. Over."

"Three-Oh, I want you to crank and contact Blue Ghost Two-Eight. Head up there and support them as he sees fit. How copy? Over."

"Three, Three-Oh, I have good copy and will get cranking." With that, Nielsen's crew began the task of untying the main rotor blade and donning chicken plates and helmets. As the main rotor slowly began to turn, the crew chief and door gunner checked the engine compartment for possible fire. When assured that all was okay, they returned the fire extinguishers and closed the pilots' doors after moving the armored plate forward on the pilots' seats. Once airborne and heading north, Nielsen contacted Rosebeary.

"Blue Ghost Two-Eight, Blue Ghost Three-Oh, over."

"Three-Oh, Two-Eight. Understand you're joining us. What is your location?"

"Two-Eight, I'm off Quang Tri, heading to Dong Ha. Over."

"Roger, Two-Four is coming back to join up with you." Rosebeary looked over and saw Ezell enter a rapid turn and head back towards Quang Tri. He knew that Ezell had been monitoring the conversation with Three-Oh, so no command was necessary. Blue Ghost Three-Nine and Blue Ghost Two-Eight continued their flight north towards Dong Ha. As they approached the town and the main bridge over the river, Two-Eight contacted Bilk Three-Four. Bilk Three-Four was an O-2 Forward Air Control aircraft flown by First Lieutenant Bill Jankowski and Captain Lyle Wilson.

"Bilk Three-Four, Blue Ghost Two-Eight, Over."

"Blue Ghost Two-Eight, Bilk Three-Four, over."

"Bilk Three-Four, Blue Ghost Two-Eight is a flight of two. A Uniform Hotel One and an Alpha Hotel One Golf. I have two other aircraft inbound to join us, but the same as us. Understand you have a pickup for us. Over."

"Blue Ghost Two-Eight, we have a pilot down two klicks north of the river west of Dong Ha in the vicinity of the big bend back to the east. Currently two Sandys are working the area over, but there's a lot of bad guy activity down there.[1] He's on the edge of a rice paddy next to the main road. His parachute is in the middle of the rice paddy. He can mark his location with a signal mirror. How copy?"

"Bilk Three-Four, Two-Eight, I have a good copy. We're going in low, so you may have to guide us. We're coming up on Dong Ha now. Over."

"Roger. Cross the river and come up the north shore. Do you have the Alpha Ones in sight?"

"Negative, crossing now."

Both aircraft turned northwest crossing the river west of Dong Ha. Kulland was at fifty feet above the trees and Rosebeary was at three hundred feet and about one thousand feet behind Kulland, in the perfect position to provide suppressive fire to cover Kulland if need be. Almost immediately, the need became obvious.

At treetop level, Kulland had green tracers chasing him across the sky. Rosebeary was laying down suppressive fire with miniguns from the nose turret but quickly realized that there were just too many positions shooting at Kulland. As he crossed the river, Rosebeary realized he was a target as well. While his front seat gunner exercised the nose turret minigun and forty-millimeter grenade launcher, Rosebeary was punching off his rockets. *At this rate I'll be out of ammo before we get to the downed pilot.*

"Blue Ghost Two-Four, Two-Eight."

"Two-Eight, Two-Four."

"Two-Four, get your ass up here. We're in a world of shit. We need you now!" Ezell could tell from the tone of Rosebeary's voice that they were in trouble.

"Two-Eight, roger, hang on."

"Three-Oh, did you monitor?"

"Roger, nosing it over. Go ahead, I'll catch up." The AH-1G was a faster aircraft than the UH-1H, and both pilots realized the situation was possibly critical. The additional firepower of Blue Ghost Two-Four was needed immediately.

"We're taking hits!" Rosebeary heard over the radio, not sure who'd said it. He suspected it was Kulland or someone in Kulland's crew transmitting.

"Did you hear me? We're taking hits!"

Then Rosebeary realized it was his own copilot talking to him. Small hammer tappings could be heard on the aircraft. The sound of a sledgehammer hitting the aircraft got his attention. The master caution light came on. The master caution light was highlighted by one large red light that came on if there was a problem and was located on the top left side of the pilot's instrument panel. This light got the pilot's attention. Below on the pilot's right console was another set of caution lights, which indicated the exact problem, such as low oil pressure or possible hydraulics failure. The front seat pilot/gunner had the same caution lights. If one came on, then the pilots would respond accordingly as they had been taught. However, with almost each tapping sound, another light was coming on. The caution panel was beginning to shine like a Christmas tree.

"Blue Ghost Three-Nine, Two-Eight, get back across the river. This is too much!" Rosebeary transmitted as the sky was full of green tracers, all concentrating on him and the UH-1H to his front. Although Kulland didn't respond verbally, Rosebeary saw him starting to turn south. His concentration on Kulland was interrupted when his own canopy was suddenly penetrated by a string of bullets. He realized his own aircraft was coming apart. As he fought to fly his crippled aircraft, he saw Kulland's engine starting to smoke. His last sight of Kulland was what appeared to be a controlled landing in a small clearing.

"We're taking fire!" Specialist Astorga screamed aboard Blue Ghost Three-Nine as he began returning fire from his M60 machine gun. He could hear Specialist Paschall shooting on the other side of the aircraft. He could also feel the sledgehammer blows on the side of the aircraft. An occasional glance into the cockpit showed a flashing master caution light and the caution panel lighting up rapidly as each of the aircraft's systems began to fail. Astorga and Paschall were firing as fast as the M60 would allow when suddenly, Astorga's gun jammed. Reaching for the charging handle, he felt first a searing pain in his leg and then a powerful blow to his chest. He passed out and collapsed in his seat.

"Astorga, get on that damn gun," Kulland screamed as he glanced back at the door gunner. Astorga wasn't moving.

"John, get on the controls with me," Kulland ordered. Laughlin said nothing but quickly followed the command. He had been watching the master caution panel, ready to turn off fuel and battery if the engine quit.

"We've got an engine fire!" Specialist Paschall yelled while firing his guns. The noise was tremendous. Kulland flashed a quick look at the engine instruments. *The engine is going to quit any second now. Got to put it down. Dammit.* He spotted a rice paddy and decided it was time. Raising the nose of the aircraft, they landed hard and fast with the nose burying itself in the soft mud.

The impact of the crash jarred Astorga awake. The blow to his chest was a bullet stopped by his chicken plate. His leg was a different story. He knew almost right away that it was broken. Half crawling and half walking, he pulled up alongside Mr. Frink's seat. Frink was pinned in the aircraft and couldn't get out. He could see that Lieutenant Kulland was slumped over in his seat, not moving.

"Astorga, here—take my survival vest and get out of here. The gooks are going to be swarming over this aircraft any minute. Get out of here. *Go, go!*" Frink said as he stripped his vest off and passed it to Astorga. Astorga was hesitant to leave and moved over to the left side of the aircraft. Paschall was pinned by his leg under the aircraft, unable to move. He was conscious. As Astorga attempted to dig him out, he heard voices moving towards him.

"Astorga, leave me. Get out of here. *Go!*" Paschall told him. Astorga began to crawl away from the aircraft, hoping not to be seen. As he made it about fifty yards from the aircraft, he looked up. A pair of boots common to the NVA were blocking his path. An NVA soldier was standing in front of him with his weapon pointed at Astorga's head. Hands began grabbing him and raised him up. The NVA soldiers quickly realized that Astorga had been shot and had a broken leg. They began riddling the aircraft with automatic weapons fire. It didn't take long before the aircraft exploded. Astorga hoped that the others were truly dead before the fire engulfed what was left of the aircraft.[2]

Having lost sight of Blue Ghost Three-Nine, Rosebeary had his own problems. The master caution panel was indicating the aircraft wouldn't be in the air much longer.

"Blue Ghost Two-Four, Two-Eight here."

"Two-Eight, I have you in sight. Three-Oh is with me and just south of the river. When you put it down, we'll be right behind you." Ezell didn't want to make a long conversation of the transmission, knowing that Rosebeary needed to concentrate on flying. From the aircraft's gyrations, it was obvious he had his hands full.

"Three-Oh, have you got him in sight?" Ezell asked.

"Roger, when he lands, you lay down the suppressive five and I'll be right behind him for a pickup," Nielsen said, never taking his eyes off Rosebeary. Turning to his copilot, he asked, "Do you see Three-Nine?"

"No, but I do see a column of black smoke north of the river behind some trees next to that village."

"Let's worry about getting Rosebeary first and then we can make a try for Kulland," Nielsen said.

"Three-Oh, this is Two-Eight, I'm going to set her down in this rice paddy before she quits on me," Rosebeary transmitted.

"Roger, Two-Eight, I'm right behind you."

"Two-Four is rolling hot," Rosebeary noticed as he touched down a stream of red tracers from a minigun ripping through the trees closest to the aircraft. Before the rotor blades had stopped turning, the fuel was off along with the battery switch. Rosebeary and his copilot popped the canopy open and began to climb out, being careful to stay low enough not to be hit by the main rotor as it wound down. Almost simultaneously, Nielsen landed next to the damaged AH-1G gunship. Another burst of minigun fire stitched the trees along with the explosions from 40-millimeter rounds and 2.75-inch rockets impacting. Ezell was unloading everything he had to cover Nielsen and the extraction. Applying power, Nielsen executed a combat takeoff with both door guns laying down suppressive fire as they cleared the trees and headed south at treetop level.

* * *

2115 Hours
Ai Tu TOC

"What do you mean the Air Force had imposed a no-fire area north of the damn river?" Lieutenant Colonel Turley asked Major Brookbank.

"Sir, we just got a call from the Air Force Direct Air Support Center in Da Nang stating that due to the down pilot location not being known exactly, they've imposed a twenty-seven-kilometer-square no-fire zone around the area. No artillery, air strikes or naval gunfire can be shot without clearance from them first," Major Brookbank explained.

"Are you telling me that none of our artillery batteries can fire right now and have stood down?" Turley asked, almost in a state of shock.

"That's about it. None of our requests for fire are being approved by the DASC."

"Did General Giai approve this? Did Metcalf know of this?"

"Neither of them approved it or knew about it being imposed," Brookbank said in resignation as Colonel Dinh, the operations officer for the 3rd Division, walked over.

"Why no artillery fire approved?" he asked.

"Sir, there's a downed American pilot somewhere north of

the Cam Lo/Cua Viet River, and the DASC in Da Nang has imposed this no-fire zone around him," Turley explained.

"We have our firebases being attacked across the north. They must have fire support or we will lose them. This cannot be. Many soldiers will die and bases lost if we do not have fire support," Dinh said in frustration.

"Sir, I understand, but the Air Force is attempting to rescue and protect this pilot," Turley said, attempting to justify the no-fire zone, although he didn't believe it was the right thing to do under the circumstances.

Dinh stood for a moment, exchanging looks with Turley and Brookbank, then he raised one finger. "Just one." He turned and walked away in disgust. Turley and Brookbank knew Dinh was correct. For the sake of one individual, hundreds of Vietnamese soldiers would be killed or captured and several firebases overrun with a great deal of terrain surrendered to the enemy. Something had to be done.[3]

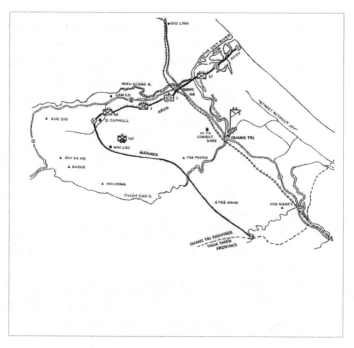

Ngo, Lieutenant General Quang Truong, The Easter Offensive of
1972. *Washington, D.C.: U.S. Army Center of Military History,*
1980.

22

CAMP CARROLL

2 APRIL 1972
56th ARVN Regiment
Camp Carroll

Camp Carroll was key to the defense in northwest Quang Tri Province. Located eight kilometers southwest of Cam Lo, the firebase, named after a US Marine that had died there in 1966, contained the elements of the 1st, 2nd and 3rd Battalions and headquarters of the 56th ARVN Regiment. There were two thousand soldiers and Vietnamese Marines and twenty-two artillery tubes, of which four were the long-range 175mm M107 howitzers and the others were a mix of 105mm and 155mm howitzers. In addition, quad .50 machine guns on two-and-a-half-ton trucks and 40mm track-mounted dusters were present. They also had a stockpile of ammunition. The firebase was laid out in a pentagon formation with three separate rows of concertina wire encircling the camp, spaced approximately one hundred meters apart with mines between the rows. Bunkers with overhead cover were interspersed in the earthen berm that was the perimeter. One road entered the camp on the west side. Over the past two days, stragglers from the 1st, 2nd and 3rd Battalions were making their way into Camp Carroll. They were reporting sighting the 24th NVA Infantry Regiment. Carroll had been subjected to rockets and 130mm indirect fire with the same intensity as everyone else. April 1 would see the first human wave ground assault on the perimeter of the firebase. Since the start of the offensive, Camp Carroll had been providing counterbattery fire as well as defensive fire for all the firebases in Quang Tri Province.

Lieutenant Colonel Pham Van Dinh was the 56th Regiment commander and had earned the nickname "Young Lion" during the TET Offensive of 1968 for his aggressive actions at Hue. However, time had not been kind to him. His fit and trim physique had morphed into the body of a pudgy politician rather than a combat commander. Tactical operations were less of a concern to him than the latest politics of the I Corps chain of command. He left military matters to his deputy, Lieutenant Colonel Vinh Phong, who had an intense dislike for American advisors.

The 56th had Lieutenant Colonel William Camper as a senior advisor. This was Camper's second tour to Vietnam and second as an advisor. His deputy, Major Joseph Brown, another US Army officer, was beginning his second tour in Vietnam and his first as an advisor. Camper was a very experienced officer and wasn't happy about being with the 56th, a unit with a less-than-stellar reputation. However, Colonel Metcalf felt that Camper was just the man this outfit needed to shape it up. For Camper and Brown, it was constant headbutting with Phong.

The day before, 1 April, the first ground assault hit the perimeter. Colonel Dinh contacted the division commander, General Giai, who told Dinh no reinforcements were available and excused himself to play his afternoon tennis match.

Major Brown had been with a resupply convoy returning from Nui Ba Ho to Carroll with the shelling became intense. Late that night, Camper's anxiety for his deputy's safety was relieved when Brown walked into their bunker, alive and well. They toasted the evening with warm Cokes. Their sleep was interrupted by small-arms fire and incoming artillery.

"Sir, that sounds like an all-out assault on the perimeter," Brown said, pulling on his boots and quickly lacing them up, noticing daylight beginning to bring in the new day.

"Yeah, it sounds like it's on three sides. As soon as the artillery stops, let's check the perimeter." And they waited. Intense small-arms fire told them that the ARVN soldiers were giving as much as they were getting and probably delivering more. Human wave assaults in the past had seldom worked on prepared firebases, and crossing three rows of concertina with mines was no easy task, as the 24th Regiment was finding out.

"Let's go," Camper said as there was a pause in the incoming artillery. Wearing their flak jackets and helmets, they sprinted to the perimeter and started moving from fighting position to fighting position, giving words of encouragement to the young ARVN soldiers manning the line. Some were wounded but none seriously. Both advisors started administering first aid as they came across a wounded ARVN. Then Camper noticed something odd.

"Major, have you seen any officers?" Camper asked. Brown looked up from the leg wound he was treating and looked around.

"Come to think of it, I haven't seen any, sir." Looking down at the soldier he was assisting, he asked in his best Vietnamese, "Where are your officers?" The soldier just shrugged. The two advisors continued to move around the perimeter and returned to their bunker. Neither had eaten yet, and they decided to get some warm C rations and coffee, which they cooked on their camp stove. Camper had a backpack with a PRC-77 FM radio. It came to life as they prepared their meal.

"Eagle Six, Star Gazer Four-Five, over." Camper hadn't ever heard that call sign before.

"Star Gazer Four-Five, Eagle Six, over."

"Eagle Six, Star Gazer Four-Five, good morning. I have a flight of two fast-movers over your location. The weather is breaking enough we might be able to help you out. Do you have targets for me? Over." This was an Air Force forward air controller on station, wanting to assist if possible.

"Star Gazer Four-Five, wait one." Camper looked at Brown. "What do you think?"

"Sir, we really don't have any targets for them. The ground attack has withdrawn and we don't know the assembly areas for them. The artillery that's been pounding us is well to the west and we don't know where," Brown pointed out.

"Star Gazer Four-Five, Eagle Six, over."

"Eagle Six, go ahead."

"Roger, Star Gazer, we really don't have any targets for you at this time. I believe you would be better employed by the guys over at Dong Ha than here. Over."

"Roger, Eagle Six. Star Gazer out." Although they'd turned down the offer, it suddenly felt lonely not having the FAC above them.

"After chow, let's go over to the 56th TOC and see Colonel Dinh. He'll be able to tell us what's going on," Camper stated as he pulled his beans and weenies C ration off the fire. About thirty minutes later, they decided to head over to the command bunker. When they reached the door, Colonel Phong was blocking the entrance. He didn't move.

"Where is Colonel Dinh? Is he around?" Camper asked. Phong just stared at him. *Oh, we're going to play "who has the bigger dick?", are we?* Camper thought. Finally, and with disdain, Phong answered, "He in staff meeting." Advisors were supposed to attend the staff meetings. Attempting to push past Phong, Camper realized the man wasn't going to move. "He not to be disturbed," Phong said. Camper felt like picking the guy up and tossing him out of the way but was smart enough to know that this wouldn't accomplish anything. Taking the high road, Camper said he would check back later and he and Brown returned to their bunker.

In the early afternoon, Camper gazed out the bunker doorway and saw Dinh emerge from the command bunker. He was walking towards their bunker.

"Hey, here comes Dinh with his staff. Let's go out and meet him," Camper said as he stood and moved to the door. Outside, he and Brown came to attention and smartly saluted Colonel Dinh, who appeared to be distressed. Dinh returned the salute, as did the other staff officers. The executive officer, Phoy, was not with him.

"Colonel Camper, everyone refuses to fight," Dinh said, looking at his feet. "I tried to bolster their spirit, but they want to surrender."[1] Camper and Brown exchanged looks of disbelief.

"Sir, you've got to be shitting me! This can't be true," Camper stammered.

"I'm afraid so. I have talked extensively with them and they all feel it is best for our soldiers," Dinh said, looking around the base camp but not making eye contact.

"Sir, we have had some artillery fire and one attack on the wire, but they haven't come close to seizing this firebase. We're in a very strong position. The weather is clearing, so we can get air support and probably reinforcements from the 1st Armored Brigade. There's no reason for us to surrender," Camper pleaded.

"I have been talking to them, but they are firmly committed. I even shot one of them to get the others to continue to carry on the fight, but they will not hear of it. Do you want to surrender with us?" Dinh asked the two startled American officers. "I have been in contact with their commander. He has assured me that if we surrender, our soldiers will be treated well."

"Are you out of your mind? No! We will not surrender," Camper shouted.

"The communist commander wants you to surrender as part of the agreement," Dinh added.

"No!" was Camper's emphatic response.

"I did not think you would. You can hide among our troops as they walk out the gate and slip away in the elephant grass. We have thought this through and feel that surrender is the best option," Dinh said as he presented a contemplating face.

"No!" Camper said again. "Major Brown and I will find a way to slip out of the camp on our own."

"If it will save face, we can commit suicide together," Dinh said. Camper was shocked.

"Colonel, Americans do not do that," Camper said. *I have got to turn this around. We're still a viable fighting force.* "Colonel, we have some light tanks here and two of the 40mm cannons mounted. Me and Major Brown can develop a breakout plan and movement plan to Mai Loc. We can break through their lines and make it to Mai Loc. The South Vietnamese Marines and American advisors are still there and it's not that far," Camper pleaded.

Dinh thought for a moment. "That will not work," he replied. It was then that Camper realized that Dinh was defeated and no matter how much he pleaded, nothing was going to move him into continuing the fight.

"Sir, in that case, we wish you luck. Major Brown and I will take our chances and make our own way. We're no longer your advisors and you no longer have any responsibility to us. You must do what you think is best for you and we will do the same." Camper was attempting to control the anger that was building up inside him.

"Colonel Camper, I understand," Dinh said. "But I have one request."

"What is that, sir?"

"Please do not tell General Giai that I surrendered," Dinh asked. Camper had to consciously restrain himself not to shoot the coward on the spot.

"Sir, I have no concerns about General Giai. I care about me and Major Brown. I will notify my senior officer and inform him of what is happening," Camper said with daggers in his stare. Dinh acknowledged with a nod and turned away, heading back to their bunker with his staff in tow. Camper and Brown were still attempting to digest what had just happened as they moved back into their bunker.

"Sir, I'll start getting stuff together to burn and get our shit packed," Brown indicated.

"Okay, I'll get on the horn to Ai Tu and inform them of this. See if they can get a bird here quick to pick us up," Camper indicated and moved to his radio. Their two ARVN radio operators were present, with questionable looks on their faces. These two had been assigned by Colonel Dinh when Camper and Brown had arrived, and a strong bond had developed between them and the two Americans.

"Underground Six, Eagle Six, over," Camper radioed. A moment later, he heard a familiar voice. Camper knew the North Vietnamese had American communications equipment and were probably monitoring all the frequencies, so he didn't want to say too much.

"Eagle Six, Underground Six India, over."

"Underground Six India, the American advisors at Camp Carroll are no longer needed with the 56th Regiment. We're leaving the perimeter for Mai Loc, over." Underground Six

India was the young soldier on radio watch. He wasn't sure of what to make of this transmission.

"Eagle Six, Underground Six India, can you clarify that? Over."

"Underground Six India, negative, can't say over the radio," Camper reported.

Turley heard this, and with everything else falling on his shoulders, it was too much. He grabbed the radio received from the young soldier.

"Eagle Six, Underground Six. Dammit, Colonel, stay at your post and do your damn job. Out!"

"Roger out," Camper said in a bit of shock. Turley almost immediately knew he'd screwed up. *Decisions such as this must be made by the man on the ground in the situation. A senior officer so far from the action cannot possibly understand the circumstances that would warrant leaving one's post. Professional officers don't do that without reason, and for some reason Camper wouldn't say,* Turley was thinking.

Camper handed the receiver to his radio operator and nodded to Brown. The message was clear—*we're getting out of here*. Picking up the gear that they would carry, Brown started pouring kerosene around the bunker, over radios and classified documents as well as personal items. Walking out of the bunker, Brown removed four thermite grenades from his belt, pulled the pins and tossed them inside. Almost instantly, the interior of the bunker became an inferno with black smoke boiling out the bunker door and side windows. As they stood outside, watching the fire consume their home, Camper noticed ARVN officers moving along the perimeter and pulling their soldiers out of the perimeter defense. Weapons were being stacked in piles around the camp and soldiers were moving to the center of the camp and sitting on the ground.

"Dai'uy, we go you, okay?" one of the radio operators asked. Camper was glad to have them with him for the two-mile trek though enemy-held land to Mai Loc. As Camper stood there viewing this mass desertion, he was appalled that so much firepower had gone to waste. Reaching for his hand mike, he transmitted, "Underground Six, Eagle Six, over."

"Eagle Six, Underground Six, over."

"Underground Six, Eagle Six, we're leaving Camp Carroll. The base commander wants to surrender. The white flag is going up in ten minutes. Over."

Turley couldn't believe what he was hearing but had suspected something like this after Camper's last call.

"Roger, Eagle Six, good luck."

Camper handed the receiver back to the radio operator. As they headed towards the perimeter, the regimental operations officer started to walk past Camper and his party. This officer spoke good English and had something to get off his chest.

"Major," Camper said, gaining the young man's attention, "you don't know what you're doing. You're a coward and should come with us and we'll fight our way out."

Bowing his head in shame, he replied, "I have to follow orders," and continued on his way.

Moving down the hill to the perimeter berm, the small party crossed over and entered the area with three rows of concertina wire and mines. Moving cautiously, they reached the third and final row of wire when the North Vietnamese spotted them and opened fire from the far tree line. They immediately returned fire. Camper was back on the radio.

"Underground Six, Eagle Six, we're pinned down just outside the perimeter. We need an extraction, over," Camper yelled. The on-duty officer, Major Jim Davis, heard the call and grabbed the receiver. Major Davis had replaced Major Wilson as operations advisor when he disappeared.

"Eagle Six, there's a CH-47 lifting ammo to Mai Loc. He has two Cobras with him. I will divert to your location. How copy? Over."

"Roger, but he better get here quick." Camper was heard over the background noise of small-arms fire.

Looking at his radio operator, Major Davis asked, "What's the call sign and frequency for that CH-47?"

The young soldier grabbed up the duty log and found the information, quickly switching the frequency to the CH-47.

"Coachman Double-Oh-Five, Underground Six India, over."

"Underground Six India, Coachman Double-Oh-Five, go ahead."

"Coachman Double-Oh-Five, we've got two American advisors at Camp Carroll who need immediate extraction. The ARVNs are surrendering, and the bad guys are approaching the perimeter. Over."

"Roger, I'm on final to Mai Loc and will proceed immediately to Carroll. I have Centaur Four-Nine as escort. What frequency are they on? Over."

Davis immediately provided the information that Coachman Double-Oh-Five was going to need.

Ten minutes later, "Eagle Six, Coachman Double-Oh-Five, over" was heard on the radio by the ARVN radio operator.

"Dai'uy, Coachman Double-Oh-Five calling," he said, not knowing who this was.

"Coachman Double-Oh-Five, Eagle Six."

"Eagle Six, Coachman Double-Oh-Five is inbound to your location. I have Carroll in sight. Where are you? Over." Camper knew that aircraft couldn't land where they were due to the enemy fire from the tree line and the mines between the wire. Camper signaled for everyone to get up and make a run back to the perimeter. In good order, Brown and his radio operator jumped up and sprinted to the next row of concertina. Upon reaching it, they turned and started shooting, covering the withdrawal of Camper and his radio operator.

"Coachman Double-Oh-Five, there's a windsock next to the pad. We're moving to it. Over."

"Roger, Eagle Six, we'll meet you." Camper and his radio operator picked up the pace. Suddenly the North Vietnamese soldiers stopped shooting but watched as they moved back up to the perimeter. Reaching the windsock, Camper could hear the *whop-whop* sound of the rotor blades approaching. He could also see the green tracers reaching up to touch Coachman Double-Oh-Five.

"Coachman Double-Oh-Five, you're taking fire," Camper called.

"Roger" was all that was said in a calm, cool, stressless voice. Unseen by the North Vietnamese forces were the two AH-1G Cobra gunships escorting the CH-47 and several hundred yards behind him.

"Centaur Four-Nine, Coachman Double-Oh-Five, taking fire from the tree line, over."

"Roger, Coachman, we have the tree line and are rolling hot at this time." The gunships immediately laid down rockets and minigun fire where the tracers had originated in the tree line. Centaur Four-Nine set up a racetrack pattern, with each aircraft covering the other as they completed their respective run. On each run, they received ground fire.

When the CH-47 touched down, its rear tailgate was already down. Brown and his radio operator climbed aboard. The big Chinook helicopter was a welcome sight to every Vietnamese on the firebase, and they started running for the aircraft. Camper lowered his weapon and pointed at the mob. That got their attention. He then started pointing. Anyone with a weapon was permitted on the aircraft. No weapon, no evacuation as Camper considered those people to be unworthy cowards. Several attempted to get on, only to be violently thrown off the tail ramp. When Camper had thirty ARVN soldiers on board with their rifles, Camper stepped aboard and gave the crew chief a thumbs-up. As they departed, he looked down and saw white flags being raised. *What a waste—what a disgrace*, he thought.[2]

Sitting back, Camper could take time to evaluate the events of the day. He closed his eyes, only to feel someone tapping his leg. Standing over him was the crew chief.

"Sir, we have to put down. We took hits in the hydraulics," the crew chief said, moving to the back ramp.

What else can go wrong today? Camper was thinking when the aircraft touched down on QL1. Camper could see out the back. He quickly identified it because of the debris, abandoned clothes, dead water buffalo, overturned carts and bodies. The cause of this chaos rapidly became evident as 122mm rockets began to land around the CH-47 and everyone dashed to a ditch on the side of the road. When the barrage subsided, Brown and Camper hurried back up to the aircraft. It appeared they would be walking when a jeep with two American advisors pulled up and offered them a ride. They didn't have to ask twice.

* * *

0900 Hours
  Pedro

"Major Hoa," Major Cockell called out as he moved during the artillery lull to Major Hoa's position. "I just got word on the advisor net that we're pulling out and going back to Ai Tu. A Ranger battalion is coming up to relieve us. Have you heard this?"

"I got word minute ago to meet with Ranger commander for the relief. No hurt my feelings to get out of here. Who is Ranger advisor?" Hoa asked.

"There are no advisors with the Ranger battalions. Only at Ranger group," Cockell said, wishing that there was an American advisor with the Rangers.

"You come and discuss how best to conduct relief, okay?" Hoa said, knowing that a relief in place could be a very dangerous and tricky move, especially when being watched by the enemy.

Fortunately, the relief came off without much interference from the NVA, and Major Cockell was glad to see Pedro in the rearview mirror of the jeep he was riding in.

23

ANOTHER FALLS

147th Vietnamese Marine Brigade
Mai Loc, South Vietnam

Camp Carroll was the primary fire support base in the western portion of Quang Tri Province. When Colonel Dinh entered negotiations with the communists, support to Mai Loc ceased. Without that support, Mai Loc could not be held. Major Joy was dead on his feet, not having slept in several days. He knew that an evacuation plan was probably going to be executed. He called his team together.

"How you guys holding up?" he asked Captains Kruger, Randall and Embrey. They had been tirelessly moving around the firebase from the command bunker to the battalion command bunkers as well as erecting AN/PRC-292 antennas, which were a favorite aim point for artillery rounds.

"Sir, we're doing okay. Any word from Boomer or Smith?" Kruger asked. Everyone was concerned about the welfare of those two advisors.

"Yeah, I just heard from Boomer. He's sitting outside the perimeter with Smith, who just linked up with him. They have about two hundred and eighty-five Marines from the 4th Battalion with them, to include walking wounded," Joy acknowledged.

"Did Boomer give you any indication of how the assaults were carried out?" Embrey asked. "Might give us a good idea of what we can expect."

"Boomer said it was classic assault, flawlessly executed. Accurate artillery preparation concentration on the main assault objective, followed by a fire-and-maneuver ground attack," Joy indicated. "I've spoken with Colonel Bao about evacuating. We're almost out of artillery ammo, we're low on small-arms ammo, and we're out of food. It appears that Camp Carroll is going to fall. Bao hasn't made a decision to evacuate, but we do have a plan. It's critical that we keep the east gate open, and the 7th Battalion is going to be tasked to do that." As he said this, he looked at Captain Embrey, who had developed a good rapport with the 7th Battalion commander. The 7th had been with the 258th Brigade and recently attached to the 147th Brigade. "The 7th has got to hold the shoulders and keep the commies far enough back that we can slip out after dark. When we exit, we'll turn northwest and link up with the survivors from the 4th Battalion and then head for Quang Tri. We want to execute after dark as the artillery observers won't see what we're doing, and if they do, their fire won't be as accurate. Once everyone passes the 7th, they'll collapse and be the rear guard. Any questions?" There were none.

"Okay, let's start getting our classified material centrally located so we can destroy it quickly when Bao gives the go-ahead to execute," Joy ordered, and the captains began the process. Thermite grenades were located and handed out to each. Fortunately, Bao and Joy mutually respected each other and had a good working relationship that was lacking at Carroll. Bao consulted on all matters, exchanging ideas with Joy on how to approach tactical situations. Seldom were they in disagreement, and they respected the other's opinions.

Communications became more difficult throughout the day as enemy artillery was destroying coax cables to the 292 antennas and the antennas themselves. In the late afternoon, the last antenna was destroyed. Communications with Ai Tu advisors was lost as the manpack antenna didn't have the range of the 292 antennas. Communications on the firebase even became difficult, with Boomer having to relay message traffic to the 7th Battalion. Colonel Bao spoke with General Giai before commo was lost with the 3rd ARVN Division Command Post.

"General, we are surrounded on three sides presently, we are almost out of artillery ammo and small arms. We have no food. We are getting no fire support from Carroll," Bao informed him.

"Colonel, you are not getting any support from Carroll as it has fallen," Giai said with anger, thinking it was the fault of the American advisors.

"General, in that case, I want your permission for us to evacuate Mai Loc later tonight. Our position is no longer defensive. We cannot repel a major ground attack in our current condition. Is there any chance of reinforcements reaching us tonight?"

"I'm afraid not. Everything has been committed in the Dong Ha Bridge area. Colonel, you are the commander on the scene. You must make the decision to stay or leave. I wish for you to remain for as long as possible, but it is your decision when to pull out. I wish you good fortune and hope to see you back here," Giai said with some resignation in his voice as he hung the receiver up.

Bao turned to his operations officer and Major Joy. "Please gather the staff. I must talk to them," he requested.

Once the TOC staff was assembled, he informed them, "The decision has been made to leave, but it will be an orderly departure. The brigade command headquarters, 2nd Artillery Battalion and detachments will move out to link up with the 4th Battalion to plan the final move eastward toward Dong Ha, and the 7th Battalion will bring up the rear. We will begin our march as soon as it is dark."[1] The staff began making the preparations in an orderly fashion for destroying materials and preparing their equipment that they would carry.

As Joy was doing the same, Major Gnibus and Captain Randall were meeting with the artillery commander. At 1800, the last artillery round was fired. Gnibus and Randall were immediately showing the artillerymen how to spike the guns with thermite grenades to render the guns inoperative. This action is very demoralizing to an artilleryman as it signals defeat, but they understood that they couldn't allow the guns to fall into the hands of the communists. Pulling the artillerymen around them, Major Gnibus conducted the class.

"First you remove the firing lock," he explained and then demonstrated as the young Marines watched. "Once the firing lock is removed, you place the thermite grenade in the breach and pull the pin. Then close the breach in the locked position. The grenade burns at forty-five hundred degrees and will melt the metal. When it cools, the result is a worthless hunk of metal. Any questions?" he asked in his best Vietnamese. Looks were exchanged but no questions asked, and Randall passed out the thermite grenades. The Marines moved to their respective guns and, in what almost resembled a religious ceremony, destroyed each gun.

Joy and the other advisors put the final touches on the burn pile and tossed thermite grenades on the stack. Adding diesel fuel greatly helped the destruction. Once they were assured that nothing would be left, they joined the column that had formed after dark for the seventeen-mile trip to safety. Joy was maintaining contact with Boomer and Smith. The 7th Battalion had been in contact all day but accomplished its mission of keeping the enemy at bay and away from the east gate. Moving in a column of two, the brigade departed the east gate and immediately came under small-arms fire, but due to the distance, it was ineffective. What was troublesome was the indirect fire that was falling on the base and harassing the column as it moved across the airfield, entering a depression on the far side, taking it out of view of the enemy. When the column reached Mai Loc Village, Colonel Bao called a halt.

"Major Joy, we will halt to allow those in the base to withdraw and join us," Bao said.

"Roger, sir. Has 8th Battalion cleared the east gate yet?" Joy asked.

"The 8th Battalion is passing through it now and the 7th Battalion is preparing to break contact and follow. Unfortunately, 7th Battalion still has three companies engaging the enemy," Bao said as he pulled out his map and spread it out on the ground. Under a poncho and with a flashlight, Bao pointed at the map and sketch of the firebase and explained the situation.

"Here is 1st Company on the south side and in contact. He reports that about sixty Marines from Holcomb have come through his lines and are joining the company, but he cannot account for half of his company," Bao said with some concern. Moving his finger, he went on, "The 2nd Company disengaged and passed through east gate okay. The 3rd Company, which was with Alpha Command Group, has gotten mixed in with the rear of the column and is separated from his command."

"Sir, you're telling me that Major Hue is not with the Command group? Where is he?" Joy asked.

"When Major Hue was assembling to join the rear of the column, he came across an enemy mortar position and killed the mortar crew and destroyed the mortar. That action separated him from the command. He is attempting to link up now," Bao explained.

"Okay, so Major DeBona and Captain Rice are still with the elements back on the firebase. They'll stay with those elements and help the company commanders get organized and disengaged. They won't leave them, you can be sure, sir," Joy explained in hopes of reassuring the colonel.

"I know they won't," Bao said with a smile. "I think it is time we move. The 7th can catch up. We no stay too long in one place. I think artillery is looking for us," he concluded, folding his map and turning off the flashlight. The poncho provided light discipline and protection from the drizzling rain that was beginning.

Artillery had been impacting around their position since they'd left the east gate. The enemy would fire two rounds, wait a moment and then shift fires as much as a klick and fire two more rounds. Fortunately, they never hit the column. After moving for another three hours, the column ran into a stream across their route of march. The stream was chest deep with steep banks about ten feet in height. This slowed the column considerably and provided the time for the 7th to join the rearguard position.

Sitting at the stream, Joy was joined by Gnibus, Kruger, Randall and Embrey. He had communications with Boomer and Smith, who were with the 4th Battalion in the lead, and with Major DeBona and Captain Rice bringing up the rear guard. As they waited, Joy's radio received a call.

"Tom Six, Vanguard Two-One, over." *This sounds like a FAC*, Joy thought. Rather than use the official call signs as designated in the codebook, Joy had his team assume false names to confuse the enemy if they were listening.

"Tom Six, Vanguard Two-One, I'm over your position, I believe. Over."

"Vanguard Two-One, you're close enough. If you're over the firebase, we don't own it. You're free to engage. Over."

"Tom Six, understood." A few minutes later, the sound of sustained minigun fire could be heard with what appeared to be streams of red molten metal shooting from the sky onto the firebase.

"Vanguard Two-One, Tom Six, over."

"Tom Six, go ahead."

"Vanguard, we sure could have used you earlier today. Can you get a message to my higher with my location? Over."

"Tom Six, that's an affirmative. Send me your coordinates and I'll forward them, over."

Joy immediately sent the coordinates for their location. He was more afraid of friendly B-52 strikes and artillery than he was of the enemy at this point and wanted to be sure that the 3rd ARVN headquarters knew their location.

By the time Joy and his advisors crossed the stream, they lost contact with the lead elements of the column. He had a general idea of the route of march, but elements were losing contact with elements to the front. Tactical integrity was breaking down; discipline was not. Physical stamina was also breaking down. Major Boomer was exhausted, becoming disoriented and hallucinating as a result.

"Sir, are you okay?" Captain Smith asked. He received an incoherent answer. He quickly surmised the problem and knew he had to do something or else Boomer would be lost. His solution was simple—he tied a strap to himself and attached it to Boomer. They continued on without speaking and with Boomer's hand on Smith's shoulder.

Meanwhile, the 7th Battalion in the rear guard had its own problems. The 7th Battalion cleared the east gate at 1930 hours and started to follow the trail left by the main column.

It wasn't hard to follow due to the number of wounded that were left behind on the route. In addition, physical exhaustion was overtaking the stragglers from Nui Ba Ho, Sarge and Holcomb. Major Hue and DeBona weren't leaving anyone behind and organized stretcher-bearers. As they came across someone, he was placed on a field-expedient stretcher if necessary and brought along. Eventually, however, they lost the trail of the main column.[2] Major Hue and DeBona halted the column and huddled for a discussion.

"We have lost the trail," Major Hue indicated.

"What do you plan to do?" Major DeBona asked. He had been in the rear of the formation, policing up the wounded, and hadn't paid much attention to the direction of march. Major Hue was up front on point and had taken the responsibility.

"I will shoot compass heading to Quang Tri and we follow that," Major Hue said, pulling out his compass and shooting an easterly heading. The partially overcast sky with drizzling rain didn't allow navigating by the stars, and the dense underbrush prevented getting a fix on a distant object. The only course of action was for the compass man to hold his compass and constantly watch the luminescent needle as he walked. If Hue had consulted his map, he would have realized that this was not the best course of action as a straight-line compass heading had them crossing the Song Dinh River four times.

Reaching the river, DeBona and Rice consulted with Major Hue.

"Hue, how are we going to get the stretchers across this?" DeBona asked.

"We can lift some above our heads with four guys per stretcher, but they need to be the tallest we got," Hue answered.

"I got a better idea," Captain Rice said, digging into his rucksack. After he unloaded practically everything, he pulled out his air mattress. Ten air mattresses were found in the column and inflated. Wounded soldiers were placed on the air mattresses and floated across each time they had to cross the river. This was a slow and arduous task, but they were determined not to leave anyone behind. They had twenty kilometers to travel. It wouldn't be until 1000 hours the next day before they reached safety and friendly forces.

* * *

Pedro

"Major Hoa, we can't take too much more of this pounding from their artillery," Major Cockell said as he dove into the trench line that was occupied by the battalion commander. Artillery fire on their position had increased significantly in the past twenty-four hours.

"I think it best we move and soon. I will leave one company here and we will move the others to the surrounding hills. They can provide supporting fire if necessary and hopefully we will keep most people out of this artillery," Major Hoa outlined. "We should have done this last night."

Hoa gave the order as he had already discussed his plan with the company commanders. His intention was good, but the NVA spotters saw them withdraw and continued to harass not only those on Pedro but those that had moved off to surrounding terrain. It was going to be a long night of moving units to keep them out of artillery fire. This was the pattern of activity for the next four days, with less than a rifle company actually inside Pedro.

* * *

0600 Hours
   3rd ARVN Division Forward
   Ai Tu, South Vietnam

Turley was running on adrenaline. His sleep pattern had now become on-off fifteen-to-twenty-minute catnaps. His fluid levels were more coffee than blood.

"Hey, sir, wake up. Wake up, sir," Swift said, gently shaking Turley's shoulder.

"Okay, I'm awake. What's wrong?" Turley asked, attempting to clear the cobwebs from his mind.

"Sir, we got a call from Metcalf. Seems we may be having our B-52 support curtailed," Swift said, knowing this was going to cause a major problem.

"Why would they do that to us?" Turley said, visibly angered.

"Sir, it seems that during the night, Firebase Lac Long, located down in III Corps, was hit by a full NVA regiment and overrun. There was only a mechanized rifle company there with a few tanks. The head shed thinks this may be the start of a major push to seize Saigon. We're still to send our requests forward, but just recognize we may not be getting what we asked for," Swift went on to say.

"Okay, wake me if you have any more cheerful news." And Turley closed his eyes and sat back in his chair.

"Hate to disturb your sleep, sir, but I might be able to help," a voice said. Turley kept his eyes closed, momentarily thinking it was a dream.

"Sir," the voice said ever so softly. Opening his eyes, Turley saw a US Marine major standing in front of him. "Major Jack Turner, sir. Can I assist you?"

Turley eased back in his chair. "Major, you're in charge. Wake me in an hour."

24

PROPAGANDA

3 April 1972

3rd ARVN Division Forward
Ai Tu, South Vietnam

General Giai was present in the TOC when Lieutenant Colonel Camper and Major Brown arrived. After they got something to eat and a cold beer, they began to tell their story to Turley and Metcalf. Jack was present as well. Giai initially listened, but as the story went on, he became more and more upset. Finally, he couldn't contain himself any longer.

"You lie!" he screamed, looking directly at Camper.

"Excuse me, sir," Camper said, attempting to maintain his composure.

"You lie. You no tell truth. Colonel Dinh is Lion of Hue. He no surrender, he fighter. You the coward. You deserter," Giai shouted. It took everything Camper could muster to keep from punching Giai's lights out.

"Sir, I'm a professional officer and I do not lie. What I've told you is the truth. You can ask these two men." He pointed at the two radio operators.

"They lie, you make them lie." Giai was furious now. Turley could see this was going downhill rapidly while Metcalf just sat there and said nothing. Turley decided to step in.

"General Giai, I think that's enough. Accusing these officers of dereliction of duty is a serious offense and is not going to be solved here. If you want, we can hold a board of inquiry to their actions back at FRAC headquarters," Turley stated, buying time.

"Yes, do that. They are cowards," Giai said as he turned and stormed out of the TOC.

"Sir, I saw a bit of what Camper and Brown were putting up with on Carroll. If this goes to a board, I would like to speak in their defense," Jack said.

"Jack, I may have to make you the Article 32 investigation officer. Let's just wait and see how far Giai is going to push this thing," Turley replied.

The next day, Major Nearly approached Turley. He was holding a tape recorder. "Excuse me, sir, but I think you should hear this," he said as he punched the play button. The voice was Colonel Dinh.

"My fellow ARVN soldiers, this is Colonel Dinh, Commander of the 56th Infantry Regiment. Yesterday we negotiated an honorable peace with my North Vietnamese counterpart and surrendered our firebase to them. Our sacrifice's in this war mean nothing now as the North rolls across Quang Tri Province. Get in touch with those forces for the National Liberation Front opposing you and negotiate a peaceful settlement. Me and my men have been treated very well and no longer have the fear of dying in a lost cause."

General Giai heard the same broadcast and was dumbfounded that Dinh would have made such a statement. A few hours later, one of Dinh's subordinates, Major Thon That

Man, a battalion commander, made a similar broadcast. "From the very first shelling, our position shook and wavered. How could we continue to fight? Our regimental commander summoned a briefing—a briefing that would decide the fate of six hundred officers and men. Within five minutes, all agreed to offer no more resistance and decided to go over to the Liberation Forces side."

When Camper heard the broadcast, he was shocked as Major Man was the only commander that had argued not to surrender. Earlier in the day, Giai had located some of the soldiers that had returned on the CH-47 with Camper. They confirmed Camper's story. Giai was embarrassed and ashamed of himself. He sought out Colonel Camper.

"Colonel Camper, I owe you apology. You no lie and you no coward. I talk to soldiers. I heard broadcast by Dinh. He coward and traitor. Please accept my apology," Giai asked. Camper was ready to tell him where he could put his apology, but both Metcalf and Turley were standing there with him and Brown.

"General Giai, I accept your apology. It was a stressful day for all of us," Camper said with as much tact as he could muster.

"Thank you, Colonel," Giai responded and turned to Metcalf. "Can we have Colonel Camper and Major Brown be advisors to 2nd Regiment?"

"Sir, I think that would be excellent," Metcalf said, glad this had blown over in a way favorable to Colonel Camper. Camper and Brown left the next morning to join the 2nd Regiment with their loyal radio operators.

25

CONSPIRACY

MACV Headquarters
Saigon, South Vietnam

The MACV staff had been receiving the daily reports from the senior advisor with the 3rd ARVN Division as well as receiving updates from the South Vietnamese Joint Command Staff. Reports indicated that there were engagements in MR-1, but nothing they needed to be concerned about for the most part. They were upset with the fact that a direct order not to blow the Dong Ha Bridge had been violated. The question was, who was this Marine lieutenant colonel directing the actions of Army advisors, and who had given him the authority to do so?

"Looking over these reports, which confirm what the JCS is telling us, I really don't see why this lieutenant colonel felt it necessary to blow those bridges," General Abrams stated.

"Sir, we're questioning the same thing. Our reports indicate that there have been probes and ground attacks on several of the firebases, but nothing to warrant the destruction. Things were bad enough without that happening," the G-3 commented.

"What do you mean?" Abrams asked.

"Well, sir, the 3rd ARVN was notified that there would be a major strike by the communists in the coming days. We still haven't gotten an answer on why they would remove a very disciplined and well-trained regiment like the 2nd ARVN from the western flank when that's where they expected the main attack to come from and replace it with a newly formed regiment that was very poorly trained and lacking discipline. The 56th is composed of mostly deserters, jailbirds and misfits from MR-3. It also appears that the relief in place was not monitored by the 3rd Division headquarters, and that the senior Army advisor along with the division commander departed that day to fly to Saigon and the Philippines for the Easter weekend," the G-3 said and paused. "Add on to that, this regimental commander getting on the radio and broadcasting that other units should surrender as well—it's almost as if the communists knew the plans for the relief in place and coordinated their attack for that very day. In addition, the number of deserters that have been noted in the 3rd Division and the speed with which they're deserting makes it even more plausible that this was all well planned ahead of time. Both the communists and the ARVNs are monitoring each other's communications. Dinh called his wife and spoke with her on March thirtieth. Could he have passed her some message, and did he initiate the call to surrender or did the communists? There are just too many unanswered questions."

"Could be," General Abrams said. "Let's get this lieutenant colonel back here and get to the bottom of his actions. See if his impression of what's going on up there is any different than the reports we're receiving."

"There's one other thing, sir," the G-3 indicated.

"Okay, let's have it."

"Sir, we have a message sent by the lieutenant colonel."

"Just read it to me."

"Lt. Col Turley, USMC, Quang Tri reports situation critical and requests immediate USMC assistance to reinforce, fight and hold position. Situation passed via SPOT (NFG net) as follows: position is being heavily shelled. NVA and ARVN tanks engaged at Quang Tri airfield. Request immediate landing BLT southern end of Quang Tri airfield. Will have USMC personnel in area with smoke. This is urgent, repeat, urgent."[1]

"Get that man back here, now," Abrams said and slammed his hand on his desk. "We are not going to put a battalion landing team ashore. Understood."

"Yes, sir. I'll get word out right away to have him brought back here."

26

TURLEY AFFAIR

3 April 1972
 MACV Headquarters
 Saigon, South Vietnam

"Jack," Turley called out, walking into the TOC.

"Over here, sir," Jack responded. He and Brookhaven were plotting some possible B-52 strikes.

"Jack, I've just received a call from Colonel Dorsey to get back to Saigon. Appears that General Abrams wants a briefing on what's going on up here. I'm leaving you in charge up here at 3rd Division Forward. Any questions? I should be back in two days," Turley said.

"Sir, you know I have no authority up here. I'm an observer for the DoD IG."

"Yeah, but you're the senior guy that knows what's going on. Call Metcalf if something requiring major attention comes up and stick it to him. Otherwise just hold the fort down. Okay?"

"Okay, sir, I got it. Go enjoy a day or two in Saigon. Bring back some beer," was Jack's final comment as Turley departed.

Lieutenant Colonel Turley slept on the two-hour C-130 flight down to Saigon. He dreamed of a hot shower, a porcelain toilet that flushed, and a cold drink prior to a good night of uninterrupted sleep on clean sheets. A clean set of utilities was planned for as well. All the things that people coming off the line after so many days in combat thought about. As the C-130 taxied to a stop, a jeep driven by a familiar face pulled up. *Now this is service,* Turley thought. Ha Si Chow, a frequent driver for the Marines, pulled up and with a broad smile greeted the colonel.

"Colonel Turley, welcome Saigon. I take you MACV headquarters," Ha Si Chow said in his broken English, which was pretty good.

"Drive on, Ha Si Chow," Turley said, tossing his rucksack and weapon in the back while he took a front seat. Ha Si Chow was experienced at driving in the Saigon traffic. His driving instructor was probably an ex-kamikaze pilot as he weaved, dodged and frightened other drivers and Turley as well with his driving ability, but they reached the compound unscathed. Turley entered the compound, checking in at the security post, and was informed that he needed to return a phone call that had come in earlier for him. The sergeant pointed him to a phone that he could use and handed him the number.

"MAU Headquarters, Warrant Officer Francis speaking."

"Gunner, this is Lieutenant Colonel Turley. Is Colonel Dorsey in?"

"No, sir, he's not in, but you're the subject of his nightmares right now."

"What are you talking about?" Turley asked, not understanding why he had been called to Saigon in the first place. *And why would I be the cause of his nightmares?*

"Sir, when he got back from the Philippines, Abrams called him to the carpet. Seems that you sent several messages through the Navy that got to Admiral McCain and back to Abrams about wanting the forces afloat to make an over-the-beach landing. Abrams hit the ceiling."

"Gunner, what are you talking about?"

"Sir, message traffic with your name as sender has really raised the flag around MACV. Seems based on your message traffic that the situation up there is critical and that Brigade 369 and Vietnamese Marine headquarters are deploying to Da Nang as we speak," Francis related.

"Okay, I'll get this sorted out. Another subject, everyone up north is doing good. We did lose Lieutenant Bruggeman, and Corporal Worth is MIA, both from the ANGLICO team. Other than those two, everyone is doing okay. A few minor wounds, but everyone is hanging in there."

"That's good to hear, sir. Lieutenant Colonel Hilgartner wants you to call him as soon as you arrive."

"Okay, I'll head up to his office. Good talking to you, Gunner."

"You too, sir. Bye."

Hanging up the phone, Turley maneuvered through the pristine halls of MACV, looking for the J-3 Operations office. As he did so, people would casually look at him as he passed them. *Is my fly open?* he was thinking as he walked into Pete Hilgartner's office with his rucksack and weapon. *Come to think of it, I'm the only one in the building with a rucksack and weapon.* As he entered, Pete looked up from his desk. He was slightly taken aback by Turley's appearance. A six-day growth on Turley's face, filthy utilities, scuffed boots, and a pungent odor were enough to startle someone in clean utilities with shined boots, clean-shaven face and the smell of Old Spice aftershave.

"Pete, how you doing?" Turley asked as he set his gear

down. Pete and Turley had known each other for years, having served together as company commanders in 1959. Pete didn't respond to the question but turned professional once over the shock of Turley's appearance and smell.

"Can you explain these messages?" Pete asked, handing Turley three flash messages. "These came through naval channels and personally embarrassed General Abrams." Turley read through the messages, all with his sender address.

"No, I can't, as I didn't send these messages."

"What are you even doing up there? You're not assigned there and you certainly aren't the senior advisor to the 3rd ARVN Infantry Division," Pete asked in an accusatory tone.

"Wow. Wait one—let me explain the situation up there." And Turley started explaining what had happened since he'd arrived at Ai Tu for his visit. When he finished, Pete didn't say much but was skeptical about the story.

"Well, General Abrams certainly wants to meet with you. You will report to Admiral Salzer first. Don't stop anywhere but go straight over. He's waiting."

"Who's he?" Turley asked.

"He's NAVFORV, and he's expecting you right now. You get going and I'll inform him you're on your way. Good luck. Oh, you might want to take these messages with you and review them to get your story straight."

Climbing back into the jeep, Turley reviewed the messages as Ha Si Chow zigged and zagged through Saigon traffic. The more he read, the more concerned Turley got.

"Lieutenant Colonel Turley, USMC, Quang Tri reports situation critical and requests immediate USMC assistance to reinforce, fight and hold position. Situation passed via SPOT as follows: position is being heavily shelled. NVA and ARVN tanks engaged at Quang Tri airfield. Request immediate landing BLT southern end Quang Tri airfield. Will have

USMC personnel in area with smoke. This is urgent, repeat, urgent."[1]

Oh shit, now I can see why Abrams wants to see me. During the hectic moments, the skippers of the destroyers were asking for situation reports. We had destroyed the Dong Ha Bridge and told him he was engaging tanks. Somewhere in the transmission, he thought we had tanks on the Ai Tu base.

Arriving at the NACFORV compound, Turley made his way to the Chief of Staff's office with his weapon and rucksack. Seated behind his desk, Captain Paddock, the admiral's executive officer, indicated that Turley could put his gear next to a chair but didn't offer the chair, instead continuing to write on a document. *A bit of a power demonstration*, Turley thought. After a few minutes, Paddock, in his starched Navy white uniform and white shoes, left and entered the adjacent office, Admiral Salzer's office. Moments later he returned.

"The admiral will see you now," Paddock said, holding the door open.

Straightening his back and with all the pride of a US Marine, Turley entered and came to a halt and attention center and in front of the admiral's desk.

"Sir, Lieutenant Colonel Turley reports."

The admiral rose from his seat, holding a handful of pagers, "Colonel, have you been sending messages?" he asked.

"No, sir," Turley responded without hesitation. This caught the admiral off guard momentarily, but the opening was all Turley needed. "Sir, if you will allow me to explain the tactical situation and my actions, I believe this will all be cleared up."

"Okay, Colonel, let's hear your story," Salzer said as he took his seat. He didn't offer Turley a seat. Turley relaxed momentarily and began to explain. It quickly became obvious that this sailor didn't understand the terrain, the geography, the ground tactics or the enemy situation in Quang Tri Province.

Finally, Turley said, "Sir, with your permission," and without waiting for the admiral's permission, Turley pulled a map out of his cargo pocket. This map had been on the TOC wall and had been kept up to date on friendly firebases and enemy movement. It had been an extra map that Turley had taken as an afterthought.

"Sir, allow me to show you on this map the situation," Turley said. Holding it, he began to explain the tactical situation, but attempting to do that and point wasn't working. Moving to the side of the admiral's desk, Turley knelt down and spread the map out on the floor. With a pencil for a pointer, he started his presentation.

"Let me start over, sir," Turley said, continuing without allowing the admiral time to respond. "Sir, these are the forward outposts along the DMZ, Alpha 1, 2, 3, and 4. They've been there for the past six years. They're outposts and not really designed or manned for a conventional battle. All were quickly overrun by the end of the second day. These firebases on the west managed to last a bit longer but were subjected to very effective enemy artillery fire and began capitulating. This firebase, Carroll, had four one-seven-five guns and an assortment of twenty-two, one-oh-five and one-five-five when the regimental commander just up and surrendered without a fight. When Carroll fell, we lost a great deal of the fire support for the other firebases throughout the western perimeter." At this point, the admiral moved his chair and leaned forward for a better view. He interrupted several times with questions as Turley walked the admiral across the map, describing the battle.

"So how did you become the man in charge?" Salzer asked. "Isn't a Colonel Metcalf, Army, the senior advisor to the 3rd Infantry Division?"

"Sir, he displaced to Quang Tri Citadel with the 3rd ARVN Headquarters and called me a day later. He said that by order of the commander FRAC, I was in charge of the 3rd ARVN Division forward."

"Can you prove that, Colonel, or is it a case of your word against his?"

"Sir, I have his Social Security number right here on a slip of paper."

"May I have that?" the admiral asked, holding out his hand. Turley now realized he was in trouble—big-time trouble. Metcalf had hung him out to dry—if 3rd ARVN collapsed, he could wash his hands clean as he had put Turley in command. If things went well, then he could take credit for it as he was the senior advisor to the 3rd ARVN Division. That scrap of paper with Metcalf's Social Security number was the only proof Turley had of his story.

"With all due respect, Admiral, no, you may not have it. This is the only proof I have that I'm telling the truth," Turley stated, expecting the explosion that didn't come.

"I understand, Colonel," the admiral said, withdrawing his hand. "Who authorized you to call in and change B-52 strikes?"

"Sir, that was a call I received from General Bowen, giving me the authority to designate any targets for B-52 strikes." And Turley followed up with the time and date of that call. The admiral was stunned by this account. It became obvious to the admiral that MACV was not aware of the dire situation in Quang Tri.

About this time, Montezuma's revenge struck. Turley had to excuse himself and quickly departed to find the nearest bathroom to relieve himself. When he returned, Captain Paddock stopped him and had him wait to return to the admiral's office. This time Paddock offered a chair and a cup of coffee. It was obvious that he and the admiral had had a discussion.

After a cup of coffee, Paddock announced that the admiral was ready to see him. Opening the door, Turley was surprised by the audience that was present. Admiral Salzer made the introductions.

"Colonel, this is Rear Admiral Wilson and Rear Admiral Price. I would like them to hear what you related to me earlier," Salzer stated. The map had been moved from the floor to a coffee table, and four chairs were placed around the table, along with cups and coffee. Turley started his presentation all over again, ticking off the events as they'd unfolded. When it came to discussing naval gunfire, the flag officers became very interested. The crowning moment was when Turley explained having Metcalf's Social Security number, as he noticed a change in their posture and attitude. At the conclusion, Admiral Salzer asked for final questions, which Turley answered.

"Colonel, you need to get over to the MACV now and see General Abrams. First you'll report to Brigadier General Lanigan, the senior Marine in Vietnam, who's on the J-3 staff. He'll arrange for you to see General Abrams," Salzer said.

Standing, Turley realized this interview was over. "Aye-aye, sir, but first I'd like to swing by and get a shower and some clean utilities if that's okay," Turley said.

"No, you go over there just as you are. I'll meet you at Lanigan's office in thirty minutes. That's all," Salzer said. Turley left and immediately stopped at the bathroom to have a second session with Montezuma's revenge. Once relieved, he found Ha Si Chow waiting out front to drive him back to the MACV compound. True to his word, Admiral Salzer was waiting for Turley outside of Lanigan's office. When they entered, the audience had grown considerably. Even Pete was there, along with five other senior officers and his map. For the third time, Turley started his presentation, but he couldn't finish before Montezuma came knocking and he had to dash out of the room. Returning, he continued his presentation with questions from the senior officers. Pete stood in the background but didn't speak. When Turley was done, Lanigan motioned from him to follow as he headed for the door and hallway. Salzer accompanied them. As they walked, again, people in starched fatigues and shined boots gawked at this filthy warrior. *What jungle did he crawl out of? The war is over for us*, they thought. *And that smell...*

The sign on the door read General Fred Weyand, Deputy Commander MACV. When they entered, General Weyand was present along with eight Army general officers. Standish Oscar Brooks was one of the officers. Spreading the map out, Turley related the events for the fourth time that afternoon. The door to General Abrams's office was open, but Abrams didn't appear. Things were going fine until he came to the discussion of how he had become the man in charge of 3rd ARVN Division forward. The Army brass got real interested at this point. An Army lieutenant colonel asked for the scrap of paper with Metcalf's Social Security number. Turley's antenna went up.

"I'm sorry, but no, you can't have it," Turley said. The room became very quiet.

"I only want to make a copy of it," the Army lieutenant colonel said, holding his hand out.

"No," Turley said again. A standstill was coming to a head when Pete stepped forward.

"Gerry, let me have it and I'll make a copy and bring the original back to you," Pete said. Turley trusted almost no one at this point, and this was the only proof he could show that he was in the right. How far this affair was going, he couldn't tell, but a court-martial could be looming at the end of this, he believed. Finally, he handed the scrap to Pete, who did as promised and returned the scrap after he had copied it.

After the final question, Weyand indicated that he wanted to talk to the others without Turley present.

"One final question if I may, sir," Brooks said, looking at Weyand, who simply nodded his head. "Colonel Turley, where is my Major Turner?"

"Sir, Major Turner has been all over the AO. He's observing firsthand how well Vietnamization is doing, or not. Right now, sir, he's an immense help to me. I'd really like to hang on to him for a while if I may," Turley replied.

"Very well, but remind him he has a report due by the first of August," Brooks said. As Turley left the room, he heard Weyand state, "Until this moment I wasn't aware that the commanding general FRAC, the team commander, had placed Lieutenant Colonel Turley in any US Army advisory command position."[2]

Moments later, Turley was called back into Weyand's office to answer questions on where the 3rd ARVN Division lines had been when he'd left that morning. Having concluded the last of the questions, Weyand asked his next and final question. "Colonel, what do you want to do now?"

Without hesitation, Turley answered, "Get back to Quang Tri, sir."

Silence hung in the room until Lanigan said he had a plane laid on for 1800 departure to Da Nang and if Turley could be ready, he had a seat. A chopper would be laid on to fly him to Ai Tu. Ha Si Chow drove like a kamikaze pilot to get Turley to a shower and shave, but Turley was on that flight along with Colonel Dorsey.

"Colonel, we're creating a Vietnamese Marine division," Dorsey said, sitting next to Turley on the C-130 that was exclusively theirs. "I'm going to be the senior advisor. I'm moving you over to FRAC headquarters to be the assistant operations officer. I cleared it with Brooks that, for the time being, Turner will be my deputy. We're going to place the three Vietnamese Marine brigades under the division. The 3rd ARVN Division will be on their own with Metcalf having to take responsibility. Any questions?" Dorsey asked. Turley had none.

27

RING OF STEEL HOLDS

4 APRIL 1972
FRAC Headquarters
Da Nang, South Vietnam

"Sir, Lieutenant Colonel Camper reports," Camper said as he stood before General Kroesen's desk.

"Have a seat, Colonel," Kroesen responded, pointing to a conference table in his office with chairs. As he stood, he went on, "I've asked you here to get some firsthand knowledge of what's been going out up north. Seems the reports we're getting out of General Lam's headquarters aren't matching up with what we're hearing." Kroesen sat down at the conference table, where a map of Quang Tri Province was already laid out. The original disposition of the 3rd ARVN Division was posted on the map as reflected on 30 March. Slowly, Camper walked through the events as they'd happened. Kroesen didn't say much but listened intently and showed some disgust when he heard that Carroll had surrendered without a fight. As

Camper talked, he confirmed what Kroesen had heard from sources at MACV about Turley's story.

"Colonel, I have one question. Where was Colonel Metcalf during this time?"

"Sir, I believe he was with General Giai at the 3rd ARVN Headquarters in Quang Tri at the Citadel. It was my understanding that he left Colonel Turley in charge at Ai Tu in command of the 3rd ARVN Division forward," Camper stated. "Sir, there's something that you may be able to help us with. An Air Force pilot ejected and is somewhere north of the Cam Lo River. The Air Force has imposed a no-fire zone around this pilot for seventeen miles. Sir, we can't get any fire support for any of the 3rd ARVN Division. Can you get the Air Force to cut this no-fire zone down? We're going to lose a lot of ground if this continues."

"Colonel, we've been trying to get the Air Force to see the folly of this no-fire zone and so far we're beating our heads against a wall. They did almost the same thing in Lam Son 719 and we did lose a firebase because of that action. I'll get on the phone again."

After an hour, Camper was dismissed and went looking for a flight back north to rejoin his regiment. General Kroesen decided it was time to speak with General Lam about what he was being told. Lam wasn't one to report bad news to his superiors. Kroesen had his aide notify General Lam that he was on his way to Lam's office.

"General Lam, thank you for seeing me on such short notice. I'm sure you're very busy, so I won't take much of your time," Kroesen said as he walked into Lam's office.

"There's always time to talk with you, General Kroesen. How may I help you?" Lam said, motioning for them to sit in the overstuffed chairs.

"General, you can help me by providing accurate and timely reports on the conditions north of Quang Tri. What your reports are saying and what is in fact happening are two different things."

"I can assure you, General Kroesen, that my staff has been providing accurate assessments of the situation," Lam said with a defensive tone.

"Then, sir, your staff is blowing smoke up your ass. I just had a long meeting with one of the advisors and he confirmed everything that Lieutenant Colonel Turley told General Abrams. You have a damn major invasion going on and are doing nothing about it."

"We're planning a counterattack right now that will destroy the communists. General Giai has more than adequate forces to maintain the Ring of Steel."

"General, he has too many forces to control as a single division," Kroesen said and raised his hand with an open palm and extended fingers. "He doesn't have the communications equipment needed to maintain contact with everyone." A finger was curled. "He doesn't have the logistics to resupply everyone." Another finger was curled. "He doesn't have the transportation to move everyone, or even a portion of his forces." Three fingers were curled. "The Marine brigades should be under the command of the Marine division and have General Khang report to you, the corps commander. Assign a sector to him and give him the Marine brigades to command and coordinate. The same with the Rangers. Put them under Ranger command and assign them a sector to control and defend. That reduces General Lam's span of control and allows him to more effectively employ his forces," General Kroesen stated, curling his last finger and lowering his hand.

"I've just reviewed the orders for the Marine division. They're inbound with the 369th Marine Brigade and are flying into Phu Bai Airfield over the next two days. The division headquarters will occupy the Citadel in Hue and be responsible for the city defenses. The 369th Brigade will take over responsibility for the area north of the My Chanh River. Colonel Pham Van Chung commands the 369th, and I've met with him, as has General Giai. His sector will have the ocean on his right flank, the Nhung River to the north and on the west the jungles of the Hai Lang District. The 5th Battalion of the 369th is coming by truck and will dismount five kilometers north of the My Chanh River and move to Fire Support Base Jane. This will reinforce our western flank," Lam said with some bluster.

"General Lam, how are they going to get up the road? QL1 is packed with vehicles, bikes, carts and people, all moving south. There's no traffic control out there. You have maybe twenty thousand refugees moving down that road."

"General Kroesen, the 3rd Division has been in the fight from the start and has had to give up some ground, but I believe the time for a counterattack is rapidly approaching. The enemy is stretching his supply lines. The close-air support is in operation since the weather has improved and we have fresh troops coming up to join us. In addition, many of our troops from the 3rd that were bypassed are rejoining their units. My staff is putting a counteroffensive plan together now. The details must be worked out but we have two goals. First, to reestablish our former perimeter of firebases, such as Mai Loc and Camp Carroll; second, to reopen Firebase Holcomb; and finally, to cross the Cua Viet River and seize Gio Linh and then cross over the DMZ. This will force the communists to move back into Laos and back north." Kroesen was having trouble swallowing this dream.

"What about your western flank? That appears to be the main attack since they haven't been able to cross at the Dong Ha Bridge. If you pull forces from the western flank to support your attack across the Cua Viet River, you're liable to open your side up for a quick attack by the communists right into Quang Tri proper," Kroesen pointed out. He could see the wheels turning in Lam's head as he hadn't considered these things. "Sir, I would recommend you rethink this and hold in the north and attack in the west. I would also caution you not to be overly optimistic. As it's conducted, it needs to be methodical and slow, clearing everything out of its way," Kroesen said as he stood to leave.

"Thank you for coming to see me, General," Lam said as he stood as well. "You've given me much to think about. I will keep you informed as we develop our plan."

"When are you anticipating kicking this operation off?"

"It'll be sometime next week. We'll let the communists expend more of their resources before we go on the offensive," Lam indicated.

"General, I look forward to seeing the final plans," Kroesen said as he departed. *Someone has his head up his ass.*

28

COMMAND BRIEF

4 APRIL 1972
MACV Headquarters
Saigon, South Vietnam

The information Turley had provided about the conditions in MR-1 were disturbing for the simple fact that South Vietnamese JCS wasn't aware or hadn't informed MACV if they were aware. Questions would have to be asked delicately so as not to offend any of the Vietnamese officers. Now the advisor channel was saying that trouble was brewing in MR-3. Abrams called a meeting with his staff and the senior officers in each of the military regions and General Kroesen.

"Let's start this off with a recap of what we know," Abrams directed, looking right at MG Carley. Seated behind Abrams were John Paul Vann and BG Hollingsworth as well as a couple of majors that hadn't been introduced as yet.

"Sir, as we are now aware, a major assault has occurred in MR-1, with the main attack appearing to be coming out of Laos and supporting attacks coming from the north down

Highway 1. It appears that these are conventional forces operating in a combined-arms manner with infantry, tanks and supporting artillery all working together in an attempt to seize Quang Tri. The ARVNs and Vietnamese Marines have had some success, some failures and some hard-fought battles. When possible, we're getting tac air support to them and the B-52s are working overtime with strikes. Naval gunfire has been excellent in providing support. We're getting attack helicopter support, but we're starting to get reports of surface-to-air missiles going after the helicopters. As you're aware, the bridge at Dong Ha has been destroyed and that has halted the enemy attacks from north of the Cam Lo River. The firebases on the west side of Quang Tri have taken a pounding from 130mm artillery, with Mai Loc being abandoned and Carroll surrendering without much of a fight. Our advisors, with about one thousand South Vietnamese soldiers and Marines, also have made their way back to Ai Tu. The 147th Brigade is being moved back to Hue for reequipping and replacement personnel," Carley outlined.

"Any comments?" Abrams asked, looking at the others seated. There was a pause in the conversation as if no one wanted to be the first. Vann couldn't let the opportunity pass.

"Sir, I predicted that this was going to start this week. They're going to hit us hard and attempt to split the country. I think the attacks up north are more of a deception plan with the main attack coming through MR-2 from Laos to Dak To to Kontum, Pleiku and the coast," Vann said.

"And what indications have you had to lead you to that conclusion, sir?" Abrams said.

"Sir, it's my opinion that Giap wants to cut the South in half. He has initiated his attack in the north as a diversionary attack, hoping that we will draw forces from MR-2 and move them north before he launches his main attack out of Laos in hopes of seizing Dak To and Kontum and driving on to the coast. We had a major contact by the 23rd Ranger Battalion just west of Rocket Ridge last week. They were conducting a reconnaissance of a B-52 strike that I had ordered and got into a major firefight. We had to use tac air to break contact. The 95th Border Ranger Battalion got into a major engagement with an NVA regiment a few days later in Ben Het. From those two fights, we've determined that the 320th NVA Division and the 203rd Armored Regiment are just across the border, and as soon as his forces can sweep us off Rocket Ridge, he'll attack towards Tan Canh and Dak To. We've also had numerous sightings of tank tracks in the area along the border. Sir, in my opinion, we should foil Giap's plan and shift forces to MR-2 to reinforce Kontum," Vann said.

"Hmmm...well, Mr. Vann, where do you recommend I take those forces from?" Abrams asked, having given Vann enough rope to hang himself.

"Well, sir, you could take them from MR-3."

"Now hold your horses there, Mr. Vann," General Hollingsworth said, entering the conversation for the first time. He was the commander of the Third Regional Assistance Group located in Long Binh. Hollingsworth was a model of General Patton, having served under Patton in World War II—well, under as a tank battalion commander. He was tough and aggressive but had a deep love for soldiers. Officers might quake at the sound of his voice, but it was seldom harsh with an NCO or a private. He knew the first name of every advisor under him and personally wrote letters to each child apologizing for their daddy being with him and not them at Christmas, pointing out that Daddy was doing important work. Like Patton, he would clash with senior officers about politics influencing tactics. "Let's not be so generous with my soldiers."

"What do you think are the enemy's intentions in MR-3?" Abrams asked.

"Sir, intel is painting a picture that the 9th VC Division, 5th NVA Division and 7th NVA Division are just across the border in Cambodia. In addition, the 24th and 271st NVA Regiments are in the vicinity of Tay Ninh Province. Traditionally it was always assumed—there's that word again, assumed—that the NVA would attack population centers first, such as Tay Ninh, and seize people. I don't see it that way. In the north, in MR-1, he's attacking less-populated areas versus going after Hue and Quang Tri. He's also shelling the crap out of civilians attempting to get out of his way on the roads. He's not out to win the hearts and minds of the people but to kill ARVN soldiers and seize ground. In the center, that's one of the least populated areas until you get to the coast. A major offensive there would not render a large population to seize but a lot of land. I ask myself, why would he attack towards Tay Ninh if he's out to seize people, in which case the target would be Saigon? Why attack through rubber tree plantations and jungles with no roads for support, when he can attack down a major road right into Saigon? I think his major attack in MR-3 will be against Loc Ninh, An Loc and Lai Khe, stopping only in Saigon."

"What's the situation in MR-3 now?" Abrams asked.

"The patrols that have gone out from Loc Ninh have been finding a lot of commo wire running from Cambodia into our AO. We know the NVA likes wire communications and this would indicate that he's going to be making a lot of phone calls. There's a Special Operations Unit at Quan Loi and Colonel Miller visited them, asking for some intel on what they were finding. In typical special ops fashion, their response was 'Only for those with a need to know'—like the senior combat advisor in the area has no need to know." Hollingsworth's death-dagger stare at the special ops representative could melt an ice cube. "On the eleventh of March, we swapped out the 7th Regiment 5th Division with the 9th

Regiment at Loc Ninh and added a two-battalion task force from the 18th Division, which we're calling Task Force 52. They're OPCON to the 5th ARVN Division for now.[1] Task Force 52 is located at the junction of Highway 17 and Highway 13, five miles southwest of Loc Ninh. It consists of two infantry battalions, one from the 52nd Regiment and one from the 48th Regiment, along with a battery of 105mm howitzers and a platoon of 155mm howitzers. There are three American advisors with them. This way, enemy movement from the west is blocked, and enemy movement from the north is blocked by the units in Loc Ninh. On March thirty-first, we had some low levels of activity, being a feint towards Tay Ninh. The day before yesterday, the 24th NVA Regiment with tank support hit Firebase Lac Long and overran it by 1200 hours. It was a pretty isolated firebase. Unfortunately, it has been the policy in III Corps to man these small isolated firebases, which are nothing more than a trip wire to the NVA. Minh has given the order to abandon the isolated firebases and pull those people back to Tay Ninh. The one Ranger battalion in Tong Le Chon, however, is going to stay in position."

"Why?" Abrams asked.

"Sir, the battalion commander is convinced that if he attempted to make it over to Tay Ninh from his location, he would be ambushed and probably wiped out attempting to move through the Michelin rubber tree plantation," Hollingsworth explained. "Case in point, the unit at Firebase Thien Ngon pulled out of their firebase, which was twenty miles north of Tay Ninh, and were ambushed by the 271st Regiment. We thought they lost their artillery tubes, but a relief element arrived the next day and found them all. The NVA didn't destroy the tubes or even the vehicles that were towing them. That screams hit and run to me and not dig in and hold, at least not in Tay Ninh. However, as of yesterday, we're seeing more activity towards Loc Ninh. I think his main attack is going to come down Highway 13 towards Loc Ninh, An Loc and Lai Khe."

Abrams was silent, digesting what Hollingsworth had just told him.

Hesitantly, Hollingsworth continued, "Sir, my biggest concern is not with the enemy but the leadership, starting right up there with General Hung."

"Go on," Abrams encouraged him.

"Sir, Hung, Minh and Vinh are all from the Delta and were brought up here together. None of them have seen much combat over the years. If we get into a big fight, I doubt if they can handle it. When the attacks started in I Corps, Hung came into Colonel Miller's office elated because he felt that no attacks would come against the 5th Infantry Division. The real concern that the team has is that once the shooting starts, and maybe even before, that bunch will surrender to the NVA," Hollingsworth explained.

"That bad?" Abrams asked.

"Sir, the other day, Vinh, the 9th Regiment commander, called Colonel Miller and asked that he come up to Loc Ninh, immediately. Miller got a flight up, expecting to find a wounded or, worse, dead advisor. He gets there and Vinh takes him aside and wants to know if the American troops will come back. Vinh thinks the North Vietnamese troops are better soldiers than his own forces. Miller even asked if the regiment would fight," Hollingsworth said.

"And?" Abrams asked.

"Vinh said they would but would eventually have to surrender. Told Miller that if they resisted, prisoner camp would be much harder on them," Hollingsworth replied.

"Well, why doesn't Hung replace him?" Abrams asked, his temperature rising.

"Miller asked that question, sir, and Hung said to do so could politically jeopardize his, Hung's, career. After that,

Hung went off yelling about US advisors sticking their noses in purely Vietnamese affairs," Hollingsworth replied.

"I suppose the conversation went downhill from there," Abrams said.

"Miller just left the room," Hollingsworth replied.

"Okay, gentlemen, it's apparent we haven't figured out where the main attack is coming in each of the military regions or which attack will be the overall main attack where we should be concentrating our B-52 strikes. Let's keep our intel flowing and identify what exactly he's up to and what his intermediate and final objectives are. The peace talks will be resuming soon, and I'm convinced he was to go into those talks from a position of strength. The more ground he can gain and control, the more weight he's going to have in Paris. Keep me posted. For right now, the priority and main effort is MR-1."

29

PEDRO

8 April 1972
6th Vietnamese Marine Battalion
Firebase Pedro

Firebase Pedro was the remaining firebase between the advancing NVA and Quang Tri City after Mai Loc and Camp Carroll had fallen. It was located seven miles southwest of Quang Tri City in a flat open plain and north of the Thach Han River. As firebases went, it wasn't intended to be a defensive strongpoint against an armor threat or even a major ground assault. It had a dirt berm and wire perimeter but no overhead covered bunkers. A Ranger battalion had been there for the past six days and was to conduct a relief in place with the 6th VNMC Battalion under the command of Major Tung. He was accompanied by two US Marine advisors, Major Bill Warren and Captain Bill Wischmeyer. The 6th VNMC Battalion advance party met with the Ranger command group and was briefed on the disposition of their forces. Once they left, Tung, Warren and Wischmeyer sat down with a map and discussed the plan for them. Tung had not shown any affection for his American advisors, and the relationship was strained. Brown and Wischmeyer had a nickname for Tung, "Fast Eddy."[1] The name just seemed to fit.

"Warren," Tung said, "I not think wise to put eggs in one basket. Pedro is basket and not good basket. NVA know all positions and holes in wire."

"I think you're right, Tung. What are you thinking?" Warren asked.

"I think best we position north and northeast on these hills with only one company here in Pedro. Command Group Bravo with one company in blocking position here on Route 557 one thousand meters east of Pedro. Command Group Alpha here." Tung pointed at the hilltop north of Pedro. "Two companies on this hill overlooking Pedro. What think you?" he asked, which was appreciated by Brown.

"I concur. The commies have Pedro well registered with their artillery. If he brings tanks, then Command Group Bravo will be able to hit them hard. The engineers should be here soon with the antitank mines. Where do you intend to have them emplaced?" Warren asked.

"We place on sides of road. Engineers can do that," Major Tung indicated.

For the rest of the day, the 6th VNMC Battalion engaged in preparations of defensive positions in the new locations they moved to occupy. Occasional incoming rockets or artillery rounds on Pedro made life hectic for those selected to be on Pedro proper. Major Tung supervised the positioning of the companies over the course of the next two days.

"Hey, Bill, did you hear what happened with the 5th Battalion this morning?" Major Warren asked Captain Wischmeyer as Brown got out of a jeep by Command Group Bravo's position. Wischmeyer had been out with Command

Group Bravo and hadn't been next to the advisor net back to the 258th VNMC Brigade advisors.

"No, sir, what happened?" Wischmeyer answered.

"Seems they walked into a shitstorm this morning. Two companies left Firebase Jane and moved west into the Hai Lang Forest to search out the NVA. Well, they found them—a reinforced company nailed them in an ambush and took out the entire Command Group Alpha in the opening volley. Captain Wells is now in command of a Vietnamese battalion minus with the NVA in hot pursuit. He's using artillery to create some space with the NVA," Warren explained.

"Jesus, didn't they know the commies were there?" Wischmeyer asked.

"Seems not. That's a large force to be sitting that close to Quang Tri undetected until now. If that's the case, it could be very possible that we're the last firebase before Quang Tri City, north of the Thach Han River. Ai Tu doesn't have much left there after the pounding they've been getting. We best get dug in for the night. Stay in touch on the radio. Need anything?" Warren asked.

"Nah, I'm good, sir," Wischmeyer lied, wishing Major Warren had a UH-1H helicopter inbound to extract them out of their present location.

"Well, I guess we should get comfortable as I think it's gonna be a long night. Why don't you come on back with me to my location?" Warren suggested.

"That's okay. I'll hang with the Bravo group. Keep you posted on what we see coming," Wischmeyer replied with reluctance.

"Okay, keep in touch and I'll see you in the morning. Be safe," Warren ordered as he departed to return to the Alpha Command Group and Major Tung.

Throughout the night, impacting artillery rounds reduced the time for sleep. In previous assignments, Wischmeyer had been a company commander and an advisor. His ears were tuned to the various sounds made by different-caliber weapons. Now he was hearing a new sound.

"Dai'uy, what that?" his Vietnamese counterpart asked as a round impacted.

"Tran, that is the sound of a main gun on a tank. We're going to have tanks coming at us in the morning. Best we make sure everyone has the light antitank weapons." And Tran and Wischmeyer set out to inspect and encourage their Marines. As dawn approached, there was a significant increase in artillery fire.

"Badger Six, Badger Three, over," Wischmeyer called Warren on their FM frequency.

"Badger Three, go ahead."

"Hey, boss, I hear tank tracks approaching our position and not just one, over."

"Roger, what's the plan?"

"We intend to hold here for as long as possible and then withdraw back to Pedro, over."

"Roger, I have Custom House Six on call whenever you want it. He's in contact with Navigate and Assassin. They're standing by."[2]

"Roger, we will be calling in the near future, I'm sure. Out."

While Wischmeyer worked the fire support, Warren was on the radio calling for Major Easley collocated with Colonel Dinh, the 258th Brigade commander at the TOC in Ai Tu.

"This is Badger Six. We have tanks approaching our positions with what appears to be two battalions of infantry. Requesting reinforcements, over," Warren called on the advisor net while Major Tung spoke directly to Colonel Dinh on his command net.

"Badger Six, roger, understood," Easley said. "Can you identify the tank unit? Over."

"Each of the tanks is flying a red-over-white triangle flag from their antennas, but I can't determine which is the command tank. Over." Almost immediately, the flags on each tank were withdrawn. It was instantly obvious to Warren that the NVA were monitoring the advisor net with someone that spoke English. *Shit, we've got to watch what we say now.*

Wischmeyer didn't have long to wait. Suddenly the impacting artillery stopped and in typical commie fashion the ground assault started, led by sixteen T-54 tanks. An entire regiment of NVA soldiers were following the tanks down the road. The tanks were two abreast, with the others in column behind them, followed by the infantry.

"Custom House Six, Badger Three, fire mission!" Aboard the USS *Bausell* and USS *Craig*, gun crews moved into action as they monitored the calls for fire.

"Badger Three, Custom House Six, go ahead. Over."

"Custom House Six, tanks and infantry in the open. Target reference point two-six. Fire at will. How copy? Over." Aboard the destroyers, fire direction centers had already plotted the target reference points the night before and immediately passed the data to the guns.

"Badger Three, Custom House Six, good copy. Understand fire at will, over." When the ships heard "fire at will," the first rounds were released.

"Affirmative, Custom House Six." Before Wischmeyer could hand the receiver to his radio operator, the first round screamed overhead and impacted. It was followed by several others that held the advance in check.

"Tran, it's time to fall back now," Wischmeyer said—needlessly as the Vietnamese Marines were already moving out of their positions. Not all were headed for Pedro, but a few headed off in a westerly direction, avoiding the firebase. An hour and several naval gunfire missions later, Command Group Bravo reached its assigned positions. Wischmeyer joined Warren in an overwatch position, observing Pedro. The approach to Pedro was littered with several tanks that had fallen victim to the minefield the Vietnamese engineers had emplaced. In their haste to get out of the naval gunfire, the tanks had accelerated their movement up the approach to Pedro while the regiment of NVA infantry had delayed their movement. The result was that the tanks had no supporting infantry.

Two tanks had taken the lead, crashing through the wire around Pedro as if it wasn't there at all. Once inside Pedro, they began an exercise in crushing positions and shooting anything and everything they saw. Because of the noise from the incoming artillery and the tanks, the screams of those trapped in the bunkers that the tanks were rolling over could not be heard. One platoon perished in this fashion. Some Marines withdrew in an orderly fashion; some just ran, not to be seen until much later.

"What can you see?" Warren asked as he moved into Wischmeyer's position. Pulling away from his field glasses, Wischmeyer handed them to Warren.

"It appears that nine tanks made it through the minefield and gunfire. They've taken up positions around Pedro and are waiting for the infantry to catch up. The two tanks that initially overran the firebase took off towards the retreating Marines to the northeast," Wischmeyer said as Warren scanned the firebase from their position about five hundred meters west and on a small knoll.

"Oh shit!" Wischmeyer exclaimed, grabbing Warren's arm.

"What!" Warren said, looking at Wischmeyer, whose eyes were the size of saucers. They were fixed on the two tanks that had just turned and were departing Pedro, heading directly towards his position.

"Time to get out of here. Tung, time to move," Warren said as he started to stand up. Tung was already on the move.

The first tank exploded. Both advisors exchanged looks of surprise and continued to move as the second tank didn't stop but pressed forward its advance, slowly gaining on the departing group. Finally, the command group took up a hide position behind a small knoll, and the tank didn't pursue but instead parked. Naval gunfire and now 105mm artillery support rained down on the enemy infantry, preventing them from joining the tanks, which were now isolated on and around Pedro.

"Badger Six, Thunder, over." Warren wasn't sure who this was.

"Thunder, Badger Six, over," Warren answered hesitantly, knowing the NVA were monitoring the frequency.

"Badger Six, Thunder, how you doing? Thought you might be getting lonely, so we thought we'd join you and help you out. We're just approaching your position from the northeast. I have eight Mike Four-Eights and twelve Mike One-One-Threes along with two companies of Marines. I have our counterparts talking, and it appears my guy will organize and lead the counterattack. Over," Captain Livingston, the advisor for the 1st VNMC Battalion, said.

Warren turned to look and saw the first of the M48 tanks in the distance. Now it dawned on him who Badger Six was. He started to speak to Tung but noted that Tung was already on the radio, talking to the commander of the relief force, Major Hoa, from the 2nd Troop, 20th Tank Regiment. A brief tank battle was initiated. Tanks played hide-and-seek with each other, exchanging fire. The M48s were experiencing first-round hits at fifteen hundred meters while the T-54s were using three rounds to get a hit, bracketing the target with two rounds and the third the kill shot only—they never got a kill hit. The fire control systems in the M48 were far superior to the T-54 system.

The overcast sky parted just enough for four A-1E

Skyraider aircraft to join the fray. They were able to destroy five tanks, some possibly disabled in the minefield earlier. The remaining three decided it was time to withdraw. One did so in high gear and at maximum speed. One, however, stopped for some unknown reason, possibly disoriented and checking his navigation. Warren watched through his field glasses as some movement to the front of this stopped tank caught his attention.

"Hey, watch this," he said to Wischmeyer, who focused his attention on the tank and noted the movement. As he did so, a lone Vietnamese Marine climbed out of his foxhole fifty feet in front of the tank. The tank commander was standing in his open hatch on top of the tank. Suddenly he looked up as the young Marine waved his M16 rifle at him. Slowly the tank commander climbed out, directing his crew to do the same. The young Vietnamese Marine had captured a T-54 tank by himself.

"I'll be dipped...," Wischmeyer said in amazement.

"That young man deserves a medal, by God," Warren said, looking at Tung, who just shrugged his shoulders and walked off.

The day ended with Pedro, or what was left of Pedro, still in the possession of the Vietnamese Marines. Members of the 6th VNMC Battalion moved back into Pedro, but Major Tung decided that they would pull out if threatened again and not be subjected to enemy tanks grinding down on top of them.

"What does Hoa intend to do tonight?" Warren asked Livingston as the three advisors sat and drank their first cups of coffee for the day. In the damp night air, it was a welcome relief after a long day, and the small campfire they had built in the bottom of a foxhole behind a hill from the NVA offered some warmth.

"He's with Tung and they're going to keep Hoa as a counterattack force. Hoa is going to stay behind these low hills and trees out of sight but keep moving throughout the night so they can't get a fix on him. He's moved once already, and artillery hit the position shortly after we vacated. What about Tung? What's his plan?" Livingston asked, sipping from his cup, attempting not to burn his lips on the metal canteen cup.

"After that display today of the single soldier capturing a tank, he's putting some of his soldiers in spider holes and going to let the tanks roll over and bust them with LAWs once they roll past. This should be interesting. It's going to take some nerve for them to stay in those holes and let the tanks pass, but if they do, they're going to bag tanks. We'll just have to see," Warren replied. "Only tomorrow will tell."

The next morning did tell. NVA tanks repeated the previous day's attack and left the infantry behind, attempting to get out from the fire support from ships and artillery. Moving against identified VNMC positions, they didn't see the spider holes until they had rolled past them and the Vietnamese Marines rose up and fired LAW rockets into the rear engines of the tanks. What was left of the NVA tanks retreated, leaving Pedro somewhat intact.

30

AMBUSH

12 APRIL 1972
12 APRIL 1972
1st VNMC Battalion
Ai Tu, South Vietnam

"We're going to head back to Ai Tu with Command Group Bravo. Major Hoa is going to stay here with Command Group Alpha," Captain Livingston said as he approached Major Warren and Captain Wischmeyer. "Seems that things are quiet now and we're going back to pull palace guard at Ai Tu."

"Want to take Fast Eddy with you?" Wischmeyer asked.

"No. That guy seems to have a corn cob up his ass. He no likey you guys?" Livingston replied, imitating pidgin English.

"We've bent over backwards to help him out, but he's just an arrogant son of a bitch. He hates the commies more but has no love for us. He'll take anything we can give him but doesn't give back in return," Wischmeyer replied with some disgust in his voice.

Reaching in his cargo pockets, Livingston pulled out two

cans of Coke and handed them over. "I grabbed some from the track."

"Thanks, we'll save them for the cocktail hour today and Tung can watch," Wischmeyer said with a smile. "You take care." He extended his hand, which Livingston accepted, and did the same with Major Warren before returning to his track vehicle, where Major Hoa was seated, looking at his map. Captain To Ton Te, the battalion executive officer and leader of Command Group Bravo, was seated next to him.

"Dai'uy," Hoa said, getting Livingston's attention. He and Livingston had the opposite relationship from what Warren and Wischmeyer were experiencing with Major Tung. Hoa motioned for Livingston to join them and look at the map. Dragging his finger across the route to Ai Tu, Hoa said, "You take this route, but I no like. Too easy to ambush here and here. You put out security front and sides, yes?" Major Hoa said.

Livingston studied the map for a moment and then agreed with Hoa.

"Te, where do you want me to be in this convoy?" Livingston asked. "Do you need me with you or should we split up? You take lead and I'll bring up the rear?" Livingston offered, then added, "Or I'll take lead and you bring up the rear."

Te looked at Livingston and smiled. "Very hard for leader to lead from rear. I take lead."

"I thought you would say that," Livingston said with a smile, shaking his head. Te was a no-nonsense warrior that everyone respected, and Livingston would have been surprised if Te had taken tail-end Charlie.

After orders were issued and everyone was mounted up, the first elements moved out on the narrow dirt trail back to Ai Tu. They hadn't been moving long when the lead vehicle stopped. Moving forward to the lead vehicle, an M113, Te inquired as to the stop.

"Dai'uy, up ahead about four hundred meters, we see people crossroad. We think NVA. We went forward on foot and heard digging and talking. We think ambush," the senior noncommissioned officer said. About this time, Livingston came forward to see what was going on. He didn't want to discuss mission details on the radio as he knew the NVA were listening on their frequency. As he approached the lead vehicle, he saw the lead platoon leader, the company commander, Te and two of the scouts behind the vehicle with a map on the ground.

"What's the situation?" Livingston asked as they approached.

"Dai'uy, scouts spotted people four hundred meters up road. They dig and cut brush for concealment. Much larger force, they think," Te indicated, pointing at the map. Although the scouts didn't speak English, they nodded their heads as Te spoke. It was one of the two locations that Hoa, Te and Livingston had discussed as being a good ambush location. The enemy didn't have security out and wasn't finished fixing their positions.

"What size force do they think is there?" asked Livingston. Te translated and asked the scouts; his eyes enlarged with the answer. "They say maybe battalion...or two."

"Te, I think we best get back to Major Hoa and ask for some assistance. Don't use the radio," Livingston said.

Turning to another NCO, Te said something in his native tongue, and the NCO immediately took off back down the road to Major Hoa's position. The NCO returned and informed Te that a company-size force from 6th VNMC Battalion would be coming to assist within the hour. An hour later, a rifle company from the 6th VNMC arrived. When the plan was ready, units moved out. The company from the 6th Battalion moved out first, conducting a reconnaissance by fire. Once the enemy started returning fire and identifying their positions, Livingston was on the radio, calling for artillery support. The M48 tanks and M113 armored personnel carriers opened up on the enemy. Te moved forward with the lead elements.

"Damnit, Te! Get your ass down," Livingston screamed as a hidden machine gun opened up on the Bravo Command Group. Livingston could only watch as the Vietnamese warrior was cut down along with the rest of the command group. Suddenly, Livingston found himself in command of a sizable Vietnamese force and knew he had to do something quick. Grabbing the senior NCO of 20th Tank, Livingston sent him down the road with four tanks to start clearing the ambush sites. Infantry soldiers accompanied all tanks, preventing any NVA infantry from closing on them. After the fighting ended with most of the NVA force being killed, Livingston started making an assessment of the action.

Major Warren joined him once things were quiet. "So what is your assessment of this?"

Livingston was tired, sitting in the back of an M113 and drinking a cold coffee. "We got a prisoner that said this as well as the attack on Pedro was carried out by a regiment of infantry and a battalion of tanks," Livingston revealed.

"You know, if they'd broken through, there would have been nothing north of the Thach Han River to stop them from getting into Quang Tri," Warren exclaimed.

"I can tell you this, the LAWs proved their worth against the T-54 tanks. They have to be close but they will kill a tank, these guys found out. That alone has bolstered the morale of the troops. That's the good side. The bad side is the damn 130mm artillery they're using is kicking the crap out of us."

31

CONFUSION

3rd Division Headquarters
Quang Tri, South Vietnam

The 147th VNMC Brigade had been at Ai Tu since 22 April, having moved from Hue, where it had been refurbished and rested. Arriving at Ai Tu, it relieved the 258th VNMC Brigade. The 147th Brigade now consisted of the 1st, 4th, and 8th VNMC Battalions and the 2nd VNMC Artillery Battalion. The 4th Battalion was assigned perimeter defense of Ai Tu, which was occupied by Brigade HQ, 2nd VNMC Artillery and the recon company. 1st VNMC deployed three thousand meters southwest between Ai Tu and Pedro. 8th VNMC was deployed one thousand meters northwest of Ai Tu.

1st ARVN Armored Brigade was responsible for the area from QL1 west for five kilometers with the Cam Lo River on the north and Ai Tu to the south. 1st Armored had the 57th ARVN Regiment and 4th and 5th Ranger Groups under their control as well as organic units. 2nd ARVN Regiment was responsible for the area south of Ai Tu to the Thach Han River. 1st Ranger Group was situated south of the Thach Han River. 369th VNMC was located near Hai Lang. 3rd ARVN Division headquarters had displaced to the Quang Tri Citadel.

The past couple of days, the situation appeared to have stabilized, with only light contract in the north or the west. The weather was and had been overcast with misty rain as the monsoon season was just getting started in its first month in the northern part of Vietnam. Colonel Metcalf was taking up residence in the Citadel with the bulk of the 3rd Division staff. Dong Ha Base was still occupied, as was Ai Tu. At 0600 hours, that all began to change.

* * *

0900 Hours
   3rd ARVN Division Forward
   Ai Tu, South Vietnam

"Sorry to have to drag you out of bed, sir," Major Jim Davis said as he handed a cup of coffee to Major Jack Turner. Davis had volunteered to come to the forward CP and assist in operations.

"That's okay. What you got?" Turner responded, looking at the map of the operational area. Unit locations were depicted in blue and enemy forces in red. He was seeing a lot of red.

"At 0600, the 304th NVA Division started shelling the 1st VNMC Battalion. Cockell called in and said they were holding okay but being pushed hard. Simultaneously, 1st ARVN Armored Brigade, located north of the 1st VNMC Battalion, came under attack as well. The shelling was constant, with little pause. Over on the east, the Ruff-Puffs have had some pressure but appear to be handling it. It appears that the 304th NVA Division's main effort was going to push from the southwest and west. The 5th Ranger Battalion reported contact with a strong enemy force west of the Dong Ha Bridge."

"Who commands that unit?" Turner asked, as the Ranger battalions were under 1st Armored Brigade command and he wasn't familiar with them.

"Sir, that's commanded by Lieutenant Colonel Ngo Minh Huong, a strong commander," Davis replied. "We also had some reports from 3rd Troop, 20th Tank, reporting that all officers and noncommissioned officers had been killed and six tanks had been badly damaged. 1st Armored Brigade reported that the 4th Ranger is falling back two miles and should be in a new position by noon. The 33rd Ranger Battalion was ordered to move up and reinforce the 30th Battalion, but when it arrived, no one from the 30th Ranger Battalion was alive or present. The 33rd Ranger Battalion has assumed the 30th's positions. Reports are that the 43rd Ranger Battalion only stayed and fought when the officers and commander threatened to kill them all if they fled. I guess the soldiers figured it was better to fight the NVA than face certain death at the hands of American bombs from the US Air Force," Davis added. "Sir, this may be the major push that division intel warned would be coming today."

"Are the Ranger battalions going to hold or run? We don't have advisors in depth with them, so do we really know what they're doing?" Turner asked.

"Sir, they're in some tough positions. I wouldn't be surprised if, throughout the day, the Ranger group is slowly forced back from the river," Davis indicated.

"Alright, talk to 1st Armored Brigade and let's establish a hasty defensive line along Route 604 extending north to Dong

Ha from a mile south of Dong Ha Combat Base along the Cam Lo River just in case they're forced back. I want them to hold their current positions if they can, but if not, this'll be the new hasty defensive line. I'll call Metcalf and explain the situation to him," Jack said, reaching for the landline phone.

"Roger, sir, I'll get right on it," Davis said as he examined the map and copied coordinates to send to 1st Armored Brigade.

Turner picked up the phone and called 3rd Division Main at the Citadel.

"Colonel Metcalf, it appears that the push that intel said was coming has started. We're getting increased pressure all along the west and northwest. Looking at establishing a new defensive line along Route 604 extending north to Dong Ha Base along the Mien Giang River. Truthfully, sir, I don't think we're going to hold much longer," Turner said.

"Why not?" Metcalf asked in a less-than-calm voice.

"Sir, we have no resupply of ammo or fuel. When the supply depot at Hai Lang was destroyed, we lost most of our tank ammunition, and with the supply depot at La Vang being taken out last week, no ammo of any kind or fuel is left."

Metcalf didn't say anything for several minutes. "Alright, lay out for me where the units are at currently," he finally ordered.

Jesus, don't you have that plotted there? Jack was thinking. "Alright, sir. In the north along the Cam Lo River west to Route 604 is the 57th Regiment with 20th Tank at the intersection of Route 604 and Highway 9. Facing west is the 5th Ranger Group, then the 4th Ranger Group, then the 258th Brigade, 2nd ARVN Regiment, and lastly 1st Ranger at Jane. All north of the My Chanh River."

Finally with resignation, Metcalf said, "Close out the forward command post. Bring everyone back here. We have comms with the regiments and the armored brigade from here. Your job up there is completed. When you get back here, you report to Colonel Dorsey at his new headquarters beside the Vietnamese Marine division in Hue."

Throughout the rest of the day, the 304th NVA Division maintained pressure on the western flanks and mostly against the Ranger group.

* * *

1300 Hours

Lieutenant Colonel Huynh Dinh Tung, commander of the 2nd ARVN Regiment, was tired but still in the fight. Located on the southern perimeter of the Ai Tu defense, Tung and Lieutenant Colonel Camper had been monitoring and orchestrating the defense in their sector. Major Brown was frequently out along the river, encouraging and assisting the ARVN commanders in their defense. Artillery had been hitting the soldiers as they dug into the riverbank. Everyone, both the ARVNs and the NVA, recognized the importance of the bridge as it was the last way to get into or out of Quang Tri. At 1200 hours, a report was received at 2nd Regiment CP of renewed NVA action.

"Colonel, could you go see situation so we can develop a plan?" Colonel Tung asked.

"You got it, Tung. Be back..." Camper grabbed his helmet and weapon and headed outside. Clearing the front entrance to the command bunker, he was surprised by small-arms fire, forcing him back into the bunker. "What the ... did anyone report enemy troops in the base camp?" Camper asked. The blank stares told him that no report had been rendered. He checked the map again and started back out.

"Hey, sir," Major Brown yelled, "I'm going with you."

Camper had no objection as Brown had been out frequently that morning and understood the situation and the location of ARVN units better than he did. A small group of ARVN soldiers joined them as they moved towards the railroad bridge over the tributary to the Thach Han River.

"*Incoming!*" Camper yelled as the mortar rounds slammed into the trees above their heads, bursting in the treetops. The entire area was sprayed with hot jagged pieces of shrapnel and splintered wood.

"Son of a bitch," Major Brown mumbled, lying on the ground with his face pressed into the dirt. Opening his eyes, he was shocked at what he could see. Camper was lying close to him, his face partially missing, it appeared, and blood everywhere. Brown quickly crawled over to him to find him struggling to breathe as blood was collecting in his cut throat, Brown rolled Camper onto his side to drain blood out of him and began administering first aid. Camper attempted to speak, but it was obvious his vocal cords had been partially cut from the wound in his neck. Brown turned to the ARVN soldiers, attempting to get assistance from them, but none would stop to help. Grabbing the AN/PRC-77 radio, Brown called the 3rd Division Forward command post.

"Underground Six, Red Ball Three, over," Brown transmitted.

"Red Ball Three, this is Underground Three India," came the response.

"Underground Six, Red Bull Three, Red Bull Six is down and I need medevac, *urgent*," Brown reported.

"Red Bull Three, send request," a new voice with some urgency came on the radio. Brown formulated his medevac request and was told to wait.

At the 3rd ARVN Division command post, a makeshift aid station had been established and manned by US Navy personnel. HM1 Tom Williamson from the ANGLICO team along with Lieutenant John Lapoint, HMC Donovan Leavitt, HM2 Francis Brown and HM3 James Riddle, all from the naval advisor unit in Da Nang were providing treatment to the wounded. One of their patients had been Lieutenant Colonel Iceal Hambleton. Hearing the call, the Army advisor, SFC Roger Shoemaker, and HM1 Williamson grabbed a M113 armored personnel carrier with a driver and headed out to retrieve Camper and Brown. From the Citadel, it would be a fifteen-minute drive.

"Red Bull Three, a medevac aircraft isn't available, but we have ground coming to your location with medical on board. ETA is fifteen minutes. They're departing now. How copy?"

The driver was reluctant to go to the bridge, but SFC Shoemaker made a convincing argument for the driver to get moving. Drawing his .45-caliber pistol from his holster, Shoemaker placed the muzzle against the Vietnamese soldier's temple. "Look, you little shit, you can drive or you can die. Which option do you choose?" The young soldier spoke no English, but he didn't need to—the message was very clear in any language.

Arriving at Brown and Camper's location, they were quickly loaded and departed south to safety. The 2nd ARVN Regiment was now without a US advisor that could coordinate for close-air support.

* * *

2000 Hours

"Sir, we may have a problem," Davis said, approaching Turner. Although Turner and Davis were the same rank, out of respect for Turner's position, Davis always referred to him as sir. The forward command post was still operational as the trucks to take them out hadn't arrived.

"Let's have it. That's all this day has been."

"At 1810 hours, the 1st Armored Brigade ordered the Rangers to move to Dong Ha Base and set up the new defensive line as well as link up with the 57th ARVN Regiment. When they arrived, they found that the 57th ARVN Regiment was gone," Davis said.

"Where'd the 57th go and why didn't they tell us?" Turner asked with a touch of anger in his voice.

"It seems, sir, that when the 57th saw the tanks that were supporting the Rangers roll past because they were being sent to clear some roadblocks, they thought they were supposed to pull out as well, so they did," Major Davis explained. "We don't know where the 57th is right now, and division rear can't answer the question either. They appear to have just melted away," Davis said with some resignation.

"Have we got contact with Colonel Twitchell?" Turner asked.

"No, sir," Davis replied.

"Where are the tanks that were with and supporting the Rangers? Please don't tell me they've disappeared as well," Turner responded with sarcasm dripping from every word.

"Sir, the tanks that were moving with the Rangers to Dong Ha Base continued down QL1 to the 20th Tank Battalion command post located just north of Vinh Phuoc River and assumed defensive positions on the north side of the Thach Han River Bridge, the last bridge to Quang Tri."

"Who ordered that move?" Turner asked in frustration. He was supposed to be in charge and yet orders were being issued by the 3rd ARVN Division CP in Quang Tri without anyone notifying or going through his headquarters.

"It appears that General Lam has ordered General Giai to open up some roadblocks on QL1 south of here, and he's sending part of the 20th to do that. I heard Giai put up a fuss about cutting some of his combat power, but Lam insisted he do it."

"I don't think Lam has ever left his command post in Hue," Turner indicated, adding, "At least the tanks didn't continue to Saigon. Let's pull everyone in and get an update on where everyone is and their status." It was going to be another long night.

Throughout the night, the NVA continued to push the attack with rockets and artillery. 1st and 8th VNMC were ordered after the staff update to withdraw closer to Ai Tu and did so in an orderly fashion.

* * *

28 April 1972

The 20th Tank was down to only eighteen tanks for the original fifty-two. The 17th and 18th Armored Cav Regiments had lost one-third of their tanks. The Rangers, for all practical purposes, were out of the fight. The northernmost unit was the 1st Armored Brigade, commanded by Lieutenant Colonel Nguyen Tran Luat.

"Underground Six, Rhino Six, over," Lieutenant Colonel Wagner from the 1st Armored Brigade called.

"Rhino Six, Underground Six, over."

"Underground Six, Rhino Six, we have tanks approaching our position and need close-air support, over." 1st Armored Brigade was located at Dong Ha Base. The NVA tanks had come west along Highway 9.

"Roger, Rhino Six, wait one," Turner said and turned to see Major Brookbank giving him a thumbs-up and then five fingers. Tuner got the message. "Rhino Six, Underground Six, you will have support over you in five minutes. Call sign is Bilk Two-One, over." During the night, the 3rd ARVN Forward CP had displaced back to the Citadel, but the staff of advisors had been integrated into the main CP at this point. Turner was just waiting to get an aircraft to fly him to Hue to join Colonel Dorsey.

"Bilk Two-One, roger. Rhino Six out." At 0830, thirty NVA tanks were seen burning. None immediately exposed themselves.

"Colonel, I think we pull back across river now," Colonel Luat said as he watched the burning NVA tanks with some satisfaction. A wide grin accompanied his comment.

"Sir, I believe you're right. It'll take them time to regroup and get reorganized. That'll provide us time to reestablish a defense on the south bank of the river," Lieutenant Colonel Louis Wagner, his US advisor, agreed.

With the pause, Luat ordered his units to pull back across the Thach Han Bridge and establish a defense south of the bridge. The Thach Han River was south of Ai Tu but north of the My Chanh River. Luat and Wagner were north of the bridge and decided to be the last to leave, monitoring and coordinating the withdrawal.

"Okay, that's the last of our vehicles. Let's get out of here," Wagner said, tapping Luat on the shoulder and heading for his vehicle, an M113 armored personnel carrier. Luat also rode in one, and the two moved together. Enemy observers saw the withdrawal and immediately called for artillery fire before Luat and Wagner could get across the bridge.

"Son of a bitch!" Wagner yelled as a round landed in the middle of the bridge and blew a hole in the center span. His driver, a young Vietnamese soldier, said nothing but made a command decision immediately: *Option one, stay on the north side of the river and be captured or killed, or option two, drive very fast and hope to jump the span.* Before Wagner could discuss this latest development with his driver, the driver gunned the engine, getting the M113 up to full speed as quickly as he could. All Wagner could do while standing in the open commander's hatch was to hang on. The M113 jumped the opening at full speed and slammed down on the far side, only to continue at top speed to the south side of the river.

"*Go, go!*" Luat yelled to his driver, having witnessed Wagner's vehicle's maneuver. Luat's driver did the same. Luat's M113 cleared the opening and landed on the far side, much to his and his driver's relief. As it continued to race down the remainder of the bridge, an AT-3 Sagger antitank missile fired from the north side of the river detonated into the vehicle. Luat was badly wounded in the legs and was immediately medevaced from the fight.

Lieutenant Colonel Wagner pulled up alongside Luat's deputy. "Tran, you're now in command." Lieutenant Colonel Tran Tinh was a good officer, but more of an administrator than a combat commander. Wagner quickly noticed that Tinh was displaying a less-then-confident attitude, which Wagner attempted to bolster.

The brigade continued to move south towards Ai Tu, but it was increasingly difficult as refugees were clogging the road. QL1 was the main and only road running north to south and a magnet for refugees attempting to avoid the fighting as well as ARVN soldiers that had panicked and run. Mixed with the people were also cars, trucks, bikes, carts, and water buffalo, and all were moving south. Arriving at the Ai Tu compound, which was astride QL1, Wagner found the reason for the mass of refugees. Someone had ordered that the gates be closed and guarded by Vietnamese Marines with orders not to open them to anyone. Wagner argued with the guards, to no avail. Finally, he got on the radio to 3rd ARVN Division main command post at the Citadel.

"Metcalf, have you got any idea what kind of a clusterfuck

this is up here? The Marines have orders not to let anyone through and the road is backed up for miles with refugees," Wagner exclaimed.

"General Giai is concerned about the number of refugees flowing into Quang Tri and moving down QL1. That's why he isn't allowing anyone else to come south," Metcalf stated.

"Well, he's doing a fine job of keeping out all tanks north of Ai Tu and is about to be overrun if we don't get through these gates. Tell him that," Wagner practically screamed.

A few minutes later, a Marine officer from the 258th came out and opened the gate enough to allow Wagner and Tinh to pass with one jeep to proceed to the command bunker at the Citadel. Reaching the command bunker, Wagner went and spoke to General Giai and Colonel Metcalf.

"Sir, the situation is that we destroyed the armor column on Route 9, but there's a lot more coming down that road. QL1 is backed up forward of Ai Tu with refugees, abandoned vehicles, and dead water buffalo, not to mention all the dead civilians from the indiscriminate artillery being thrown. All that's stacked up in front of our unit, and we can't get through. If that gate isn't opened, then we stand a good chance of being sitting ducks when the armor column starts moving again," Wagner pointed out.

"Colonel, we will counterattack soon and cannot allow all the refugees to come into Quang Tri. They will present an impossible situation for us. No, we must keep the gate closed," Giai said. Wagner looked to Metcalf to talk some sense into the Vietnamese general.

"Colonel...," Wagner pleaded, but Metcalf just shrugged. Wagner continued to plead his case for another thirty minutes, but Giai wouldn't budge. Wagner was beside himself with frustration. He could just picture the NVA armor rolling up behind this mass of refugees and opening fire on them as well as the remains of 1st Armored Brigade.

Returning to Ai Tu, Wagner met with Colonel Bao, the commander of the 147th VNMC Brigade, which had responsibility for the defense of Ai Tu.

"Sir, I've talked to General Giai and he won't budge on opening the gate," Colonel Wagner explained to Colonel Bao. Major Joy was present; Tinh had returned to his command vehicle.

"Colonel, if we don't open the gate and let these people through, Colonel Tinh's force is going to be hit in the rear by the approaching armor. He won't be able to assist in the defense here. Numerous civilians will be killed as well. Sir, if you allow the civilians to flow through, we can get Colonel Tinh's force through and assist in your defense here," Major Joy pointed out. He wasn't sure if he did any better at convincing Colonel Bao to open the gate than he had at convincing General Giai.

After a few minutes, Bao said, "I will order that the gate be opened. General Giai is not on the scene and I have not been able to get him here to observe for himself. Once Colonel Tinh's force is through the gate, we will close it. Have him report to me when he is through."

By 1600, the roadblock of refugees was clear and QL1 was again open, just in time for new orders. Major Joy had the foresight to send all of his advisors except Major Huff and Captain Kruger to Quang Tri City to establish a new command post to support the possible withdrawal.

"Major Joy," Colonel Bao said, getting the major's attention as he watched the last of Colonel Tinh's force move through the gate.

"Yes, sir," Joy replied. He liked Colonel Bao, who he found to be a dedicated combat commander, unlike some of the ARVN commanders he had seen.

"We are receiving the 7th Battalion from the 369th Brigade.[1] They are moving north from Firebase Jane. Two companies have closed into Quang Tri, but one company is bogged down in an ambush south of the city. Also the ten M48 tanks from the 20th Tank that went south earlier today will be coming back to us. I suspect that they will be here after dark. Let's talk with Tinh and see where we can best use them," Colonel Bao stated, but he didn't look happy about receiving reinforcements. Joy had worked with him long enough to read that something was wrong.

"Okay, sir, that's good, but what are you not telling me? Why not let Tinh just position those returning tanks?" Joy asked.

"We are keeping the 4th and 5th Ranger Battalions and 20th Tank, but 1st Armored Brigade is to move southeast of Quang Tri and assume a new defensive position. I'm issuing the orders to 1st Armored Brigade now," Bao indicated.

Bao then returned to the CP, while Joy took off to find Wagner. "Hey, sir," Joy said, approaching Wagner's vehicle.

"I understand we're moving on to the south, Major," Wagner said before Joy could say anything else.

"Yes, sir, I just spoke with Bao and he's not happy about it, but he wasn't able to get it turned around. When you get down there, you may find the 57th ARVN Regiment, but don't count on it. Last I heard they were supposed to be between the Thach Han and QL1 bridge on the south side of the river there."

"I'll contact Metcalf and see what he can tell me when we get down there," Wagner said as he climbed into his track. "That is, if he knows anything," he added with sarcasm.

By 2000 hours, the 1st Armored Brigade had established a defensive position one mile south of Quang Tri City and settled in for the night.

32

QUANG TRI BRIDGE

29 APRIL 1972
2nd Battalion, 2nd ARVN Regiment
Quang Tri Bridge

The 2nd Battalion, 2nd ARVN Regiment, had assumed the defense of the Quang Tri Bridge on the north side of the river and was securing the north approach to the bridge. Lieutenant Colonel Camper had been medevacked and Major Brown had departed with him, so no advisors were with the 2nd ARVN Regiment. At 0100 hours, they were attacked with the usual artillery barrage followed by ground assault. One thing the NVA had been demonstrating throughout the battle thus far was their ability to coordinate ground assault with artillery support. By 0300, the 3rd Battalion, 2nd ARVN, was in contact. Reports sporadically flowed into the command posts at 3rd ARVN Division, but with no advisors now with the 2nd ARVN Regiment, an accurate assessment of the situation couldn't be made. Throughout the night, US Air Force FACs maintained close-air over the area, destroying five enemy tanks in the process. More could have been done if an advisor had been on the ground. Communications within the ARVN structure was faulty at best.

"General, we don't have an accurate picture of what's going on at the Quang Tri Bridge. I don't have any advisors in the 2nd Regiment, and comms with the regiment aren't good. I recommend we get another unit there that we can talk to and who can give us a better assessment of the situation," Metcalf pointed out.[1]

"Who do you recommend we send?" Giai asked. Metcalf moved to the operations map that supposedly had the accurate locations for each of the units.

"The 2nd Troop, 18th Armored Cav, is the closest to the bridge. They should be sent to reinforce the 2nd ARVN Regiment," Metcalf recommended. Giai walked over and studied the operations map for a few minutes.

"I think that would be wise. I will order it now," Giai said and went to find his operations officer.

Arriving at first light, the troop commander reported that no one was at the bridge to reinforce. His transmission was monitored by the NVA, and immediately an order was issued to attack as no one was defending the bridge. The 2nd Troop engaged the NVA forces attempting to get onto the bridge and notified the 18th Armored Cav commander, who notified 3rd ARVN Division.

"General Giai, we've got to reinforce the 2nd Troop now," Metcalf pointed out. "If we lose that bridge, the door to Quang Tri is wide open."

"Who do you recommend?" Giai asked.

Does this guy ever make a decision on his own? Metcalf thought. "Sir, the 147th Marines are here," he said, pointing at the map. "Send them. I'll notify Major Joy to get them ready."

"I concur. They're the best at this point," Giai stated and so ordered. Major Joy got the word before Colonel Bao.

"Major Joy here, sir."

"Major, this is Colonel Metcalf. The 147th is about to get an order to move and join up with 2nd Troop 18th at the Quang Tri Bridge. Seems no one was there when the troop arrived and now we have a full-scale attack on the bridge. Can Bao move now?"

"Sir, I believe he's getting the order right now, and we will be moving shortly, I'm sure," Joy said as he watched Colonel Bao issue orders.

"Good, let me know when you're at the bridge and can give me an assessment," Metcalf directed and hung up. Joy replaced the receiver and looked at Colonel Bao, who motioned him to approach.

"I take it Metcalf called you," Bao stated.

"Yes, sir, he said there was no one at the bridge and only a cav troop was holding it now."

"That is what I heard. I will send 7th Battalion as it is the closest to the bridge. General Giai also wants me to send some of 20th Tank, which I have attached to 7th Battalion. Can we get some air support as well?"

"Sir, I'll send Major DeBona with the 7th. He's been working with them all along and can provide air support. I'll have to see if we can get naval gunfire to support."

Almost immediately, 147th VNMC moved into action, ordering the 7th Battalion to get to the bridge. 20th Tank sent vehicles as well.

"Pegasus Six, Pegasus Three," Major DeBona transmitted.

"Pegasus Three, Pegasus Six," Major Joy replied with his new call sign. At this point it was well known that the NVA had captured US radios and codebooks. To confuse them, advisors were dreaming up different call signs depending on the mission and time of day.

"Pegasus Six, we are in position north of the objective with two companies plus tanks. The troop appears to be holding and we are stepping off. How copy?" Major DeBona said. Prior to his departure, they had discussed that the 7th Battalion would send two companies with supporting tanks to approach the Thach Han Bridge from the north and come in on the flank and rear of the NVA units. This would cause the enemy to fight in two directions, which was never a favorable situation to be facing. Joy was monitoring the radio traffic between the 7th Battalion and the regiment CP. All appeared to be going well for the 7th.

Late that afternoon, everyone was breathing a bit easier as the bridge appeared to be secured when artillery rounds began hitting around Ai Tu. The massive explosions told everyone in the command post that things had just turned for the worse.

"What's that?" Joy said as the dust settled around him, only to be raised again by another explosion.

"I think the ammo dump just got hit," Smith exclaimed, moving cautiously towards the door to be greeted by another explosion. "Yep, they hit the ammo dump." The ammo dump at Ai Tu had well over a thousand rounds of artillery ammunition as well as small arms. Once the ammo was hit, a chain reaction occurred as exploding rounds set off other rounds. No one dared to approach the inferno.

"Major Joy," Colonel Bao said, getting Joy's attention.

"Sir, I don't think we can stay here now. With the ammo dump exploding, it's not safe for the troops to be near it, and we're not going to have much ammo left after it is safe to go near it," Joy said before the colonel could voice the same opinion.

"I will notify General Giai that this position is no longer tenable. We must pull back," Bao said with some resignation in his voice.

QL1 still had a mass of refugees as another roadblock

south of the bridge had been established by the NVA. The mass that had been at Ai Tu had migrated south of the city and become the target of NVA artillery observers. It was evident that the mass on QL1 were civilians, but NVA forward observers called for artillery fire nonetheless. The civilians had no chance of survival as artillery rounds slammed into them. The advisors that witnessed this slaughter all concluded this was a war crime. Inexcusable. Bodies, whole and in pieces, littered the road. Children, women, the elderly lay scattered on the road and in the adjacent fields and ditches. Over two thousand civilians were killed.

* * *

0200 Hours
    30 April 1972

"Pegasus Six, Pegasus Five," Major Huff called. He had been with the 8th Battalion since it had taken up its position out of Ai Tu.

"Pegasus Five, Pegasus Six, go ahead."

"Hey, Six, we got a guy that we policed up a couple of hours ago that was at Carroll. He managed to escape. He's telling us that there's an NVA regiment with twenty tanks in an assembly area southwest of Ai Tu. He showed us on the map where it's at. Think we can get some tac air on it or naval gunfire? Over."

"Five, send me the coordinates and let me see if I can get a FAC over you, over." And Major Huff sent the coordinates of the enemy position.

A few minutes later, the response came. "Pegasus Five, Pegasus Six, over."

"Six, this is Five, over."

"Five, this is out of range for naval gunfire, and our artillery is critically low on ammo. A FAC has the info and is moving to the location. It appears that this isn't near you, so you won't be able to observe, but I'll get a cav team out in the morning to give us a BDA. Over."

"Roger, Six, sounds good. Five out." Tac air was called in and struck the enemy position. In a panic, NVA soldiers ran into the 1st Vietnamese Marine Battalion positions in order to escape the napalm and bombs.

* * *

At first light, Colonel Chung, commander of the 369th VNMC Brigade, received a call from General Giai. "Colonel, it appears that there is a roadblock on QL1, north of your position to Quang Tri. We need that road cleared. I want you to send a force up to clear the road. Who could you send?" Giai asked.

"I can send the 5th Battalion along with some M48s and M113s. I will alert them and get them moving," Chung replied. At the same time, Metcalf was on the advisor phone, talking to Major Price.

"Colonel Metcalf here. Giai is having the 369th send a unit up QL1 to clear the road to Quang Tri. I understand you're the advisor with that unit. Is that correct?"

I've only been the advisor with this unit for the past four months and he's asking me, Price thought. "Yes, sir, and have been for the past four months," Price replied, but the sarcasm was lost on Metcalf.

"Alright, I want you to keep me posted on their progress. We need that road opened or a lot of folks are going to be cut off above the O Khe River," Metcalf ordered and hung up before Price could respond.

Major Price and the battalion commander discussed their

plan prior to departing. As the convoy of M48 tanks and M113 APCs rolled out, Major Price chose to ride in one of the lead vehicles. The first vehicle was an M48 tank, but with an infantry squad scouting ahead of the vehicle. Approaching the bridge, the scouts triggered the ambush that they had been anticipating. They hadn't anticipated that the ambush would have recoilless rifles. The recoilless rifles were supported with RPGs and automatic weapons. Dismounting from the M113, Major Price, carrying his AN/PRC-77 FM radio, moved forward to observe the ambush site. What he saw was what he'd expected; what he heard was not, as the sound of a tank was clearly heard.

"Thunder, Thunder, fire mission, over." Thunder was the USS *Newport News* sitting one mile off the coast and within range of this ambush site with her nine eight-inch guns.

"Station calling Thunder, identify and send."

Major Price sent the fire mission. As the USS *Newport News* sounded off with a broadside, Price contacted a FAC working the area and was told it would be an hour before any aircraft would be available. As he communicated with the FAC, he heard a sound that everyone dreaded. "*Incoming!*" he yelled. The Vietnamese Marines might not have spoken English, but that was one word they all understood. Almost immediately, NVA 130mm artillery rounds began impacting in the vicinity of the convoy. Suddenly, those artillery guns became a higher priority to Price than a single tank or the ambush site.

"Blink Four-Five, Rover Three, over," Price transmitted to the FAC.

"Rover Three, Blink Four-Five, go ahead."

"Blink Four-Five, we are receiving artillery fire. Can you see the guns? Over."

"Rover Three, I'm at eight thousand and have negative

sightings. Let me drop down and see if I can. Wait one," Blink reported.

Great, drop down and take an SA-7 right in the ass, Price thought, but he had to get the NVA artillery stopped. He scanned the sky, attempting to see the OV-10 Bronco. Silently, he prayed that the Bronco wouldn't be hit by an SA-7 as one aircraft had already been lost.

"Rover Three, Blink Four-Five, over."

"Blink Four-Five, Rover Three, over."

"Rover, are you ready to copy?"

"Roger, Blink, send," Price said as he pulled out a grease pencil and prepared to write on his map. Blink sent the coordinates of what he had found, two artillery guns. Quickly Price sent the new coordinates to the *Newport News*, which adjusted its guns to lay on the new target.

"Rover Three, Blink Four-Five, over."

"Go ahead, Blink."

"Rover Three, looks like you nailed it. Over."

"Blink, thank you much for—" Price didn't get to finish as two more artillery rounds landed very close to his position.

"Blink, Rover, we have more incoming. There must be more guns. Over," Price yelled into the receiver.

"Rover, roger. I'll take another look. Wait one," Blink replied.

Wait one? Where does he think I'm going? flashed through Price's mind as two more rounds impacted. *Son of a bitch, they're trying to bracket us.*

"Rover Three, Blink Four-Five. I have new coordinates for you. Are you ready?"

This kept up for an hour. As the FAC would find two guns and help destroy them, two more guns in a separate location would open fire. Finally two F-4 jets arrived on station and began using napalm on the ridgeline along which the guns were located. That silenced the last of the artillery holding

Price up. The 5th Battalion remounted the track vehicles and proceeded north across the bridge. Major Price was feeling pretty good that few casualties had been taken and none serious. He was confident that the last of the problems were over. He was wrong.

Moving up QL1 and having crossed the O Khe River Bridge, the 5th Battalion approached the hamlet of Hai Lang. Hai Lang had been an ARVN camp adjacent to QL1. Thinking that it was still an ARVN outpost, the column approached, only to receive a hail of enemy fire. Dismounting again, Major Price called Blink Four-Five. "Blink Four-Five, Rover Three, over."

"Rover Three, Blink Four-Five, over."

"Blink Four-Five, I have a target for you, over."

"Rover, send it." And Price sent the coordinates and a description of the target to Blink.

"Rover Three, Blink Four-Fiver."

"Go ahead, Blink."

"Three, contact Spectre Two-Oh on four-oh-five-five. How copy?" Blink said. Spectre Two-Oh was an AC-130 Spectre gunship eager for some work, and Price was eager to give him some work.

"Spectre Two-Oh, Rover Three, over."

"Rover Three, Spectre Two-Oh, understand you have a target for me. Over."

"Roger." Price sent him a description and the coordinates of the compound. Moments later, Spectre appeared at about two thousand feet and engaged with his 20mm Gatling guns. His 105mm howitzer that was computer-controlled targeted the compound as well. The extreme accuracy of this weapon was devastating to the NVA. While Spectre was engaging, a flight of F-4 Phantom jets arrived and commenced pulverizing the hamlet with bombs and napalm. Once the Phantom jets had expended their ordnance, Spectre resumed his engagement, but the NVA that hadn't been killed had had enough and attempted to flee in every direction, like mice released from a box, right into the waiting Marines of the 5th Battalion. At this point, the 5th Battalion, low on ammo and fuel and with the road clogged with refugees, decided that they couldn't reach Quang Tri. They were ordered back to the north side of the O Khe Bridge and assumed a defensive posture.

As the morning wore on, General Giai felt that the situation north of the Thach Han River was such that he needed to do something. He had spoken with Colonel Bao about the situation at Ai Tu and agreed with his assessment.

"Colonel Metcalf, I have instructed all commanders to come to the division command post at twelve hundred hours for a meeting. I have made some decisions but do not wish to transmit them as the enemy is listening to our communications," Giai said.

"And the purpose of your meeting, sir?" Metcalf asked.

"The situation is such that our defense north of the Thach Han River is very, how you say, shaky. I want to get them back here and go over new plan." And Giai went over his new plan with Metcalf. "I spoke with Colonel Bao earlier. I agree we cannot hold Ai Tu now that the ammo dump has been destroyed. I have instructed him to withdraw back to Quang Tri and provide a defensive force and secure lines of communications south out of the city. His unit should begin the move shortly."

* * *

1200 Hours

. . .

At 1200 hours, the brigade commanders were present at the 3rd ARVN Division command post located in the Quang Tri Citadel. Giai stepped to the front of the room and everyone quieted down. He surveyed the commanders and could see they were all tired, but so was he.

"Gentlemen, I believe the situation has reached a point where it is no longer feasible to attempt to defend our salient north of the Thach Han River but need to pull back and assume new positions around Quang Tri. I say this because I believe that the enemy will start a new push very soon, with the main attack coming from the west and supporting attacks from the north. We are experiencing a shortage of supplies at this point. We lost the ammo dump at Ai Tu and have less than one thousand artillery rounds left. Ambushes along QL1 are preventing resupply convoys from coming north, so we are low on fuel, ammo and food. We have a major refugee problem moving south on QL1, which further hampers our ability to move supplies north, and they need food as well. We have lost a great deal of artillery, especially with the loss of Carroll, which had the 175mm howitzers. Some of that artillery is now being used against our own people. We have seen an increase in his air-defense weapons, which are hampering our ability to be resupplied by helicopters. And lastly, I fear that his western attacks may encircle us and cut us off from exiting to the south," Giai said, pausing to let his remarks sink in. No one said anything. "The plan now is for 147th VNMC Brigade to move and defend north of Quang Tri against 304th NVA Division. The 56th, 57th and 2nd ARVN Regiments and the Ranger battalions will defend on the south bank of the Thach Han River," Giai instructed, pointing out specific locations and sectors for each unit. There were no commanders for either the reconstituted 56th Regiment or the Ranger battalions present.

"The 1st Armored Brigade and the 17th and 18th

Armored Cav will open QL1 to the south towards Hue and prevent enemy forces from blocking the highway," Giai concluded. There were no questions.

Major Joy and Colonel Bao had attended the meeting. At the conclusion, Colonel Bao contacted Lieutenant Colonel Phuc, deputy commander of the 147th Brigade, and told him to get Major Huff and come to the Citadel. In the meantime, Joy and Bao conducted a recon of Quang Tri City. They needed a location for the 147th command post. The decision was to take over the compound that MACV Advisory Team 19 had occupied. When Phuc and Huff arrived, they were briefed and told to go back to Ai Tu and execute the plan to bring the regiment to Quang Tri. Bao decided to remain in Quang Tri City and prepare to establish his new headquarters.

"Sir, wouldn't it be best if you went back to Ai Tu and supervised the movement?" Major Joy commented.

"Lieutenant Colonel Phuc can supervise the movement. I'll get things set up here," Bao responded.

"Sir, you should be at the point where you can best influence events. Being here to set up the command post, should something go wrong—"

"Major Joy," Bao said in his most fatherly voice, "everything is in order. It is a simple move and will occur smoothly. Not to worry."

Prior to reaching Ai Tu, 3rd Division issued the execute order before Phuc and Huff could return. With both the commander and deputy commander absent, there was some confusion as to what to do. The operations officer attempted to contact both Phuc and Bao but was unsuccessful. The order was issued based on intelligence that a major attack would be launched that evening by the 304th NVA Division. In the absence of guidance, the operations officer prepared and issued the orders for the regiment. The order of march was the brigade headquarters and brigade artillery battalion with the

1st VNMC Battalion, followed by 8th VNMC Battalion, and the 4th VNMC Battalion serving as rear guard. This was an orderly process. The advisors, Major Huff and Captain Kruger, destroyed classified documents with thermite grenades and joined the 4th Battalion as they withdrew. Captain Kruger and Major Huff directed air strikes, naval gunfire and artillery, keeping the NVA at bay as the 4th cleared the southern perimeter of Ai Tu Base Camp in an orderly fashion.

All was going according to plan, but that soon changed. When the 147th Regiment lead elements reached the two bridges over the Thach Han River, they discovered that the ARVN engineers had blown the bridges earlier. The 147th was trapped north of the river. Getting people across the river was going to be difficult in the swift water but not impossible. Getting eighteen howitzers and twenty-two vehicles across, on the other hand, was going to be impossible.

"Shit," Kruger exclaimed when he saw the bridges. "How are we going to get the tanks across?"

"Unless we find a ford site, we ain't," Huff said, turning to the company commander. Shortly afterwards, scouts were heading down the river, looking for a fording site.

"Good news, Dai'uy," the company commander said as he approached an hour later. "We have crossing site one klick north of bridge. Tanks can cross there."

"Great, but what about trucks and howitzers?" Kruger asked, ever hopeful.

"No can do" was the answer. North of the bridges, eighteen tanks were able to ford the river. As the fording operation commenced, a recoilless rifle opened fire and destroyed one tank waiting to cross. Another tank climbing out of the river struck a mine and was destroyed.

"Well, we got sixteen safely over the river. Now for the fun part. Do you think these guys know how to swim? This water is high and swift. We could lose some," Kruger pointed out.

"Let's string a line across the river and have them enter upstream to swim," Huff replied. "If they get pushed down, the line may offer a safety measure they can catch and pull themselves over. I'll swim over with a light line and pull over a heavy rope. Let's get this set up."

With that, the two American advisors began stringing a line across the swift-flowing Thach Han River. The rains had filled the river, which was now running swift and cool. Huff entered and easily swam to the far side, pulling a light line with him. Reaching the other side, he pulled over a much larger line and tied it off. Kruger then started the young Marines across. Most of the Marines were able to cross the river with their equipment, but the heavy equipment remained on the trucks with the artillery howitzers.

Reaching the far side, 147th Brigade occupied its assigned defensive positions by nightfall with 1st VNMC Battalion on the west, 4th VNMC Battalion on the eastern and southern approaches, and 8th VNMC battalion on the north. As 147th moved south across the Thach Ha River, word reached the ARVN units that a withdrawal was in progress. Some units panicked and abandoned their positions although they were south of the Thach Han River. Command of the situation was completely absent. Within the Citadel there was a total breakdown in the division staff and the Advisory Team 155. The 3rd ARVN Division command center was in a bunker fifty yards away from the Team 155 bunker, and the only interaction was between Colonel Metcalf and General Giai. Division staff officers weren't capable of talking to their American advisors. The division was receiving reports from each battalion and not from regimental headquarters. The advisor team was getting reports from advisors in the field that were different from what the division staff was receiving from commanders. Chaos was in control.

One advisor that had only arrived the week before took

matters into his own hands. Major Borman, a new naval gunfire officer for MR-1, quickly found it impossible to operate effectively by running from the advisor command center to the division command center. He strung a telephone line between the advisor bunker and the artillery officer for 3rd ARVN Division. Borman would receive calls for fire from Marine advisors and FACs and was able to coordinate with his Vietnamese counterpart. However, there was no formal fire support plan. Formal guidance from Metcalf was "Everything outside this circle around the Citadel is a free-fire zone."[2]

* * *

1 May 1972

"Colonel Metcalf, we have a new intelligence report," Giai said, handing a message to Metcalf, who couldn't read Vietnamese. "It say we get hit with ten-thousand-round artillery barrage starting at 1700."

"We should alert the units and prepare as much as we can here to protect the command bunkers. Let the units prepare their positions as best they can," Metcalf advised. Giai absorbed the recommendation but didn't respond. Metcalf returned to the advisor compound to discuss the upcoming barrage with the advisors.

"Where Colonel Metcalf?" the division chief of staff asked as he walked into the advisor team command post. It was 1215 hours.

"Sir, he's in the back. I'll get him for you," the team watch officer said.

"Please, I must speak," the chief of staff stated. A few minutes later, the watch officer came back and indicated that Colonel Metcalf would be right out. The chief of staff had seldom ever been in the advisor team command post, so everyone on watch was curious as to what this was all about.

"Colonel, how can I help you?" Metcalf asked, wiping the crumbs from his mouth.

"Colonel, may I use your radios to make announcement? We have difficulty with ours."

"Sure," Metcalf said, not sure what was going on and pointing to the advisor command radio. The operator handed the chief of staff the mike.

"General Giai has released all commanders to fight their way to the My Chanh River."[3] Without another word, the chief of staff turned and walked out of the advisor command post. After the shock wore off, Metcalf grabbed his helmet and headed to the division command post to observe the chaos. A shouting match was in progress between the division staff and General Giai. General Lam, the corps commander, was on the radio countermanding the order to withdraw as soon as he heard it. Evidently Corps had been notified of the intended withdrawal, but it wasn't clear to Metcalf who had notified them. When General Lam attempted to countermand the order, the staff told Giai he could stay and die, but they were out of there. Metcalf began to think that the chief of staff had ordered the withdrawal without discussing it with Giai. Within an hour, there was confusion everywhere as units pulled out with no withdrawal plan. Every man for himself was the order of the day for the ARVN units. Brigade 147 commenced to withdraw as well but in an orderly fashion while remaining a cohesive fighting force. Metcalf gave the advisors an option to run or stay with their units. They stayed, for the moment. From the advisor command post, the advisors could only watch as the Vietnamese scrambled to get out of Quang Tri.

Giai loaded up an M113 and departed along with two other M113s carrying part of the division staff. He had coordinated with Major Joy to link up with the 147th Brigade at 1300 hours and move down QL1 with them. When it became obvious that no linkup was going to happen, Metcalf suggested that the advisors with the 147th could fly out with him. All stayed with their units. At the advisor command post, there were over one hundred people that needed extraction. Metcalf was on the phone with MG Kroesen at FRAC headquarters, explaining the situation. FRAC hadn't been informed by General Lam or the I Corps staff. To everyone's surprise, General Giai returned in his M113. It seemed the roads were so blocked with refugees, vehicles, and panicked soldiers that he couldn't get through. Stepping out of his M113, he approached Colonel Metcalf.

"Colonel, you call helicopter to come get me. I go now," Giai said in the form of an order. Metcalf returned to the command post and requested air evacuation for everyone. MG Kroesen, understanding the situation, forwarded a request for the evacuation. While they waited and destroyed documents, Major Borman attempted several times to contact the 147th Brigade, with no success. Finally, the commercial phone rang and he answered.

"Major Borman, naval gunfire support officer. How can I help you?"

"Hey, it's Major Clibber here at I Corps in Hue. How's it going up there?"

Borman immediately recognized it was a social call and ripped the phone off the wall.

* * *

1630 Hours

. . .

The sound of rotor blades beating the air into submission could be heard as three USAF rescue helicopters with two AH-1G gunships and tac air arrived over the Citadel to take out the one hundred and twenty personnel remaining. The first CH-53 landed, and immediately Giai was aboard. Metcalf and Borman were the last US personnel out of the Citadel, only one step ahead of NVA soldiers moving in.

33

THE LONG RETREAT

1 MAY 1972
147th Regiment
Long Hung, South Vietnam

When the planned linkup with Giai didn't occur, Colonel Bao decided they could wait no longer. Bao hadn't been informed that Giai had returned to the Citadel and was flying out. He surveyed QL1 and didn't like what he saw. Vehicles bumper to bumper, three abreast, stalled, damaged and out of gas. ARVN soldiers with no weapons or equipment fleeing south. Civilians walking with carts, strollers, and some personal baggage. Oxcarts lumbering on the edge of the road, and bodies torn to pieces by the NVA's indiscriminate artillery strikes.

"Major Joy, we no go down road. I call it Highway of Horror. Let's have a meeting with battalion commanders and plan our next move," Colonel Bao said, and Joy called the advisors together to hear Bao's guidance.

"We will move east two thousand meters to avoid QL1 and then turn south and head to Hai Lang area. There are no friendly forces north of us, so we must move quickly but tactically. We have about ten klicks to move, so let's move out in ten minutes," Colonel Bao said.

No one opposed his guidance, and all acknowledged they understood the plan. Joy took a position with Bao and the other advisors returned to the battalions. As the artillery had left their howitzers at the river, they were now basically an infantry unit and provided security around the brigade command element. The order of march remained the same, with the brigade command group and artillerymen in the lead, followed by 1st Battalion, 8th Battalion and 4th Battalion. The route of march wasn't easy, with several small stream crossings required. It was after dark when they reached the Hai Lang area. People were tired.

Bao pulled in his subordinates as they closed in on the Hai Lang area. Some commanders were for pushing on towards Hue. Others were for stopping for the night. A very heated discussion was observed by Joy and the other advisors, but Bao commanded, and a tight perimeter defense was established for the night. Part of the discussion revolved around the fact that, of the sixteen tanks that had gotten across the river, ten M48 tanks had been lost in the move south. Some were lost to enemy fire and some in the attempts to cross the streams. Only six of the original eighteen that had left Dong Ha were still operational. Joy determined that the main concern was security if they were hit by a large NVA force.

"Colonel, if I may," Joy spoke up.

"Yes, Major," Bao allowed.

"Sir, would they feel better if I can get a Spectre gunship up over us for the night?" Joy asked, and immediately he observed some renewed confidence in those commanders that had pushed for moving on through the night.

"Please do, Major," Bao said.

Joy immediately went to his radio and contacted Major

Borman, who had been attempting to get Joy on the radio and was setting up in a new location in the vicinity of Hue. When he received the call, he was relieved that Joy and the others were okay. He was on the phone moments later, forwarding Joy's request for Spectre gunship support for the night. The request was granted and the droning sound overhead throughout the night was reassuring.

Wanting to know the status of others in the withdrawal, Joy contacted Major Robert Sheridan, VNMC Brigade 369 senior advisor.

"Badger Six, Black Bear Six, over," Joy transmitted, using the new call signs they'd all decided to use once the withdrawal had started, knowing all the US communications equipment left behind was now in the hands of the enemy.

"Black Bear Six, Badger Six, over," Sheridan responded.

"Badger Six, what is your status? Over," Joy asked.

"Black Bear Six, we're moving at this time. Not staying in the same place two nights in a row. Still holding our objective but moving around a lot. Charlie likes to target our one-oh-fives, so we keep them moving. This way is open but a lot of traffic on the Red Ball. We have indications that you may have company in the Hai Lang area. What is your status? Over."

Red Ball was the code for QL1. The 369th Brigade was keeping the O Khe and My Chanh bridges open and secured as the refugee flow moved down QL1. Colonel Chung antici-pated being hit hard in the coming days as his unit was guarding the only bridges over the O Khe and My Chanh Rivers. His Marines were placing antitank mines along the sides of the road, registering suspected assembly areas and attack positions with naval gunfire as well as artillery and preparing defensive battalion blocking positions along the south side of the My Chanh River.

"Badger Six, we're holding for the night. Will move at first light and come your way. We're good and have a guardian angel overhead. Will call you when we move out and head your way. Black Bear Six out."

* * *

2 May 1972

Troops began stirring as the eastern sky showed traces of light. No one got much sleep as the brigade had fifty percent manning throughout the night. Stand-to was at 0400 and everyone was expected to be awake and in their hasty fighting positions, ready to repel any attack. None came during the night, not even probes. Spectre was even quiet for most of the night. Joy and some of the other advisors were enjoying a hot cup of coffee that they had made with their canteen cups, heat tab and instant C coffee. The edible portion of the C rations had run out two days ago.

"Everyone ready to move out?" Joy asked. He received affirmative nods from everyone. *No comments—they must be tired. I am.* "I talked to Sheridan last night. They're holding the bridges at O Khe and My Chanh. He did say for us to be aware that they have reports of NVA forces in this area," he concluded.

"Great, that's all we need—a running gun fight to get to the bridges," Boomer commented.

"Let's hope it doesn't come to that. So far Colonel Bao has done pretty good holding it all together. Last night got a bit testy, but they're tired," Huff chimed in. As they continued to discuss the plan for the day, Colonel Bao's deputy trotted over in a low crouch.

"Major Joy, Colonel needs to see you," he said. Joy took a final swallow of his coffee and left with the deputy.

Approaching Colonel Bao, who was on a radio, Joy waited until the colonel was done.

"Major, 1st Battalion is reporting tank noise close to their positions and to the west. We will maintain everyone in their positions now until we hear no more," Colonel Bao explained.

"Sir, I'll get the advisors back to the units," Joy responded.

Arriving back at the group, Joy told them what Bao had just related and they all departed to get back to the units. An hour later, Joy got a call from Kruger with the 8th Battalion.

"Black Bear Six, Sugar Bear Three," Kruger called.

"Go ahead, Sugar Bear."

"Black Bear, we have tanks moving towards the O Khe Bridge across our intended route of march. Over."

"Sugar Bear, roger, I've just been informed by my counterpart. He wants to hunker down for another hour and see what develops. Over."

"Roger, Black Bear, Sugar Bear out."

Joy made a net call and informed the other advisors of the turn of events. They didn't have long to wait. Within an hour, the perimeter was receiving light small-arms fire from the northwest. It quickly built into a major firefight when heavy automatic weapons and RPGs began an engagement from the east. The Marines of the 147th Marine Brigade quickly realized they were surrounded. As the volume of fire increased, so did the caliber of the enemy weapons. Soon recoilless rifle fire was impacting around the remaining tanks and M113s. The crews began to panic. Vehicles took off, breaking out to the perimeter, only to be quickly destroyed. When the Marines saw the armor and ARVNs leaving, they began to leave as well. Despite the best efforts of the chain of command, all discipline and cohesion broke down.

Joy and Huff were in one M113 that bolted. "Stop," Joy screamed, but the driver wasn't listening. "Jump," Joy yelled to Huff, and both went over the side of the runaway APC. It disappeared in a cloud of dust. As the following APCs came upon Joy, he yelled to the other advisor to jump and join him. He had a radio. All but two Army advisors did so. One civilian that had worked for DoD and been caught in Quang Tri when the withdrawal had started also made the jump.

Joy made the jump with his radio, knowing that was his only connection to safety at this point. He contacted a FAC that had been working above his position.

"Blink Four-Five, Black Bear Six, over," Joy called.

"Black Bear Six, Blink Four-Five. Be advised you have tanks approaching your position approximately ten minutes out. I'm bringing a surprise to them, but you need to move. Over."

"Blink Four-Five, we're surrounded. Can you get us a ride out? Over." *If I don't ask...*, Joy was thinking.

"Black Bear Six, Blink Four-Five, wait one."

* * *

Major Sheridan crouched lower in his foxhole as an intense artillery barrage fell on the 369th Brigade overwatching the O Khe and My Chanh Bridges. Major Jim Beans was the advisor for the 9th Battalion and north of the O Khe River bridge. Sheridan was in a position south of the My Chanh River Bridge. Major Price, with the 5th Battalion was three thousand meters south of Price's position and on the north side of the My Chanh River.

"Badger Six, Badger Three" came loud over the radio. The sounds of automatic weapons could be clearly heard, and they sounded close. They also heard the distinctive sound of an AK-47 mixed with the sounds of multiple M16s.

"Badger Three, go."

"Badger Six, we have infantry and tanks approaching —*shit.*" And the radio went silent.

"Badger Three, Badger Six," Sheridan said, getting no response. "Badger Three, Badger Six, over."

"Badger Six, we're pulling back. Be advised we have bad guys between you and me. We're moving to the bridge." Looking over the rim of his foxhole, Sheridan could see that a running gun battle was being conducted north of the bridge. Panic-stricken civilians as well as demoralized ARVN soldiers were all racing to get across the one remaining bridge over the My Chanh River. Suddenly a T-54 tank pulled onto the road and turned north in an apparent attempt to cut off the retreating Marines of the 369th Brigade. Before he could fire his main gun, a pair of M72 LAWs slammed into the side, causing the interior ammunition to explode. None of the crew members exited the tank.

Come on, guys, get your asses back across the river, Sheridan thought as he watched.

* * *

As Joy and Huff waited for an answer on their request for extraction, Joy worked with the FAC to deliver air strikes. On another radio, Huff was talking to Major Borman, working naval gunfire support.

"Do you hear that?" Huff asked.

Joy cocked his head to hear better. "Sounds like a helicopter to me," he said.

"Black Bear Six, Blue Star Two-One, over," Captain Mike Dougherty transmitted.

"Blue Star Two-One, Black Bear Six. Over," Joy answered.

"Black Bear Six, understand you would like a lift. Pop smoke."

On that, Huff grabbed a smoke grenade and tossed it to the edge of a small clearing next to them. Boomer, Smith, Huff and Kruger turned and took up a defensive stance.

"Blue Star, smoke out," Joy announced and watched as the grenade first sputtered and then began to pour out the colored smoke. Now he waited.

"Black Bear Six, I have goofy grape, over." Everyone looked at Joy as he responded.

"Blue Star, that's affirmative."

"Roger, coming down." And the UH-1H entered into a rapid and steep descent.

* * *

Captain Mike Dougherty lifted off expecting a lot of sightseeing and not much action, at least for his aircraft. Normally his mission was one of observing the actions on the ground from on high. Tom was his copilot for the day.

"Okay, I have the aircraft," Mike said.

"You have the aircraft" came the proper response from the copilot as he looked over to confirm that Mike's hands were on the controls. He was sure Mike had the controls when the throttle was suddenly cut, the collective bottomed out and the cyclic pushed over, causing the aircraft to suddenly drop in a tight left descending turn. Tom's stomach went to his throat and he was thankful he was able to hold his breakfast down. Without having to be told, the crew chief and door gunner brought their guns up and began looking for targets. Anything shooting at them was considered a target.

As Mike watched the clearing rapidly become larger as he executed his descent, he noticed the wind by the blowing smoke and set his approach to maximize the lift it would offer on his takeoff. He also noted the tanks that were moving towards the intended pickup zone.

"When we touch down, get those guys on board ASAP. If they're on the skids, that's good enough," Mike told the crew.

He didn't want to be on the ground for longer than four seconds.

"Black Bear Six, Blue Star, over."

"Blue Star, Black Bear, over."

"Black Bear, when I touch down you have four seconds to load. We have company coming fast. Over."

"Blue Star, I understand." Joy didn't need a long explanation.

* * *

"Listen up. We have four seconds to load, so when we see the back of his skids touch down, we run for him. Got it?" Joy yelled. Everyone understood and watched as the UH-1H approached, coming rapidly over the trees. Suddenly the nose of the aircraft pitched upward and the tail dropped to almost touch the ground. Everyone thought the aircraft had been hit, but they realized the pilot was executing a rapid deceleration when the nose came back to a normal landing position and all forward motion of the aircraft ceased except for a left pedal turn, placing the aircraft between the advisors and the enemy fire.

"*Go, go, go!*" Joy yelled as the advisors all moved to the aircraft from the opposite side from where he was standing. Joy quickly jumped into the cargo area and began pulling others inside.

"One thousand one, one thousand two, one thousand three, one thousand four, coming up," Mike yelled as he pulled up on the collective and pushed forward on the cyclic. The aircraft began to move and so did the ARVN soldiers, mobbing the aircraft in an attempt to get on. Huff and Kruger were behind Boomer and Smith in reaching the aircraft. Huff had one foot on the skid and one hand on the door frame when he felt the aircraft start to move. Looking back, he saw

Kruger running to the aircraft and reached out for him, catching his hand. As the aircraft gained treetop altitude, Kruger was hanging below the aircraft only by the strength of Huff's grip.

"We've got to land!" Joy yelled to the pilot when he saw the situation. Mike was already aware as the gunner had told him that Kruger was hanging on by a grip. Mike was looking for a spot to put the aircraft down without landing in the middle of an NVA regiment. Finally, he spotted an opening that he hoped wouldn't be occupied. As he came in for a landing, the tree line opened fire, with the gunner and crew chief returning fire. Kruger leaped for the aircraft as soon as his feet touched the ground, and he and Huff scrambled aboard. The master caution light told Mike he had taken some damage to the aircraft, and fluctuating instruments indicated he was losing some engine power. He attempted to climb out of the clearing, but the aircraft wasn't gaining the power it needed.

"Kick some off," Mike commanded. Four ARVNs had climbed onto the skids when Mike had first landed. They had gotten in Kruger's way and prevented him from reaching the aircraft in the dash to safety. "Kick them off *now*," Mike yelled. The gunner reared back and hit the first squarely in the jaw, causing him to release his grasp on the aircraft. The advisors dispatched the other three. Everyone breathed a sigh of relief when the aircraft passed over the My Chanh River. A few minutes later, the aircraft began a slow approach to a clearing with several jeeps and M113s.

Joy turned to face into the cockpit to thank the pilots for coming to get him and his team. The look on his face was one of shock when he saw the copilot. Captain Dougherty was the personal pilot for Brigadier General Thomas Bowen Jr., the deputy commander for FRAC, who was occupying the copilot seat.

* * *

"I think we have the last of the stragglers from the 147th, or as many as we can get," Sheridan said to Major Price. "If we don't destroy this bridge, then the next uniforms we see are going to be the NVA. Colonel Chung said to blow it when I thought we should. We should now."

"I'll take that engineer platoon and go blow it. It should be easy, being that the roadbed is only wood planks. Be back in an hour. Keep that artillery between us and the advance elements of the NVA," Price said as he departed and joined the ARVN engineers.

The first impediment to reaching the bridge was navigating through all the refugees that were streaming across it. Some of them were Marines from the 147th. Others wore the uniform of the ARVN Army. As they got closer to the bridge, the tide of humanity thinned out as it was obvious that the NVA had closed the road, preventing anyone else from coming south. It was also obvious that the NVA had deliberately targeted the civilian refugees with artillery fire. Torn, mangled bodies attested to the fact all around the northern approach to the bridge. Price was appalled at the cost in human life he witnessed. When they reached the bridge, no time was wasted in setting the demolitions.

"Dai'uy, is this all the demo you have?" Price asked the Vietnamese captain. In his mind, what they had wouldn't do the job.

"Yes, there no more," the captain responded.

"Okay, let's set the charges and blow it," Price replied, almost sure it wouldn't be sufficient to really damage the bridge. The engineers went about their tasks and placed all the charges under the center span. When they had placed it all, the engineers moved back to the south side of the My Chanh River.

"Fire in the hole!" Price yelled, and the Vietnamese captain said the same thing in his native tongue. The explosion was impressive, but ineffective. Only the wood planks across the center section were destroyed and others moved. The bridge could be quickly repaired.

"Damn," Price said. "We've got to bring this thing down. Let me think." As he stood there, his mind ran through some possible scenarios. *We could call an air strike on it, but that's going to take time that we don't have. We could go back and get some artillery rounds and use those tied to the bridge, but again, time. We could...use the five-gallon cans of diesel fuel and gas that are on our vehicles and burn it.* "Dai'uy, we burn it. Unload all the fuel from the APC gas cans as well as the jeeps and bring it to the bridge," Price told him.

As the Vietnamese started grabbing the gas and diesel cans, Price rummaged through his jeep for a flare gun that he carried. "Have them pour it all together along the support beams," Price directed, and the Vietnamese moved quickly to carry out the order. They didn't want to be around the bridge any longer than necessary. When the last can was empty, Price stepped up and fired the flare gun into the area. The gasoline caught fire immediately, but the diesel was slow to ignite. When it did, the column of smoke was seen for miles and for days. No one would be crossing the My Chanh River Bridge.

34

HOLD THE LINE

The situation across the entire country was not good. All four military regions were under siege, although the fight in MR-4, which was the Mekong Delta region, was still an unconventional fight. The fall of any one region could open a floodgate of enemy forces achieving success. General Abrams called a meeting to focus on events in MR-1.

General Carley took the podium. "Morning, sir," he said as General Abrams entered the room. Since the first of April, they had dropped the "good" from "good morning" as nothing good was happening or would for the rest of the day. Abrams nodded his head in acknowledgment and signaled to get on with it.

"First slide," Carley called. A slide appeared on the screen to his right, showing the location of friendly and enemy forces in Military Region I. "Sir, as you can see on this slide, friendly forces in the north have been pushed back to south of the My Chanh River. The 369th Vietnamese Marine Brigade is defending in the vicinity of the QL1 bridge, which has been destroyed. There are no remaining bridges over the My Chanh River at this time. The 147th Vietnamese Marine Brigade is located in the Citadel in Hue and is regrouping. They really bore the brunt of the fighting in the exodus from Quang Tri City. The 3rd ARVN Division is also located at Hue, but reports are inconclusive as to the effectiveness of this division any longer. One regiment, the 57th ARVN Regiment, 3rd ARVN Division, had problems from the very start and seems to have disappeared into the mass of refugees attempting to move south on QL1. The 56th Regiment surrendered at Camp Carroll without a fight on day one. The 1st Armored Brigade, the 17th and 18th Armored Cav Regiments, and the Ranger and Airborne units are all south of the My Chanh in some degree of strength and organization. We haven't been able to determine what levels those are as of yet. Advisors with the Marine units have rejoined or are in the process of rejoining those units that they were separated from. We're unaware of the status of Army units that were north of the My Chanh River as contact with most of the advisors has been lost. The 1st ARVN Infantry Division is in the vicinity of FSB Eagle as it was never committed to the fight. 1st ARVN Corps headquarters forward is located in the Citadel in Hue, while the main headquarters is in Da Nang," General Carley outlined.

"Okay, what are the key lessons we can take away from this debacle? Because, gentlemen, any way you slice this, it is a debacle," Abrams said in frustration.

"Sir, I've had Lieutenant Colonel D'Wayne Gray from ANGLICO looking into this matter as well as evaluating our fire support structure. If I may…"

"Yeah, let's hear what he has to say," Abrams said, now

sounding resigned. *I'm going to have to brief the President later today. I hope this guy can give me something useful*, he thought as Lieutenant Colonel Gray took the podium.

"Sir, the debacle in MR-1," Gray started, noticing Major General Kroesen bristle at that opening remark, "can be attributed to a couple of factors. First, the NVA have excellent artillery weapons that outgun our 105mm howitzers as well as the 155mm howitzers. Second, they've learned to integrate their artillery and ground forces into a combined-arms force. That is on their side. On our side, we have control of the sky for the most part and can overcome their air-defense systems for the most part. What's severely hurting our side is lack of decisive leadership at the highest level—"

Abrams quickly interrupted, "Colonel, are you saying that General Lam is the problem?"

"In large part, yes, sir. Actually, most of the higher chain of command above battalion levels is the problem—with exceptions, General Giai being an exception as well as the Marine Brigade commanders. Lam is slow to make a decision and will countermand decisions already made by him or subordinates, which adds to the confusion. He doesn't have a grasp of the situation on the ground in his sector. I'll go so far as to say that if he's given command of the defense of Hue, it will fall to the enemy as well," Gray said.

"That's a mighty bold statement about a senior officer, Colonel," a bit testy Abrams added.

"Sir, he is not in my chain of command, nor is he in my military. I was told you wanted my opinion on the current situation. This is my opinion," Gray stated politely but firmly. *I'm approaching my twenty years for retirement, so what are you going to do, General? Bend my dog tags and send me to Vietnam?* he thought as he and Abrams exchanged looks.

"Anything else?" Abrams asked, breaking the ice.

"Yes, sir. I have looked at the fire support structure in

place. It's inadequate across the board. This morning, with General Carley's permission, I sent a message to Fleet Marine Force Pacific, requesting additional naval gunfire officers, air observers, and enlisted communications personnel. Within forty-eight hours, we should have two hundred more Marines flown in to meet this request. I'll form them into naval gunfire teams and assign them to ARVN Airborne and Marine units," Gray outlined.

"Damn it, people! We are drawing troop strength down, not increasing it," Abrams said with a raised voice and a frustrated expression.

"Sir, these additional service members are coming to us on temporary orders and do not count against our overall troop strength," Gray noted.

That seemed to calm Abrams down a notch. "Alright, continue, Colonel."

"I also feel we need to establish effective targeting and coordination centers for a total fire support package of artillery, naval gunfire, naval tac air and Air Force tac air as well as strategic bombing by B-52s. The Vietnamese are clueless on how to do this. This is going to take your doing, sir, to pull the senior Army advisor and Air Force commander together to make this work. But it will solve what I see as a disconnect between the ground battle and the air support," Gray explained.

"I think I can handle that," Abrams said, chuckling that he was now taking direction from a lieutenant colonel—a Marine lieutenant colonel at that. "Is there anything else, Colonel?"

"Just one more thing, sir. We're going to have to replace a lot of lost equipment. I've given a list to the J-4 already," Gray stated as Abrams turned to look at his J-4.

"I got it, sir, and am working on getting the stuff," the J-4 stated, not really wanting to show Abrams the amount of equipment and ammunition that had been lost, or the cost of replacing that equipment. Replacing an M16 rifle that a soldier lost was pretty cheap; replacing a tank battalion was pretty expensive.

"Sir, if you have no more questions for me, I'll be followed by General Williams, who will cover the latest intel," Gray said as he picked up his notes.

Stepping behind the podium, Williams asked for his first and only slide.

"Sir, this slide shows the disposition of enemy forces as of twenty-four hours ago. The main attack through Quang Tri Province has halted at the My Chanh River with no bridges currently over the river. The 304th NVA Division is located across the My Chanh Line with its command post in the Quang Tri Citadel. The 324B Division has moved to the west of Hue and is applying pressure on Firebases Bastogne and Checkmate as of this morning. We've tracked the 324B as it came out of the A Shau Valley on the twenty-ninth of April and has been moving down Route 547, which runs from A Loui in Laos through the A Shau and terminates in Hue. We believe that this is now considered the main attack for the NVA as the capture of Hue will be severely demoralizing and a great political victory for the NVA," General Williams said before he was interrupted by Abrams.

"That damn valley has been a thorn in our side since this war started in 1954. Always an enemy stronghold. We put a special forces camp in there in March of '66 and it got overrun. The Marines went in June of '67 and got run out by September of the same year. The 1st Cav thought they could do better and went in a year later in April of '68, and they lasted less than six months. We've sent in special forces teams, and some we never heard from again. Even when we bomb the place to rubble, it doesn't seem to faze them." He paused. "Sorry, I'll get off my soapbox. Please continue."

"The 324B Division beginning in March is attempting

to encircle Hue, moving around the western and southern area of Hue. The 1st ARVN Division found some assembly areas in the vicinity of FSB Bastogne and Veghel, with the 29th NVA Regiment located in that area," Williams explained.

"Pretty gutsy of the division. We haven't seen aggressive action from any of the others in the recent past," Abrams observed.

"Colonel Hillman Dickinson is the senior Army advisor with the 1st ARVN Division and rates the division commander, a Major General Pham Van Phu, as an aggressive, top-notch officer," Carley interjected, catching a look from Abrams.

"Sir," Williams said, hoping to keep the briefing on track, "the 1st ARVN Division has been aggressive for the past months, with little fanfare as it was all up north. On the fifth of March, the 1st and 3rd ARVN Regiments conducted airmobile operations into six landing zones and utilized artillery and B-52s on known and suspected targets."

"Who flew them out there? Please tell me it was Vietnamese Air Force helicopters," Abrams asked.

"Ah, no, sir. It was US Army helicopters," Williams answered, clearly noting the disappointment on Abrams's face. "The 1st ARVN has continued to be active in sector against the 324B but has lost some ground. From April twenty-eighth to twenty-ninth, the 803rd NVA Regiment attacked FSB Bastogne and took it. That night of the twenty-ninth, Checkmate was abandoned, which now has opened the way to Hue."

"What's standing in their way?"

"The 1st Division is still viable and occupies Birmingham and Eagle. A battalion of the 39th Rangers is at Evans and holding them at bay in the north," Williams said.

"What is Lam doing about this?" Abrams asked.

"Nothing, sir." This wasn't the answer that Carley wanted to give, but there it was.

"Time to replace Lam. I'm calling President Thieu and getting this changed now. Lam has cost us enough," Abrams said as he stood to leave the room.

* * *

As strategy discussions were being conducted in Saigon, combat actions were happening along the My Chanh River. The use of B-52s had taken the fight out of the NVA along the river and provided a pause in the fighting. However, right now, a more serious problem faced the command.

"General Lam, something has got to be done about this situation in Hue," Colonel Metcalf said. He and General Giai had come to Da Nang to meet with General Lam.

"What is the situation you speak of, Colonel Metcalf? Is it a military matter or meddling again by American advisors in Vietnamese affairs?" General Lam asked with sarcasm dripping from every word.

"Sir, the situation in Hue is a military problem. Bands of deserters are roaming the streets, robbing stores, raping women, killing each other, and there's nothing the local police can do about it as the deserters have all their weapons, grenades and antitank rockets. You've got to do something," Metcalf attempted to impress on Lam.

"Those deserters are mostly 3rd Division soldiers, so General Giai should handle this situation," Lam indicated pointing at Giai.

"General, the 3rd Division is for all practical purposes dissolved. We exist on paper only. I have no organized forces to use in this matter," Giai said with some resignation.

"Then let us not worry about Hue and think about how you will defend against another attack," Lam instructed.

"Defend with what? Have you not heard a word we've said? The 3rd Division doesn't exist except on paper any longer. Someone else is going to have to conduct a defense," Metcalf practically screamed. Lam turned and faced him.

"This is no longer General Giai's problem. As of now, he is relieved of his command and I am placing him under arrest for deserting his post in Quang Tri. He was ordered to stand and fight and he did not do that," Lam said as he pushed a button on his phone. The door opened and in walked his chief of staff with two ARVN military police soldiers.[1]

Metcalf was shocked. He began to say something, but Lam held up his hand. "Colonel Metcalf, your service is no longer needed. I believe you have a message waiting for you to return to FRAC headquarters. Good day, sir. You are dismissed," Lam said, gloating. *Now they will be blamed for the loss of Quang Tri and not me*, he was thinking when the phone rang.

"Yes?" he answered.

"Sir, President Thieu is on the phone and wishes to speak with you."

* * *

The morning was slightly overcast, but Lam hardly noticed as he walked out of his office. The day before, his staff had cleared all his personal belongings and placed them in boxes. There would be no ceremony. He would simply leave the building and return to Saigon and to whatever position was waiting for him. He wouldn't even have an opportunity to meet with his replacement, Lieutenant General Ngo Quang Truong.

Truong had grown up in the airborne community. The day before, May 3, he had been notified that he would be taking command of Military Region I. He had already alerted his staff and was ready to leave that afternoon from his assignment in the Mekong Delta and fly to Da Nang. He had followed the events up north since the beginning and anticipated that Lam would be relieved and he would be placed in charge. He brought his staff with him and immediately moved them into the Citadel in Hue while he stopped at the current 1st Corps headquarters in Da Nang. General Kroesen met him when he arrived.

"General Truong, welcome to Military Region I," Kroesen said, extending his hand.

"Thank you, General. I look forward to working together," Truong responded. "Please have a seat," he added, pointing to two overstuffed chairs.

"General, I won't beat around the bush. You have your work cut out for you up here. I won't be assigning a senior advisor to your headquarters, but I'll be your senior advisor. I'm not going to tell you how to conduct this fight but will give you all the support I can and honest opinions and advice when you ask for it," Kroesen said.

"General Kroesen, I appreciate your advice and opinions. I know you have extensive experience in Vietnam and I think we will work well together," Truong said, pausing for a moment. "My immediate concern is the defense of Hue and establishing a defensive line. Second is examining our command structure to see if some units are controlling too many assets and some not enough. Third, we have got to get a better handle on logistical support and distribution."

Kroesen nodded in agreement. "There's also another issue that I'm afraid you will need to address."

"And that is?"

"The refugees and deserters that have flowed into Hue have taken over the city, overwhelming the police and looting and terrorizing the people. In addition, the refugees that have flowed south are overwhelming the local government with requests to assist them," Kroesen stated.

Truong was a soldier and had always been a soldier. He was uncomfortable having to deal with local government issues and certainly wasn't comfortable committing military forces that he needed in the defense to mopping up and controlling a city. For a long moment, he sat, deep in thought. Finally, he turned to his aide and said something in Vietnamese that General Kroesen didn't understand. The aide's eyes grew wide, his facial expression changed and he quickly excused himself from the room.

"That problem will begin to correct itself in about five hours, General," Truong said with a slight smile.

"I don't speak enough Vietnamese to understand what you just ordered, General," Kroesen explained.

"I have just issued my first order as commander of 1st Corps. Hue is, as of noon today, under martial law. Curfew will last from 1800 to 0800 each day, and anyone on the streets will be detained or shot. All deserters will return to their units and begin training or be shot after twelve hundred hours tomorrow. I also have ordered one hundred armored cars with machine guns to start patrolling the city," Truong said matter-of-factly. "My staff will coordinate with the local government and province chief to locate a place we can move the refugees to. The deserters we will consolidate at Camp Evans and begin their retraining. Now, General, if you will excuse me, I want to get up to Hue with my headquarters and assess the situation. Can we meet tomorrow and discuss my plans?"

"General Truong, I would like that very much," Kroesen said as he stood and extended his hand. *This guy is going to make this happen.*

* * *

Lieutenant Colonel Turley had been reassigned to FRAC headquarters as the operations officer. Forces that were available were the Marine and ARVN Airborne Divisions, the 1st ARVN Infantry Division and the 2nd ARVN Division. The Marine division had been assigned its own sector extending from the Gulf of Tonkin across QL1 and terminating at the Bo River. Division CP set up in the village of Huong Dien north of Hue. The Marine Advisory Unit under the command of Colonel Joshua Dorsey set up adjacent to the Division CP with a communications section, combat operations section and a fire support center. Battalion advisor billets were abolished, with the battalion advisors now serving at the brigade level along with a fire support coordinator. As needed, advisors would be sent to respective battalions to offer assistance.

The 147th VNMC Brigade, which had seen the bulk of the fighting coming out of Quang Tri, had lost most of its equipment and had taken huge personnel losses. Truong had ordered the 147th VNMC Brigade move to Hue and refit. A relief in place was conducted in an orderly fashion between the 147th and the 258th VNMC Brigades. Ranger units were equally missing weapons and bodies, and what was left was moved to Camp Evans. The loss of so many officers greatly affected the ability to reconstitute the units. 1st Ranger Group was ineffective for combat, it was felt, while estimates were that at least a month would be needed before the 4th Ranger Group would be considered combat-ready. It was questionable whether the 5th Ranger Group would be reconstituted as its losses were so high. The 3rd ARVN Division was disorganized, lacking leadership, equipment, and personnel. Remnants of the 57th Regiment that had managed to get back were milling around in Hue. Former members of the 56th Regiment that had managed to escape from Camp Carroll were also in the city. The 2nd Regiment had very few stragglers make it to Hue. 1st Armored Brigade was almost wiped out. Only one M48 tank managed to return to Camp Evans under its own power along with six M41 tanks and fifteen APCs. This was all that remained of a force of one tank regiment and three armored cav squadrons.

Personnel losses were equally disturbing, with approximately eleven hundred killed out of a force of two thousand. Truong had requested the Airborne Division. His plan was for them to secure the northwest and northern portions of the defensive line. The 1st ARVN Infantry Division was located south and southwest of Hue and the 2nd ARVN Infantry Division was in the southern portion of MR-1. The 1st ARVN Infantry Division had acquitted itself very well in the Lam Son 719 operation, as had the Vietnamese Marines and the 1st ARVN Airborne Division. Truong saw them as the main force of 1st Corps from the defense of Hue.

NVA forces north of the My Chanh Line were the 304th, 308th and 324th NVA Divisions, the 202nd and 203rd Armored Regiments and supporting units. The fear was that two divisions could control north of the My Chanh Line and others could maneuver to the west and attack towards Hue.

Truong instituted changes in the forces almost immediately. Meeting with General Kroesen the next day, he outlined what he was going to do.

"General, I wanted to get your opinion on some moves I intend to make today. This will also keep your staff and Lieutenant Colonel Turley informed as well. The 258th VNMC Brigade headquarters is displacing to Phong Dien and will relieve the headquarters for 369 Brigade. The combat battalions will stay in place in both cases. The 39th Ranger Battalion will assume command of Camp Evans and begin a retraining program there for Rangers and some deserters we are moving there. I have ordered Lieutenant Colonel Ngo Van Dinh, commander of the 2nd VNMC Battalion, to concentrate his battalion at the My Chanh River Bridge and prevent any reconstruction of this bridge. He and I spoke with his brigade commander and we all agree that with the bridge destroyed and him preventing its reconstruction, any attack to seize Hue is going to come from the western foothills and out of the A Shau Valley," Truong outlined.

"And the 147th?" Kroesen asked.

"It will remain in Hue with the 4th and 8th VNMC Battalions to replace equipment and people," Truong said and turned to Turley. He added, "Lieutenant Colonel Turley has been most helpful in assisting Colonel Dorsey with our supply needs." Truong paused, then added, "I understand your new antitank weapon will be arriving soon with a mobile training team as well...called TOW, yes?"

"Yes, sir. They should arrive any day now and we'll start training the Marine and Airborne units on their use. We haven't been authorized to give them to the ARVN units but only the Marine and Airborne units. We can't afford to allow this weapon to fall in the hands of the enemy. If that happened, it would be on its way to Moscow or Peking within hours," Turley said, expecting some pushback from Truong.[2]

"I understand, Colonel. We will make good use of this new weapon," Truong replied as he turned to face Kroesen again. "For right now, General, I see our most difficult problem being the enemy's artillery. His 130mm guns outrange everything except the 175mm howitzers. His guns are well hidden with only two to three guns on one location and only one location firing at a time, but when the FAC flies over, they stop shooting and another position starts shooting."

"I can understand your frustration, General. The problem is reports that they may be receiving SA-7 anti-aircraft missiles and that's forcing the FAC to stay at altitude, which makes it difficult for them to spot the guns."

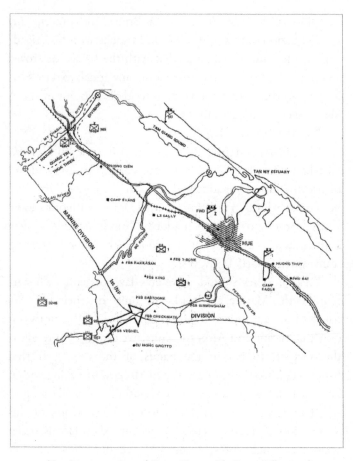

*Ngo, Lieutenant General Quang Truong, The Easter Offensive of
1972. Washington, D.C.: U.S. Army Center of Military History,
1980.*

35

SLICK GOES DOWN

2 MAY 1972
F Troop, 4th Cav
Camp Evans, South Vietnam

"Okay, we got some work to do," Captain Dan Tyner said as he approached the group of nine pilots lounging around one of the Centaur slicks. "Here's the deal. We have two advisors to pick up along with a downed FAC pilot and a couple of wounded Vietnamese Marines. They're located north of here along Highway 1. Let's take the two snakes and the slicks. Jessie, why don't you take slick lead, and, Rose, you take Chalk Two."

"What, no little birds on this one?" asked one of the LOH drivers.

"Nah, we'll give you a break on this one. Should be fairly easy, and we know where they are, so we don't need you hunting for them," Dan added. "Let's crank."

As the two Cobra gunships and two UH-1H slicks came to full power, CWO William Jessie called the flight. "Centaur

Lead on the go." And the two slicks departed with the Cobras right behind them. The aircraft climbed to fifteen hundred feet, a safe altitude above effective small-arms fire. As they arrived over the pickup zone, a green smoke grenade ignited, marking the location.

"Centaur Four-Five, Lead, over."

"Lead, Four-Five, go ahead," Captain Tyner replied.

"Four-Five, I have the green smoke and will make my approach north to south. How copy?" Jessie asked. Mr. Chuck Rose was right behind him, piloting the second slick.

"Roger, north to south, We'll cover." Tyner watched as Jessie entered a steep descent towards the pickup zone. Almost immediately, the NVA opened fire on the UH-1H helicopter.

"Lead's taking fire," Jessie reported, which was obvious from the green tracers reaching up from the surrounding trees. Tyner pushed his nose down and began punching off 2.75-inch rockets at positions firing at Jessie.

"Four-Five, Four-Seven, I'm covering your six," Russ reported as Tyner pulled out of his dive and Russ commenced his own. *Hope Tyner gets back around to cover my break*, Russ thought as he commenced depositing rockets and 40mm grenades on the enemy positions. As Russ entered his dive, he could see Jessie landing in the pickup zone and the advisors moving to the aircraft.

Aboard Chuck Rose's aircraft, he could see several Vietnamese dressed in civilian clothes, attempting to board Jessie's aircraft. "Crew, if the Vietnamese attempt to swarm us, shoot them," Rose ordered. The gunner and crew chief raised their guns. The Vietnamese civilians got the message without a shot fired. An advisor quickly grabbed Rose. "Don't fly over the tree line to the left."

"Roger, I'll let my lead know," Rose said, switching to the unit UHF frequency.

"Lead, Two-Five, over."

"Two-Five, go ahead."

"I got an advisor on board and he says do not, repeat, do not break left and go over that tree line." Jessie didn't acknowledge the call. Rose waited.

Before Russ completed his run, Jessie was pulling pitch and departing the pickup zone.

"Centaur Lead, coming out," Jessie announced. As he did so, he initiated a left turn. All Rose could do was observe. As Jessie climbed and passed over the tree line, an explosion of sorts could be seen on the tree line and a long object went skyward. It hit Jessie in the lower side of the tail boom in the oil cooler compartment. The aircraft exploded with only the rotor head intact, spinning off into the distance.

"What the—" Russ called out and continued his break.

"Lead is down, Lead is down," reported Mr. Rose, aircraft commander for the second slick. "Two is taking fire." Moments later, Rose called, "Mayday, mayday, Two is going down." And the smoking engine confirmed that Chalk Two was in fact going down, slowly. Rose was milking the crippled aircraft for all she was worth and managed to move towards the beach before he had to set the aircraft down. As he did so, they flew over QL1. "Oh shit, tanks," Rose transmitted. Then things got quiet except for the master caution warning and the caution panel indicating that the engine had just stopped functioning. Mr. Rose executed a low-level autorotation to a wide-open rice paddy field. *All is good*, he was thinking when a dike in the rice paddy appeared where he intended to touch down. "Ah shit" was all he could say as he popped his collective and eased the aircraft over the dike, which left little for a soft touchdown. They landed hard. The crew were seen unassing the aircraft and taking small-arms fire as well.

"Four-Five, Four-Seven, over," Russ called. No answer. Tyner's aircraft had a 20mm, three-barreled Gatling gun on the wing pylons and every time he fired, it knocked out his radios. Russ took the lead and began suppressing the enemy positions. However, he was getting low on ammo. Switching to the UHF Guard frequency, he made a blanket call.

"Attention on Guard, any aircraft with ordnance, we have a bird down and need assistance. This is Centaur Four-Seven, over."

"Centaur Four-Seven, Centaur Three-Six, over." Captain Fred Ledfors was in a little bird just off Camp Evans and heard the distress call.

"Centaur Three-Six, Centaur Four-Seven, I need some help. Centaur Two-Five is down and has bad guys around him. I'm low on ammo and Four-Five's radios are out. Over."

"Centaur Four-Seven, what's your location?" Ledfors asked. Russ passed the coordinates and Ledfors arrived soon afterwards. Being a little bird, he had to make multiple trips to pick up the survivors, moving them to safety and returning for another pickup.

36

AIRBORNE DIVISION

8 May 1972
I Corps Headquarters
Hue, South Vietnam

General Truong was in command and exercised command without wasting time. After his discussion with General Kroesen, he immediately requested additional forces.

"Sir, General Du Quoc Dong is here," Truong's aide said, holding the door to his office open.

"Send him in, please," Truong said, coming from around his desk as General Dong walked in. They were both members of the South Vietnamese Airborne community and had served together several times. However, as with all South Vietnamese senior officers, their political alliances were different.

"General Dong, welcome to Military Region I. We are very happy to have the airborne division supporting us up here. Please sit," Truong said, pointing to an overstuffed chair in his office. "Tea?"

"No, thank you, General," Dong replied, taking a seat.

Truong took another overstuffed chair across the coffee table from Dong.

"General, have you been briefed on the situation up here?" Truong asked.

"I have and believe I understand it fully. You simply can not accomplish your mission without my division supporting you. The 3rd ARVN Division is a shell, and the 1st is barely holding its own against the forces coming out of the A Shau Valley. The Marines are holding the line and the Rangers are broke. The armored cav squadrons have very few tanks left. Do I have that about right?" Dong asked in a smug manner.

Standing and walking over to a wall map, Truong said, "You are not far off the mark. The My Chanh Line is thin." As he spoke, he used his pen as a pointer and traced it along the map. "Currently the Marines are holding the My Chanh Line and their defense is very thin. Only because the bridge was taken down is the enemy not pressing his attack. The RFPF is blocking Highway 555 on the right flank from the sea to here, where the Marines' positions start. Along the My Chanh River, the Marines are controlling the south bank west to here," Truong said, stopping his pen.

"I'm placing your 2nd Brigade under the operational control of the Marines until your headquarters is up and operational. That will allow the Marines to shift forces to the east and thicken their lines. I will have the Marines position your 2nd Brigade on the left flank but will leave the Marines responsible for the bridge over the My Chanh. As your other brigades arrive, I will have them move to positions adjacent to the 2nd Brigade. This will position your forces between the Marines and the 1st ARVN Division," Truong explained.

"I do not like that I will not have control of my own brigades. Why am I even here, then?" Dong hotly contested.

"Calm down. They will only be operational for the Marines until your headquarters is established at FSB Sally here. In addition, I am placing the 4th Regiment of the 2nd Division under your operational control until such time as you have all your brigades here," Truong indicated. This seemed to placate Dong.

"The 2nd Brigade is arriving today. It has been fighting in the vicinity of Kontum. It will need a few days to rest and refit. The 3rd Brigade had been palace guard in Saigon but in April they were moved up to Lai Khe in III Corp and have been fighting for a month to open Highway 13 to An Loc. They will be coming out of there in a day or two and will need some time to refit and resupply. Once that is done they should be able to move into the line right away. They will arrive up here about the 22nd of this month. The 1st Brigade is at An Loc and fighting, but I expect that as soon as Highway 13 is open, they will be coming up here. What shape they will be in I am not sure. I do know that the 6th Battalion will have to be completely refitted. The 1st Brigade will need a refit and rest period," Dong said, expecting some pushback on the requirement for rest. He did not receive any.

"We will have them in reserve, in that case, in the vicinity of Hue when they arrive. When do you think you will be ready to go over on the offensive?" Truong asked, catching Dong off guard with that question.

"I'm not sure. Maybe two weeks after the 1st Brigade gets here," Dong responded.

"Fine," Truong said, pointing at the area west of QL1, he continued, "In the meantime, and as your force grows, we will position you between the Marines on the My Chanh and pull you south to the 1st Division. Once we take your 2nd Brigade away from the Marines, I will move the 1st Ranger Group up to reinforce them. The 1st Ranger Group has been refitted and rested." When he finished, he came back to his seat but only sat on the armrest.

"So I take it that we are going to just sit and not do anything until all our forces are here," Dong stated.

"Hardly. I am not going to give the enemy a chance to rest and resupply himself. Oh, no," Truong said, standing again and moving to the map. "We are going to spend this month making limited attacks on the enemy. We are planning right now a helo assault for the Marines' 369th Brigade to land in the Hai Lang area. This is ten kilometers southeast of Quang Tri. Once on the ground, they will attack south into the rear of the enemy defenses along the north side of the My Chanh," Truong explained with a smile.

"Good. I was worried that we were going to just sit here with indecisions," Dong said.

"This morning, the 1st Division sent over plans for an airmobile assault on Bastogne with one regiment while its two other regiments move to seize the high ground overlooking Bastogne. This will allow them to also control Birmingham and be well positioned to eventually move to take Fire Base Checkmate. No, General, we are done sitting and letting him have his way," Truong said, moving to the front of his desk and leaning back on it.

Dong stood, correctly determining that this was the end of their meeting. "General, it is going to be a pleasure to serve with you. Together we will take it all back," Dong said, extending his hand, which Truong accepted.

37

REFIT AND RETRAIN

FRAC Headquarters
Da Nang, South Vietnam

General Truong was wasting no time bringing his forces back to fighting strength and condition. His decree that deserters in Hue return to their former units or Camp Evans if they could not find their former unit had an immediate effect. Word quickly spread that he was serious after the first day, when several were shot. Looting and lawlessness had ceased in Hue. Now it was time to refit and rebuild the force.

"Sir, we believe General Truong will be begging in your meeting with him for trainers and equipment," Colonel Crowley, Kroesen's logistics officer, indicated. "He would be very happy if the 196th would just leave everything in place when they leave so he can have it," Crowley snickered, looking over at Brigadier General David, the Operations officer for FRAC.

"Of course, he would want it all in like-new condition, I'm sure," David said.

"Oh, of course," Crowley responded.

"Okay, you two," Kroesen said, cutting off the sarcasm. "What are we looking at logistically that he wants?"

"Sir, he's looking for 105 howitzers, trucks, armored vehicles, crew-served weapons for the larger items as well as M48 tanks. On the small stuff he wants gas masks, artillery ammunition, fuses, and claymores to name a few that we know of. His logisticians will be accompanying him with a complete list, to include amounts. I can almost guess that he wants enough to reequip the 3rd Division plus," Crowley said.

"Who's the plus?" Kroesen asked with a furrowed brow.

"The plus right now is probably the 2nd Airborne Brigade that arrived two days ago from the Central Highlands after slugging it out around Kontum and the 1st and 3rd Airborne Brigades when they arrive. We just finished refitting the 1st Ranger Group, but that was pretty easy," Crowley indicated.

"Sir, he's also going to be asking for the TOW system," David said with some resignation.

"General Abrams has already spoken to me on that note. We will train the airborne and Marine units on the system and give the weapons to them, but only them. The ARVN divisions do not get them. He's afraid that if they go to the ARVN divisions, as soon as they fire the last round they'll run and leave the weapon behind, or they'll run and leave the weapon and missiles behind. No, no training and weapons for regular ARVN units on that system," Kroesen explained.

"He's going to ask that the TOW systems be vehicle-mounted as well," David said matter-of-factly.

"Well, of course. Let's ask for the moon and see what the Americans will give us," Kroesen said in frustration.

"Their rational for the vehicles is that due to the physical size of the average Vietnamese soldier, the system is too heavy for a four-man team. They need a vehicle to transport it," Crowley explained.

Kroesen thought about it for a moment, then said, "Sort of makes sense, I guess. What about mobile training teams?"

"Sir, he will be asking for some as well. We can pull something together fairly quick and help there. Specifically, he will ask for us to train the trainers initially on artillery fire direction procedures, call for and adjustment of close-air support, engineer demolitions, use of the M202 system—" David said before he was interrupted.

"My God, how difficult is it to fire the M202 that he needs a mobile training team?" Kroesen asked with frustration.

"Sir, the ARVN is afraid of the thing. They doubted the M72 until they took it into the fight, or I should say were forced to use it. The same with the M202. For these guys, that's a heavy weapon to lug around. In fact it's four times the weight of the M72."

"Any idea where they're going to be doing the training with the mobile training teams?" Kroesen asked.

"Some of it they want to do at Camp Evans. That's mostly refitting the deserters and stragglers that they've rounded up. One to two weeks of retraining is what they're looking at. Small-unit tactics, discipline, that sort of stuff. The more technical stuff they'll do at the training center. I've spoken with Lieutenant Colonel Nguyen Due An about billeting our people and the facilities for the training and he assured me all would be in place and ready when they arrive," David said.

"Good," Kroesen said, pausing for a moment. "All this is good, but the real central problem to all this is the leadership. That is a twofold problem. The first is the quality of the leadership and the second is the positioning of the leadership. Have you noticed that many of the battalions are commanded by majors? They're good officers, aggressive for the most part, but they don't have the experience to be an effective battalion commander. Where are all the lieutenant colonels? They sure as hell are not commanding the battalions. They have in a couple of cases captains and in two cases first lieutenants commanding battalions. That lack of experience at the lower levels is really hurting their ability."

"Sir, maybe we should propose a two-week leaders course to Truong. Bring company and battalion commanders in while their units are going through a one- or two-week refit and we have an MTT teach leadership to the commanders," David recommended.

"Not a bad idea. I'll run that by him," Kroesen said, jotting down a note. "The second leadership problem they have is the generals. A bunch of incompetent, indecisive politicians...and don't repeat that outside this room. I've already spoken to Abrams about Lam. He needed to go, but he's wired tight with Coa Ky. If I could attribute this disaster to one person, it would be him, but he managed to pile the shit on Giai, who is now facing a court-martial and is under house arrest. Truong even made a behind-the-scenes case to keep Giai but was turned down. Someone must be the fall guy and Lam managed to dump it all on Giai. There's just too much rotten wood in the wood pile at the top. And if we say anything about it, 'Oh, you Americans, meddling in Vietnamese matters' is what we're going to hear. I spoke with Hollingsworth down in III Corps and he hears that all the time from the Corps and 5th Division commander," Kroesen said in frustration as his intercom buzzed.

"Yes," he said, picking up the receiver. "Alright, I'll be right there." Kroesen stood. "Let's go see what they're asking for."

38

TAKE THE FIGHT TO THEM

12 May 1972
369th VNMC Recon
My Chanh River

The moonless night provided the darkness necessary to cover their movement. Captain Luc, the recon company commander, and First Lieutenant Thu Xuan, the commo officer, slipped into the waters along with a small element of Marines and quietly and slowly swam the river. Once over, they moved with all the stealth they could muster to establish a communications site. They all knew if they were discovered, there would be no rescue. Their mission provided guidance for what was about to happen at first light.

* * *

0600 Hours
USS *Okinawa*

. . .

"Alright, let's get this briefing started," Lieutenant Colonel Ed Hertberg said, taking center stage. "General Truong has had enough of being pushed back. It's time to push the enemy. This operation is going to be the first. A helicopter assault across the My Chanh River and then a ground assault south into the rear of the frontline enemy forces along the My Chanh River. The defensive line along the My Chanh River has stopped the commie advance. Now's the time to kick their butts. Helicopters from HMM-164 will support the lift of over thirteen hundred Vietnamese Marines from FSB Sally. CH-53 aircraft will carry fifty Vietnamese Marines and the CH-46 aircraft will each carry twenty Vietnamese Marines. We will pick the troops up at FSB Sally. The first lift will depart Sally and fly treetop level, no higher than forty feet for the CH-46 and no higher than fifty feet for the CH-53 aircraft. The first landing zone is LZ Tango, and we have a 0930 H hour. We will have a naval gunfire and artillery prep from H minus six to H minus two. We depart at 0800 and all aircraft should be airborne within forty minutes. We will have Cobra escorts as well as LOH support. You guys fly whatever line you need to avoid enemy fire. The Cobras will adjust accordingly to cover you. Cobra flight leader is Centaur Six. After the first lift, return to the ship and refuel. We will then return to Sally and pick up the second lift and insert them into LZ Delta with an H hour of 1136 hours. Complete the second lift and return to the ship," Lieutenant Colonel Hertberg said. "Chalk assignments are as indicated on the board, along with crew assignments. See you on the flight deck."

The day before, Jack Turner approached Colonel Dorsey. "Sir, if it's okay with you, I'd like to go along on this mission. Give me a good chance to evaluate the Vietnamese in a helicopter assault," Jack said.

"Yeah, good idea. Also, if you would provide a bit of

advice to whichever unit you go in with," Dorsey replied. "You know they're going into the Hai Lang District, don't you?"

"That's where an NVA regiment was reported, yeah, but that regiment is now all along the My Chanh River in a defensive posture facing south. We're going in behind them and attacking into their rear," Jack said.

"Well, Captain Hodory is going in with the 3rd Marine Battalion. Why don't you go with the 8th Battalion?" Dorsey recommended.

"Sounds good, sir, I'll get my kit and head over there for the night. See you when I get back," Jack said, picking up his utility cap.

"Just make sure you get back, Major," Dorsey said, half in jest, half serious.

* * *

Captain Richard Hodory, the assistant advisor to the 3rd VNMC battalion, prepared himself mentally as the CH-46 bobbed and weaved over the terrain, avoiding ground fire, which didn't appear to be significant as the aircraft approached LZ Tango. He knew they were close to landing when the crew opened fire with the onboard weapons and the aircraft commenced decelerating in preparation for landing. As the wheels touched, the back ramp was lowered and the twenty Vietnamese Marines were anxious to get off the large target. Exiting the aircraft, Hodory noticed a tree line about four hundred meters to the south and in the direction the battalion was moving. It was also where a concentration of enemy fire was coming from. The landing zone had been devastated with air strikes, artillery and naval gunfire, but still the enemy was persistent and dug in along the tree line.

"Dai'uy, there, there," the Vietnamese company commander that Hodory was moving with shouted, pointing.

The message was clear even if the language wasn't. *Place artillery fire on the tree line.* Orbiting above was a UH-1H with members of Naval Gunfire Support Element Bravo. A quick call and they responded with aviation support, hitting the tree line. The assault went on, and Hodory continued to adjust fire on the enemy positions using whatever assets were available. As they crossed the four hundred meters of open ground, however, at some point Hodory realized that the best support he could ask for in close proximity was attack helicopters.

"Blue Ghost One-Three, Panther Three, over," Hodory transmitted as he lay behind a low dike in the middle of the rice paddy.

"Panther Three, Blue Ghost One-Three, over," First Lieutenant Chris Cole transmitted as he zipped on the flanks of the ground assault. Chris was the scout leader with the Blue Ghosts, more formally known as F Troop, 8th Cav. F Troop had been in the I Corps area for over a year but operating mostly south of Hue. Chris was operating today with another OH-6 helicopter, two AH-1G Cobras, one which had a 20mm Vulcan strapped under one pylon, and a UH-1H command aircraft. The Naval Gunfire Support Element Bravo, call sign Avenger Six, was flying in the back of that aircraft.

"Blue Ghost One-Three, Panther Three, when this prep stops, can I get you to come over and recon ahead of my elements? Over."

"Panther Three, roger. I'm planning on doing that just as soon the prep stops. We'll sweep ahead of you all the way to the river, over."

The little bird working ahead of the Vietnamese Marines was a welcome sight to those Marines, and their confidence in moving forward increased significantly. By the end of the day, they had crossed back over the My Chanh River. In terms of major operations, it wasn't one, but it was a step north. One that the North Vietnamese would have to answer. While the forces inserted into LZ Tango were making progress, the situation at LZ Delta was very different.

* * *

1045 Hours
FSB Sally

"Flight, this is Lead. We pick these guys up and head for LZ Delta. H hour for Delta is 1136," Lieutenant Colonel Hertberg transmitted from the lead aircraft. Once the troops were aboard, the flight of CH-46s and three CH-53 helicopters departed and assumed a low-level flight attitude, which was as low as possible and as fast as you could fly while maintaining a formation. Up ahead, Hertberg could see the fire support prep being placed on and around the landing zone. *I hope this is as easy as Tango*, he was thinking when the last round impacted at the H-minus-two-minute mark. Commencing his deceleration, Major David Moore, the squadron executive officer flying Chalk Two, made the announcement that no one wanted to hear.

"Chalk Two taking fire, taking fire. LZ is hot." Small-arms fire was being directed at some of the aircraft from the north side of the landing zone.

"Lead, Centaur Four-Five, go short in the LZ. Centaur rolling hot." And Centaur gunships began to lay rockets, minigun fire, 20mm cannon fire and 40mm grenades across the north end of the landing zone. To everyone's horror, the CH-53 took a hit in the tail rotor and had difficulty landing, but it did get on the ground, not to be removed. Three of the CH-46s reported hits but managed to limp back to the ship.

"Centaur Four-Five, Lead, over."

"Lead, Four-Five, go ahead."

"Centaur Four-Five, on my command, hit the CH-53. We can't recover it and we can't afford to leave it here. I take responsibility, over."

"Lead, Centaur Four-Five. I understand you want us to destroy the down CH-53. Is that correct?"

"That's affirmative, Centaur Four-Five."

"Roger." And with that, Centaur Four-Five rolled into a steep dive and released two rockets into the disabled helicopter. The immediate explosion of JP-4 fuel left a lasting impression on everyone.

* * *

Jack had never really liked sitting in the back of a CH-53 going in on a combat assault in training, and this was his first time doing so in combat. All his previous experience in combat had had him in a CH-46, and he didn't care to be in the back of one of those either. *Get me out of this thing quickly, dear Lord*, Jack was thinking as tiny bullet holes appeared in the skin of the aircraft, above the heads of the Marines seated there. The flight engineer had just given them the two-minute warning when he began shooting. Suddenly the aircraft lurched to one side. *Shit, something hit us*, Jack thought when the back of the aircraft slammed into the ground. *At least the ramp is down.* Jack was on his feet and leading the charge out the back. The Vietnamese Marines quickly exited right behind him. As soon as they exited, everyone took up a prone position, waiting for the aircraft to depart.

Getting his bearings while lying on the ground, Jack spotted the 8th Battalion commander. Major Nguyen Van Phan was behind a small dike, looking at his map. Jack pushed up and trotted over to him. "What's the plan, Major?"

"Can you put fire on tree line?" Phan asked, pointing at a tree line south of their location at three hundred meters.

"Sure can," Jack said turning to the ANGLICO team chief that was moving with Jack. Jack didn't need to say anything as the team chief understood.

"Avenger Six, Custom House Four, over."

"Go ahead, Custom House Four."

"Roger, contact our friends and place fire on this tree line," the lieutenant directed.

"Roger, Custom House Four. Break, break, Vigilant Shepherd, Vigilant Shepherd, Avenger Six, over," the Naval Gunfire Support Element transmitted. Sitting a mile offshore, its gun crews at their stations and just waiting, the USS *David* (DE 1050) answered the call.

"Avenger Six, Vigilant Shepherd, over."

"Vigilant Shepherd, Fire Mission, troops in tree line with overhead cover." The team chief passed the coordinates, and Jack and Phan watched as the naval gunfire from the USS *David* ripped through the trees and tore into the enemy bunkers and trenches. When the *David* reported end of mission, Phan ordered his Marines to move out, and they did, quickly moving against the enemy position before they had time to recover from the pounding they had just taken.

When Jack reached the enemy position, he immediately looked to see what intelligence he could glean from the destruction. Not much was left. Most communications equipment was in pieces. The NVA relied on wire communications, so there were few radios to get frequencies from that hadn't been destroyed. A few prisoners were being rounded up.

"Black Watch Six, Highlander Six, over," Jack heard on his advisor radio.

"Highlander Six, Black Watch Six, over." Major Cockell was with the 9th Vietnamese Marine Battalion on this operation along the south shore of the My Chanh River and serving as a blocking force.

"Black Watch Six, Highlander Six. We're starting across the river to link up with you, over."

"Roger, Highlander Six, I'll pass that to my people. We believe these guys are part of the 66th NVA Regiment. We have a couple of prisoners and they're a bit surprised. We're finding a lot of ammo, weapons and equipment. Have one burning tank and I understand my neighbors on my flank have two burning tanks over there. I'll see you at the linkup point, over," Jack said.

"Roger, see you at the linkup. Highlander Six out."

By the end of the day, the 3rd and 8th VNMC Battalions along with the 9th were back across the river and congratulating each other on a successful operation. Possibly a bit too soon.

39

GATHERING OF COMMANDERS

17 MAY 1971
11th Aviation Group HQ
Da Nang, South Vietnam

"Gentlemen, if you will take a seat, we will get started," Lieutenant Colonel Cass, commander of the 11th Combat Aviation Group, said as he entered the room. Gathered were the aviation unit commanders from those units operating in MR-1. Seated were Major Dan Kingman of the 48th Assault Helicopter Company, call sign Blue Star Six, as well as Major Larson, Centaur Six from F Troop, 4th Cav, who had just recently taken command. The Blue Ghost commander, F Troop, 8th Cav, was present, as was the commander of 4th of the 77th ARA, call sign Blue Max. Although the unit was designated a group, it barely represented a battalion's worth of aircraft. Once everyone settled, Cass took a seat in the front. It was obvious he was going to chair his meeting.

"Okay, I want to go over a few things that I think we need to address and make some changes. First is intelligence. We have responsibility for Night Hawk around Da Nang and keeping the rockets from hitting this place. They're coming from Rocket Ridge and we aren't doing a real good job of finding them and preventing them from impacting. I have discussed this with the S-2 and it appears that our S-2 section was designed to be administrative versus an operational organization. Well, that is changing starting today," Cass said. He then turned to Major Wycoff, the S-2. "Major, you explain it."

Wycoff was an aviator but also branched Military Intelligence. He had been newly assigned to the group and from the start he didn't like what he was seeing in the group intelligence section. "Gentlemen, our section has been an administrative organization for the past year, simply passing on intelligence that we get from the Air Force and Mi detachment. Truthfully about ninety percent of that intelligence is bogus or has no meaning for us. I've discussed this with the colonel, and here's what we are going to do. First, the S-2 shop will prebrief and debrief each Night Hawk crew with each mission. We will pass on to them what we as an intelligence section have developed based on previous reports. After each mission, we will debrief the crews to get the latest combat information that we can develop into combat intelligence. Second, we will send out a mission tasking order each day by 1200 hours announcing the prebrief time and launch time. We will vary those times and vary the duration of each mission. We will no longer launch at the same time each day and fly the same route. We're going to start mixing things up. Third, a unit will have the mission for a month at a time and we would like the same crews each night. This will provide the crews with the opportunity to sleep during the day and have input during the prebrief based on what they've been seeing. Any questions," Wycoff asked. There were none.

Cass resumed, "Okay, next on the agenda is flight altitudes. The air-defense threat is such that we will no longer be flying at altitude. Low-level or nap of the earth only. We're hearing that they may be moving into the area with this SA-7 Stella anti-aircraft missile, and it can take you down up to about eight thousand feet."

"Sir, how are the C&C birds going to exercise navigation control on cav missions? Right now we fly at fifteen hundred feet and provide navigation guidance to the little birds," Major Larson questioned.

"I recommend you either follow behind the gunships and provide navigation guidance or go to altitude over a secure area and provide guidance. Over unsecured areas, I want you low-level," Cass replied.

"Sir," Kingman said, gaining the colonel's attention. "Sir, low-level will work for the lift ships, but that N-O-E crap that Mother Rucker is putting out is not going to work for a lift. Can you just imagine six to twelve Hueys moving forward, hiding behind trees on a combat assault? I don't think so. That may work for the cav in a recon roll, but not for the lift birds. And as far as the SA-7s are concerned, I seriously doubt that the enemy is going to bring them here or that the Soviets or Chinese would give them to the NVA for fear of us getting our hands on them."

"Excuse me," Major Larson said with some disdain in his voice. "I lost a crew on 2 May and the other birds in the flight say it was a missile of some type and not an RPG. The SA-7s are here and we're going to see a lot more of them."

"Well, for now let's keep everything at low level. I don't want to lose anyone needlessly," Cass said. "Okay, the last item. I'm preparing a report to send to Aviation Systems Command about our aircraft. In my opinion, our current aircraft are just not adequate any longer. They have served us well in the low-intensity conflict which this war has been for the past five years, except during Lam Son 719. As then and now, we are no longer in a low-intensity conflict but a mid- to high-intensity one, and the Huey, even the Cobra, is not up to the task. Our engines are vulnerable, our crews are vulnerable, our fuel cells are vulnerable. We need redundancy in the engines. We need better armor protection for the crew chiefs and door gunners. We need crash-worthy fuel cells that won't burst into flames if they take a round through them. We need a modular package concept if something needs to be replaced rather than waiting on individual parts. What do you all think?"

"Sir, no one can object to those improvements, but we aren't going to see that in our time. Hell, it'll take twenty years to bring a new aircraft online," Kingman said.

"Not so," Larson spoke up. "The Cobra only took eighteen months from paper to production."

"True, but it's really a skinny Huey with a Charlie-model rotor head and a Mike-model engine. He's talking about a whole new aircraft," Kingman replied.

"I am," Cass stated. "And unless we raise the flag now, it will never happen."[1]

40

SPOILER ATTACK

20 MAY 1972
369th VNMC Command Post
My Chanh Line

On 4 May 1972, Lieutenant General Ngo Quang Truong took command of I Corps. He was determined to go on the offensive. To do that, he had to reposition forces. One of the first actions he took was to realign sectors of responsibility. He announced his plans to his commanders and senior advisors with his decision that day.

"Gentlemen, my first concern is consolidating and stabilizing our defense of Hue. In the past, the Marine brigades have been scattered in support of Army units. No more. The Marine brigades will now be consolidated under a Marine division," Truong said, much to the joy of those Marine brigade commanders and their advisors. Colonel Metcalf, however, didn't look happy. Since Lam had departed, he had been placed back as the senior Army advisor to the 3rd ARVN Division but would no longer exercise control over the advisors for the Marine brigades. Colonel Joshua Dorsey would now control all advisors to the Marine brigades as well as serve as the senior advisor to the Marine division.

Truong continued. "The Marine division will be responsible for the eastern portion of the My Chanh Line from the coast across QL1 to the foothills of the Annamite Cordillera. The Marine division will also have control of the Regional and Popular Force units responsible for the coast. The 2nd Marine Battalion will establish defensive position overlooking the My Chanh Bridge and prevent anyone from rebuilding the bridge. 2nd Brigade of the 1st Airborne Division is attached to the Marine division until such time as the airborne division headquarters is in place. That brigade will be the westernmost unit on the Marine division's flank and the left flank of the 2nd Marine Battalion. As the 1st Airborne Division comes online they will occupy between their 2nd Brigade and the 1st ARVN Division. Understood?" All indicated they did.

Colonel Nguyen The Luong commanded 369th VNMC Brigade and had been in command since the beginning of May. He and Colonel Dorsey had hit it off pretty well and had a good working relationship.

"Colonel," Dorsey said, acknowledging Colonel Luong when he walked into the 369th VNMC Brigade command post. Luong returned the salutation with a smile upon recognizing who had said it.

"Dorsey, what you think about our situation?" Luong asked.

"Colonel, I think we're sitting pretty good. Your strongest battalion is on the eastern flank along the My Chanh River. The 369th Brigade has the Regional and Popular Front Force along the coast watching Route 555. The 258th Brigade and 39th Ranger Battalion are positioned on the west flank to the Annamite Cordillera with the airborne brigade coming up today. I'd say we're sitting pretty good. If he makes a major attack, it's going to be from the west, I believe, or down QL1," Colonel Dorsey said. "The operation we conducted on the 13th set him back, I'll bet, preventing him from doing anything along the My Chanh Line for a while," Dorsey concluded.

"I believe you are correct, Colonel. Now we wait and see what he does," Colonel Luong replied. He didn't have to wait long.

* * *

0630 Hours
21 May 1972

"Sir, Captain Hodory is on the line," Sergeant Swift said, holding the receiver to the TA-1 phone out. Swift had been at Alpha 2 before the invasion had started and at Ai Tu command center when it did start. With the reshuffling of US Marine advisors, he had been assigned to the 369th Brigade advisor team fire support cell. "He wants to speak to you and says it's urgent," Swift added, handing the phone to Major Regan Wright, the artillery advisor to the 369th VNMC Brigade.

"Wright here," he said as he took the receiver and listened.

"Sir, Hodory here. We're starting to get reports from the Ruff-Puffs that they're receiving ground probes and hear tanks along the coast road," Hodory said. No USMC advisors were with the Ruff-Puffs, and Hodory, with the 3rd VNMC Battalion, was the closest.

"What time did the probes start?" Wright asked.

"About an hour ago. They thought at first it was just harassment, but now that they hear tanks, they're thinking maybe an attack. Do you think—" His words were cut short by a loud explosion.

"Hodory," Wright called out, "what was that?"

"We got incoming. Can you get a scout team up and tell us what is—" Another loud explosion.

"Hodory, are you okay?" Wright asked with concern.

"Sir, I think we have the beginning of a major attack. This is sustained and accurate artillery. I'll call you back." And the line went dead. Major Wright was more than mildly concerned.

"Sergeant Swift, let's see if we can get a scout team up and over the Ruff-Puffs to see what's going on." Turning to the VNMC officer on watch, he asked, "What are you hearing from the Ruff-Puffs?"

"No contact with them. Frequency being jammed and landline is down," he answered.

This is not good, Wright was thinking when he heard the calls for fire coming over the radio from Captain Hodory to the fire direction center. Naval gunfire would soon be employed in support of the Ruff-Puffs, but they had no advisor that could adjust the fire for them. *Hodory must be adjusting based on what he's hearing*, Wright thought.

Captain Hodory had forgotten to mention that he had moved from the 3rd VNMC Battalion CP to the last position on the eastern flank of the division, overlooking the area covered by the Ruff-Puffs. In addition, he could see where the Ruff-Puffs were adjusting their mortars and artillery support, so he simply added naval gunfire to those impacting rounds. Not the best way to employ supporting fires, but at least it might have added weight to the fires employed by the Ruff-Puffs. As he watched the action unfold, he realized that the Ruff-Puffs, as gallant as their effort was, were not going to be able to stop the attack. Scampering back to the 3rd VNMC

Battalion command post, he found the battalion commander, Major Le Ba Binh.

"Major, the Ruff-Puffs aren't going to be able to hold much longer. I recommend that you pull your flank around to face this attack or they're going to be able to roll you up," Hodory advised.

"I have ordered 1st Company to reinforce 3rd Company. They move now. Brigade say they have aero scout team coming to assess situation. They contact you shortly. Centaur Four-Five is call sign," Major Binh said. "We go 3rd Company and observe from there," Binh added, putting his helmet on and grabbing his M16.

Moving back to the right flank of 1st Company, Hodory and Binh watched as 3rd Company reinforcements began arriving. Hodory was very pleased with the manner in which the 3rd Company commander positioned the reinforcements, not along the My Chanh Line but perpendicular to his forces and extending their defensive line to the south. It wasn't long before retreating Ruff-Puffs began passing through his lines. Those that did were quickly integrated into the line to strengthen the defense.

* * *

0900 Hours

Captain Hodory and Major Binh were observing the actions in the Ruff-Puff sector as the first enemy artillery began to fall on his positions. The command post for the Ruff-Puffs was one of the first targets to be destroyed.

"That didn't look like artillery," Hodory blurted out as he watched the blast exit the windows in the TOC. Binh tapped his shoulder and pointed to the left. He said one word: "Tank." Hodory quickly grabbed up his binoculars.

"No, not one tank, but many," Hodory exclaimed and began counting. "Oh shit, I count six and I think there are more behind them," he said, handing Binh the field glasses. Binh began to look a bit concerned as he scanned the field when an OH-6 helicopter passed over their heads, fast and low.

"Panther Three, Centaur Four-Five, over."

"Centaur Four-Five, Panther Three," Hodory responded.

"Panther Three, Centaur Four-Five is a heavy pink team. We were told to look over the area along Route Triple Five."

"Centaur Four-Five, that's affirmative. Be advised the Ruff-Puffs are being pushed west into my position, and I count six"—Major Dinh quickly held up eight fingers—"correction, eight tanks along the Triple Five."

"Roger, we'll be on the lookout. Are we cleared to engage?"

"You are cleared along the Triple Five. We'll mark our front line with panels, and smoke when you call for it," Hodory transmitted.

Binh was immediately on his radio, notifying his company commanders to place their orange panels along their front line. As Hodory watched, one of the two AH-1G gunships began firing his rockets and breaking off his attack. As he did so, the second AH-1G began firing his rockets in front of the aircraft making its departure. The second aircraft departed in the opposite direction. Hodory couldn't see the OH-6 aircraft that were doing the scouting, but he could hear their guns firing. After thirty minutes, Hodory got the call he didn't want to hear.

"Panther Three, Centaur Four-Five, over."

"Centaur Four-Five, Panther Three, go ahead."

"Panther Three, we have expended and are breaking

station. We have observed twenty-five tanks moving along Triple Five and heading in your direction supported by infantry—at least a battalion plus if not a full regiment. I didn't see any friendlies in the area forward of your position," Centaur Four-Five reported. He added, "We'll pass this to your higher. Good luck. Centaur Four-Five out."

* * *

1000 Hours

"Hodory, Wright here," the major announced over the TA-1 field phone.

"Yes, sir, we're in contact now with infantry. Two tanks have been destroyed by LAWs. We estimate a reinforced battalion if not a regiment. We're taking mortar fire and tank fire. Major Binh is pulling back his 1st and 3rd Companies to reestablish a new defensive line perpendicular to the My Chanh Line. With these tanks, we're not able to hold our current positions, sir."

"Let me know when you have your new positions, and we'll keep the artillery coming. We have a FAC on station and he'll be bringing in fast-movers along the Triple Five. Contact him and adjust fire," Wright instructed. He didn't realize that Hodory was already working with the FAC. Unfortunately, the anti-aircraft fire was so intense that the FAC was at eight thousand feet and wasn't able to observe the close-in fight, so the air strikes were hitting the follow-on forces and not the tanks in the immediate vicinity of Captain Hodory. The FAC attempted to explain that he had been briefed that morning that the NVA might possess a new air-defense missile called an SA-7 Strella, similar to the US air-defense weapon, the Redeye missile. He was taking no chances and remaining at altitude.

* * *

1200 Hours

Casualties began to increase for the 3rd VNMC Battalion as they were slowly pushed west, which they did in an orderly, disciplined fashion, something Hodory hadn't seen or heard about from the ARVN soldiers. At the 369th Brigade command post, Colonel Dorsey and General Lan, the Marine division commander, were meeting with Colonel Luong. Major Sheridan, the senior advisor to the 369th Brigade was present as well.

"The situation is that the Ruff-Puffs were forced to pull back and withdraw due to the pressure from the enemy supported by tanks. Some moved south along Route 555 and established a blocking position. Others moved west into the 3rd Battalion lines and the enemy followed. It appears that they are attempting to roll up the flanks of the brigade and open the My Chanh Line," Colonel Luong explained. When no questions were presented, he continued, "The 3rd Battalion has adjusted his forces to face this threat. I have also ordered the 9th Battalion to begin reinforcing 3rd Battalion. The enemy infantry are the main problem as they have been reluctant to move their tanks with the air support we are getting. As long as they hide under the trees, they think they are safe. When they are moving, the FAC can easily spot them and brings in air strike. The pressure on the 3rd Battalion is mostly infantry now with artillery support," Luong explained.

"Why have we not knocked out his artillery?" General Lan asked, looking at Colonel Dorsey for answers.

"Sir, there are a couple of factors. First, he has dispersed his artillery. Two guns fire from one position and then stop, while two guns in another location begin firing a few rounds, followed by two more guns in a third position. This way there's not a lot of telltale smoke for the FAC to spot. Second, the FACs have been warned about this Strella missile and they're flying at eight to nine thousand feet, making it difficult for them to see targets. Third, and this has been suspected from the beginning of this campaign, is the fact that Soviet advisors may be with the artillery units and directing the action. This is typical Soviet tactics and very effective shooting, if I might add," Colonel Dorsey outlined when Sergeant Swift handed Major Sheridan a slip of paper.

"Sir, we just got a report from Captain Hodory. It appears that the air strikes are taking their toll on the infantry. He reports that the combination of 9th Battalion reinforcing 3rd Battalion and the air strikes have stopped the attack and eased the pressure. Major Dinh is preparing to start pushing the enemy back. He says further that the enemy tanks have been holding back and not advancing," Major Sheridan said.

"Same thing was seen in the beginning—a lack of coordination between the tanks and the infantry," Colonel Dorsey observed.

"Lucky for us, sir, that they just can't seem to get it together for a coordinated attack," Major Sheridan added. General Lan and Colonel Luong continued to study the map as Colonel Dorsey and Major Sheridan stood back and allowed the two Vietnamese officers to discuss the situation. Dorsey and Sheridan were there to make recommendations and assist, not command. Command decisions had to be made by the two Vietnamese officers, who were very capable commanders in Dorsey's opinion. When they were done with their discussion, General Lan announced his decision.

"I'm going to order the armored cav to advance up Route 555 and link up with the Regional and Popular Force forces. The armored cav should be here by morning. It appears that the 3rd Battalion can hold and push the enemy back for now.

In the morning, they can coordinate a counterattack with the armored cav. The armored cav will be under the command of Colonel Luong and 369th Brigade. Do you think that is satisfactory, Colonel Dorsey?" Lan asked.

"Sir, I think that is most appropriate and should drive them back across the My Chanh. I'll see about keeping the Air Cav up scouting the area to make sure they don't attempt to slip out or around our forces," Dorsey added.

* * *

"What's going on over in the 3rd Battalion AO?" Jack asked Major Phan as Jack walked into the command post from having walked the defensive line. All morning, they had been hearing sounds of a fight and the sounds appeared to be getting louder.

"Situation in 3rd Battalion not good. NVA attack with infantry and tanks and got across My Chanh on Route 555. Pushed Ruff-Puffs back. Have turned the flank of 3rd Battalion," Phan said, looking at his map. Jack squatted down next to him to get a good look.

"Shit, if they turned the 3rd Battalion's flank, they could well turn ours if 3rd Battalion folds," Jack said, pointing to the map.

"I think we reinforce 1st Company with platoon from 3rd Company on this right flank. We be ready if 3rd Battalion folds," Phan said.

"Good idea, Phan. I'll go and bring that platoon over to 1st Company and show them where to dig in," Jack said as he stood to head out the door. The 1st Company commander wasn't happy about losing a platoon but understood the situation and the order. Grabbing the platoon leader, Jack started leading the platoon to its new fighting position, where they began digging as soon as they arrived.

* * *

1600 Hours

The sound of a helicopter shutting down could be heard outside the 369th Brigade command post. A few minutes later, Major Kingman, commander of the Blue Stars, walked into the TOC, looking for the senior advisor.

"Hi, Blue Star Six, 48th Assault Helicopter Company. Understand you have some wounded that need to be evacuated," he said, approaching Major Sheridan.

"Yes, and glad to see. Let me give you a rundown of what we got," Sheridan said, moving to the map board. "This morning they hit the Ruff-Puffs along Route 555. We call it the Triple Nickel for short. They caused us to withdraw. We had to adjust our line, with the 3rd and 9th Battalions doing the heavy lifting. They had tanks with them but didn't bring them forward, only their infantry, about a regiment minus, we figure. Anyway, we hit them with air strikes, artillery and Cobras and have been able to reestablish our initial defensive line. We have a lot of wounded that we evacuated, and that's where you come in," Sheridan explained.

"We've been doing a lot of medical evacuation missions as there are almost no more medevac units left in-country. Where exactly is the pickup point so I can pass that to my aircraft? I have six inbound, so we should be able to get your people out fairly quickly," Kingman said. Sheridan gave him the pickup location, which Kingman plotted on his map.

"Okay, I'll get on the radio and pass this along to my ships. Oh, I brought in a US Army sergeant with some kind of new weapons system. He's getting his stuff out of the aircraft. I'll send him in when he's unloaded," Kingman indicated.

"What kind of new weapon system?" Sheridan asked.

"I'm not sure. Some sort of antitank system. He called it a TOW. He'll have to explain it to you. I'll call you when I'm airborne."

Kingman departed. A few minutes later, a US Army buck sergeant entered and asked to see Major Sheridan.

"I'm Major Sheridan," he said, approaching the three-stipe sergeant. Right away, he noticed the combat infantry badge and combat patch from the 196th Light Infantry Brigade.

"Sir, Sergeant Bill Tillman. I was told to report to you for instructions," Tillman said. Bill was from Ridgeway, Colorado and was not happy in his assignment as gate guard at the Da Nang air base. One night in a slightly intoxicated state he'd told the battalion command sergeant major what he could do with the gate guard duty. The sergeant major didn't appreciate the guidance and sent young Tillman to a five-day course on this new weapons system. Unfortunately, in school he had never actually fired the weapon due to the expense of the missile that it fired.

"Okay, instructions for what.? To be honest, Sergeant, this is the first I've heard about you. Why are you here?" Sheridan asked.

"I guess you didn't get the word, sir," Tillman said with some frustration. "Sir, I've been instructed to come here and employ the TOW system. I was told to report to you and you would give me a Vietnamese squad to help me set up and I would show them how to use the system," Tillman replied.

"Who told you to report to me?"

"A Lieutenant Colonel Turley, sir. He's at FRAC and told me that you could use the system." Miller noticed a smile creeping across Sheridan's face.

"Okay, tell me about this TOW system. What's it do?"

"Sir, it kills tanks. It kills them out to a range of three thousand meters. And it does it in the day or the night, in good weather and bad weather. TOW stands for tube-launched, optically tracked, wire-guided missile," Tillman said with some pride.

"Okay, I'll get you a squad, and tomorrow I'll move you out to the unit that has had contact with tanks. How many of these systems are in-country?"

"Sir, there are two ground systems, this one and one down at Da Nang, and four systems mounted on gunships. Two operating in the Kontum area. I understand all those have scored kills," Tillman added.

"Okay, for tonight, why don't you just stay here at the command bunker and we'll send you out in the morning?" Sheridan explained. "Right now the fighting has died down. There were tanks earlier today, but things are getting quiet now. Sergeant Swift will show you where you can bunk tonight," Sheridan explained.

"Sounds good, sir. Until the morning."

* * *

0100 Hours
22 May 1972

Jack had been with 8th Battalion since the helo assault. He was enjoying a few hours of sleep when he was rousted awake by Major Phan. "Wake up! 3rd Battalion just got hit and with tanks!" Phan screamed.

"What? How? When?" was all Jack could say as he attempted to clear the cobwebs from his head. "Where are they now?" Jack questioned.

"They one klick behind us, moving toward brigade CP," Phan answered.

"Phan, I would recommend you pull one platoon from each company and form a reserve facing rearward and position them here. This is the likely avenue approach into our rear," Jack said, pointing at the map. Phan said nothing but studied it for a moment.

"Good. Now we have four companies. You command 4th Company," Phan said, looking right at Jack.

"Me? Why me?"

"I have no captains left, and it your idea. You go now and take command. I notify companies to move a platoon to this location. You be there." Phan left to return to the command post as Jack was thinking, *What have I gotten myself into now?*

The position Jack had chosen was where the supporting artillery battery of 105mm howitzers were located. He figured that would be the primary target of the tanks once they got in the rear area. Arriving, he found the artillery battery crews were on their guns and just waiting for orders. He approached the battery commander.

"Dai'uy, what have you got in the tubes?" he asked.

"I have beehive in two tubes and point detonated in three tubes. We ready," the young Marine captain said.

"Good, we'll have infantry here shortly and I'll position them around your battery," Jack said.

"Thank you, Major. I was afraid I would have to defeat this attack all by myself," the captain said, showing some sarcastic humor. Jack just smiled and patted his shoulder.

* * *

0115 Hours

"Sir, wake up. Wake up, sir," Sergeant Swift yelled, attempting to wake up Major Sheridan.

"Yeah, I'm awake. What's up?" Sheridan asked, startled and semiconscious.

"Sir, it's Captain Hodory on the phone. They're under a full attack. Tanks and infantry together. He says some of the tanks have broken through their lines," Swift stated.

"Oh shit," Sheridan blurted out as he groped for his boots. "Do we know where they are right now?"

"Reports are coming in from the 9th Battalion that some are in their rear area," Swift responded, adding, "and heading this way."

"Where's the sergeant with that antitank system?" Sheridan asked as he headed for the door of the advisor hut to the command post.

"Sir, he's setting up his weapon on the edge of town on that small rise. Said it was the highest point around that he could get off clear shots," Swift said. The sounds of small-arms fire accented by the explosive sound of tank rounds was not ignored by Sheridan.

"Sergeant Swift, break out those M72s in the bunker. We may need them before this is over," Sheridan directed. As they entered the command bunker, Sheridan headed right to the operations desk. Colonel Luong was talking with his operations officer and studying the map.

"Good morning, Major Sheridan. Sorry we wake your sleep," Luong said in an almost cheerful voice.

"Morning, sir, what's the situation?"

"Not good. 3rd Battalion has had tanks break through but is holding infantry. They were surprised. OPs/LPs not report. Think maybe they taken out earlier. Last report from 3rd Battalion indicates they destroy seven tanks with M72. 9th Battalion reports tanks are in the rear area now and we believe they come this way."

"Sir, I'll see if we can get Spectre up and over us to find them," Sheridan said and moved off to the Air Force liaison radio. Off in a corner, he noticed Major Wright was getting a crash course from a young Vietnamese

Marine on how to operate the M72 light antitank weapon.

* * *

0200 Hours

"Dai'uy, *fire!*" Jack yelled as a tank crested the adjacent hill next to the artillery battery. Jack was in the process of positioning the arriving infantry platoons when they heard the sound of a track vehicle. They just weren't sure what type or whose track vehicle it was. The battery commander unloaded one tube and substituted an illumination round for a beehive round, increased the tube to maximum elevation and fired. The burning one-million-candle-power flare revealed the tank approaching. Jack grabbed a gun commander and pointed. Words didn't need to be exchanged as the gun commander lowered the tube and aimed the gun. He looked at Jack, smiled and nodded. That was all Jack needed.

* * *

"Don," Sheridan called out to Major Donald Price.

"Yeah, whatcha need?" Price answered.

"Find that sergeant with that antitank weapon and see if he needs any help. Those tanks are heading this way and he may be able to take out one or two," Sheridan said as he reached for the Air Force liaison radio.

"Roger, I think know where he's at. I'll find him," Price said as he picked up an M72 and headed for the door.

A few minutes later, Sheridan returned to talk to Colonel Luong. "Sir, Spectre will be on station in about an hour," he informed the colonel.

"Good," Luong said and pointed at the map. "I have just ordered the 8th Marine Battalion to prepare to counterattack and reinforce the 9th and 3rd Battalions. We will be thin along the My Chanh Line, but cannot be helped."

"How long before they're in position?" Sheridan asked. He was hoping they were going to send some Marines to provide security to the brigade command post, which had only the brigade reconnaissance company providing security.

"They move by foot, so a few hours. Trucks may attract the tanks," Luong replied.

Just great, Sheridan thought as the sound of the battle drew closer. *How did they get tanks across the My Chanh River?* he was wondering, as he had been since the first reports. Throughout the wee hours of the morning, reports of continued heavy fighting were received as well as reports of tanks moving in the direction of the command bunker.

* * *

0600 Hours

The clear sound of an explosion was heard, as was the cheer that followed shortly afterwards. *What are they cheering about?* Sheridan wondered as he moved to the door to investigate. Outside, he heard more cheering and it was coming from the top of the bunker.

"Price, what are you so damn happy about?" he asked, looking up at the rooftop. Major Price looked over the edge.

"This damn weapon is awesome. That tank is fifteen hundred meters away and the top just flew off it. We got to get some more of these," Price said as Sergeant Tillman appeared from around the corner of the command post.

"Sorry about the house, sir. Forgot about the back blast area," Tillman said sheepishly.

"What house? What are you all talking about?" Sheridan asked in a confused state.

"Sir, when I fired at that tank, I forgot about the back blast. It was strong enough that it blew one of those thatch houses down," Tillman explained.

"Wait, you just killed a tank fifteen hundred meters out?" Sheridan said in amazement.

"Sure did, sir, and I think that's the first kill by a ground-mounted TOW ever in combat," Tillman said with some pride and a wide grin. "Got to get back and look for some more."

"Well, try not to destroy any more homes in the process," Sheridan said with a smile and gave Price a thumbs-up. Returning inside, he informed Colonel Luong of the success of the system.

"Good, he has more targets coming," Luong said, pointing at the map. Reports indicated that the tank force was indeed only fifteen hundred meters away if not closer. Again the TOW could be heard firing. Another round of cheers went up from the Vietnamese Marines outside. "The 8th Marine are in position and starting their counterattack," Luong added. All they could do in the command post was wait and provide support where needed with artillery.

"Sir, Captain Hodory is on the line," Swift said as things began to quiet down. The TOW hadn't fired in over an hour and no small-arms fire could be heard.

"Sheridan here. How you doing, Captain?"

"Sir, we're good. The 8th hit them hard and the infantry are pulling back. The armored cav is on the Triple Nickel and pouring it into the retreating forces. From what I can tell, they came across the My Chanh with PT-76s initially and then drove their tanks across at a fording site. The river isn't deep there, so I doubt the hull was even covered. How are you doing up there? We just couldn't stop the tanks." Hodory almost sounded apologetic.

"We got a bit of excitement. The closest the tanks got was four hundred meters to the command post. This new weapon system we got was knocking them out long before they got here. Reports are that we knocked out ten tanks before they started retreating. As soon as the 3rd can reclaim its old positions, Luong wants to get the Ruff-Puffs back in position as well as the 3rd, 9th and the 8th. Truthfully, the My Chanh Line is a bit weak right now until we get everyone back in position," Sheridan pointed out.

"Roger, sir. I'll get with Binh and get on it. You have a good day, sir." And Hodory signed off.

41

AIRBORNE MOVES UP

22 May 1972
2nd Brigade, 1st ARVN Airborne
Camp Evans, South Vietnam

"Welcome to the 2nd Airborne Brigade, Lieutenant," Major Pete Kama said as the newly assigned first lieutenant walked into the advisor bunker. Major Kama was the senior advisor to the 2nd Airborne Brigade. He was an Army officer with considerable time in airborne and special forces units. He was also fluent in Vietnamese. Sitting with him were several other American service members. "Let me introduce you to our team, Advisor Team 152. Gentlemen, this is First Lieutenant Tony Shepard, USMC. Tony has been assigned as part of the ANGLICO team," Kama said. Tony felt a bit awkward standing there in clean fatigues with some of the dirtiest guys he had ever seen staring at him.

"Okay, I'll go first. I'm Captain Scott Schick, Senior ANGLICO for the 2nd Brigade," Scott said, standing and extending his hand, which Tony accepted. "I've been expecting you."

"Sir," is all Tony could say before Scott continued.

"This is Lance Corporal Mike Jurak and Corporal Parton, our team's radio operators." They both stood and acknowledged Tony's presence. From their uniforms, Tony quickly summarized they were also Marines.

"Hi, Terry Griswold, but call me Buddha," the giant standing on the far wall said. "This is Sergeant First Class Wright. We're the advisors for the reconnaissance company," Buddha said. From his size, Tony wondered if he had to use a cargo chute on a jump. The man was huge.

"Well, I'm just glad to finally get here. I was starting to wonder," Tony said to break the ice.

"You can have this cot over here. Just stow your stuff under it. Want a beer?" Buddha asked.

"I'll take you up on that," Tony said, tossing his rucksack on his cot, along with his helmet, flak jacket, load-bearing equipment and sidearm.

"So who did you piss off to get this assignment?" Captain Schick asked.

"They drafted about two hundred of us. One hundred from San Diego and one hundred from Kaneohe. Gave us a twenty-four-hour heads-up to get our affairs in order and shipped us over. Since I'm airborne-qualified, I came here," Tony explained.

"So you aren't permanently assigned here?" Major Kama asked.

"No, sir, we were all sent TDY, as you Army types say," Tony answered with a slight grin. He knew what was coming next.

"Son of a bitch!" Buddha said. "You're getting per diem pay on top of your combat pay for being here. Damn, some people have all the luck," he mumbled.

"Hey, it's only another twenty-five dollars a day," Tony said, knowing he was tossing salt in the wound.

"Shit, that's, what, another seven fifty a month you're pulling down. Some things in life are just not fair," Buddha was fuming.

"What branch are you, Lieutenant?" Kama asked.

"Field artillery, sir," Tony responded.

"Good," Kama replied and looked at Schick. "Do you think we could use him for crater analysis?" Schick and Kama both turned to look at Shepard.

"I'd be happy to do that, sir, if it will help," Tony responded.

"Oh, I'm sure it will help, Lieutenant, and I'm sure you'll get lots of opportunities to practice your skill. See, we're on the western flank of this defense and the A Shau Valley is on the other side of the hills out to the west. They have 122-millimeter rockets and 130-millimeter artillery. We're the closest thing for them to shoot, at and they do love to shoot at us," Schick said. "Come on I'll take you on a tour of this place and then we can get some chow. On the menu tonight is your choice of C rations and rice. In fact, we get rice every night... and breakfast." Schick said, picking up his steel pot and weapon.

Camp Evans had been a major US compound for five years and held a division and support troops. Since the drawdown, however, the firebase had fallen into disrepair to some extent but would still be a formidable defensive position if the NVA wanted to take it on. Schick took him over to the brigade command post and showed him where the ANGLICO team hung their hats when they were on duty. Generally they came on duty only when a unit was out and needed naval gunfire support, which was limited now that the brigade was on the maximum range of naval gunfire. If they were needed, a runner was sent to fetch them.

"Right now we have patrols out. Each battalion is assigned a sector, with one battalion held here on the firebase. Vietnamese artillery is handling the calls for fire currently. Right now they're planning to conduct an airmobile insertion for the 26th, but it's going to be to the west as well. VNAF helicopters will be taking them in and Jurak and Parton are going on that mission. Jurak is qualified as a forward observer as well as radio operator, so he can handle it. The 3rd Airborne Brigade has been fighting down around AN Loc in III Corps and is coming up tomorrow. The 1st Airborne Brigade along with the 81st Airborne Rangers are fighting it out down south in An Loc but will be coming up here shortly. When that happens, then we fall back under 1st ARVN Airborne Division and have responsibility for the western side of the force. I've been told that the 3rd Brigade will stay in reserve at LZ Sally and 1st Brigade will join us on the line."

"Sir, I heard talk of a counteroffensive coming," Tony said.

"Yeah, they're planning for that, but they've got to build up our forces before that happens. When it does, you'll be moving with the recon company. Good company commander that you will meet tomorrow. He—"

"*Incoming!*" someone yelled, and both Tony and Schick dropped to the ground as rounds started landing and exploding. Lying there, Schick looked over at Tony. "Well, it looks like you can start today with crater analysis, Lieutenant."

Tony continued to lie on the ground until the shelling stopped. Captain Schick got up and headed for the command post. Tony went and began to analyze the craters created by the incoming shells. Right off, the debris told him the shells were 130-millimeter Soviet shells. The craters' shapes confirmed it as well, as Soviet shells exploded as soon as they hit the ground, whereas US shells buried themselves partially before exploding, creating a bigger crater. Next, he noticed the angle of the craters and began to take a back azimuth from the angle to obtain an idea of where the rounds had come from.

Two kilometers away on a small rise and well camouflaged, a North Vietnamese spotter watched Tony's actions. He quickly determined what Tony was doing and picked up his radio mike. He began his message to the firing battery. *I will make it easy for this guy to determine where the firing battery is*, the spotter was thinking when the first round sounded coming out of the tube.

Tony heard the distant sound of an artillery gun firing, followed by another and another. The second sound was muffled by the sound of the artillery round, which was mimicking a freight train coming right at Tony, who did the only thing possible and lay as flat on the ground as he could. Artillery rounds began impacting all around him. With each round, Tony pressed himself closer to the ground. With each impact, Tony felt the ground shake but heard nothing. His hearing had shut down from the noise and concussion of the blasts. Finally the ground stopped shaking, and he slowly raised his head. He could only see out of one eye but felt no pain. In a flash he was up and sprinting for the door of the command post bunker. Blowing through the doorway, Captain Schick caught him.

"*Wow*, slow down. Let's get a look at that cut. Here, sit down," Schick said. Tony heard none of it but allowed himself to be guided to a seat and his helmet removed. A Vietnamese medic came over and began wiping Tony's face and head. With each stroke, more of Tony's sight returned as the blood was removed from his eye.

"Damn head wounds bleed like a son of a bitch," Schick said as the medic did his thing. Tony caught bits and pieces of that comment as his hearing was returning. Something had sliced Tony's scalp to the bone and he never felt it when it had happened. While the medic stitched Tony's head, Major Kama came in and looked at the newly arrived Marine lieutenant. "Well, did you determine where the guns are at?" he asked.

"Yes, sir," Tony said, which surprised the major. "They're over there." And Tony pointed to the west of Camp Evans. The major had to laugh at that observation.

In response, the major said, "Well, Lieutenant, that is the easiest Purple Heart you are going to get. Take the rest of the day off."

42

HIT 'EM AGAIN

   147th VNMC Brigade
   Tan My

General Lan was not about to let up pressure on the forces across the My Chanh River. The NVA attack from the day before convinced him that something needed to be done and done quickly to keep them from attempting another attack. The order came down shortly after midnight for the 7th VNMC Battalion to move to Tan My Naval Base, due east of Hue. The 6th and 4th Battalions were ordered to move to a pickup zone posture and wait. That morning, Lieutenant Colonel Do Ky, the division G-3 operations officer, Colonel Dorsey and a small staff flew out to the USS *Blue Ridge* with General Lan to coordinate the upcoming operation.

The plan was for the 147th VNMC Brigade to conduct both an over-the-beach amphibious landing and a helicopter assault. The 7th Battalion would conduct the amphibious assault with the 4th and 6th Battalions conducting the helicopter assault portion. Once they arrived at Tan My, the 7th loaded landing craft that took them to the *Schenectady* (LST-1185), the *Manitowoc* (LST-1180), the *Cayuga* (LST-1186) and the *Duluth* (LPD-6).

"Welcome aboard," Brigadier General Miller, commander of the 9th Marine Amphibious Brigade, said as General Lan stepped aboard the *Blue Ridge*.

"Thank you, General. It is my first time aboard this ship." The *Blue Ridge* was a newly commissioned ship and in Vietnamese waters for the first time. Especially designed and built to be a command-and-control ship, its communications and electronics were state-of-the-art. It was capable of supporting the onboard Marine amphibious brigade command element as well as the ground force command element.

"If you will follow me, sir," General Miller said, directing General Lan and his staff off the flight deck. Once in the command center for the ground assault force, General Lan's staff immediately began the coordination for the operation with the assistance of US Navy communications personnel. Besides an amphibious landing and helicopter assault, a B-52 strike would take place along the beach and landing sites just prior to the landings and insertions. As they planned and coordinated, the Vietnamese Marines moved to the awaiting ships.

"Excuse me, sir," First Lieutenant John Paparone said, getting Major Boomer's attention as the Vietnamese Marines boarded the USS *Duluth* (LPD-6), "but have any of these Vietnamese Marines ever conducted an amphibious assault?"

"Why you asking?" Major Boomer replied.

"Well, sir, I command the AmTrac platoon attached to BLT 1-4. I have been tasked to deliver them ashore. Just want to know how experienced they are at doing this and being around the LVTs," Paparone explained.

"Well, I doubt if any of them have ever done an amphibious assault," Boomer replied. "Maybe we should get them below and do some familiarization on them. Whatcha say?"

"Sir, I think that's an excellent idea. Let me get Lieutenant Bob Williams as he commands the AmTrac platoon attached to BLT 1-9 and will bring in the second wave," Paparone said, turning to find his senior NCO. The rest of the day was spent training the Vietnamese Marines on the use of the LTVs that would take them to the beach.

Outside of Hue, the 4th and 6th VNMC Battalions moved to a stretch of Route 555 that they would use the next day for their pickup zone. It was fairly routine for them, so Major Joy and Major Price had little to do in preparation for the mission. They had worked with the CH-46 and CH-53 helicopters of HMM-164 before. That afternoon, Blue Ghost Six arrived to coordinate scout support of the operation as well as gunship coverage for the escort and fire support on the landing zone. All was ready for the next day.

* * *

0750 Hours
24 May 1972

Lieutenant Colonel Hertberg looked across the flight deck of the *Okinawa* as his CH-46 aircraft lifted off. His eighteen aircraft were all waiting their turn to depart and follow him towards Tan My to pick up the 4th and 6th VNMC Battalions, consisting of five hundred and fifty Vietnamese Marines. Between the USS *Duluth* and the USS *Cayuga*, twenty AmTrac vehicles plunged into the clear waters of the Gulf of Tonkin as the sounds of naval gunfire could be heard and the smoke and dust rose above Wunder Beach, thirty-six hundred yards to the west. Lieutenant Paparone's unit made up the first wave and Lieutenant Williams's unit the second wave. Major Boomer was beside Lieutenant Paparone when they closed within two thousand yards of Red Beach. The LVT's noise was loud but didn't drone out the sound of the final B-52 strike on the beach.

"There goes the B-52 strike," Paparone said. "I wouldn't want to be on the receiving end of that." This was his first time in combat, and he had never seen or been this close to a B-52 strike. He was mesmerized watching the few trees that silhouetted the beach flying several hundred feet in the air. Approaching the surf line, explosions from impacting mortar rounds began throwing up water spouts around the LVTs. This surprised Paparone, as he thought no one could survive the amount of naval gunfire and B-52 bombing that had hit the beach.

Lieutenant Williams watched as the first wave went ashore and noted the incoming mortar fire. He also noted some small-arms fire across the beach. Rolling out of the surf, the second wave move up the beach. Suddenly Williams found someone grabbing his leg. It was a Vietnamese Marine who had no desire to get off the LTV. As the rear ramp dropped, most of the Marines were hesitant to depart, and Williams and his crew had to throw some off the vehicle. This same scene was being played out on other vehicles in both the first and the second wave. Once all the Marines were off, Paparone and Williams returned their vehicles to the ships.

On the beach, Major Boomer was moving with the battalion commander as they secured their initial objectives.

"Major Ninh," Boomer said, getting his attention. "You best report that you have secured your objective." This was Ninh's first amphibious assault, and although an experienced combat commander, he was a bit shaken by the experience, and seasick. Boomer watched as light resistance across the sand dunes was met and eliminated by the advancing Marines.

Before long, the body count was fifty dead enemy, with few casualties of their own. It was obvious that the B-52 strike had successfully accomplished its task.

* * *

0940 Hours

"Flight, this is Lead, coming up," Lieutenant Colonel Hertberg announced as his aircraft began to lift.

"Lead, this is Centaur Six," Captain Jim Bryant transmitted.

"Centaur Six, Knightrider Six, go ahead," Lieutenant Colonel Hertberg responded.

"Knightrider Six, Centaur Six. I have a red team[1] screening along your flight route as we discussed. Little birds will mark the LZ with green or red smoke and report condition. Over."

"Roger, understood. We're off at this time, flight of eighteen plus three."

"Roger, I have you in sight," Captain Bryant said. He was at fifteen hundred feet and observing the red team, looking back to see the Marine CH-46s and CH-53s departing the pickup zones. Over friendly lines, as well as over the open water, fifteen hundred feet was a good altitude to fly at. Over Indian country, you would be a perfect target for the newly introduced Strella SA-7 anti-aircraft missile. The flight route, it was decided, would depart the pickup zone, fly out over the water and then approach Landing Zone Columbus from the east, minimizing the time over Indian country for the helicopters. Columbus was identified as the intersection of Route 662 and Route 555, the Triple Nickel.

"Centaur Seven-Zero, Centaur Six."

"Centaur Six, Centaur Seven-Zero," WO Mike Russell

responded. Mike was the lead AH-1H for the day's mission. He had previously flown for the aerial rocket artillery battalion in the 101st Airborne Division, but when they had stood down, Mike had transferred to the Centaurs.

"Seven-Zero, Centaur Six, what's the status of the red team? Over."

"Six, all's quiet for now. We're just crossing the beach. Over."

"Seven-Zero, roger, let's hope it stays that way," Centaur Six said as the flight continued. As the scouts cleared the landing zone, they marked it with smoke grenades.

"Centaur Six, Seven-Zero. Smoke out."

Sabre Six scanned the area and finally saw the smoke drifting up in the morning breeze.

"Knightrider Six, Centaur Six."

Knightrider was flying low across the beach at this point. "Centaur Six, Knightrider Six, over."

"Knightrider Six, Centaur Six, you have green smoke at your twelve o'clock approximately two klicks. How copy?"

"Roger, understand green at twelve two klicks," Colonel Hertberg acknowledged and looked at his copilot with a grin. "Notify the flight we have a cold LZ." Switching to his intercom, he said, "Hey, Major Price."

"Yes, sir."

"Just heard from the scouts. We have a cold landing zone. Thought that news may brighten your day," Hertberg said.

"Sir, you have no idea how much that brightens my day," Major Price said and turned to tell the 4th VNMC Battalion commander the good news. Looking at the faces of the Vietnamese Marines in the aircraft, he saw that the expressions of apprehension were replaced with smiles as they all understood the meaning if not the words.

As the aircraft touched down, the Vietnamese Marines exited through the rear ramps without having to be tossed off the aircraft. No one was shooting at them. Major Price watched as the 6th VNMC Battalion touched down, and although he couldn't see Major Turner, he knew he was somewhere in the mix. Everyone was feeling pretty good at this point with the entire brigade on the ground and no enemy contact for the helo assault force. The euphoric mood didn't last long, however.

Small-arms fire could be heard to the south between the brigade and the My Chanh Line. Initially it was sporadic, but the intensity quickly reached a crescendo.

"Devil Dog Six, Devil Dog Four, over," Major Price transmitted.

"Four, this is Six, we're in contact," Major Turner responded. "Appears we've hit the back end of the guys manning the My Chanh. I'm calling in an air strike."

"Roger, Six. I'll work the guns. Break, Centaur Seven-Zero, Devil Dog Four, over."

"Devil Dog Four, Centaur Seven-Zero, over."

"Centaur Seven-Zero, I have contact, request fire support."

"Roger, pass it over."

Major Price sent the call for the fire mission request. Moments later, 2.75-inch rockets began slamming into positions occupied by the 18th NVA Regiment, 325th NVA Division. When Centaur Seven-Zero had expended, Blink Three-Seven, a FAC at eight thousand feet in an OV-10 Bronco, dropped down and marked the area that Seven-Zero had been firing into. Blink placed two rockets into the tree line and now-exposed trench line. The rockets were followed by two F-4 Navy jets unleashing their bombloads. The 147th VNMC Brigade quickly overran the NVA positions.

* * *

Ten days later, as the brigade closed in on its assigned area south of the My Chanh, Colonel Dorsey met with the team at the brigade TOC. The brigade had cleared the area to the north side of the My Chanh River, but maneuvering back and clearing out the defending NVA took several days.

"So how did the operation go?" he asked as they started an after-action review. He had left the *Blue Ridge* when the operation was being wrapped up but before it was completed. General Lan had been made aware of another problem and wanted to get back to his command headquarters as quickly as possible once he was satisfied that the 147th Regiment was established ashore and moving to complete its assigned mission.

"Sir, the amphibious assault went very well considering it was the first time for not only the Vietnamese but most of the US Marines on the AmTracs. Only about ten percent of the US Marines had ever been in a real no-shit combat landing. It was a first all around," Major Boomer said, sipping his coffee, which he'd secured as soon as he'd walked into the command bunker.

"Good, and the helicopter assault?" Dorsey asked, looking at Price and Turner.

They exchanged looks to see who would answer. Turner fielded the question. "Sir, it went smooth. The choppers flew at low level. We took no ground fire coming in and the LZ was cold, so the Vietnamese exited the aircraft with no problems," Turner said. "We did lose one aircraft, Army," he added.

"Oh? What happened?" Dorsey asked.

"Sir, it was the C&C aircraft for the medevac missions. We had six UH-1H aircraft from the 48th working medevac missions. Their CO, Major Kingman, was at a thousand feet and medevac missions were called to him and he was directing aircraft to respond. Seems an SA-7 nailed him. The crew never had a chance. Aircraft exploded in midair as the tail boom separated," Turner concluded.

"Sorry to hear that. Kingman was doing good work for us," Dorsey said.

"Sir, we did manage to police up two prisoners, who informed us that they had recently come down from the north and weren't expecting this reception. We got a body count of approximately three hundred and sixty-nine enemy and three tanks destroyed in addition to releasing about a thousand civilians under communist control. Not a bad week's work," Major Price concluded.

"Well, glad it turned out okay, but time to get back to work. The 258th Brigade was hit the other morning by a regimental attack supported by tanks on the western perimeter. In addition, General Lan is already planning his next move. May need you three to get over there and help out. My jeep is outside, so let's load up and head up to the Division TOC to see what we can do. Oh, and Lieutenant Colonel Turley is now the advisor to the Division G-3. Thought you might like to know."

43

AIRBORNE ASSAULTS

26 May 1972
2nd Airborne Battalion
Camp Evans, South Vietnam

"Hey, Jurak," Parton said, getting his partner's attention, "can you take this extra battery? I have three but would feel better if we carried four."

"Hell, we're only going to be gone for two days, three at the most. You expecting to stay out for a week?" Lance Corporal Jurak asked. He really did not want the extra weight in his rucksack.

"I just want to be sure we have enough juice in case the Vietnamese pilots decide not to come and extract us. I would feel a lot better if we were doing this with American aircraft. You never know about these Vietnamese pilots," Parton said.

"We just stick close to the battalion commander and all will be well, I'm sure," Jurak said, not truly believing his own words. "Besides, we fly into the landing zones and then 1st Battalion is coming to link up with us using track vehicles.

What could go wrong? Don't answer that," Jurak ordered quickly.

In the distance, the sounds of rotor blades beating the air into submission could be heard and a flight of twenty Vietnamese Air Force UH-1H aircraft appeared in some semblance of a formation. As soon as the aircraft touched down, the ARVN soldiers began moving towards them and climbing aboard. Jurak and Parton followed the battalion commander into an aircraft and sat on the floor while the battalion commander took the jump seat between the two pilots.

Once in the air, Jurak and Parton wished that they were in a US Army helicopter. The Vietnamese pilots not only in their aircraft but the others didn't seem to be able to maintain spacing and formation. At one point, Jurak was sure he could walk over to the aircraft flying next to his, it got so close. *Two rotor blade separation my ass*, he was thinking when the other aircraft flared away. As they approached the landing zone, artillery was impacting, but no gunship support, which bothered him a bit.

"Where the hell are the Cobras?" Parton asked as they exited the aircraft.

"The ARVNs don't have Cobra gunships and all the Huey gunships have been shot down or are operating down south. The mountains up here cause them to fly too high for the density altitude and carry too small of a load. They learned the hard way last year in Lam Son 719 that Charlie-model gunships don't work that well up here," Jurak enlightened his battle buddy as the UH-1H aircraft departed.

"Let's go," Parton said, noticing the battalion commander moving out.

"Let's make contact with the FAC," Jurak instructed.

Parton pressed the switch on the mike. "Covey Five-Four, Waterman Four-Five, over."

"Waterman Four-Five, Covey Five-Four, over."

"Covey Five-Four, Waterman Four-Five, we're on the ground and just checking in with you. Over."

"Waterman Four-Five, roger, I believe I have your flight of choppers departing the landing zone. I'm at eight thousand over you, how copy?"

Parton looked up and thought he could see the OV-10 Bronco aircraft but wasn't sure. He couldn't hear it.

"Covey Five-Four, I do not have you in sight—"

"*Incoming!*" Jurak screamed and knocked Parton down as the first round came screaming in on the landing zone. It was accompanied by several others that indicated accurate adjusted fire. Casualties quickly started to mount.

"Covey Five-Four, Waterman Four-Five. We have incoming. Appears to be adjusted fire. Can you spot the guns? Over."

"Waterman Four-Five, wait one, I'm coming down." And Covey Five-Four executed a wingover and went into a plunging dive. As he did so, he saw the rounds impacting on the landing zone and came to the conclusion that he needed to look west and north to find the guns. Slowly he pulled out of his dive and began scanning for telltale smoke from the guns.

"Waterman Four-Five, is it mortars or artillery? Over." He asked because that would make a difference in where to look due to the range differences.

"Covey Five-Four, it's mortars" was the answer.

"Roger." And he began looking in the range of five to ten kilometers from the landing zone, knowing the effective range of the 120mm mortar was about six kilometers. It didn't take long to find the telltale smoke. Winging over, Covey Five-Four dropped like a rock and, while remaining upside down, punched off a smoke rocket. This aim was true and the rocket impacted within one hundred yards of the mortar position.

"Waterman Four-Five, I have target. Fast-movers inbound."

Those were the nicest words Jurak and Parton had heard all morning. Another round impacting brought their thoughts back to the landing zone until they caught a glimpse of two Navy A-6 Grumman bombers coming across the tree-tops. The sticks of bombs they dropped silenced the enemy mortar position, and anything else that may have been around.

"Covey Five-Four, Waterman Four-Five, over."

"Go ahead, Four-Five."

"Roger, thank those guys for us. That was awesome, but a bit of overkill, wasn't it, to dump a full load? Over."

"Their original mission was canceled, and they didn't want to land back aboard with that load on board or drop it in the ocean. Consider it an early Christmas present," Covey Five-Four indicated as he climbed back up to altitude and resumed his chicken hawk surveillance routine.

For the next two hours, the battalion conducted medevac operations with US helicopters. The aircraft had a blue star on the nose, extracting the wounded, and the dead. Eleven body bags were loaded on one aircraft. Seven wounded individuals were loaded on the other six sorties. The days of medevac-specific aircraft taking the wounded out were over. Regular lift ships now undertook the task, and medical treatment didn't start until the wounded reached an aid station or a hospital.

"Blue Star Lead, Blue Star Six."

"Six, this is Lead, go ahead."

"Roger, Lead, this is Six. I'll provide navigation guidance for you. You stay low-level and I'm climbing—"

"Six, this is Lead. You were cut off. Say again, over." There was no response.

"Blue Star Six, Blue Star Lead, over." Again no response.[1]

For the next two days, the battalion moved, finally linking up with the 2nd Battalion. As they moved, they began to pinch the NVA forces against the 258th Marine Brigade. Soon the enemy found themselves encircled between the Airborne units and the Marines. Loose and discarded NVA equipment began to tell a story. The enemy was withdrawing, and not in the most disciplined fashion.

44

COUNTEROFFENSIVE

6 JUNE 1972
I Corps Headquarters
Hue, South Vietnam

General Truong was wasting no time. He wanted a counteroffensive, and he wanted it now. For the month he had been in command, his time and energy had been devoted to stabilizing the situation in Hue with the deserters, establishing a defensive line south of the My Chanh River and rebuilding and rearming the forces. Now it was time to take the fight to regain Quang Tri. His staff had been working on a plan for the past month and now were ready to present it to Truong, the subordinate commanders, and General Kroesen. When Truong and Kroesen walked into the briefing room, everyone stood.

"Keep your seats, gentlemen," Truong said. He pointed at a seat next to his own for General Kroesen but didn't take a seat himself, surveying the room instead. He wanted to see who was attending this briefing. In the back, he saw several new American faces. One he recognized.

"Major Turner," Truong called out.

Standing, Jack said, "Yes, sir."

"Major Turner, who are all those young American officers seated with you?" Truong asked.

"Sir, we have received several ANGLICO teams to support your upcoming operation. Each of these officers is a team chief that will be supporting your operation. A team will be with the 1st ARVN Airborne Division, the 1st ARVN Division and the 2nd ARVN Division in addition to 1st Vietnamese Marine Division," Turner explained. "In addition, sir, we've placed teams at FRAC to integrate artillery, air and naval gunfire to support your operation. Major Borman will be located there to coordinate these assets. Naval gunfire teams will be flying out of Da Nang and Phu Bai as well."

"Gentlemen, I'm very glad to have you joining us," Truong said with a smile and then turned to take his seat. "Please begin."

A Vietnamese colonel took the stage and called for his first slide. Most of the Americans in the room didn't speak Vietnamese but could follow the gist of the brief from the slides presented. Jack was filling in the blanks quietly in the rear.

"Sir, we currently defend south of the My Chanh River as indicated with the 147th Marine Brigade on the right from the coast west to the O Lau River; 369th Marine Brigade from the O Lau River west to Xa Phong Hoa; and the 258th Marine Brigade from Xa Phong Hoa west to QL1. 1st Airborne Division defends from QL1 west to the Annamite Cordillera foothills. 1st Infantry Division is in reserve at Eagle, with one Airborne brigade in reserve at Evans. The Ranger groups will screen the western flank of the corps sector. Next slide." Before the slide came up, Truong turned to the 258th Brigade commander.

"You understand that the 2nd Battalion is responsible for the bridge on QL1 and that is still your responsibility," Truong asked.

"Yes, sir, and we will hold the bridge," the commander replied.

Satisfied, Truong then turned to Kroesen and had a conversation to which no one else was privy. As the next slide came up, Truong nodded for the briefer to continue.

"Sir, the enemy before us is the 304th NVA Division reinforced with tanks. Their main headquarters is in the Citadel in Quang Tri at this time. The 324B NVA Division is on our western flank, operating out of the Annamite Cordillera. The 308th NVA Division is opposing the 1st Airborne Division," the colonel said, pausing to see a reaction from Truong. There was none.

"Next slide," the colonel called. "Sir, the concept of operation...on order, the 1st Marine Division will attack across the My Chanh River. Both the helicopter assault and amphibious operations will be executed to strike deep behind the enemy front lines to disrupt his logistics, destroy his artillery and commence the encirclement of Quang Tri City."

Turning to General Kroesen, Truong asked, "General, is the Navy ready to support this operation?"

"I can assure you, General, that the US Navy is standing by to assist in this operation with both naval gunfire and lift helicopters as well as tactical air strikes," Kroesen said.

"Good," Truong said. "Gentlemen, we started in May, taking baby steps that allowed us to test the mettle of our forces and provide us with small victories that built confidence in our soldiers and put fear in the minds of the enemy. Our first operations were almost raids into the frontline troops' rear areas. We got in quick, attacked the frontline troops in the rear and pushed through them as we pinned them between our attack and our defense along the river. We did that two times, each a bit more aggressive, and we caused him to be looking in both directions, not sure where to position his forces. When we have placed doubt in his mind, now we move on to bigger operations to seize back Quang Tri. Any questions?" Continuing, he said, "After lunch, we will discuss the logistic requirements to launch this operation. Shall we?" Truong motioned to the door for him and General Kroesen.

45

20TH TASS

29 June 1972
20 TASS Flight Ops
Da Nang, South Vietnam

The 20th Tactical Air Support Squadron was providing the forward air controllers at this time over the entire area of MR-1. Originally flying O-1 Bird Dog aircraft back in 1965, they had transitioned over the years to the OV-10 Bronco. The Bronco was a twin-engine split-tail aircraft with a pilot and observer seated in tandem in a central nacelle.[1] Armed with a variety of weapons in the FAC role, the aircraft would generally carry an internal machine gun and wing-mounted rocket pods carrying seven to nineteen 2.75-inch rockets to mark targets for the supporting attack aircraft.

"Morning, Captain," the operations sergeant greeted Captain Steven Bennett as he came through the door for his morning brief.

"Morning, Sergeant. I hope we have an interesting

morning this morning," Bennett replied, noticing another captain in a US Marine Corps uniform.

"Well, sir, you'll have company today," the sergeant said as the Marine approached Captain Bennett, extending his hand.

"Hi, Mike Brown, spotter. Mind if I ride with you today?" Captain Brown asked.[2]

"Not at all. Glad to have the company, and we just might be able to get some naval gunfire in today. Have you ever been up in a Bronco before?" Bennett asked the Marine Corps aerial observer.

"No, I haven't, but the good sergeant here has already given me two barf bags because he said you'd be sure that I'd have to use them," Brown admitted. "And he lent me a helmet. Got my own map," he added.

"In that case, let me get my brief and we'll go hunting." Once Bennett had his mission brief, they walked out to the aircraft together and Bennett explained the mission for the morning and the aircraft systems. The aircraft crew chief was at the aircraft and had two ladders positioned for the pilots to climb up. While Bennett walked around and conducted his preflight, Brown climbed up and got situated in the back seat, with the crew chief explaining what he could touch and what he shouldn't touch.

"Sir, this is the ejection handle. Do not touch it unless Captain Bennett tells you to do so, and be sure your feet and legs are up against the seat when you do," the crew chief explained.

"Got it, but doubt we'll be using it today," Brown said hopefully. A few minutes later, Bennett was strapped in and started the engines.

"You all set back there?" Bennett asked as the engines ran up to full power.

"All set" was Brown's reply.

Bennett switched to the VHF radio. "Da Nang Ground,

Bully Oh-Four, over." The OV-10 had three radios that the pilot could use: an FM radio to talk to ground personnel, a VHF, and a UHF radio for air-to-air or air-to-airfield communications.

"Bully Oh-Four, Da Nang Ground."

"Da Nang Ground, request clearance to taxi," Bennett said. As the ground and tower knew where all the OV-10s were located on the airfield, it wasn't necessary to state your location.

"Bully Oh-Four, you are cleared to taxi to runway one-seven left, over." With that, Bennett applied power and released his brakes, making his way to the runway. Holding short of the runway, he contacted the tower.

"Da Nang Tower, Bully Oh-Four, holding short of one-seven left for takeoff."

"Roger, Bully Oh-Four, you are cleared to take the active and depart, over."

Bennett made a visual clearance of the approach end of the runway and applied full power as he turned to look down the ten-thousand-foot runway. His takeoff roll used only a quarter of the runway before he was airborne and turned to head north. As they flew north and continued to climb to eight thousand feet, Brown sat back and enjoyed the scenery. The crystal-clear water of the Gulf of Tonkin was only marred by the number of sharks he could count cruising just off the surf. White puffy clouds were scattered at six thousand. AFVN radio was playing the latest rock music on the radio station out of Da Nang. Pilots generally kept the ADF receiver tuned to the station as another navigation aid to get back to Da Nang if need be.

"That's the Quang Tri Citadel up ahead," Bennett pointed out to Brown. "We're going to be putting in a couple of air strikes for the Vietnamese Marines operating northeast of there. They were inserted on the eleventh, I believe, and are trying to root out the bad guys from the Citadel."

"I had a couple of good friends down on Alpha 2 when this dogfight started. They got pushed all the way back. One, a lieutenant, didn't make it, and we have another that's MIA at this time. Hope they find that kid alive," Brown responded.

"We should be able to contact the ground advisors and see what they have for us this fine day," Brown said, switching to the FM frequency radio.

* * *

"Hey, sir, I got a FAC upstairs looking for targets," Sergeant Swift said, looking over at First Lieutenant Stephen Biddulph. Swift was just glad to be out of the command bunker and doing something he found much more worthwhile. They had been in an intense firefight all day, attempting to dislodge the NVA, who were just as determined to stay.

"Great, have him hit that tree line with as much as he can," Biddulph directed. He was new to being an ANGLICO, and Swift had come along to teach him the ropes of dealing with the Vietnamese Marines.

"Bully Oh-Four, Tiger Two-One, over," Swift transmitted.

"Tiger Two-One, Bully Oh-Four."

"Bully Oh-Four, from my location on a two-one-five azimuth four hundred meters in the tree line. Troops in trenches. How copy?"

"Tiger Two-One, I have it. Rolling hot." With that, Bennett turned slightly to his left, looking at the ground as the aircraft entered a left bank. "Hang on, here we go," Bennett said over the intercom, and the aircraft immediately rolled onto its back and went nose low, losing altitude rapidly. As the altimeter wound down and the vertical speed indicator registered a fifteen-hundred-foot-per-minute rate of descent,

Brown could clearly see the red smoke marking Swift's position and the tree line. Going lower, the green tracers from the tree line could be easily seen as they began to rise up towards the aircraft, slowly at first and then increasing in speed the closer they came. Reaching one thousand feet, a 2.75-inch rocket left the aircraft and streaked to the tree line, impacting in a white ball of rising smoke.

Bennett was talking to two F-4 Phantom jet fighters that were loitering at ten thousand feet, waiting for him to mark the target. Pulling out of the dive and rolling upright, Bennett quickly cleared the area so the jets could initiate their bombing runs. At the same time, Brown was clearing his stomach into one of the barf bags provided back at Da Nang. *Oh, this is going to be a long day*, Brown was thinking when Bennett snap-rolled the aircraft into another dive and plunged towards the tree line again, adjusting his rocket impact. Brown pulled out a second barf bag. He knew he was going to need it.

"How you doing back there, Mike?" Bennett asked with a humorous tone in his voice.

"Oh, just fine," Brown managed to get out as the aircraft turned right side up and pulled out of the dive. He lied.

The OV-10 had a flight time of around three hours, and for three hours Brown and Bennett directed one air strike after another on the enemy defending around the Quang Tri Citadel. After the first thirty minutes, Brown had emptied his stomach of all contents, so the dry heaves were no problem, along with the occasional passing out.[3]

"Bully Oh-Four, Tiger Two-One."

"Go ahead, Tiger Two-One."

"Bully Oh-Four, new target located one klick north of the previous target. Troops in the open, how copy?"

"Tiger Two-One, Bully Oh-Four, understand new target. Be advised it'll be an hour before I get another flight and I'm going to have to break station for fuel in one-five minutes, over."

"Bully Oh-Four, any chance we can do something? New target is heavy automatic weapons and a mortar. Over."

"Tiger Two-One, wait one," Bennett said and switched to intercom. "Mike, did you catch that last from Tiger Two-One?" he asked.

"Yeah, sounds like he's in need of some help."

"What say we make a couple of strafing runs to help him out? Going to have to break station soon to go back for fuel, and there are no more fast-movers coming up for another hour."

"Fine by me," Brown said.

"Tiger Two-One, Bully Oh-Four, over."

"Bully Oh-Four, go ahead."

"Tiger Two-One, I have no fast-movers for you, but I can make some runs at it with what smoke rockets I have and my guns. How copy?" Bennett transmitted.

"Bully Oh-Four, be my guest."

"Roger, making my run." And with that, Bennett rolled the aircraft over into a steep dive for the target. Descending, he could see where the enemy fire was coming from and punched off two rockets. They were only smoke rounds, but the NVA didn't know that, and if they did, then they would expect some bombers coming in right afterwards. Bennett followed up with his machine guns, strafing the area. Instead of climbing back to altitude as he normally would, he maintained a lower altitude and came back around, strafing the enemy position. He did that three more times.

"Mike, this is the last run as I'll be out of ammo after this one," Bennett informed Mike as he opened fire and flashed over the enemy position. Pulling four positive g's, Bennett initiated a climb back to eight thousand. Passing through two thousand, there was a loud bang and the aircraft shook. A large hole suddenly appeared in the canopy between Brown and Bennett.

"Mike, are you okay? I think we took a hit," Bennett said as he tested his controls. He was heading towards the beach.

"Yeah, I'm fine. How's the aircraft?"

"Well, we must have taken a big hit as the landing gear is down and the left engine is running rough. I'm going to keep it at two thousand over the water in case we need to bail out. I think we can make it back to Da Nang," Bennett said with a degree of confidence. Passing over the beach, they both heard the transmission on Guard.

"Bronco over the water southeast of Quang Tri, be advised, you are on fire." Both turned to look and Brown spotted the flames coming out from under the left-side engine on the bottom.

"Steve, we have a fire on the left-side engine," Brown stated.

"Okay, we need to bail out. Check your gear and get ready," Bennett said. Both began checking to make sure all was in order prior to ejecting from the aircraft, which could explode at any minute.

"Steve, I got a problem. My parachute has a gaping hole in it from where some shrapnel must have gone through it," Mike said.

Oh shit. No one has ever done a water landing in a Bronco and lived. Well, this will be a first, Steve thought. "Okay, no problem, we're going to ditch. Tighten your seat belt. Note where the ejection handles are for the canopy. Place both hands on the console in front of you and brace yourself." Brown executed the commands and waited, then commenced his descent from two thousand feet.

Wish the damn landing gear hadn't dropped down, Bennett thought as he passed through five hundred feet. At three hundred feet, he slowed the aircraft down to just above stall speed and lowered his flaps, attempting to land at the slowest speed possible. The fire was now consuming the left engine. The twin tail stuck the water first, pitching the nose of the aircraft down hard. The nose dug into the water and the aircraft cartwheeled to a stop. Water immediately started flowing into the cockpit.

Brown managed to retain consciousness in the crash. He didn't remember jettisoning the canopy, but it was gone. Mike was totally disoriented as to which way was up. *Got to get out of this thing, but which way?*

"Exhale," a voice told him, and he did. He watched as the bubbles slowly rose to the surface with him right behind them. Once he cleared the surface and was treading water, or attempting to with his clothes, boots, flight helmet and pistol all weighing him down, he looked around for Bennett. *Where is he?* But Bennett was nowhere on the surface. Ducking underwater, Brown could see Bennett slumped over in the front seat of the crushed cockpit as the aircraft slowly sank in the clear waters of the Gulf of Tonkin.[4]

It wasn't long before he heard and saw the CH-53 Air Force rescue helicopter approaching his location. The aircraft that had first announced he was on fire had called for a Jolly Green Giant aircraft to come to the crash site.

Water wings, got to inflate them, he remembered. Unlike Navy life vests, the Air Force and Army used what were referred to as water wings. They were two small pouches worn on the service member's sides in a harness. When inflated, they created what appeared to be two orange half-circles under the swimmer's armpits.

46

AT THE DOOR

3 July 1972
  Recon Company, 2nd Airborne Brigade
  Hai Lang, South Vietnam

The ride from Camp Eagle up to Hai Lang had been uneventful for Lieutenant Tony Shepard and Lance Corporal Jurak. Lieutenant Terry "Buddha" Griswold stood on the lead tank along with Captain Ut, the recon company commander. It was not the most comfortable of rides sitting on the top of an M48 tank, but it did beat walking. Tony had always thought that he was in great shape physically, but the last two months in Vietnam, living on C rations and rice, combined with frequent bouts of diarrhea, had reduced his muscle mass and his stamina. Riding the tank, he stood at the back of the turret as he had no more butt padding. Every jar seemed to be a punch in his pelvis.

The distance up QL1 was only five kilometers. Tony could only picture the horror that those five kilometers must have been for the civilian Vietnamese that raced ahead of the invading North Vietnamese Army. A bulldozer had preceded them up the road, pushing aside destroyed autos, buses, oxcarts and motorcycles. It had also pushed bodies out of the road—some were children, some women, some Vietnamese soldiers. All were decomposed. The North Vietnamese spotters had no qualms about registering artillery on groups of civilians. Tony knew that no one would be interested in investigating this as war crimes. The standards for war crimes in the Asian lands were different than the norms in Western civilizations, he was sure.

Arriving at Hai Lang, everyone dismounted from the tanks. Tony and Jurak joined Buddha and Ut.

"From here we move up this ditch to the outskirts of town. We pass through the lead battalion after dark. Move very quiet. Okay?" Ut said. Ut had been the recon company commander for almost three years and was very proficient at this job.

To avoid detection, the unit would move on foot up to the point battalion. From there it was a five-kilometer infiltration to the Citadel in Quang Tri under the cover of darkness. As the unit moved, they frequently had to freeze in place as illumination rounds were lighting up the night sky and individuals moving could be easily detected. Following the ditch, which was about six feet deep, provided some cover as they moved.

"Freeze!" Tony whispered loudly as he heard the first popping sounds of an illumination round above their heads before it ignited. Those around him did as ordered even though they may not have understood English. In the light of the flare, everyone and everything appeared in black, white and gray. All color normally associated with the Vietnamese countryside was lost. Once the flare burned out, Ut gave the hand signal to start moving again.

Suddenly, a burst of machine-gun fire opened up, passing

over their heads by no more than two feet. All were immediately grateful to be down in the ditch. From the sounds of the gun, Buddha surmised it was a .51-cal anti-aircraft gun. "Ut, do you think they spotted us?" Buddha asked.

"No, they just shoot to scare everyone. We good," Ut said and continued to move forward, in a lower crouch position.

Halfway to their planned hide position, an enemy tank suddenly appeared and fired its main gun, but this engagement appeared to be ineffective as he only fired one round and its trajectory was across the path and not down the ditch. As they converged on the tank, which was still running, it was discovered that the crew had fired the one round and then abandoned the vehicle. Shortly after, they came upon a group of new trucks in perfect condition, also abandoned. It became clear that the enemy was on the run. At approximately 0330 hours, they reached their initial position and settled in for the rest of the night, placing camouflage over themselves before it was light. As the light of dawn crept over the land, they were glad they had camouflaged themselves.

"Hey, Tony, are you seeing what I'm seeing, man?" Buddha asked.

Approximately two hundred meters in front of them was a trench line full of NVA soldiers.

"Oh crap," Tony exclaimed. Ut passed the word that no one was to move for fear that movement would alert the enemy. At times, NVA soldiers would approach to within fifty meters of their position to relieve themselves and then stroll back to the trench line. For a reconnaissance unit, they weren't going to be able to do much reconning from this position because of the close proximity to the enemy. Tony, however, was able to spot an interesting target.

"Hey, Buddha, you see what I see in the church steeple?" Tony asked, slightly moving his head. Buddha eased his head up ever so slowly.

"Oh shit. That bastard is sitting up there like a damn hawk," Buddha exclaimed as he watched the spotter. In the top of the steeple was a spotting team, which made sense as it was the highest feature around. The spotter would be a valuable target to take out.

"See if you can take him out with an air strike," Buddha directed.

In a low whisper, Tony contacted the FAC.

"Covey Five-Four, Waterman Six, over."

"Waterman Six, Covey Five-Four."

"Covey Five-Four, mission, over."

"Roger, Six, send it," Covey said, and Tony commenced to send the request for an air strike to take out the spotter.

A few minutes later, Covey transmitted, "Waterman Six, Covey Five-Four, over."

"Go ahead, Five-Four."

"Waterman Six, I have a flight of two Foxtrot Fours inbound. Echo Tango Alpha is one-five mikes. Over."

"Roger, Covey Five-Four," Tony responded. Nudging Captain Ut, he said, "Watch this, Dai'uy," excited to lay a punch on the guy that had shelled the road.

Eight thousand feet above, Covey Five-Four was in contact with a flight of US Air Force Phantom Jets.

"Tango Echo, Covey Five-Four."

"Covey Five-Four, Tango Echo, over."

"Tango Echo, Covey Five-Four. I'll mark the target for you. Pretty easy to spot. Target is a church steeple with enemy spotters in the steeple. Over."

"Ah, Covey Five-Four, did you say church steeple? Over."

"That's affirmative. Artillery spotters are in the steeple adjusting fire. Over."

"Covey Five-Four, in accordance with Air Force directive twenty-two point one, subparagraph six, that's considered a cultural site and I'm not permitted to hit that. over."

"Tango Echo, you have got to be shitting me. They're hitting friendly forces from that location. We have eyes on target. Over."

"Understood, Covey Five-Four, but I'm not authorized to engage. Tango Echo breaking station. Out"[1]

"You mother..." Covey Five-Four knew he would be wasting his breath. He switched back to Waterman's frequency.

"Waterman Six, Covey Five-Four, over."

"Covey Five-Four, go ahead."

"Waterman Six, we have a problem. Seems the Air Force is afraid to hit a cultural site, so they wouldn't. Sorry."

"Covey, are you serious? Shit, we should have gotten a Navy flight or Army attack helicopters. They would have shot the shit out of that place," Tony said in anger. The rest of the day was spent watching the spotter call missions for his batteries. For the rest of the day and into the early evening, the recon force remained in position. As night fell, Captain Ut decided it was time to move.

"We go. This no good. We go," Ut directed, and the unit slowly and quietly slipped out and moved off. Their new location was in a building only three hundred meters from the walls of the Citadel. Vegetation provided good concealment and the unit hunkered down, running intel-gathering patrols and direction air strikes from this location. Within the range of naval gunfire, Tony spent a lot of time talking to the four and as many as six destroyers offshore and responding to calls for fire.

"Waterman Six, Covey Five-Two, over."

"Covey Five-Two, Waterman Six," Tony responded, wondering where Five-Four was today.

"Waterman Six, need you guys to hunker down. We're coming in with a special weapon. Over." *Shit*, thought Tony, *has someone decided "enough of this crap, let's just nuke the*

431

place?" He had never received a call like this before. "TOT is one minute," Covey Five-Two said. Tony spread the word quickly for everyone to get down and then he waited.

Finally he heard the roar of a jet passing over, but no explosion. When nothing happened, Tony looked up in the direction of the Citadel. A huge white cloud almost like a fogbank was over the Citadel and moving towards Tony's position. *What the f—* he was thinking when he realized what was coming.

"Gas! Gas!" Tony said in a loud whisper, alerting everyone to what was coming. Before anyone could pull out the seldom-ever-used gas masks, everyone was coughing, choking and had a full-on flow of snot and mucus coming from their noses and eyes. Normally individuals carried a C ration can of peaches or fruit cocktail in their gas mask container along with a mask. All the "special weapon" managed to do was piss off everyone on the ground, enemy as well as friendly forces. The armchair commandos at Air Force headquarters had struck again without consulting the frontline troops.

Buddha was still bothered by the spotters in the church steeple. He thought about recommending that a patrol slip in and take them out, but Ut didn't jump on that idea for fear that it would tip off the enemy that someone was close by. Buddha's chance to do something appeared in the morning. A tank had pulled up right next to the church.

"Tony, do you see that tank?" Buddha asked.

Tony eased over to Buddha's position.

"Oh yeah," he said in a low, slow voice. "Jurak, give me the radio. Covey Five-Two, Waterman Six, over."

"Waterman Six, whatcha got for me?"

"Covey Five-Two, tank right next to the church with the spotters, over."

"Roger, understand tank and that's all I need to know, over." The message to Tony was clear. A few minutes later,

Tony heard, "Waterman Six, Covey Five-Two. I have a flight of one inbound. He's one hundred percent accurate and delivering a midsize. How copy? Over."

Tony got the message. "Hey, Buddha, tell Ut we have a strike coming. It's using one of the new laser-guided five-hundred-pound bombs to hit that tank. He needs to let his people know," Tony instructed.

Meanwhile, Covey Five-Two was having a mission brief with an aircraft designating the target. "Mystic One, Covey Five-Two, over."

"Covey Five-Two, Mystic One. I have positive on target." Mystic One was an Air Force F-4 jet at thirteen thousand feet and over a mile from the target. What the EWO, electronic warfare officer, in the back seat was looking at was a return indicating the target was identified and the laser receiving in the nose of the bomb had a lock.

"Covey Five-Two, we have a lock. Weapon release." And the aircraft suddenly became five hundred pounds lighter.

Tony and Buddha sat observing the tank as Ut came up and stood with them. He had never seen a laser-guided bomb in action, so his curiosity was piqued, along with the two Americans'. They never saw the bomb, but the explosion left no doubt in their minds that a bomb had been dropped. The turret of the tank spinning in the air was an indication of mission success. The steeple on the church collapsing was just an added bonus.

"Maybe a five-hundred-pound bomb was a bit of overkill for a tank," Tony said with a grin.

By the ninth of July, the NVA figured out something was amiss and started actively patrolling, looking for the recon team.

"We're starting to get a lot of people moving around here,' Buddha explained, seeing two patrols moving on opposite sides of their location.

"They may be attempting to triangulate our position with radio fixes," Tony exclaimed. Captain Ut recognized when it was time to retreat and live to fight another day.

The retreat turned into a running gun battle, with Tony calling in one air strike after another to keep the NVA at bay. When air wasn't available, naval gunfire was requested. The problem with naval gunfire was that it had to pass over friendly Marine positions, and the Marines didn't like naval gunfire passing over their heads. They finally linked up with friendly forces from another brigade, who provided trucks and returned them to Camp Evans. The joy of being back in friendly territory with comrades was not to be. Corporal Parton was hit with machine-gun fire on 1 July and died on 4 July at the hospital in Da Nang.

47

BRIEF THE NEW BOSS

10 July 1972
1st Corps Headquarters
Hue, South Vietnam

General Truong had ordered his staff to pull together a briefing for the new FRAC commander, Major General Howard Cooksey, who had replaced General Kroesen. General Cooksey was a bit different from most general officers in that he was commissioned through officer candidate school in 1943 as opposed to attending West Point or ROTC. He only had one previous tour in Vietnam in 1969 as the deputy commander of the 21st Infantry Division. This was all a bit new to him. This was also Truong's first meeting with him.

As Cooksey entered Truong's office, Truong immediately noted that Cooksey was considerably taller than him. He also noted that Cooksey's demeanor appeared to be less than pleased. "Good morning, General Cooksey. It is a pleasure to finally meet you in person," Truong said, offering his hand, which Cooksey accepted.

"You too, General. I understand you have a briefing for me this morning to bring me up to speed on what's been going on in I Corps," Cooksey replied. Cooksey was well aware of the events that had occurred since April as he had been briefed by his own staff when he'd assumed command of FRAC. He was also well aware that the US was pulling out of Vietnam and he really didn't want to be the last to leave and be blamed for this debacle that was unfolding. He had been told that this assignment would be good for his career. That was considered a lie by him. *Hell, I've gone from OCS to two-star general and I'm realistic enough to know my career isn't going much further. The ring knockers wouldn't allow me to rise much further,*[1] Cooksey had thought when the assignment had been fed to him.

"Yes, my staff is ready to brief you now if you would like," Truong acknowledged.

"I hope their English is better than my Vietnamese," Cooksey said as a passing joke.

"I believe my briefer speaks very good English as he is a graduate of the University of California at Berkeley," Truong replied with a serious tone and motioned for them to move into the briefing room.

Once everyone was seated, Colonel Van Tan stepped up to the podium and the first slide appeared, listing dates.

"Sir, our defense of Hue kicked off on 5 May when all forces crossed over the My Chanh River and established our defensive line with the Regional Popular Forces on the right flank, the 369th Marine Brigade in the center and the 258th Brigade on the left flank. The 39th Ranger Group was south of the 258th, guarding the western approach to Hue. The 1st ARVN Division was in the vicinity of Camp Eagle, checking NVA advances towards Bastogne, Checkmate and Birmingham. Enemy forces seized Veghel on 2 May and Bastogne on 5 May. These attacks were carried out by the 324B NVA Division coming out of the A Shau Valley," Colonel Van Tan stated and paused.

Cooksey just acknowledged with a nod. He knew all this and was waiting for the real reason for this meeting. *What are they going to ask for?* he was thinking.

Colonel Van Tan continued. "On 13 May we initiated our offense with a combination amphibious assault and an airmobile insertion behind the enemy's front lines, disrupting his flow of supplies and reinforcements. The amphibious assault was preceded by a B-52 strike just ahead of the landing. The landing was unopposed. These forces moved through his frontline forces and returned to our lines." As Tan spoke, he pointed out the location on a projected map the location of the landing zones.

"In response to our actions, the enemy launched a major counterattack against the RFPF forces on 21 May, crossing the My Chanh River initially with PT-76 amphibious tanks and them with T-54 tanks and infantry at a shallow ford site. This attack drove the RFPF back and allowed the enemy to push into the rear area of our frontline troops during the night."

Tan paused, then continued, "It should be noted, sir, that the TOW system that was provided just that day performed in an excellent manner, killing tanks in the early-morning hours at a range of fifteen hundred meters."

"Glad to hear that it worked," Cooksey said. *Note to self, they're going to ask for more of those*, he was thinking as his aide was making a note.

Tan didn't miss a beat. "Sir, on 24 May, we launched another airmobile assault combined with an amphibious. Our forces commenced an attack to the south and over the next ten days severely hurt those frontline defending enemy forces along the My Chanh River. Any questions, sir?" Tan asked.

"Colonel Dorsey," Cooksey said, turning in his chair to address Dorsey.

"Sir," Dorsey said, standing up.

"In your opinion, how were the amphibious landings and the airmobile insertions executed?" Cooksey asked. Truong was visibly upset that the question was directed to the senior Marine advisor and not to Colonel Tan or himself.

Ah crap, you're putting my ass on the spot flashed through Dorsey's mind. "Sir, in my opinion and based on the reports from the advisors on the ground, I think they were executed very well. I was present for the planning process. I was in the command center during the execution, and in my opinion the command and control was very good," Dorsey said. This seemed to satisfy Cooksey as he turned back to Colonel Tan. Tan looked at Truong, who gave a simple hand motion to move it along.

"General, on 5 May, the 1st Airborne Division began to arrive in the area and took up positions at LZ Sally. When they were ready, the 2nd Brigade was moved up attached to the 1st Marine Division. It was positioned west of QL1. As the other two brigades arrived, they were moved up as well and are now positioned with two brigades along the My Chanh and one brigade in reserve," Tan indicated and paused for Cooksey to look at the map again. When it appeared that he was done studying the map, Tan continued.

"On 21 May, the 2nd Airborne Brigade moved from LZ Sally to Camp Evans. They conducted their first offensive operation 26 May with an airmobile inserting and mechanized linkup across the O Lau River. This was considered a successful operation, with three hundred enemy killed and nine prisoners. Our losses were eleven killed and forty-two wounded."

Cooksey mentally questioned the presentation of numbers, as seldom were casualties and killed ever discussed despite Washington's fixation on releasing such information on the nightly news. Not missing a beat, Tan droned on.

"On 18 June we initiated the current operation, Operation Total Victory, to retake Quang Tri. The 147th Brigade attacked up Route 555. The 369th attacked across the My Chanh on pontoon bridges and moved across the rice fields. The 258th attacked up QL1. By 27 June we had established a new defensive line from the coast to the west, with the 1st Airborne Division moving up on the left flank of the 1st Marine Division. Responsibility for the capture of Quang Tri at this point shifted to the 1st Airborne Division," Tan outlined, pausing to let Cooksey grasp the situation.

"How much resistance did you get?" Cooksey asked, looking at Truong.

"On the twentieth, the 6th Battalion was hit hard by a battalion with tanks, as were the 1st and 5th Battalions. That was an eight-hour fight, and thanks to Major Turner with his ANGLICO team, we were successful in turning the enemy back," Truong acknowledged and gave the hand signal for Tan to continue.

"The morning of 23 June, the left flank of 2nd Airborne Brigade was hit by two regiments supported by tanks. The enemy attempted to attack across the Thac Ma River. This was a coordinated attack with supporting artillery. Our force defending the south shore of the Thac Ma River managed, with the help of close-air support, to defeat this attack," Tan outlined.

"Sir, on 27 June, we exercised an amphibious feint north of Quang Tri. We observed movement of armor and air-defense systems to the coast and away from the intended landing zones. On the twenty-eighth, the 1st Marine Division attacked with the 3rd, 5th, 7th, and 8th Battalions moving forward. On the twenty-ninth, an airmobile insertion was made by the 1st and 4th Battalions ahead of our attacking ground advance," Tan said, pointing at the map.

"So you're making progress, but what about the 1st

Airborne Division? What have they been doing?" Cooksey asked.

"Sir, simultaneously, 1st Airborne Division crossed the My Chanh and has been moving on a similar line as the Marine division. They have had to ward off several attacks from the west by enemy elements coming from Tchepone and Khe Sanh into their flank. They have cleared QL1 and as we speak are approximately two kilometers from the Citadel at this time," Tan stated. That seemed to suddenly brighten Cooksey's mood.

"Very good," Cooksey said, looking at Truong, who acknowledged the compliment with a nod. "So it's the first of July now. Where do you go from here and when do you think you'll take the Citadel?" Cooksey asked.

Truong spoke up. "We will close the noose around Quang Tri with the Marines moving on it from the north, east and southeast. The airborne division will cut off any possible reinforcements from the northwest and take the city. We anticipate that we will control the Citadel by 1 August. They have been instructed to hold at all cost and no retreat. It will be a fight to the finish," Truong said.

"Well, they will be the first to stay and defend it," Cooksey said in an apparent slap at the South Vietnamese defense of the Citadel. Taking the high Cooksey as he was about to start asking for replacement equipment.

2

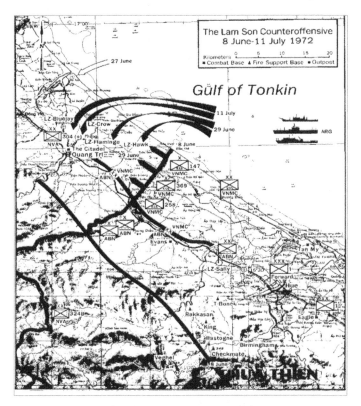

*Melson, Charles D. and Curtis G. Arnold. US Marines in Vietnam:
The War That Would Not End, 1971–1973. Washington, D.C.:
History and Museum Division, Headquarters, US Marine Corps,
1991.*

48

MARINES, TAKE THEM IN

10 July 1972
  USS *Tripoli*
  Gulf of Tonkin

"Now hear this, the smoking lamp is lit," was announced over the ship's loudspeakers, and immediately cigarettes came out and Zippo lighters began snapping. Refueling operations were completed. Sergeant Randy Newman, USMC, was in the HMM-165 operations office when Staff Sergeant Jerry Hendrix walked in.

"What can I do you for, Staff Sergeant?" Newman asked, looking up from the manual typewriter he was hunting and pecking on, attempting to complete the never-ending paperwork. The lieutenant's chicken scratch handwriting wasn't making his job any easier.

"Tomorrow I'm scheduled to fly on a CH-46 chopper and I was wondering if you would mind switching aircraft with me. You're on a CH-53 with Staff Sergeant Nelson, and I'd like to fly with him. Staff Sergeant O'Halloran is on the CH-46. Do you know him?" Hendrix asked.

"Yeah, I know Tom. I have no problem flying with him. Sure, I'll switch with you. No problem," Newman replied and returned to his typing.

"One more question. Who are the pilots on the CH-53 for tomorrow?" Hendrix asked. Newman looked up from his typing and without a word grabbed a clipboard hanging on the bulkhead next to his desk. He began leafing through the pages.

"Ah, let me see...oh...Captain Keys is the pilot and the copilot is listed as Captain Bollman. There's also a combat photographer listed in the crew, a Lance Corporal Stephen Lively. Besides Nelson, there's the gunner, Corporal Kenneth Crody," Newman added.

"Crody...he's that new kid that came aboard just before we left Subic, isn't he?" Hendrix asked.

"Yeah, was surprised to find that we were sailing for the Tonkin," Newman said, resuming his typing. "Told his mom last time he talked to her, 'Don't worry, Mom, Marines aren't ever sent to Vietnam. I'll be fine.'"[1]

"I guess he never expected to get to Vietnam either," Hendrix said as he walked out the door into the passageway.

* * *

1800 Hours
    Aviation Battalion
    Marble Mountain

"Alright, listen up, ladies," Major Spencer yelled above the voices of the pilots, who were all wondering what this meeting was about. Flight crews from several units were present. The

48th AHC, Jokers, were present, as were crews from F Troop, 4th Cav (Centaurs); F Troop, 8th Cav (Blue Ghosts); and F/79th ARA (Blue Max). Never before had this group been assembled to work a common mission. Also present were some US Marine Corps pilots. When the noise died down, he continued. "Tomorrow the Vietnamese Marines are launching a major counterattack. They'll be conducting a helicopter assault northeast of Quang Tri." Low moans could be heard. "We're supporting the operation with gun cover." Smiles appeared on the faces of many gun pilots because they were going to be shooting at someone. "The Marines will be inserted by elements of the HMM-165 and HMM-164, flying off the *Tripoli* and *Okinawa*, I believe. They'll pick up the Marines and insert them. Our job is to fly escort for the CH-46s and CH-53s as well as cover the insertion. There will be a tac air prep and naval gunfire prep before the insertion. The naval gunfire prep will commence at 0600 and an ARC light will hit fifteen minutes before touchdown. L hour, as our Marine friends say, is 1200 hours. The landing zones are labeled LZ Blue Jay and Crow and are located two thousand meters northeast of Quang Tri City. All fine and good, but I still expect there'll be plenty for us to do. Aircraft commanders' brief will be at 0600 hours in Flight Ops, so you best be getting some sleep. Any questions?" the major asked.

"Sir, do we know how many aircraft we're putting up for this?" Mr. Kerr asked.

"George, the Marines are putting up twelve CH-46 and three CH-53 aircraft," the major indicated. "The 48th will put up four aircraft on this one, as will the 4th Cav and 8th Cav. Blue Max will put up six aircraft. The 4th Cav will lead the assault with two OH-6s out front leading, followed by Blue Max flying six abreast. When they cross the river and the LOHs find targets, Blue Max will dump everything. That's six aircraft with four nineteen-round pods each for a total of four hundred and fifty-six rockets, each the equivalent of a 105 round," he explained. That brought smiles to several faces. "The Marine aircraft will fly in flights of three aircraft each. The 4th will fly right side and the 8th will fly left side on the first lift. The 48th will bring in the second lift while the 8th and 4th peel back to get the next lift, and so on and so forth until we have everyone inserted. Any other questions?"

"Sir, those are some big aircraft for an initial assault...big targets," Mr. Cleveland voiced. Mr. Cleveland was on his second tour in Vietnam and his second tour with the 48th. "What's the call sign for the Marine aircraft?"

"The lift flight leader for the CH-46s is Spanish Fly, and Lucky Lady for the CH-53."

"Sir, who's flight leader for the attack aircraft?" a voice in the back asked.

"That will be Centaur Four-Eight, Captain Haynie," came the response.

Again the voice asked, "Where will you be, sir?" directing the question at Major Spencer.

"I'll be in a UH-1H watching the flight and have a couple of UH-1s on standby for down aircraft recovery."

* * *

0600 Hours
  11 July 1972
  USS _Tripoli_ (LPH-10)

The sounds of naval gunfire could be heard rolling across the calm Gulf waters. Destroyers had moved in overnight and taken up firing positions just offshore. Between the USS _Tripoli_ and the beach, the destroyers _Eversole_ (DD-789), _Hepburn_ (DE-1055), _Hoel_ (DDG-13), _McCain_ (DDG-36),

Mullinnix (DD-944) and *Ouellet* (DE-1077) had taken up positions off the beach while the USS *Newport News* (CA-148), USS *Oklahoma City* (CG-5) and USS *Providence* (CLG-6) supported with their larger eight- and six-inch guns. All told, there were fifteen ships off the northern coast of Vietnam that morning, all firing fire support.

On deck, the crews for the CH-46s of HMM-165 began their preflight inspections. While Corporal Crody checked fluid levels, Staff Sergeant Hendrix and Staff Sergeant Nelson mounted weapons and loaded ammunition.

"Hey, Nelson," Hendrix called out, "how many of those little Vietnamese Marines are we taking on board?"

"Probably about fifty-five. They're considerably smaller than our musclebound guys and carry a lot less pogey bait, so we can get a few more in than the usual thirty-five or so," Nelson responded.

"So we'll be inserting what?" Hendrix said as he started a mental math problem. "We should get about eight hundred and forty troops in on the first lift, with one-half of the total flight bringing in equipment, rations, ammo, artillery tubes."

"Well, just be sure and tie down everything you want to stay on the aircraft, because I'll guarantee these guys will rob us blind if we're not careful. Everything needs to be secured before they get on or it's getting off with them," Nelson added.

As the noncommissioned officers bantered, Captain Keys and Captain Bollman approached the aircraft. Both were in full flight gear with the visors on their helmets down as required by standard operating procedures.

"Morning, ladies. How's she look, Corporal?" Captain Keys asked as he started through the cabin door.

"Sir, she's ready. All systems look good," Crody indicated, wiping his hands on a towel that he kept on the aircraft. "We're ready to go."

"Good, let's get loaded up and do it," Keys said as he and Bollman climbed into their seats and Bollman pulled out the checklist for starting procedures.

Crody, Hendrix and Nelson moved to their respective positions and watched as the eyes in the back of the aircraft. Just a routine day, although Crody had never thought he would be serving in Vietnam. He was supposed to be in the Philippines, as he had written to his mother. As each aircraft came up to full power, the flight leader was notified and launched. Each aircraft in turn departed off the deck and joined the leader in flight, heading for the pickup zone, which was south of the My Chanh River.

Looking forward, Captain Keys watched as the flight leader turned to final approach. Before him in a large open area, South Vietnamese Marines were lined up in chalk order, fifty men to a chalk, ready to get aboard an aircraft. Off to the side, loads for the CH-53s were also lined up in chalk order with crews standing by to hook up the sling loads of ammunition, food, or heavy equipment such as artillery howitzers if appropriate for the second turn.

"Prelanding check is complete," Captain Bollman said as Keys maneuvered the aircraft to his assigned touchdown point. Slowly, the back ramp opened and the Vietnamese Marines began the process of loading the aircraft. Nelson supervised the loading.

"Nelson, we need to get all fifty on board, so pack them like sardines," Captain Keys transmitted over the intercom.

"No problem, sir. These guys appear to know what they're doing, or maybe they just like each other a lot and like being butthole close, but hey, to each his own if you know what I mean...I'm not judging," Nelson added. Keys and Bollman just exchanged looks and shook their heads. Lively was snapping pictures of the smiling Vietnamese Marines. *Wonder what they're so happy about*, he thought.

"Sir, we're up," Nelson indicated when the last Marine was aboard and the ramp was coming up.

"Roger, stand by" was Keys's response.

* * *

"Spanish Fly Lead, Centaur Six, over," Major Spencer transmitted. Looking forward, he could see the pickup zone and the aircraft from HMM-164 and HMM-165 approaching to land.

"Centaur Six, Spanish Fly Lead, go ahead."

"Spanish Fly Lead, Centaur Six, I've just been informed that the prep on the landing zones has been curtailed due to the historical structures surrounding the landing zones. We can expect a hot landing zone. Over."

"Centaur Six, I have a solid and just received the same word. We're taking it contour and one-five-five knots, over."

"Roger, when you hit the RP, we'll move ahead and prep, over."

Major Spencer orbited at altitude over the pickup zone as the Vietnamese Marines loaded the aircraft in an orderly and expeditious manner. He knew the flight was beginning to lift off as the dust clouds swirled around the first three aircraft as they applied power.

"Spanish Fly Flight Lead is on the go." And the lead aircraft lifted off, followed by twelve CH-46s and three CH-53s in groups of three with one-minute separation between groups. All had troops on board. The CH-53s would make a second turn to pick up sling loads and heavy equipment.

"Alright, crew, here we go, coming up," Captain Keys announced on the aircraft intercom. "Stay on the controls with me," he said to Captain Bollman, who lightly placed his feet on the pedals and his hands on the cyclic and collective. Ahead, he watched the other aircraft departing in order as his aircraft was one of the last aircraft to depart in a group of five total aircraft.

"Crody, how we looking back there?" Keys asked.

"All good back here, sir," Crody responded as he scanned the faces of the Vietnamese Marines in the aircraft. Flying contour inside a CH-53, which didn't have windows to look out of, usually produced some airsickness. *At least if someone pukes, they're packed so close together they'll just puke on each other and not my aircraft*, Crody thought when the first round penetrated the side of the aircraft.

As the two OH-6 aircraft approached the river, which was the forward limit of friendly troops, they flew lower and lower to treetop level. Suddenly, green tracers could be seen arching skyward as the two little birds crossed the river.

"Blue Max, Centaur One-Two taking fire," First Lieutenant Pete Holmberg announced as he maneuvered his OH-6 aircraft around trees. The seven Blue Max aircraft didn't need to be told to engage but started punching off rockets as they proceeded across the river. Each time a rocket was fired, it was answered by two more anti-aircraft guns. At first it was obvious that only AK-47s were engaging as these were the frontline infantry soldiers, but the deeper the OH-6 aircraft proceeded, the larger the caliber of the weapons that engaged. Suddenly Blue Max was receiving fire from .51-cal and 23mm anti-aircraft guns. The airburst from a 37mm anti-aircraft gun got everyone's attention, and all the aircraft proceeded to get on the deck. Flying at altitude was not the way to go on this mission.

Holmberg swooped across LZ Blue Jay and dropped a smoke grenade to mark the landing zone of the first of the Marine Corps aircraft. Centaur and Blue Ghost escort Cobras rolled hot, engaging targets along the tree line, and there was no short supply of targets. The tree line appeared to be decorated with blinking Christmas lights, there were so many muzzle flashes. Green tracers crisscrossed the landing zone. Surprisingly, the Marine pilots weren't reporting a lot of hits, but everyone was announcing taking fire.

* * *

As the ramps on the CH-46 aircraft dropped, Major Nguyen Dang Ho, the 1st VNMC Battalion commander, and his US Marine advisor, Captain Lawrence Livingston, were the first off the aircraft and onto the landing zone. The young Vietnamese Marines on their aircraft followed reluctantly behind them.

"Dai'uy," Major Ho called to Captain Livingston. Livingston already knew what the major was going to ask for.

"Got it," Livingston called back and grabbed First Lieutenant Biddulph, the ANGLICO attached to his team. "Get naval gunfire on that tree line."

"Roger, sir, the *Newport News* is standing by. Rounds will be hitting in about one minute."

As Livingston and Biddulph discussed laying in the naval gunfire, Major Ho maneuvered his battalion towards the tree line. He understood fully that his battalion needed to clear the two trench lines that were placing intense fire across the landing zone. Livingston slid up beside Ho to hear his instructions to the company commanders. When Ho was done, he turned to Livingston.

"When prep is complete, we go. I lead."

Livingston had a lot of respect for Ho as he had led from the front on other occasions and was going to do it again. Five minutes later, a white phosphorus round exploded on the tree line, indicating the prep was over.

"We go" was all Ho said as he jumped up and started moving towards the tree line, leading his battalion. The naval gunfire had been effective, but the soldiers of the 320B NVA

Division were in well-prepared positions and determined to continue defending the Quang Tri perimeter. Casualties were beginning to be noted in the 1st VNMC Battalion.

"I'm hit!" Lieutenant Biddulph called out as he went down. Livingston turned and could see that the lieutenant had taken a couple of rounds through his legs. A Vietnamese Marine that was assigned to assist Biddulph was already digging through his pockets and pulling out a first aid kit.

"Stay here—I'll come back for you as soon as we take the trench line," Livingston told him and hastened off to get back with Major Ho. Closing in on the trench line, the Vietnamese Marines were exercising good fire-and-maneuver tactics, Livingston noted. He finally found Major Ho and stated to move to his location. The blast from the ChiCom grenade put him on his back. The burning pieces of shrapnel seared the wounds that they created. *Oh damn, that hurts* was all Livingston could think about for the moment. Picking himself back up, he reoriented himself and moved up to where Major Ho was located.

* * *

"Taking fire," Sergeant Nelson yelled over the intercom, and his gun started hammering away at potential targets. Very quickly, Hendrix and Crody were also laying down suppressive fire, as were all the aircraft.

"Centaur Six, Spanish Fly taking fire," the flight leader announced as he approached LZ Blue Jay, the furthest north of the two landing zones.

"Roger, Spanish Fly, we are suppressing," Major Spencer replied. *Truthfully, I'm not sure if we're suppressing anything. We need more gunships,* he was thinking.

"SAM. SAM. SAM," someone yelled over the air-to-air frequency. On that warning, the flight of helicopters flew even lower, attempting to avoid the SA-7 man-portable surface-to-air missile. By doing so, all the aircraft became more vulnerable to small-arms and heavy machine-gun fire. Every aircraft was reporting taking fire and hits, but no mayday calls had been heard.

"Spanish Fly RP," the flight leader announced, and a white phosphorus round exploded on the landing zone, having been dropped by the lead, Holmberg.

"Blue Ghost and Centaur are rolling hot," a Centaur aircraft declared as the six AH-1G Cobra escort gunships started firing rockets at specific locations that were engaging the flight. Flying low-level, the gunships had to get much closer to the target to accurately hit it. Firing slightly above the target meant the rockets went harmlessly over it, while under-shooting the target had the rockets impacting short and dangerously close to the aircraft. As more lift ships approached, they began dropping off Vietnamese Marines in Landing Zone Crow. The last five aircraft were on final to the landing zone when Joker Three-Six made his first pass over the landing zone and expended half his ordnance. His wingman had done likewise, and both were lining up to make another pass as they went by a CH-53. It was decelerating for its touch-down point and was at one hundred feet. As Mr. Kerr passed the CH-53, off to his right, he saw the flash and instinct took over. He immediately turned his nose towards the flash as the SA-7 rocket went past him and struck the right-side engine on the big CH-53.

"SAM, SAM, SAM," Kerr yelled as he opened fire with a burst of minigun fire.

Aboard the CH-53, Hendrix and Crody never saw what tore through the right-side engine and exploded inward into the passenger compartment of the aircraft. The SA-7 missile exploded on the right-side engine, causing the engine to come apart with the turbine blades ripping through the passenger cabin like shrapnel from an exploding artillery round. Immediately, the aircraft began to burn while Keys fought to bring it down in a controlled crash.

"May—" was all that Bollman could say before the aircraft was on the ground. It was obvious to everyone that the aircraft had catastrophic damage. They landed short of LZ Crow with no friendlies around them.

"Get out," Keys screamed into the intercom. Bollman glanced to the rear to see if everyone was getting out. No one was moving as all were engulfed in flames. Jettisoning the pilots' doors, both pilots scrambled to get out of the burning aircraft. As Bollman hit the ground, Staff Sergeant Nelson tumbled out the side crew door. His flight suit was on fire and Bollman half crawled and half ran to get the flames out. Nelson was, however, badly burned.

"There," Keys yelled, pointing at a bomb crater in the middle of the landing zone. In a crouched run, both pilots, dragging Nelson, made it to the bomb crater and hunkered down along with seven Vietnamese Marines and Corporal Lively, the US Marine photographer just along for the ride. Lively had dragged a badly burned Vietnamese Marine into the crater. They could hear the firefight on the landing zone as the South Vietnamese Marines engaged a determined NVA force.

"Okay, let's keep our heads down. Let the Vietnamese Marines do the fighting and we'll just be quiet," Keys directed. Even if the seven Vietnamese Marines didn't understand English, they got the message anyway but elected to join their fellow Marines in the fight and slipped away.

"I'll start treating Nelson," Bollman stated as he tore the first aid pouch out of his survival vest.

"Give him some morphine. That might help with those burns," Keys said, digging into his own first aid kit as well.

The four Americans and the one wounded Vietnamese

Marine hid in the bomb crater for the rest of the day and at times watched NVA soldiers paw through the burned wreckage of their aircraft. No one did anything to give away their position. As the next lift approached, intense automatic weapons engaged the flight. *Why are there only six Cobras supporting this mission?* Keys wondered.

* * *

Mr. Kerr was beside himself as he watched Lady Ace Seven-Two burst into flames at one hundred feet and plunge to the ground in a controlled crash.

"Son of a bitch!" he screamed as he lowered his nose and opened fire with the 20mm three-barreled gun hanging under the left-side wing pylon. The tree line in front continued to twinkle with small lights as he engaged and passed over the enemy with tiny hammer taps on the side of his aircraft.

"Joker Two-Five, Two-Nine, over," Lieutenant Lester transmitted. Kerr started looking around to find him. Two-Niner's transmission was distorted with wind.

"Joker Two-Niner, where are you?"

"Joker Two-Five, I'm over the water. My canopy's been blown off. We took a hit and the damn thing flew off."

"Roger, Two-Niner, can you make it back to home base?"

"Affirmative, just going to be a breezy flight. Joker Two-Niner breaking formation."

Kerr could now see Two-Niner turning south over the water. He was easy to identify as he was the only aircraft with no canopy over the cockpit. Ahead, Kerr saw the Marine helicopters heading back to sea and the USS *Tripoli*.

"Centaur Six, Joker Two-Five, be advised the LZ is hot. I say again, LZ is hot. One aircraft down in LZ at this time." Kerr really didn't need to inform Major Spencer that the landing zone was hot. The location of the landing zone was obvious now, and a burning helicopter marked a location just southeast by a few hundred meters of the down crew. *Can this day get any worse?* Kerr asked himself as he pressed the trigger to fire the 20mm gun.

* * *

Keys, Buck Bollman and Lively watched as a UH-1H helicopter approached, coming in much lower and faster than their lift had. *Good, the guys are talking and doing it better,* he was thinking as the tree line opened up with tracers, all directed at the UH-1H recovery aircraft. As the AH-1G gunships flashed past, he noticed one was missing. *Hope that crew made it.* His attention turned back to the UH-1H, which was twisting, turning and bobbing, attempting to avoid as much of the enemy fire as possible.

"Centaur Six, Centaur Four-Nine, get out of there," one of the Centaur gunship pilots yelled over the radio. The UH-1H responded accordingly, making an immediate and tight one-hundred-and-eighty-degree turn to the south and safety.

"All aircraft, this is Centaur Six. Return to base. All lift ships are in mission complete. Over."

* * *

Sitting high in the sky, Captain Knapp was piloting an Army RU-21 fixed-wing aircraft on a reconnaissance mission. The RU-21 was the military version of the civilian twin-engine King Air, except the RU-21 was packed with radio monitoring equipment. Many pilots considered flying these missions almost boring as they generally flew a racetrack pattern for hours. This was not going to be a boring day for Captain Knapp.

"Mayday, mayday. Any aircraft, this is Lady Ace Seven-

Two on Guard" crackled over the UHF radio Guard channel. Almost immediately, Knapp responded.

"Lady Ace Seven-Two, this is Vanguard Two-One-Six, over."

"Vanguard Two-One-Six, this is Lady Ace Seven-Two. I'm in a downed CH-53 northeast of Quang Tri with five souls. Two badly injured, over," Keys responded.

"Roger, Lady Ace Seven-Two, can you authenticate? Over."

"Roger, over."

"Lady Ace Seven-Two, authenticate Alpha Tango Oscar, over."

"Roger, wait one," Keys transmitted on his PRC-91 survival radio and dug in his pocket to extract the KAL-61 authenticating code. Loading in the letters that Knapp had passed to him, he found what he was looking for.

"Vanguard Two-One-Six, Lady Ace Seven-Two, I authenticate Bravo, over."

"Roger, Lady Ace, what is your location?" Knapp asked as he began to head for some location northeast of Quang Tri, hoping that Lady Ace would come back with some more definitive coordinates. Circling at eight thousand feet was not the easiest way to see five people on the ground. As Knapp approached the area, he lowered his altitude but still maintained three thousand feet due to the air-defense threat, to include the newly identified SA-7 ground-to-air missiles that had been introduced. For the next two hours, he would keep circling, looking to find Lady Ace Seven-Two, with no luck.

"Lady Ace Seven-Two, Vanguard Two-One-Six, over."

"Vanguard Two-One-Six, Lady Ace Seven-Two."

"Lady Ace, do you have anything to mark your position with? I can't find you," Knapp transmitted.

"Roger, Vanguard Two-One-Six, I can see you up there. I'm putting out a marking panel. Wait one." Keys reached into his survival vest and extracted the bright orange marking panel, spreading it out in the bottom of the crater.

"Lady Ace Seven-Two, I have your position" came over the radio almost immediately. "Lady Ace Seven-Two, I've been in contact with Jolly Green and will move over the beach to escort him in. Be prepared for extraction. Call sign King Two-Seven. How copy?"

"Vanguard Two-One-Six, I have good copy and am standing by," Keys reported, and the smiles on everyone's faces told him they understood Vanguard Two-One-Six had departed to get the cavalry.

As Vanguard Two-One-Six reached the coast, the Jolly Green helicopter was easy to spot, as were the two A-1E Skyraiders flying escort for Jolly Green.

"King Two-Seven, this is Vanguard Two-One-Six. I'll lead you to them and let you know when I'm over them," Knapp reported.

"Vanguard Two-One-Six, this is Sandy. We'll cover you on your pass as well as King. How copy?"

"Sandy, much appreciated. Heading in now," and with that, Knapp turned back towards the beach and the Lady Ace survivors. Sandy took up positions between him and the Jolly Green helicopter and they all proceeded to approach the coast. Once they were over the beach, however, the anti-aircraft fire became intense.

"Sandy, Vanguard Two-One-Six is taking fire!" Knapp announced as green tracers came up from the tree lines.

"Roger, Vanguard Two-One Six, get out of there. We have the orange panel," Sandy announced as he opened fire with his four 20mm automatic weapons and commenced unleashing rockets. Knapp did as he was told as he had done all he could, being an unarmed aircraft and low on fuel. Sandy continued to engage targets but held off the Jolly Green helicopter as the intensity of anti-aircraft fire was too great.

Finally, the bad news had to be given to Lucky Ace Seven-Two.

* * *

Keys and company had been sitting in the crater, watching the approaching RU-21 followed by two A-1E Skyraiders and the intense fire that greeted them. Sandy was putting down a good volume of fire, which was being met by an equal return of anti-aircraft fire.

"Lucky Ace Seven-Two, Sandy, over." Keys anticipated what this call would bring.

"Sandy, Lucky Ace, over."

"Lucky Ace, we can't get in. The intensity of the fire is too much to bring the chopper in. Returning to base and will see what we can come up with. Good luck." Keys didn't have to translate but just looked at the faces and could tell they all understood.

* * *

Flight crews from the morning mission of escorting the Marines into LZ Blue had returned to rearm/refuel when word came that a down crew from the morning mission had been located. Major Spencer came into Flight Ops, where many of the pilots were waiting for their afternoon mission.

"Alright, listen up. The Marines lost a CH-53 this morning on that mission. An RU-21 got a mayday call on Guard from the crew that made it out of the burning aircraft. They in turn contacted the Rescue Coordination Center, who sent out a Jolly Green with Sandy to get the crew. They couldn't get in because of the level of anti-aircraft fire. They're now asking if we can get in there since we have smaller aircraft. Do I hear any volunteers for this one?" Major Spencer asked.

"Sir, I'll take my bird," First Lieutenant Frank Walker, an LOH pilot, volunteered. Seven more pilots stepped forward and were selected: Captain Fred Ledfors, another LOH pilot; CWO Charles O'Connell with his copilot; Captain Stephen Moss in one Cobra gunship, and First Lieutenant Russ Miller and his copilot, CWO Terrance Hawkinson, were selected for the other AH-1G. Other pilots jumped up and were selected for backup. Captain James Elder was selected to fly air mission control in a UH-1H with Captain Jack "Beetle" Bailey as copilot.

"Good, step over here and let me brief you on where they're at," Spencer said as he laid a map on the table. The group studied the map and decided on a route that offered the best chance of getting to the downed crew with the least exposure to the enemy. Over the course of the past months, pilots had learned that the NVA had spotters positioned out from the actual troops and air-defense weapons, looking for inbound aircraft. Those spotters would provide a degree of early warning to the anti-aircraft gunners. Walker pointed out a route that he thought would minimize the time the spotters had to detect and alert the guns. Chief Warrant Officer Moss agreed as he had flown escort on the original missions.

"Okay, let's get in the air and go get them. I'll be in the C&C bird," Captain Elder said as Major Spencer finished the briefing.

Departing Tan My, the scout team of two OH-6 helicopters, two AH-1G Cobra helicopters and one UH-1H helicopter headed out over the clear waters of the Gulf of Tonkin. Flying at wave-top height, they finally turned in towards the beach and remained in a contour flight attitude, following the folds of the terrain and flying under the height of trees where possible. *How long will our luck hold out?* Walker thought as he and his fellow OH-6 weaved around trees and bushes at high speed. He didn't have to wait long for the answer.

Suddenly, green streaks crossed in front of his nose. A light tap could be heard on the right side of Walker's aircraft, a long red line appearing along the right side as one of the AH-1G Cobras laid down a burst of minigun fire, protecting his right side. On the left, he could hear his own gunner, Specialist Bollman, exchanging fire with his M60 machine gun, and Sergeant Joe Beck in the back was firing his M60 as well. Suddenly, Captain Ledfors broke hard left to avoid a .51-cal machine gun that he was about to pass over and laid a burst of minigun fire from his aircraft. His gunner, Sergeant Leon Ring, had a sufficient number of targets to service as well. Before the NVA could lock on to him, two 2.75-inch rockets slammed into the enemy position. As Walker looked back towards the down crew's location, he saw the orange panel. He also heard the sharp rap of what sounded like a hammer on the side of his aircraft. Executing a tight deceleration pedal turn, Walker set the aircraft on the ground right next to the down crew, which didn't need an invitation to get on board.

"Get Nelson on board," Keys screamed as he and Bollman grabbed the young staff sergeant and pushed him into the aircraft. Lively was shoved in next to Nelson and told to hang on to him. The remaining wounded Vietnamese Marine was placed next to Lively. Ledfors now landed behind Walker. Keys and Bollman ran back to that aircraft and jumped in, not bothering to put on seat belts.

"Go, go!" Bollman yelled as the Vietnamese was loaded. Walker didn't need to be told twice and applied power, but the aircraft wouldn't move. They were overloaded. The OH-6 was designed to carry four people, not six along with the weight of machine guns, grenades and ammo.

"Kick off everything except two hundred rounds," Walker ordered, and the crew quickly complied. This time Walker could get the aircraft light on the skids but not get off the ground. Easing the cyclic forward and pulling max power, he felt the aircraft slide along the ground. In doing so, it picked up speed and at some point hit translational lift, which greatly helped get the aircraft into the air. Skimming over mangroves along the river, both aircraft were off the ground and dancing between the trees, seeking safety. Crossing back over the beach, both aircraft along with their Cobra escorts began to reach for altitude and home.

49

SPECIALIST MIKE HILL

13 JULY 1972
48th Assault Helicopter Company
Marble Mountain, South Vietnam

"Hey, Gary, how about letting me take your position today?"
Specialist Mike Hill asked. Gary Warrick was a door gunner on
a UH-1H flown by the Blue Stars. Hill was a crew chief but
never got to go out on missions as he crewed the AH-1G
Cobra gunship, which only flew with two pilots. He was
getting bored sitting around and hearing the UH-1H crews
talking about their exploits on the combat assaults. His aircraft
was currently in maintenance and would be for a couple of
days, it had been so heavily damaged two days prior by enemy
gunfire. All things considered, the pilots were fortunate to get
the aircraft back to Marble Mountain.

"Yeah, let's be sure and clear it with Captain Norbeck and
if he says okay, then fine by me. I'd like a down day," Gary said,
and the two headed off to find Captain Norbeck. They found
him in Flight Operations, talking to another officer.

"Excuse me, sir," Warrick said, addressing Captain Norbeck once he saw that Norbeck was done talking.

"What's up, Warrick?" Norbeck asked.

"Sir, this is Specialist Hill and he's a crew chief on the Cobras. He'd like to fly in my place today as a door gunner if you have no objections." Captain Norbeck had no objections once he was sure Hill knew how to operate the M60 machine gun. Arriving at the aircraft, Gary checked Mike out on the guns and his responsibilities as the door gunner. Once satisfied, Gary left Mike to return to his rack for some nap time.

As Norbeck started out the door, Captain Wilson walked in with a Marine Corps major. "Let me introduce you to our flight leader," Wilson said, addressing Major Turner. "This is Captain Norbeck. Captain, Major Turner—he'll be flying in my ship. He's a DoD inspector looking at Vietnamization. He's also fluent in Vietnamese."

Extending his hand, Norbeck said, "How do you do, sir? So you're fluent in Vietnamese, sir, and evaluating Vietnamization?" Norbeck asked.

"Yup, several tours over here over the years. They sent me to language school for a year as well," Jack explained.

"Good luck with that evaluation, sir. You'll learn a lot today, I'm sure," Norbeck said, sarcasm dripping off every word.

"Captain, I'm told it's a quiet pickup zone," Jack said.

"Sir, if it's quiet, why are we going in to pick up wounded with three aircraft?" Norbeck asked. Jack didn't have an answer. "If you'll excuse me, I have an aircraft to preflight," Norbeck said as he moved towards the door.

"Hey, Norbeck," Wilson called out. "Something bothering you?"

Turning back and looking over his shoulder, Norbeck said, "I just don't have a warm and fuzzy feeling about this one." He turned again and walked out the door.

"Sorry about that, Major. He's normally not like that. Something must be bothering him."

"We all have bad days," Major Turner said, showing that he had taken no offense at the captain's comments.

"Well, sir, let's head out and crank her up. I like to get in the air before the flight. We'll be flying at treetop level and fast as I'm not taking any chances with the SA-7s," Wilson added.

Arriving at the aircraft, Captain Norbeck proceeded to brief the crew and make introductions.

"Gather around," Norbeck said. "This is Specialist Mike Hill, who will be flying as door gunner today. We're a flight of three today and we're going into a PZ to the northeast of Quang Tri to pick up wounded Vietnamese Marines. We'll fly in a left echelon going in. Get them loaded as quick as you can and give me an up when they're on board. I'm told it should be a cold PZ. That doesn't mean that we won't take fire on the route, so be on your toes. Any questions?"

"Sir, who's flying chase today?" Hill asked.

"That's Captain Wilson and he'll pick up any down crews. If we go down, the other aircraft won't wait around for us but he'll come in and pick us up. No more questions? Let's get ready and crank her up." Norbeck explained. Captain Harvey Wilson had taken over command of the 48th upon the death of Major Kingman.

"Blue Star Flight, Flight Lead on the go," Captain Norbeck transmitted and started his climb to treetop level. Since May, when Major Kingman had been shot down by an SA-7 missile, everyone had been flying low and fast. Captain Wilson was not only the chase aircraft but also the C&C aircraft for the mission and had Jack on board to coordinate the mission with the ground commander and advisor. As the aircraft approached the My Chanh River, all three of the aircraft got as low as they could because once north of that river, they were over Indian territory, as the pilots called it. Wilson was two klicks behind them and coming fast as well.

"Blue Star Flight Leader," Wilson called Norbeck, "you should be seeing green smoke any minute now marking the pickup point."

"Roger, I have the green smoke at my one o'clock. Break. Flight, this is Lead. I'll land to the green smoke. Maintain echelon left formation," Norbeck transmitted.

"Three taking fire. Left side." Norbeck glanced to his left and saw the telltale muzzle flashes from the tree line. The Cobra escort of two aircraft was beginning to hit the area with rockets and minigun fire.

"Hill, open fire," Norbeck instructed, and Hill immediately laid down a steady stream of M60 machine-gun fire in front of Chalk Two's nose in an effort to protect Chalk Two.

"Hill, be careful. You shoot Lieutenant Nelson's aircraft and he's going to be pissed," Norbeck half joked, fairly confident that Hill wouldn't do such a thing, hopefully.

As Norbeck approached the green smoke grenade with a group of Vietnamese soldiers crouched near it, he commenced his deceleration, which lowered the tail of the aircraft. Suddenly the ARVN soldiers rushed to the aircraft when it was ten feet in the air. To keep from hitting them, Norbeck increased his deceleration further, raising the nose and lowering the tail. Then the tail rotor hit the ground.

"Shit," Norbeck yelled as the aircraft suddenly and violently pitched to the left towards Chalk Two.

In Chalk Two, Specialist Joe Acuna was serving as the door gunner and watching the aircraft to his right, Captain Norbeck's aircraft. Suddenly, Acuna froze in horror as the main rotor blade of Captain Norbeck's aircraft was coming right at him. Almost as quickly, the aircraft stopped less than a quarter of a rotor blade away and settled none too softly on the ground.

"Sir, Chalk One is down," Acuna said before Captain Norbeck could even get off a transmission. Although Norbeck was on the ground and shutting down his aircraft, the Vietnamese continued to climb on, thinking that they were getting a ride out. The wounded on stretchers were still lying on the ground, totally forgotten by their more able fellow soldiers.

"Acuna, if they start to swarm us, lay down a burst of fire in front of them. I want the stretchers first. If there's room, I'll take walking wounded," Nelson instructed. The crew chief on the left side of the aircraft was still firing on the tree line from where they were taking fire. No Vietnamese soldiers were on that side of his aircraft; instead, they were hiding and attempting to get on the right side of Chalk Three, protected from the enemy fire.

"Two, this is Lead. Get out of here. We'll get on the chase bird. Break. Chase, this is Lead, I'm down and need extraction. Watch it as they're swarming the aircraft," Norbeck transmitted. "Alright, crew, get out of here and move to the back behind the tail boom. Chase is inbound to get us. Now move." As Norbeck and his crew unassed the downed aircraft, the Vietnamese couldn't comprehend why the aircraft had been shut down and the crew were getting out, especially as Chalks Two and Three had departed. Some Vietnamese that hadn't gotten on Chalks Two and Three began to drift back towards the downed aircraft. Some showed signs of being wounded; many didn't.

"Major, Flight Leader is down. We're going in to pick them up," Wilson said on the aircraft intercom system.

"What happened to him?" Jack asked, watching the trees flashing past the aircraft.

"Sir, the Vietnamese swarmed the aircraft and he crashed. They tried that with Chalk Two and Three, but they threatened to shoot them if they did," Wilson said.

"I'll call the advisor on the ground and see if he can get

control of those people," Jack said, switching from intercom to FM transmit. Before he could get a response back from the advisor on the ground, Wilson was executing a deceleration flare next to the downed aircraft and the American crew.

Norbeck and his crew moved behind their aircraft and maintained a low posture as gunfire was still being heard around the pickup zone. Then the sound of a UH-1H could be heard. The chase aircraft popped over the trees and made a rapid deceleration, touching down by Norbeck.

"Get on quick," Norbeck instructed his crew, and they moved to the aircraft. So did most of the Vietnamese, seeing this as a way out. Mike Hill jumped in and took a position on the floor directly behind the pilot's seat with his back against the seat. Almost immediately, hands were grabbing at his legs as Vietnamese soldiers fought to get on the aircraft, attempting to pull themselves aboard or hang on as others pulled or pushed them back. The cargo bay quickly filled.

"Major, kick some of them off. We have too many on and not enough power," Captain Wilson yelled to the crews and Jack. Jack and Norbeck had no problem following that order. Jack grabbed a Marine by his shirt collar and tossed him off the aircraft. Norbeck punched a soldier in the face as he attempted to climb on. The crew chief and gunner were physically kicking Vietnamese Marines off the skids. Finally, Jack felt the aircraft move slightly as it came light on the skids and moved forward, pushing some soldiers out of the way with the nose of the aircraft. As the aircraft slowly rose, several Vietnamese attempted to jump on the skids, only to be pushed, kicked or punched off by the crew.

Suddenly a gunshot was heard, very close and very loud. "Alright, what jackass just shot the aircraft?" Captain Wilson asked, thinking that a Vietnamese Marine had accidentally discharged his weapon in the aircraft. At the same time, he felt warm liquid on the back of his neck. "Did some son of a bitch hit the hydraulics?" His question was met with silence.

Finally, Jack said, "Captain, someone just shot this crewman. He's dead."

"What!" Wilson asked and turned in his seat to see what was going on behind him. The Vietnamese on the aircraft were silent but staring in his direction. He then noticed the blood on the radio console.

"How?" Wilson asked, surveying the Vietnamese to see who had a weapon. None did.

"Captain, the round came up from below us. I think one of the guys that were tossed off shot at us and it came through the floor. Looks like it hit this young man in the knee and his head. He's dead."

The remainder of the flight was very quiet.

50

SKILL, NOT LUCK

14 July 1972
48th Assault Helicopter Company
Marble Mountain, South Vietnam

"Okay, gents, today's mission is resupply for the ARVN Marines. Upon completion you will loiter at FSB Sally for further missions," Captain Brian Rinehart, the Ops officer, announced before he was interrupted.

"Hey, sir, why aren't the South Vietnamese helicopters resupplying these guys? As one said to me the other day as I attempted to pull into a POL spot, 'My country, me first,' so let them resupply their own," Chief Warrant Officer Dan Grossman asked. Dan was well into his extension, having already flown a year in-country.

"We fly what they send us, okay? We will put up six aircraft today. When you complete your respective missions, loiter at FSB Sally and wait for further missions. Crew assignments are on the board," he concluded. As everyone stood to leave, Captain Harvey Wilson came into the room.

"Wait one, guys. One more thing, watch yourselves with the ARVNs. I spoke with Colonel Metcalf and told him that if the ARVNs attempted to swarm the aircraft like they did yesterday or shoot at the aircraft like they did yesterday, we will shoot them. We're not going to lose another crew member like we did yesterday with Mike Hill. Be safe, gentlemen," Captain Wilson said. As the pilots were all looking at the mission board, a few expressed their opinion of the South Vietnamese Air Force, which provided all the helicopter support to the Vietnamese Army.

"The damn South Vietnamese Air Force won't fly shit. Every mission that's tough, we get, and they get the VIP missions," Mr. Cecil grumbled. He was considered one of the old pilots.

First Lieutenant Roger Nelson walked out to his aircraft with his copilot for the day, Chief Warrant Officer Ron Riviera. Mr. Riviera had plenty of experience and hours to be an aircraft commander but had only recently joined the unit. At the time, several units were being sent back to the States, but pilots with less than six months in-country were being retained and sent to other units. Mr. Riviera was one such pilot, having flown in other parts of Vietnam, and was getting familiar with the operational area before he was made aircraft commander. Roger had been in a similar position only months before as he'd transferred into the 48th from the 116th Assault Helicopter Company when it had been rotated back to the States.

"Schnellecht, Flemke," Nelson called out to the gunner and crew chief as he approached the aircraft. Nelson's normal crew chief and gunner were conducting a periodic inspection on Nelson's assigned aircraft, so they would not be flying on this day. Schnellecht and Flemke were the assigned gunner and crew chief on the aircraft that he would be flying on this day.

"Yes, sir," Flemke responded for the duo as they both approached.

"If the ARVNs start to look like they're going to swarm the aircraft, you lay down a burst of machine gunfire right in front of them. If one raises his weapon, you shoot him. Understood?" The two crew members exchanged looks and acknowledged the order and prepared to depart. Everyone understood what had happened the day before, and no one was taking any chances.

The morning resupply went without incident, and by noon all six aircraft were refueled and sitting at FSB Sally, awaiting further missions for the afternoon. They didn't have to wait long before a messenger came from the TOC.

"Who's Flight Lead here?" the Army staff sergeant asked.

"That would be me, Sergeant," Roger Nelson responded.

"Sir, they need you up at the TOC for a briefing," the staff sergeant stated. "Colonel Metcalf would like to talk to you," he added. That brought several concerned looks from the group of pilots Roger had been talking with. As Roger and the sergeant walked up to the TOC, nothing was said. Entering the TOC, Roger saw Colonel Metcalf and Captain Hoffman, the liaison officer from the 48th, and a major that he assumed was another advisor.

"Roger, come over here and let me brief you on what we got," Hoffman said as Roger approached. "Roger, this is Colonel Metcalf, the senior advisor to the 3rd ARVN Division."

"Afternoon, sir," Roger said respectfully.

"And Major Nelson," Hoffman added.

"Sir" was all Roger said in acknowledgment of the major.

"Here's what we got," Colonel Metcalf said, taking over the briefing. "We've got several wounded at this location that we need to get out." Metcalf pointed at a map mounted on the side of the TOC. Roger pulled out his map and plotted the location. "To be honest, previous attempts to get to them have failed." Metcalf turned from the wall map and looked at Roger for some reaction. When there was none, he continued, "We would like to see if you guys can do any better with your five aircraft." He quickly added, "If it's too hot, then abort the mission." Roger studied the map and went through a mental planning process.

"Sir, how many wounded do you have in there that we would need five aircraft?"

Looking at Major Nelson, Metcalf replied, "We're not sure at this point. Comms with them have been intermittent."

"Sir, you understand we're not medevac aircraft. We have no medical supplies or medical equipment on board to speak of. If we get them out, where do you want us to take them. Here?" Roger stated.

"Here will be good, and our medics can check them over. And when we know their condition, we'll have you shuttle them to Da Nang for treatment."

"Okay, sir, I'll take a stab at it, but I'm only taking my aircraft and the Cobras in on the first attempt to assess the situation. If I get in okay, then I'll have the others follow me back in," Roger said. "The other aircraft can loiter east of the highway until I see what the situation is like. And, sir, if they swarm the aircraft like they did yesterday, I've ordered my crew to shoot them. I will not have a crew member killed by them swarming the aircraft."

"These guys are ARVN Rangers and I don't think that will happen, but I'll make a call and emphasize that it better not happen. Major Nelson will be going with you to see that it doesn't happen," Metcalf added. Nelson simply nodded in acknowledgment.

"Glad to have you aboard, sir," Roger said with a lack of enthusiasm. Having Nelson aboard meant one less wounded soldier could be brought out.

"The landing zone will be marked with purple smoke. Good luck. Give us a call when you lift off," Metcalf said, indicating the briefing was over.

"Lieutenant," Major Nelson said, getting Roger's attention.

"Sir?"

"Let me get my stuff and I'll meet you at your aircraft," Nelson said as he headed out the door.

"Roger, if you need anything, just call me," Hoffman said with a look of concern.

"Ordering the enemy not to shoot at me would be nice," Roger replied, attempting to add some levity to the situation. Something just didn't feel right about this mission.

Experienced pilots developed a sixth sense about certain missions. Some missions gave no concern and came off with no hitches. Some missions, however, gave rise to a foreboding feeling even before the aircraft was started. Fortunately, that foreboding feeling only enhanced a pilot's awareness of the potential dangers in the mission. Sometimes the feelings were false and afterwards everyone rested easy, wondering why they had been so wound up for the mission. At other times, that feeling was the difference between life and death. As Roger walked back to his aircraft and the waiting group of pilots, the sixth sense was telling him something.

"Gather around," he called to the pilots as he laid his map out on the floor of his aircraft. As he did so, crew chiefs and gunners were already beginning to don their chicken plates, untie rotor blades and open pilot doors. Once the aircraft commanders were gathered, he began his brief.

"We have a mission to fly to this location." Roger read off the coordinates, which the other pilots started plotting on their maps. Once it appeared that everyone had marked the location, he continued. "There are ARVN Rangers located there, and they have a lot of wounded. Previous attempts to get the wounded out have not been successful, so we've been asked to go in and get them. My plan is that we'll take off and fly to a loiter point east of QL1. I'll leave you there and take the snakes with me and make the first run to the pickup zone. Let me see how it is and I'll report back and call each of you in separately or as a flight if it looks okay. The pickup zone will be marked with purple smoke," Roger explained, noticing Major Nelson walking up.

"This is Major Nelson, one of the advisors, and he'll be flying in with me and talking to the ARVNs. I've been assured that they will not swarm the aircraft. Any questions? If not, let's crank 'em up."

The Cobras were Sabre aircraft as the gunships of the 48th were all down for battle damage from two days prior. As Mr. Riviera went through the start-up procedures, Roger looked over at the Cobras to see if they were also starting their engines, which they were. What caught his attention, however, was the flight of six South Vietnamese helicopters that were on the other side of FSB Sally and appeared to be taking an afternoon siesta. *Wonder what mission they have today?*

"Hey, Lieutenant, if you could tune in this frequency, I'll be able to talk to the ground commander at the pickup zone," Major Nelson said, handing Roger a slip of paper with a radio frequency written on it. Roger immediately tuned his number two FM radio to the assigned frequency.

"Sir, I have you tuned to the ground commander on FM 2."

"Thanks."

"Flight, Blue Star One-Five is on the go." And Roger pulled pitch and departed. The four Sabre AH-1G aircraft came up last but quickly moved to positions on each side of the six departing UH-1H aircraft. It was known now that the NVA had the SA-7 anti-aircraft missile, so the flight stayed low-level and at maximum speed, attempting to negate the effectiveness of the SA-7. Approaching QL1, Roger broke off from the rest of the flight.

"Two, this is One-Five. Take the flight over to the east side and hold for me. I'm going to start my run, over."

"Roger, One-Five, good luck."

"Skill, not luck," Roger replied, using the company motto. His copilot, Mr. Riviera, was doing the navigating along the flight path that Roger had predetermined.

"Blue Star One-Fiver, Sabre Four-Five has you covered with a flight of four."

"Roger, Four-Fiver," Roger responded with a comforting feeling as he stayed as low as possible above the sparse terrain covered with brush and scattered clusters of trees.

"Okay, hold this heading until we drop over that ridgeline up ahead, then turn north. Should be a valley there we can run up until I tell you to turn to your left," Riviera instructed Roger. Riviera tracked their progress along the planned flight route to the pickup zone while Roger did the flying. Roger was holding about fifty feet of altitude over the ground and ninety knots of airspeed. He took the upcoming ridge at an angle to minimize the time he silhouetted the aircraft on the skyline. As he dropped into the valley, his stomach tightened when he saw the destroyed South Vietnamese helicopter. It looked like a recent casualty of war.

"That must have been one of the previous attempts" was all Riviera said as they passed over the wreckage. "Okay, make a left turn and let's skip over that next ridge and turn right, skirting the ridge," Riviera ordered. Roger expertly executed the order and, again reducing the silhouette, slipped into the next valley. As he crested the ridgeline, the remains of another smoldering South Vietnamese helicopter were evident.

"How many aircraft did they lose trying to get into this place?" Schnellecht asked, peering over his gun as the burn wreckage passed on his side.

"They lost five this morning," Major Nelson answered.

"Five!" Roger said in surprise. "Would have been nice if you'd told me that before we launched, sir," Roger said. Now his sixth sense was aroused to a new level.

"Would you have taken the mission, Lieutenant?" Nelson asked.

"I would have liked to have all the facts, sir," Roger replied. *We aren't going to make it on this one.*

"Blue Star One-Five, Centaur Four-Five, over."

"Go ahead, Centaur."

"Did you see that down aircraft?"

"Roger." Nothing more needed to be said between the two aircraft nor between the crew.

"Why aren't we taking fire?" Flemke asked as he surveyed the landscape.

"I don't know, but pray we don't" was all Mr. Riviera could say. Then, "I have green smoke at one o'clock."

Roger looked up and started to make a slight course correction towards the smoke. *Oh shit* flashed through his mind.

"Sir, didn't Metcalf brief purple smoke?" Roger asked Major Nelson.

"Yeah, they're attempting to lure you into a trap. They did that this morning. The pickup zone is at your eleven o'clock. I just called them for the smoke." Roger made an immediate course correction. As he did so, two klicks out he could see purple smoke just beginning to appear on the edge of a small clearing on the top of a knoll. That was when he noticed another downed South Vietnamese helicopter on its side in the trees.

"I got purple smoke," Mr. Riviera said, pointing to the area. As he did so, both Flemke and Schnellecht opened fire.

"Taking fire!" both transmitted in unison.

"One-Five, Four-Five, you're taking fire. We're engaging."

Roger didn't need to respond but kept concentrating on the pickup zone. Green tracers were flashing past his windshield. Occasionally, he would hear the familiar sound of a hammer tapping the aircraft. Explosions from the 2.75-inch rockets that the Centaurs were laying down along his flight path were almost reassuring. The explosions from the impacting mortar rounds were not. The day was already hazy, and the dust created by the explosions wasn't helping the situation any. As Roger began to execute his deceleration into the pickup zone, the explosion from the impacting mortar round was not reassuring. As he touched down, Vietnamese Rangers carrying stretchers and some walking wounded started climbing into the aircraft. Major Nelson was yelling something in Vietnamese that Roger mentally translated as "hurry up" but couldn't be sure as he didn't speak Vietnamese. Roger just knew that as they sat there loading the aircraft, the enemy was readjusting his mortar to place the next round where Roger was sitting. Ten seconds ticked off when the next mortar round impacted on the other side of the aircraft from the first round. *Shit, they have me bracketed. The next round will hit us.*

"Blue Star One-Five, get out of there," Centaur Four-Five yelled over the UHF frequency they were all monitoring.

Roger looked back to see the last Vietnamese being loaded. "Coming up," he announced and started increasing his power.

"Blue Star One-Five is coming out." As the aircraft broke ground and moved forward, green tracers again appeared from the surrounding tree line and brush. Centaur laid down minigun fire and suppressive rockets as Roger increased his speed.

"Sir, they just laid a mortar round where we were sitting," Flemke yelled as he continued to engage the muzzle flashes from the brush on his side of the aircraft. Suddenly a loud banging noise was heard.

"Shit!" Schnellecht yelled.

"What! What happened?" Roger asked.

"Oh, a damn empty stretcher just blew out the door. It hit the rear stabilizer but missed the tail rotor. Son of a bitch nearly took my head off." Roger breathed a sigh of relief as they continued to speed towards FSB Sally to drop off the wounded ARVN Rangers.

"How many did we get out?" Roger asked, concentrating on his flying.

"We have twelve," Major Nelson responded. "You got them all in this one lift. Nice job, Lieutenant."

"Sir, I'm not sending any more aircraft in there. We got lucky on this one, and the Cobras have expended everything," Roger stated.

"I understand. I'll let the TOC know of your decision," Major Nelson said.

"Flight, Blue Star One-Five, meet me at Sally and take some of these wounded to Da Nang. I have twelve on board and will transfer four to two of you. We're done for the day."

51

INTO THE BACKYARD

The past week had seen heavy fighting as the Marines consolidated their position northeast of Quang Tri. The helicopter assaults into Landing Zones Blue Jay and Crow had seriously reduced the supply lines from the north. With the Marines being so successful on the eastern flank, the 1st ARVN Airborne Division was able to push north to the southwestern outskirts of Quang Tri City.

"General Lan, with the NVA determined to hold Quang Tri, this gives us an opportunity to exploit his positions along the coast. We could cut off his supplies flowing south from the Cua Viet River and thus start strangling him," Colonel Dorsey said. He and General Lan were studying a map of the area.

"If I sent the 147th Brigade up the Triple Nickel, then we could cut his supply lines. They could then swing west on the south side of the Cua Viet and destroy his artillery and air-defense systems," Lann said, thinking out loud. He paused for a moment, then said, "Let's send the 147th with two battalions and tanks north. The third battalion, we'll fly to this location for them to link up and then the 147th can attack southeast, seizing this road junction. This will cause the enemy to drive across the Thach Han River or north over the Cua Viet River."

"So order it," Lan directed his Operations officer.

* * *

The 5th VNMC Battalion was on deck aboard the USS *Denver* (LPD-9) and in the process of loading the six CH-46 aircraft so assigned. Jack Turner was along for the ride on this one as he wanted to see how the linkup would be executed between the 5th VNMC Battalion and the rest of the 147th Brigade. Lieutenant Colonel Ho Quang Lich, the 5th Battalion commander, had met with Jack earlier and indicated that he would like Jack close to him on the operation. Major Joy was on the ground with the 147th command post and the 2nd and 3rd Battalions, and Jack expected this to be a smooth operation. Loading the aircraft was moving smoothly, with rotor blades turning and Vietnamese Marines loading. Jack wanted to be one of the first off the aircraft, so he waited until all the Vietnamese were aboard. At two minutes out from landing, everyone on board double-checked their equipment and chin straps. Touching down, the rear ramp was open and they poured out under the sound of incoming artillery. Incoming on the suspected enemy positions, that was.

"Grizzly Six, Cub Six, over." Joy had assigned the code names for the mission and was chuckling when he assigned Jack the call sign of Cub.

"Cub Six, Grizzly Six, over."

"Grizzly Six, we're on the ground. Light resistance, Victor and Lima are secured. Over."

"Roger, we just crossed the Lima Delta and are four klicks from you. Will keep you posted on our progress, over."

"Grizzly Six, I have good copy. See you when you get here, out." Jack cut the conversation off. Handing his mike back to the Vietnamese Marine assigned to carry his radio, he began observing the leadership of the battalion as they moved amongst the young Marines. It was obvious to him that the entire chain of command knew their business and placed the welfare of their soldiers very high on their priority list. As NVA soldiers were pushed out of their foxholes and trenches, the Vietnamese Marines began to consolidate their positions. Some light enemy fire was being received, but nothing that worried anyone. Four hours later, the first elements of linkup force arrived. Jack went looking for Joy.

"Nice to see you made it," Jack needled Joy.

"Someone had to come get you guys," Joy responded. "You ready to move out now?"

"Yeah, I think we are. Where to?" Jack asked as Joy spread his map out on the ground, pointing at it with a grease pencil. "We're here at Van Hoa now and are going to swing southwest and drive towards Bich Khe, with one battalion. One battalion will continue south to take the bridge over the Vinh Dinh River. This will cut their supply lines. In addition, we will block any reinforcements from getting in by one battalion going due west to cut Route 560. The airborne guys are on the west side of Quang Tri, and with the 258th on the south, 369th on the southeast and east, this will pretty well close the door on them except the northwest side. They may be able to get north to Dong Ha and move back west on Highway 9," Joy outlined.

"Sounds good. Do you want me to stay with the 5th Battalion or move with someone else?" Jack asked.

"The 5th Battalion is going to be moving west to cut the 560. Why don't you move with the 2nd Battalion?" Joy suggested. "They're lead battalion for this next move, and there's no advisor with them. They're going to Bich Khe."

"Sounds good," Jack said as he stood up. "Can your driver run me over there in your jeep?"

"God, do I have to do everything for you?" Joy asked with a shit-eating grin. "Of course, just send him back—the battalion commander over there will probably want to keep him," Joy said, pointing to some tanks over in the 2nd Battalion area. Jack also noticed the M48 tanks.

As Jack approached, the 2nd Battalion commander, Lieutenant Colonel Nguyen Xuan Phuc, recognized him almost immediately. "Ah, Major Turner. I told you come me," Colonel Phuc called out in his pidgin English.

"Glad to be with you, Colonel. I will help any way I can," Jack said resorting to his Vietnamese, which was much better than Colonel Phuc's English.

"Jack, you Vietnamese better than my English. You no need practice. I need practice. We speak English, okay?" Phuc ordered.

"Okay, Colonel, we speak English," Jack said, chuckling. He noted the ANGLICO team that was sitting on the ground with their radios and walked over to them.

"Well, if it isn't none other than Lieutenant Steller," Jack said, extending his hand. Lieutenant Tony Steller had met Jack several times, but this would be his first time working directly with Major Turner.

"Hey, sir," Tony said, standing up. His radio operator, Sergeant Mike Jurassic, stood as he had been reading a well-worn, dog-eared copy of *MASH: A Novel about Three Army Doctors*. Jack waved at him to sit down. Accepting the handshake, he asked, "Are you going to be moving with us for a time, sir?"

"Yeah, I flew in with the 5th Battalion, but Major Joy asked that I travel with you for this next leg," Jack responded.

"Great, sir," Tony said as Jack removed his rucksack. "Colonel Phuc and I have plotted out some TRPs for this move down Route 560, and those have been sent to Major Borman. He already sent them to the ships." Tony grabbed his map and spread it across the ground. Squatting down, Jack studied the map and the target reference points that had been plotted.

"We're located here, sir, Yankee Delta three-five-three-five-eight-nine, and we're going to be moving south across this stream and rice paddy to the village of An Long. From there it's a sweep through that heavily vegetated area and to Route 560," Tony explained as he pointed at an area of dense trees about a klick southwest of their current position.

As they discussed the points, Colonel Phuc called out,

"Major Turner, we go," and the command group started to pick up rucksacks and move. The tanks led moving slowly with the infantry dispersed around them. Jack hefted his rucksack, out of which he had stripped out everything nonessential, and set a pace close to Phuc. Lieutenant Steller was right alongside Jack, as was Jurassic. Tony maintained contact with Major Borman, and Jurassic had the FAC and any attack helicopters that came on his frequency tuned in. Jack surveyed the land as they moved, noting the scattered clusters of houses surrounding large areas of rice paddies. The rice paddies were filled with water as the monsoons were ending in this part of Vietnam. To the south across the rice paddy were large tracts of cemeteries. Because of the cemeteries, a restriction on the use of indirect fire in that area was in place. Some of those cemeteries had been there for centuries. Tree lines were a combination of palm trees, elephant plants and other tropical foliage. Mixed in with that tropical flora were also trench lines and covered bunkers. The question was always which ones were occupied. As the lead elements of 2nd Battalion approached Route 560, they found out.

The first mortar rounds impacting caught Jack by surprise. He found himself lying in water, where he had taken an automatic prone position without thought. Tony was right beside him.

"Did you hear that coming?" Jack asked, looking around.

"No. Tube must be far away," Tony answered as one of the tanks opened fire towards the town of An Long. When it did, a high volume of automatic fire began pouring out from the houses on the south side of their avenue of approach. Suddenly one of the tanks exploded as a Sagger AT-4 rocket streaked out of An Long and slammed into the side of the tank. Phuc's companies were all heavily engaged, even his tanks. The 1st Company was engaging forces in An Long, 2nd Company was engaging elements to the south, and 3rd Company was attempting to maneuver north around An Long. Khe looked for the ANGLICO team and spotted Lieutenant Steller talking on the radio. He was sure Tony needed no advice on where to place the naval gunfire.

"Have we got any tac air?" Jack asked.

"It's coming, sir, but about twenty minutes out as it was on standby at Da Nang," Tony said, ducking his head a couple of times as the sound of a passing bullet could be heard. Tony knew that if you heard the bullet, it didn't have your name, but instinct made you duck. "I do have a couple of Cobra gunships a few minutes away. One has what they call a Hydra rocket that's supposed to be able to take out a tank," Tony volunteered.

"Really!" Jack said with some surprise.

"Yes, sir. They've just been introduced in-country. Can we use them on something?" Tony asked.

"Let me see what I can find for you." Saddling up next to Phuc, who was now squatting behind a dike in the rice paddy, keeping it between him and the small-arms fire, Jack asked, "Colonel, have you had reports of any tanks?"

"Yes, 3rd Company reports two tanks moving south on Route 560 towards his position," Phuc said.

"Show me on the map," Jack ordered, pulling his map out of his side cargo pocket. Looking at Phuc's map, Jack noted the position of the reported tanks. Having plotted the location on his map, he made his way over to Tony. "Here's a position for possibly two tanks moving up Route 560. Pass that to the Cobra jockey and see if they can take it out."

"Roger, sir." And Tony was making the call.

* * *

"Station calling Centaur One-Six, this is One-Six, over." Centaur One-Six was supporting the operation for the day and had just refueled. He was low-level to avoid the SA-7 anti-aircraft missiles that had been effective in taking out a few heli-copters. Following the LOH made it easy for the Cobra to maneuver to the target.

"Centaur One-Six, this is Oscar Two-Six. Over," Tony transmitted.

"Oscar Two-Six, go ahead."

"Centaur One-Six, we have two tanks at Yankee Delta three-two-six-five-nine-oh. Can you take them?"

"Oscar Two-Six, understand Yankee Delta three-two-six-five-nine-oh. Over."

"Centaur, that's affirmative. Over."

"Roger, we're going up and have a look. Please notify your people. Don't want any friendly fire," Centaur One-Six said. "Break, Centaur Double Deuce, did you monitor?" Double

Deuce was an LOH traveling with Centaur One-Six and One-Eight, the other AH-1G.

"Centaur One-Six, I monitored and will check it out," Double Deuce said as he proceeded to look for the tanks. He didn't have to look long.

"Centaur One-Six, Double Deuce. Over."

"Go ahead."

"One-Six, there's a cluster of buildings at that location. The tanks are alongside one of the buildings. If you approach from the east, you'll spot them easily at about one klick out and there will be no friendlies if you over- or undershoot. Over."

"Roger, Double Deuce, we're coming in," Centaur One-Six reported as One-Eight closed up with him. Maintaining their airspeed and low altitude, they quickly spotted the tanks.

"One-Eight, you take the right and I'll take the left, over."

"Roger." And both aircraft punched off two rockets each. The 2.75-inch Hydra rocket carried the M247 warhead that was designed to take out a tank. It wasn't a precision-guided rocket, which would have been nice, but if it hit the tank, it would do some serious damage. From where Jack and Tony were located, they could see the Cobras engage and watched as the rocket streaked towards their targets, which were hidden from view to Tony and Jack. The resulting explosion told them that the rockets had probably hit the mark.

"Oscar Two-Six, Centaur One-Six, scratch two tanks, over."

"Roger, Centaur One-Six. I have more targets for you if you're ready to copy," Tony said and spent the next few minutes passing coordinates and targets to the pair of Cobra gunships. Jack had moved up to be with Colonel Phuc and discuss where it would be best to employ the tac air when it arrived. The 1st and 2nd Companies had reached the edge of An Long while the 3rd Company was attempting to maneuver to the north side of An Long but meeting resistance from the tree line behind An Long. Colonel Phuc and Jack with the ANGLICO team had been following 3rd Company.

"Here, the 3rd Company is reporting heavy automatic weapons in bunkers with overhead cover," Phuc said, pointing at his map. "That is that heavily vegetated area." Writing down the coordinates, Jack trotted over to Tony's position.

"Have you got tac air yet?" Jack asked.

"They were just coming up on station when I talked to the FAC last," Tony answered.

"Okay, the 3rd Company is receiving heavy automatic weapons fire and one of your tanks just took a Sagger missile from there. Here are the coordinates. Turn the tac air loose on them," Jack instructed as he handed the coordinates to Tony.

"Hey, Jurassic, switch me to the FAC," Tony called out to Jurassic, who switched Tony's radio.

"Wolfman Four-Five, Oscar Two-Six, over," Tony transmitted. Wolfman was an aerial observer seated in the rear seat of the OV-10, freeing the pilot up to fly. Call signs for the OV-10 were Covey.

"Oscar Two-Six, this is Wolfman Four-Five. Whatcha got for me? Over."

"Wolfman Four-Five, bunkers in tree line with overhead cover. Coordinates Yankee Delta three-two-six-five-nine-oh. How copy?"

"Oscar Two-Six, I have good copy. Coming down for a look. Can you observe? Over."

"Wolfman Four-Five, affirmative." Tony and Jack watched as the OV-10 Bronco suddenly appeared from the scattered clouds. From where they sat, it appeared that the OV-10 was upside down in a steep dive. At a thousand feet, the aircraft snap-rolled upright and punched off a rocket. Following the rocket down, Jack and Tony watched it impact in a cloud of white smoke on the edge of the tree line.

"Wolfman Four-Five, that's the spot, over."

"Roger, let your people know we're making the runs from northeast to southwest, over," Wolfman Four-Five transmitted. As Jack and Tony watched, they saw nothing at first, then they spotted movement from the east as two F-4 Phantom jets came over, low and fast. They saw the aircraft before they heard the sound. As they watched, objects began to fall from under the aircraft. The string of bombs uprooted trees, dirt and a body or two as well. Each plane made two passes and expended their ordnance. The shooting from the tree line stopped long enough for the lead elements of 3rd Company to enter the treed area. Then the fighting started all over again. The entire area was multiple trench lines and connecting bunkers. Dusk would be fast approaching. Jack approached Colonel Phuc.

"Phuc, it'll be dark soon. We can get in one more air strike. I recommend you pull your people back and let us hit the area one more time. We can go back in tomorrow. An Long is firmly in your control now. I suspect it will be more difficult to clear the treed area," Jack recommended. Phuc thought about Jack's recommendation for a minute.

"Okay, I'll pull 3rd Company into An Long. We hit this tomorrow with all three companies. Bring in the tac air," Phuc said. Jack passed the request to Tony, who dished up another flight of bombers to hit the treed area once more for the day. While that was happening, Jack was on the advisor radio net, talking to Joy and the other advisors.

"Grizzly, this is Cub, over."

"Cub, Grizzly, go ahead."

"We have consolidated for the night in An Long. The vegetated area at Yankee Delta three-four-five-eight contains a detailed bunker complex. We're putting in one more air strike now and will go back in tomorrow early. How copy, over?"

"Cub, I have good copy. 5th Battalion moved north and

cut Route 560 at Dai Ho and is set for the night there in a blocking position. He managed to police up some 130mm guns. 3rd Battalion is located vicinity of An Kiet and Tu Hui and has cut the Triple Nickel. He also controls the bridge over the Vinh Dinh River. Over," Joy transmitted.

"Roger, Grizzly, understand we are good for the night. Cub out," Jack transmitted and handed the mike over to his Vietnamese Marine radio operator. Colonel Phuc had set up his command post in an abandoned building on the outskirts of An Long. It was one of the few concrete-block-and-tin buildings in an almost total thatch village. Typical of the farm villages in the area, pigs and chicken wandered everywhere and only the Vietnamese owners could tell you whose pig belonged to whom. Jack just assumed it was all community property. Most of the villagers had fled when the NVA had first attacked. Those that remained had been rounded up and placed in two of the thatch houses as they were probably NVA sympathizers, and no one was taking chances at this point. They were guarded.

To the north, the sounds of gunfire and explosions told Jack that the 5th Battalion was in for a long night. NVA forces were attempting to break through down Route 560. The stream of what appeared to be molten metal flowing down from the sky indicated that a Spectre gunship was on station above them. Jack couldn't see the plane, just the stream of molten metal. *And to think, between each tracer round, there were five nontracer rounds*, Jack thought as he watched. Throughout the night, 2nd Battalion maintained flares in the sky over the jungle that they would enter in the morning. The intent was to place the enemy in a glow of light and not one's own forces. The light from the flares was blanketing the enemy's positions and the open area between their position and An Long. An occasional shot rang out from the tree line, but the Marines maintained their discipline and didn't engage, thus they didn't reveal their positions.

Jack spent a couple of hours moving from position to position within An Long, stopping to talk to each of the company commanders and joking with the young Marines. Seeing him raised their confidence level. His presence alone told them that American airpower was close at hand, something the NVA didn't have. The American also brought medevac helicopters, they knew, in case someone was wounded. Jack returned to the CP and briefed quickly Colonel Phuc on what he had seen. Phuc asked a few questions and then told Jack to get some sleep as the next day was going to be long. Jack took his advice and stretched out on the ground with his rucksack for a pillow.

"Hey, sir, wake up...wake up, sir," a voice said as Jack opened his eyes and stared into darkness. "Want some coffee, sir?" Mike Jurassic asked, holding out a canteen cup of steaming coffee.

Still in a daze, Jack reached out for the cup. "Yeah, thanks. What time is it?"

"It's 0400, sir. Colonel Phuc wants stand-to at 0500 and has already requested the first air strike for 0600. He wants to wake up Charlie. The lieutenant has already called the request in and is just waiting to see if the Air Force is up that early. The lieutenant told him naval gunfire wouldn't be good as we're on the gun target line presently," Jurassic informed Jack.

"Hmm...not a good idea to be in that position. Give me a minute and I'll get my ass up and talk to Phuc. Thanks for the coffee," Jack said as he propped himself up against the wall of the hooch they commandeered. Once Jack finished his coffee and stepped out for the traditional morning piss, he went looking for Colonel Phuc. He found him in the next hooch, which was being used for the battalion CP.

"Ah, good morning, Jack. You sleep good?" Colonel Phuc asked.

"Sure did. I guess I needed it," Jack responded. *Why is he always so jovial?* Jack wondered. "What's your plan for today?"

"We stand-to soon. Then air strike at first light, then sweep through the area. Charlie very quiet last night. All three companies on line until we find him. He not in rice paddy, so we stay in jungle and find him. Maybe have 2nd Company peel south towards Bich Khe when we have this cleared." As Phuc talked, Jack was looking at the map. He noted that once they cleared this forested area, 1st and 3rd Companies would have to clear the village of Ha My before they would reach Route 560. 2nd Company coming out of the forested area would face an open rice paddy, with another forested area six hundred meters to the southwest and a few scattered hooches in between.

"Colonel Phuc, can I recommend that before 2nd Company starts out towards this forested area, we hit it and hit it hard with artillery? They'll be exposed across this open area to both that forested area and these hooch's if anyone's in there, and I suspect anyone chased out of here"—he indicated the woods they were about to pass through—"will withdraw to near the woods that 2nd Company will need to clear to get to Bich Khe," Jack said.

Phuc looked at the map. "I think you right. We do that. Also, when we clear Ha My, we have this forested area to clear at Route 560. I hold 2nd Company in those woods," he said, pointing at the next objective for 2nd Company, "until we clear Ha My and cross 560. They hold and provide support while 1st and 3rd companies push south along 560 to Bich Khe. We have plan now." Phuc grinned and turned to his Operations officer to get the word out to the companies. As Jack studied the map, what troubled him wasn't the fight in the jungle areas, as air strikes and artillery could be used there.

What troubled him was that between Bich Khe and the bridge over the Vinh Dinh River was a large area of historical cemeteries where he couldn't employ air strikes or artillery. He knew that Charlie would have no sentimental qualms about setting up positions in the cemeteries. That was where the hard fight would be, Jack was sure.

52

CHANGE OF RESPONSIBILITY

27 July 1972
1st VNMC Division Command Post
Huong Dien, South Vietnam

The division's brigades had accomplished the initial order. The 147th Brigade had cut Route 560 and sealed the northwest, western and southern portions of the area around Quang Tri. The only route open still was QL1, which was under air attack constantly. If it moved, it died. Night was the only time for the NVA to attempt to resupply. ANGLICO air observers were up with the sun, calling in air strikes and naval gunfire on those NVA forces northwest of Quang Tri, with special attention to armor and artillery positions.

This morning, Lieutenant Colonel Turley had arrived at the 1st VNMC Division headquarters along with staff officers from I Corps headquarters. They were all there for a mission change. Turley and Dorsey were sitting together when the briefing started, with General Truong taking the center stage.

"We are tightening the noose around Quang Tri, but not

fast enough. The Airborne Division has pushed to within two hundred meters of the Citadel but is stopped. Their many months of fighting in the Central Highlands and III Corps before coming to us has worn them down. They can push no more. Therefore, I want the 1st Marine Division to take responsibility for clearing Quang Tri," Truong said.

To many, this was a surprise, but not to Dorsey or Lan, who had met with Truong the day before. Orders had been issued in the night for the 258th VNMC Brigade to move up and conduct a relief in place with what was left of the airborne brigade banging on the door of the Citadel. As the Vietnamese intel officer went over the enemy order of battle, Turley and Dorsey slipped out the door to meet with the rest of the advisors, which Dorsey had brought into the division headquarters for two reasons: first, to brief them on what was about to happen, and second, to give them all a bit of a rest and some real chow. A mess tent had been established thanks to some support from one of the aviation units. As the advisors ate their first "American" meal of real eggs, steak, hashbrowns, biscuits and gravy, Dorsey conducted the briefing.

"Gentlemen, continue to eat, but let me have your attention," he started off. When things quieted down, he continued. "The corps commander wants to make some changes that are going to affect us. He's moving the airborne brigade on the southeast side of the Citadel to the west and having 258th conduct a relief in place as I speak. The airborne folks will continue to push up the west side of QL1 to Route 604 and the river. The 258th will take up a position on the southeast side of the Citadel. The 147th Brigade has done a good job of closing off Route 560. I understand you had a bitch of a time in the cemeteries, Major," Dorsey said, looking right at Joy.

"Yes, sir, we couldn't use any artillery or tac air in there. The attack helicopters with miniguns helped a lot, but we held them off using rockets and forty mike-mikes," Joy said.

"Good call. Don't get too comfortable up there. I suspect that since the 147th has control up there, they'll be pulled out soon and sent someplace else," Dorsey told Joy but also informed the group. Looks were exchanged, with everyone waiting for the other shoe to fall as they thought this was an opening statement for more heavy fighting. "The 325th NVA Division units are the ones holding out in the Citadel. They were introduced to the theater within the last month, it appears from some of those we've captured. Truong wants to wrap this up as quickly as possible and his staff is working up a detailed plan now, but I don't foresee a major thrust until the first part of September. Part of his plan is to get the Seventh Fleet to stage an amphibious landing feint up north on the coast to draw off some of the artillery support that's hitting our forces in and around Quang Tri. He also needs time to decide who can be brought up to relieve us so we can take the Citadel." A few moans and bodily movements could be observed and heard.

"What's the matter?" Dorsey asked. "You don't want to be the first in the Citadel?" No one answered. "I don't blame you. It's going to be a bitch of a fight clearing Charlie out of there. Few of us have had any experience in urban warfare, and that's what this is going to be. I've asked Colonel Turley here to discuss it with us as he's had some experience at this. Listen up as it may help you a lot. Gerald."

As Dorsey sat down, Turley came forward. "I'm no expert on urban warfare. I had some experience with it when we cleared out of Quang Tri, and in Tet of '68, when we took back Hue. I can tell you lots of mistakes that were made in Quang Tri. First is relying on naval gunfire. No offense to the Navy, but in a lot of instances you're going to need high-angle trajectory indirect fire, and naval gunfire doesn't give you that. Artillery and mortars are your primary indirect fire weapons. Make sure your units have plenty of mortar ammunition and are good at shooting it. The NVA are good at it, as he's demonstrated for the past four months. Second is the use of tac air. Requests to use tac air against targets in the Citadel are not going to be approved. The Vietnamese high command considers the Citadel a historical monument and doesn't want it destroyed, at least not by us. If you can get attack helicopters to come in at high angle and use their rockets, especially flechettes, that's your best bet. But we all know that flechettes against anyone with overhead cover is worthless," Turley went on to explain.

"For the close-in fight, hand grenades are the best. Be sure your people have an adequate supply of them, and each day, each man should have four on his body, minimum. By noon you'll need to resupply them." He continued his discussion with other points that were unique to urban fighting, which was something seldom executed in the previous years as most fighting, except TET of '68, had been jungle warfare. When he finished, everyone knew that the next couple of months would not be easy.

* * *

0800 Hours
    28 July 1972

"*Incoming!*" Major Joy yelled, dropping to the ground as the 130mm rounds started slamming into the positions occupied by the 147th VNMC Regiment. Lying several feet from him was Captain David Harris, ANGLICO chief for the 147th.

"Captain Harris, have you got comms with the FAC?" Joy called out. Harris had been integrating a new officer into the team. First Lieutenant Edward Hayes was on the far side of Harris.

"Yes, sir, I do. I'm calling him now," Harris shouted out, taking the hand mike from Hayes.

"Lieutenant, can you get to my rucksack? We're going to need another battery before this day is over, I think," Harris asked.

"Yes, sir," Hayes responded and began low-crawling towards the rucksacks that were stacked together a few feet away.

"Wolfman Four-Five, Oscar Three-Seven," Harris transmitted.

"Good morning, Oscar Three-Seven. Wolfman here, over."

Son of a bitch is in a chipper mood. His ass should be down here, Harris was thinking. "Wolfman Four-Five, we have incoming artillery. Appears to be coming from the northwest. Can you spot it? Over."

"Oscar Three-Seven, that's a negative as we're to the east. We're turning back and will take a look. Wait one," Wolfman Four-Five directed.

Where the hell does he think I'm going? Wait one my— Harris was thinking before he was interrupted.

"Oscar Three-Seven, Wolfman Four-Five, we can see several artillery positions in the vicinity of Dong Ha and they're all firing. We're bringing in some fast-movers that are one-five mikes out. Over."

"Roger, the quicker the—" Harris did not finish his sentence as the artillery round impacted several feet away and Harris's world went dark.

"Dai'uy, Dai'uy," a voice in the night kept saying. Then the searing pain shot through Harris's body, alerting him to the fact that he was alive, but hurt. He attempted to open his eyes but could only detect some light and blurred images. He could, however, hear voices, but nothing was making sense. As he slowly regained consciousness, he began to understand what had happened.

"Dave, can you hear me?" It was Major Joy's voice.

"Yes, sir. I can't see you but, yes, I can hear you," Harris said through clenched teeth as he was racked with another spasm of pain.

"Dave, I'm giving you some morphine and we're getting you on a medevac bird as soon as we can get one in here," Joy said with the sound of incoming rounds in the background, but not terribly close.

"How bad, sir?" Harris asked.

"You're going to be fine. Just lay there and let me patch you up some. Nurses back at Da Nang are going to love getting their hands on you. Clean sheets, a hot bath and a ticket home," Joy said, attempting to set Harris's mind at ease.

"Where's Lieutenant Hayes, sir?" Harris asked. Joy didn't respond.

"Sir, Hayes, is he okay?" Harris asked again with concern.

"You just worry about yourself right now, okay? You're going to be fine," Joy said.

"Hayes didn't make it, did he, sir?" Harris asked, surrendering to the question.

"I'm afraid not," Joy replied with remorse.

53

THE PRIZE

147th VNMC Battalion
Quang Tri, South Vietnam

The past month had seen a slow tightening around Quang Tri. The 147th moved south from Bich Khe down Route 560 and crossed the Vinh Dinh River, pushing up to the outskirts of the city. They had cleared the area south of the Vinh Dinh River with the 3rd Battalion pushing up to the northeast corner of the city.[1] The 7th Battalion moved behind the 3rd Battalion and then east, clearing the area south of the Vinh Dinh River up to the Thach Han River, turning south to approach the outskirts of the city from the northwest. The 1st Ranger Group had relieved the 147th of responsibility for the area previously occupied north. South of the city, the 258th, with four battalions consisting of the 1st, 2nd, 5th and 6th Battalions, continued to push north, clearing the city and coming to the southern walls of the Citadel with the 2nd Battalion on the south and southwest and the 6th Battalion on the southeast. The 369th Marine Brigade was held in reserve to the southeast of the city. Everything was in place to start the final push.

Jack had moved earlier in the month from the 147th Brigade to the 258th Brigade and had been advisor to the 6th Battalion for the past month. He and Major Do Huu Tung had a good working relationship, and Jack found Tung to be a very capable officer and commander. For the past month, all the battalions had slowly fought street to street and house to house, clearing the city. They were now positioned within a stone's throw of the walls of the Citadel. Tung had his command post established off the southeast corner of the eighteenth-century fortress.

The walls of the Citadel were thirty inches thick and stood fifteen feet high. In some places the walls had been penetrated and existed only as piles of stones, but most of the wall remained. Within the piles of stones that had once been the walls, the NVA had built a tunnel network, to include fighting positions, communications lines and command posts. This intricate network went throughout the Citadel, making progress very slow for the attacker.

* * *

9 September 1972
6th Battalion Command Post

"Are you ready for this?" Jack said, walking up to Tung, who was putting on his load-bearing equipment and helmet. Tung turned.

"How you say? Ready as I will ever be." Tung smiled as he said it. He thought it was funny, and he was improving with his English. "The amphibious feint should be commencing about now." Tung looked at his watch and noted the time of 0700 hours. As the second hand passed the twelve o'clock position, the sounds of Navy guns clearing their throats could be heard, followed by the sound of their rounds impacting the beach area. "We have three hours before we launch our attack," Tung said. "I think good time we check troops and talk with platoon leaders. They see us and it calms their nerves. We go." And Tung headed out the door.

Jack enjoyed Tung's "troop morale" walks as they gave him an opportunity to get a feel for the confidence level of the Vietnamese Marines as well as observe the interaction of officers and enlisted. As the Vietnamese Marines had learned from the American Marine advisors and trainers over the years, a professional relationship existed between the officers and enlisted men. There was a strict separation of social class between the two. The Vietnamese NCOs were the linchpin between the officers and the enlisted men, and even then there was a demonstration of social distancing. When it came to combat, however, the officers, NCOs and enlisted all fought as one. To Jack, this was the icing on the cake that was the Vietnamese armed forces.

Moving from company to company, Tung would first stop and talk to the company commander, who would generally call his platoon leaders over to hear Tung speak. Tung was always accompanied by the company commander and if possible the senior NCO in the company, who ensured that the enlisted demonstrated the proper level of respect to Tung. The main question that the Marines were asking was what was the rumbling and noise they were hearing coming from up north along the beaches. Tung told them all that an amphibious assault was going in north along the beaches by the Cam Lo River and would drive down from the north. He didn't tell them it was a feint in case one of them got captured or, worse, was an NVA sympathizer.

To the north, naval gunfire was striking the approaches to the beach. Further inland behind the beaches, B-52s were dropping their loads, and even further inland, tac air was striking any targets that the FAC could locate. This demonstration alone was enough to get the attention of the NVA, who began to move and reposition artillery to cover the beach area. Launching from the ships, a flotilla of landing craft could be seen forming up for an assault, and the information was passed to the NVA higher headquarters. This generated more movement in an attempt to reinforce the beach area. When a helicopter force was observed launching off the decks and heading towards the beach area along with the flotilla approaching on line, the NVA were convinced this was a major landing and had to be addressed. Fire support for the Citadel diminished greatly and anti-air support reoriented to the beach area. As soon as the B-52 strike ended, NVA troops rushed to the area of the landings to repel the attack, only to expose themselves to intense naval gunfire. At ten thousand yards from the beach, the flotilla turned away, with the helicopter assault terminating at five thousand yards. That was the signal to attack. It was H hour.

Jack and Tung had positioned themselves behind the 1st Company as they were designated the main effort by Tung. 2nd Company and 3rd Company would provide support to 1st Company, which had the mission to breach the wall and hold the shoulders while 2nd the 3rd Company exploited the breach and entered the Citadel. That was the plan, but plans are only good until the enemy gets a vote.

As the 1st Company stepped off, they came under intense small-arms and automatic weapons fire. Accurate mortar rounds began to drop on them as well. All day, the fighting continued, with 1st Company making small progress, but progress nonetheless. The ANGLICO team trailed right alongside Jack but had little to do in such tight fighting, with only yards separating friend from foe. Hand grenades were the most effective explosive ammunition for the Vietnamese Marines, and a frequent and steady resupply was supervised by the unit first sergeants. 2nd and 3rd Company were committed early as the enemy continually appeared through their defensive network on the flanks of 1st Company and engaged. It was up to 2nd and 3rd Companies to hold those flanks for 1st Company as it slowly made its way to the wall. Everyone breathed a sigh of relief when night fell and the fighting stopped. Jack left Tung to make a call to Major Easley, who was serving as the senior advisor to the brigade. He and Easley discussed the events, and Easley related actions by the other brigades.

"In the north, the 3rd Battalion has managed to push into the outskirts of the city and is meeting moderate resistance, as has the 7th Battalion. We're the only ones up against the side of the Citadel. 2nd Battalion has a few blocks to go before they'll be against the wall on the southwest corner. 1st Battalion has pushed close to the Thach Han River and has a few more blocks to go to reach the river."

Jack headed over to the command post to talk to Tung about the operations for the next day. "Tung, what's the plan for tomorrow?" Jack asked, walking into the CP. Tung stood next to a drawing of the Citadel that one of the Marines that was from Quang Tri had drawn by hand and Tung had given to the company commanders to use. The 1:50,000 map typically used wouldn't be of use in such a close-in fight. Tung was smiling.

"What?" Jack asked, looking at Tung.

"Squad from 1st Company inside Citadel." Tung beamed. "They gathering intel and return before morning to brief us. I think it big risk to ask them to remain. We see what they find," Tung said, unable to contain his joy at having an element inside, the first to do so.

Several hours later, Tung sat with the squad leader and each member of the squad and had them explain with the hand-drawn map what they'd seen and where they'd seen it. Jack sat in on the debrief and listened. When Tung was satisfied, he dismissed the squad and turned to Jack.

* * *

10 September 1972

"It be light soon. Today I order everyone hold positions. No attack," Tung said, and Jack started to protest until that smile crossed Tung's face. *What's he up to now?* Jack thought.

"Everyone rest today. Resupply with ammo and water. No time for plan today. But tonight, we take Citadel," Tung said and began drawing on the hand-drawn maps. A night attack on a strong defensive position in an urban environment had never been done before by the South Vietnamese Marines, or any South Vietnamese force for that matter. *Oh, this is going to be gutsy*, Jack was thinking. Tung didn't discuss his plan with anyone again for fear that it might fall into the hands of the NVA.

At 1900 hours he called his company commanders to the command post and issued the orders. The order was the same: 1st Company makes the breach, followed by 2nd and 3rd while 1st Company holds the breach. Once he was sure all the company commanders understood the mission, he told them what time they would launch. They were stunned when he told them.

"Set your watches. I have 2000 hours ... now," Tung said and looked to see that everyone was setting their watches. "We attack at twenty-one hundred hours. Brief your men," he directed. One of the company commanders spoke up.

"Sir, that's in one hour," the major said with some surprise.

"No, Major, that is fifty-nine minutes. I suggest you make good use of what time you have left," Tung replied as each of the commanders scrambled to return to their respective units.

Tung wanted to maintain some element of surprise, so he launched the attack without employing his mortars. Earlier in the day, he had provided the mortars with suspected and known positions based on what the squad had given him. Those positions were plotted for the mortars to shoot if called upon. As quietly as possible, the 1st Company began moving forward towards the walls of the Citadel on the southeast corner. While two platoons of the 1st Company fought to create a breach in an opening, one platoon scaled the wall on which 3rd Company was placing supporting fire. Before the sun rose, the platoon was on top of the wall and placed plunging fire on the defenders in front of 1st Company. Sunrise witnessed a company-size position occupied by 1st Company within the Citadel proper. 2nd and 3rd Companies were holding the shoulders.

* * *

1st Battalion

While 6th Battalion was rejoicing at taking a portion of the Citadel, 1st Battalion was taking its objective for the day, the bridge on QL1 over the Thach Han River. Easley was in the 258th Brigade CP when the call came in from Major DeBona, who had been moved to the 1st Battalion.

"Panther Six, Panther One, over," DeBona transmitted.

"Panther One, Panther Six, go ahead." Joy had changed call signs when Dorsey had reassigned advisors between battalions. Since 369th Brigade was in reserve, Dorsey felt there was no need for an advisor team to be there, and this created an opportunity to provide a rest for some by rotating teams. He did the same with the ANGLICO teams.

"Panther Six, we've seized our objective. They're not giving it up, however. We've had one counterattack and it appears they're massing for a second. We're calling for tac air. How copy?"

"Panther One, I have good copy. Your counterpart confirms same. My counterpart is clearing for use of tac air deep but not in immediate vicinity of the bridge, over."

"Panther Six, roger, that's our intent. We can't afford to have a stray hit the bridge at this point. Over," DeBona said.

"Panther One, roger, but now that you have it, we've got to hold it. Do we need to move up reinforcements at this time? Over."

"Negative, Panther Six. Reinforcements are not needed as of yet. I'll keep you posted. Panther One out."

* * *

1050 Hours
15 September 1972

"Panther One-Six, Panther Six."

"Panther Six, One-Six, over," Jack transmitted. He sounded tired. The last six days had been long and exhausting. The 6th Battalion had expanded its one-company position to the entire battalion being inside the Citadel, of which the enemy wasn't surrendering one inch. Jack was attempting to comprehend how the enemy could have held out so long without resupply from the outside and just how many enemy soldiers were within the walls.

"Panther One-Six, this is Six. Our friends to the north, your previous unit, have reached the north wall and crossed the bridge over the moat. How copy?"

"Roger, understand we hold the north wall now. About time someone else got inside this place with us. So what's the plan now? Over."

"Panther One-Six, they're going to clear to the east first and then link up with you, and together you both can push to the west side. My counterpart is talking to their boss and you should be seeing a FRAGO coming down in the next thirty minutes, over."

"Okay, I can hear a fight on the north side of this place. Not a big one, however. I'll keep you posted. Anything else? Over," Jack asked.

"Nothing further. Be safe. Panther Six out." Jack returned the handset to his radio operator and patted the kid on the shoulder. The young Marine had stuck to Jack like glue for the entire time. Jack wondered if it was out of devotion to duty or the fact that if everything turned to shit, being with Jack was the best bet when it came to getting on an extraction helicopter. A few minutes later, Tung came over to Jack.

"Colonel Phuc said hello to you. He now here. We go meet to link up," Tung said and Jack stood up.

"Lead on, sir," Jack said and they departed with a squad of infantry providing some escort. The trek across the compound was a short one of only a few hundred meters, but it still took almost an hour to get there. Arriving, they waited for Colonel Phuc. Major Huff was with him. Seeing Jack, Huff came right over and extended his hand.

"Damn, it's good to see you," Huff said. "Got any cigarettes? I'm out."

"Yeah," Jack said, digging into his cargo pocket. "Keep the pack. I don't smoke—I just keep them to pass to the troops. Got plenty more in my rucksack. How is Phuc doing?"

"Doing good. A bit cautious for my taste but doing good," Huff said. "At least he's aggressive, in a cautious way," he added.

"Yeah, he must be seeing an end to this and wants to be around," Jack replied.

"Let me ask, Jack—you're assigned to something entirely different, aren't you, and just got tossed into the advisor role, right? When do you assume your old job?" Huff asked, taking a long drag on his cigarette and allowing the smoke to fill his lungs.

"I came over here to assess the Vietnamization program. Didn't think I'd get to see it up close and personal as this. Have to admit, I have more than enough to write my report. Going to ask to be released from this as soon as we take this place so I can return to Saigon, write my report and fly home," Jack said.

"Can I ask how that report is going to read?" Huff asked.

"It's going to say something to the effect that the Vietnamese Marines are the cream of the crop of the Vietnamese armed forces and have adapted very well to the program thanks to the advisor effort over the years. The Vietnamese Airborne units are a step below and demonstrate high morale and a high level of ability to carry on the fight. The ARVN forces vary from good to pathetic, lacking in decisive leadership, quality soldiers and effective training, resulting in morale and discipline being absent. In addition, without the support of the US Air Force, Naval Air and US Army helicopters, the Vietnamese armed forces will not defeat the North Vietnamese in a conventional attack," Jack concluded.

Huff stared at Jack for a moment, dropping what was left of the cigarette and grinding it out with his foot. "I think you nailed it, buddy," Huff said and extended his hand. "Let's finish this," he added.

EPILOGUE

At 1700 on 15 September, the Citadel was under the complete control of the South Vietnamese Marines. The next day at around noon, the South Vietnamese flag was raised above the walls. This didn't end the fighting, however, which would continue until January 1973, when a cease-fire was put in place. During the period between September 1972 and January 1973, fierce fighting continued. South Vietnamese forces attempted to push the North Vietnamese forces towards the Cam Lo and Cua Viet Rivers. To the west of Quang Tri, the enemy retained the west side of QL1. The monsoon season got into full swing in October and greatly hampered air support but also swelled the rivers throughout the region to impassible obstacles.

November brought a decrease in the fighting as both sides were anticipating a cease-fire being initiated due to the Paris peace talks. US advisors and ANGLICO teams remained with the South Vietnam forces at the time, but the level of activity was very low for the most part. In December, NVA forces launched a major attack against the 7th VNMC battalion but were repulsed. This was an attempt by the NVA to hold the

Marines south of the Vinh Dinh Canal. It was successful from that standpoint, at a high cost in NVA soldiers killed. On Christmas Day, 1972, Sub Unit One lost its last member when First Lieutenant Dwight G. Rickman flew out of Phu Bai to observe the Can Viet River. He never returned.

On 26 January, fully expecting a cease-fire to be declared any day, General Lan made a last effort to reach the Cua Viet River. His attack was to seize the former naval base at the mouth of the Cua Viet River. The attack had two mechanized columns, one moving up the beach and sand dunes and the other moving through the tree line that was three kilometers inland. The NVA put up stiff resistance, destroying twenty-six tanks and M113 carriers with AT-3 Sagger wire-guided missiles over the course of eighteen hours. During the night of 28 January, a final assault was made and broke through the enemy lines. At daybreak, the flag of South Vietnam flew over the former naval base. The USS *Turner Joy* (DD-951), which had been involved in the Gulf of Tonkin incident, fired the last naval gunfire support mission at 0745. At the same time, all US airpower became grounded, and at 0800 the cease-fire went into effect. US advisors left shortly after that the next day.[1]

Men in suits signed the Paris Peace Accords. North Vietnam was allowed to retain the land mass that they had seized as of January 28, which accounted for approximately twenty-five percent of the former country. South Vietnam retained about eighty-eight percent of the population. The cease-fire was short-lived, allowing US and allied forces to depart the country. On 30 January 1973, the fighting commenced again with an attack by the North Vietnamese against the 4th Marine Battalion company outpost at the Cua Viet River. Fighting would continue for another year and longer, with South Vietnam eventually being overrun by the communist North in 1975.

WOULD YOU LIKE TO READ MORE FROM MATT JACKSON?

THE NEXT BOOK, BATTLE FOR AN LOC, 1972 IS DUE IN 2023

FIND IT ON AMAZON

SIGN UP TO RECEIVE UPDATES FROM MATT JACKSON BOOKS!
https://frontlinepublishinginc.eo.page/mattjacksonbooks

KEEP READING FOR CHAPTER ONE

BATTLE OF AN LOC, 1972

UNDAUNTED VALOR BOOK 5

By

Matt Jackson

PRELUDE TO BATTLE

Central Office of South Vietnam
Snoul, Cambodia

Rain pelted the stucco roof on the building. The rumbling sounds penetrating the walls was not the sound of thunder but the sounds made by one thousand pound bombs being dropped from a flight of three B-52 aircraft. Since the Cambodian Incursion in 1970, South Vietnamese forces had frequently returned to Cambodia. Each time they would call upon US air power to strike known and suspected People's Liberation Army of Vietnam (PLA) ammunition and supply sites as well as troop concentrations. General Hoang Van Thai, Deputy Secretary for the Central Office of South Vietnam or COSVN paused in this briefing. Before him stood General Tran Va Tra, Commander B-2 Front and his three division commanders and key regimental commanders. They encircled a table with a map spread out of the northern part of Military Region III. The area encompassed Tay Ninh on the southwest, An Loc in the north center, Song Be on the northeast. Also scattered along the landscape was Lai Khe south of An Loc on Highway 13. Running through An Loc and Lai Khe was Highway 13 which crossed the Vietnam-Cambodian border outside the border town of Loc Ninh.

Loc Ninh sat 15 kilometers south of the Cambodian border along Highway 13. Surrounded by high hills covered in heavy vegetation, the bulk of the town was on the northeast side of Highway 13. An airfield was located on the southwest side of the town. It was oriented northeast-southwest. At the southwest end was the advisors compound occupied by the 9th Regiment command post, 5th ARVN Division. The compound for the Province chief was located on the northern end of the runway. An artillery compound was positioned between the two compounds.

"Gentlemen, our mission is to seize and secure An Loc. Once that is accomplished, a provisional government will be established there. Be prepared to exploit success to Saigon. To do this we will attack with the 5th VC Division crossing into Vietnam and seizing Loc Ninh and destroying the forces there," he indicated looking up at Colonel Bui Thanh Van, the division commander. "At the same time," he paused to look at the 9th Division Commander, Colonel Nguyen Thoi Bung, "the 9th Division will attack and seize and secure An Loc." The 9th Division commander smiled and nodded is head in acknowledgement of being given the prize. Continuing, "The 7th Division will move south of An Loc and establish a block position on Highway 13 preventing reinforcements from reaching An Loc. I would recommend that a strong position be established in the vicinity of Dong Phat where this rubber processing plant is located or in the hills around there just to the south. I will leave the final location up to you General Nguy as you will be the man on the ground," General Hoang

Van Thai said. His gaze shifted to the western portion of the map.

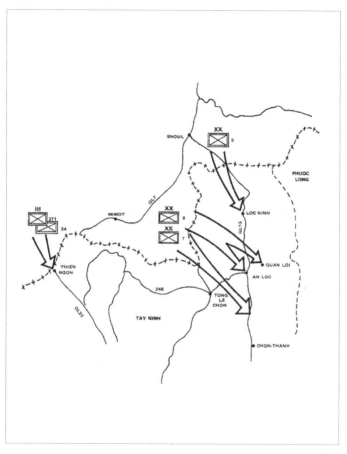

Lieutenant General Ngo Quang Truong, Indochina Monographs: The Easter Offensive of 1972 *(Washington, DC: U.S. Army Center of Military History, 1980).*

"Now we must use some deception here to maximize the element of surprise. We should allow the enemy to rely upon their assumptions. They will assume that we will attack on traditional avenues of approach through Tay Ninh in the west as we did in TET 68. They will think we are attempting to control people as we did then instead of the true purpose of this attack which is to destroy the South Vietnam army." Hoang Van Thai looked over at the commander of the 24th Independent VC Regiment. "Colonel you will attack in this area and overrun this firebase at Lac Long. Prior to your attack, we need a soldier to be captured that will state that he is part of a reconnaissance unit and they were reconning a road from Tay Ninh to the border. We should also let them find a cache site in the area to further convince them we are making our main attack towards Tay Ninh. Understood?" The commander acknowledged. Turning to the commander of the 271st NVA Regiment, " The action of the 24th will trigger a reaction and I anticipate that will be an order to move the forces at Thein Ngon. When they start to move you are to ambush them but do no become decisively engaged. Understood?"

"Yes sir," was the 271st Regimental commander's response.

Looking up from the map, the 24th Regimental commander asked, "What is the date for my ground attack Sir?"

"The 2nd of April will do nicely. That will give time for the ARVN command to shift forces towards Tay Ninh before we launch our main attack on 5 April against Loc Ninh," General Hoang Van Thai explained. "Any other questions?"

"Sir do we know the distribution of forces around Loc Ninh?" It was the 5th VC commander.

"Yes, right now in Loc Ninh is the headquarters for the 9th Regiment, 5th ARVN Division. The commander is a Colonel Nguyen Cong Vinh. He is well liked because is he is very easy and does not enforce high standards of discipline amongst his soldiers. There is a squadron from the armored cav, a battalion of the 1st Regional Forces and the 7th Ranger Battalion. Outside of Loc Ninh proper there is what they are calling

TF52. It is located at this firebase Hung Tam Base, here approximately ten kilometers to the southwest of Loc Ninh. The commander is Lieutenant Colonel Nguyen Ba Thinh. He is considered very capable. The task force is composed of 2nd Battalion 52nd Regiment and 1st Battalion, 48th Regiment. It has a reconnaissance company, a battery of 105mm artillery, a platoon of 155mm howitzers and an engineer company. Two battalions of the 9th Regiment are located in Loc Ninh with two batteries of artillery. Two companies of the 2nd Battalion with two 155 artillery pieces and four 155 tubes is located at the Cam Le Bridge south of Loc Ninh. There is the 1st Armored Squadron with two companies of infantry and some 105 and 155 artillery located just south of the border at Firebase Alpha. The 7th Border Ranges Battalion is also here at Alfa," the general outlined as he pointed our each location on the map.

"One other important piece as well," General Hoang Van Thai announced breaking everyone's train of thought. "There is at Loc Ninh, members of the American Advisory Team 70 which is located in Lai Khe. There is also an advisor team to the district commander. They will no doubt have the ability to call upon the US Air Force for support with air strikes. Their command post must be eliminated quickly, and their communications cut off even quicker. If we can capture the advisors alive all the better. Any other questions?" Van Thai asked.

"Sir, what is the disposition of forces in An Loc?" the 9th VC Division commander asked. He should already know what he will be facing in An Loc. Why is he asking now, General Hoang Van Thai was thinking.

"In An Loc as of right now is the 7th Regiment minus one battalion; the 8th Regiment, and the 3rd Ranger Group along with two battalions of Binh Long Regional and Popular Forces. They can be reinforced from Lai Khe so we need to be sure and block highway 13. Understood," Van Thai emphasized looking at the 7th Division commander. He responded with a head nod.

"Our biggest threat to success if going to be the American air force and their helicopter forces. These we must neutralize and do it effectively," Van Thai indicated as he looked an officer with air defense markings on his uniform. "The 271st Anti-Aircraft Regiment will reinforce your regimental anti-aircraft forces. In addition, members of the regiments will begin training on the new Soviet anti-aircraft missile system, the SA-7 shoulder fired missile. These will be effective against the American attack helicopters especially as they slow and attack from altitude. Worse case this missile will force them to fly very low and be subject to our direct fire weapons such as the 12.7 and 23mm guns. Questions?" he asked. As there were none he continued, "Colonel," catching the immediate attention of the air defense officer, "How do you intend to array your weapons?"

"Sir we will create a series of rings around An Loc. The outer ring will be spotters who can tell us when aircraft are approaching. They will be twenty kilometers out from An Loc. The next ring will be our 37mm and 57mm self-propelled guns. These will be six kilometers out from the An Loc village. Each of our large guns will have its own rings of 23mm guns with each of those having a ring of 12.7 guns. In this manner we will have early waring of approaching aircraft, defense in depth for our troops and our major guns," the commander explained.

"Good," is all Van Thai said. "Now any equipment they you can capture do so. Tanks, armored personnel carriers and artillery pieces are all valuable assets. If you can capture rather than destroy, do so. Code books and radios are another important item that we want to seize and utilize if possible. Capture if possible. Understood?" Everyone answered in the affirmative.

"Alright then, let us move forward and prepare ourselves for this victory," Van Thai announced as he turned and left the room.

Order Battle For An Loc, 1972 Today - Be one of the first to read.

AC. Aircraft commander; also alternating electrical current.

ADA. Air defense artillery.

ANGLICO. Air Naval Gunfire Liaison Company. Usually deployed two to three man teams with a ground force commander to coordinate naval gunfire and close-air support.

ARA. Aerial Rocket Artillery, commonly referred to as Blue Max.

ARVN. Army of the Republic of Vietnam. Soldiers of South Vietnam were referred to as ARVNs.

BC. Battalion commander.

C rations. Canned food that could be eaten cold or hot, used by the military from World War II until the late 1970s or early 1980s.

CWO. Chief warrant officer.

C&C. Command-and-control aircraft.

DC. Direct electrical current.

det cord. White cord approximately 1/4-inch around that is highly explosive and used to quickly cut trees or blow up other objects.

GCA. Ground control approach, a technique used for

landing aircraft, with a ground controller watching an approaching aircraft on radar and giving the pilots information as to runway alignment and altitude.

klick. Measurement of distance used by the military, consisting of 1,000 meters (one kilometer).

LZ. Landing zone, the designated location for the insertion of troops. Once an established firebase is present, it is named with the prefix LZ.

MP. Military police.

medevac. Medical evacuation.

NCO. Noncommissioned officer, those enlisted personnel in the military with a rank between E5 and E9; commonly referred to as sergeants in the Army, Marine Corps and Air Force and chief in the Navy and Coast Guard.

NDP. Night defensive position, usually established by company-sized or smaller units for their stationary position after dark.

NVA. North Vietnamese Army.

PX. Post exchange, the military version of Walmart.

PZ. Pickup zone, a location to pick up passengers or supplies.

RLO. Real live officer, a term applied to commissioned officers, versus warrant officers, who are appointed officers.

SF. Special Forces.

S-2. The title for the officer responsible for the overall planning, coordination, collecting and analysis of intelligence information.

S-3. The title for the officer responsible for the overall planning, coordination and execution of actions by an organization.

S-3 Air. The title for the officer responsible for coordination with aviation elements to support the actions of an organization.

thermite grenade. A grenade that is designed to destroy objects through heat rather than explode; burns at approximately 4,000 degrees.

TOC. Tactical operations center.

WO. Warrant officer, junior to CWO.

XO. Second-in-command of a unit.

REFERENCES

Andradé, Dale. *Trial By Fire: The 1972 Easter Offensive, America's Last Vietnam Battle*. New York: Hippocrene Books, 1995.

Brooks, Steve SP4, *Hurried Withdrawal*, Headquarters, XXIV Corps pdf. 24 April 1972

Cosmas, Graham A. *MACV: The Joint Command in the Years of Withdrawal, 1968–1973*. Washington, D.C.: Center of Military History, United States Army, 2006.

Dorr, Robert F. "The A-37 Dragonfly in Vietnam: When Light Attack Was the Real Thing." Defense Media Network, September 5, 2013. https://www.defensemedianetwork.com/stories/the-a-37-dragonfly-in-vietnam/.

Lavalle, A.J.C., ed. *Airpower and the 1972 Spring Invasion*. Washington, D.C.: Office of Air Force History, 1985.

References

Melson, Charles D. and Curtis G. Arnold. *US Marines in Vietnam: The War That Would Not End, 1971–1973.* Washington, D.C.: History and Museum Division, Headquarters, US Marine Corps, 1991.

Momyer, William W. *The Vietnamese Air Force, 1951–1975, An Analysis of its Role in Combat.* Washington, D.C.: Office of Air Force History, 1985.

Nalty, Bernard C. *Air War Over South Vietnam: 1968–1975.* Washington, D.C.: Air Force History and Museums Program, 2000.

"Operational Report: Lessons Learned of the 11th Combat Aviation Group for the Period Ending 31 October 1972." Washington, D.C.: Office of the Adjutant General (Army), 1978. https://apps.dtic.mil/sti/pdfs/AD0531174.pdf.

Schultz, Ken. "Teacher Shows How–Blasts Red Tank." *Pacific Stars and Stripes,* June 2, 1972.

"Senior Officer Debriefing Report of B.G. James F. Hamlet, RCS CSFOR-74," dated 25 June 1972; accessed as DTIC AD523510. https://apps.dtic.mil/sti/pdfs/AD0523510.pdf.

"Senior Officer Debriefing Report of M.G. Robert N. MacKinnon," dated 22 December 1972; accessed as DTIC AD523712. https://apps.dtic.mil/sti/pdfs/AD0523712.pdf.

"Surrender at Camp Carroll," http://www.willpete.com/surrender_at_camp_-carroll.htm.

Truong, Ngo Quang. *The Easter Offensive of 1972*. Washington, D.C.: U.S. Army Center of Military History, 1980.

Turley, Gerald H. *The Easter Offensive: The Last American Advisors, Vietnam, 1972*. Annapolis: Naval Institute Press, 1985.

USMC Combat Helicopter & Tiltrotor Association. "KIA Incident: 19720711 HMM-165 Vietnam." https://popasmoke.com/kia/conflicts/vietnam/incidents/19720711.

USMC Oral History Interview: Major Robert Cockell, Senior Advisor, 1st Bn., VNMC, #5092, updated.

Webb, Willard J. and Walter S. Poole. *The Joint Chiefs of Staff and The War in Vietnam, 1971–1973*. Washington, D.C.: Office of Joint History, Office of the Chairman of the Joint Chiefs of Staff, 2007.

Whitcomb, Darrel D. "Mission to Dong Ha—Mission to Al Hammar." Air University, 2004. https://www.airuniversity.af.edu/Portals/10/ASPJ/journals/Chronicles/whitcomb.pdf.

Willbanks, James H. *The Battle of An Loc*. Bloomington: Indiana University Press, 2015.

Willbanks, James H. *Thiet Giap! The Battle of An Loc, April 1972*. Fort Leavenworth, KS: US Army Command and General Staff College, Combat Studies Institute, 1993.

INTERVIEWS

Information provided in interviews with the following may or may not appear directly in the context of this publication, but all provided background for the development of the story. In all but two cases, individuals were referred to me by others.

Boomer, General Walter E. USMC (Ret), interview by Matt Jackson, August 24, 2022.

Eisenstein, Joel, interview by Matt Jackson, January 9,2021.

Everette, Sergeant First Class Sean, Interview, NCOIC PAO Outreach and Communications, Defense POW/MAI Accounting Agency, Washington D.C.

Holmes, Ron, interview by Matt Jackson, October, 2021.

Jackson, Jim, interview by Matt Jackson, October, 2021.

Jackson, Steve, interview by Matt Jackson, October, 2021.

Jim Lowe, interview by Matt Jackson, October 2021

Manlove, Don, interview by Matt Jackson, October, 2021.

O'Byrne, Michael, interview by Matt Jackson, October, 2021.

Purvis, Donnie, interview by Matt Jackson, October ,2021.

Shirley, Dwaine, interview by Matt Jackson, October, 2021.

Sprouse, Tim, interview by Matt Jackson, October , 2021.

Swift, Joe, interview by Matt Jackson, October,2022.

Thompson, Neal, interview by Matt Jackson, October, 2021.

Williams, Colonel Mike USMC (Ret), interview by Matt Jackson, November, 2021.

Charlie Zinger, interview, by Matt Jackson, October 2021

NOTES

Chapter 1

1. In accordance with Vietnamese custom, this person should be referred to by the given name, which is the last name as the family name always comes first. In this case, Duan is the given name.
2. Le Duc Tho was the chief negotiator for North Vietnam at the Paris Peace Accord Conferences.
3. The National Liberation Front was commonly known as the Viet Cong.
4. Joel Achenbach, "Did the News Media, Led by Walter Cronkite, Lose the War in Vietnam?" *Washington Post*, May 25, 2018, https://www.washingtonpost.com/national/did-the-news-media-led-by-walter-cronkite-lose-the-war-in-vietnam/2018/05/25/a5b3e098-495e-11e8-827e-190efaf1f1ee_story.html.

Chapter 2

1. The Cooper-Church Amendment was attached to the Foreign Military Sales Act 1971 and stopped funding for troops and advisors in Laos and Cambodia. It became Public Law 91-652. https://en.wikipedia.org/wiki/Cooper–Church_Amendment.
2. Graham A. Cosmas, *MACV: The Joint Command in the Years of Withdrawal, 1968–1973* (Washington, D.C.: Center of Military History, United States Army, 2006), 342.

Chapter 3

1. Information provided in General MacKinnon's brief was extracted from "Senior Officer Debriefing Report of M.G. Robert N. MacKinnon," dated 22 December 1972; accessed as DTIC AD523712. https://apps.dtic.mil/sti/pdfs/AD0523712.pdf.

Chapter 7

1. A common Korean term for a gofer or errand boy, used frequently throughout the Army and USMC.
2. Fougasse refers to a defensive weapon consisting of one fifty-five-gallon drum of diesel fuel that is buried in the ground on an angle with the top facing towards the enemy. Three blocks of C-4 explosives are placed under the bottom of the barrel and an ignitor is placed on the top. The C-4 is electrically detonated, blowing the fuel out of the barrel and igniting it in the process. Normally considered a last line of defense.

Chapter 8

1. There appears to be a question as to who commanded the Advisor Team 155. One source indicated Colonel Metcalf and another a Colonel Murdock. I chose the name indicated in *US Marines in Vietnam: The War That Would Not End, 1971–1973* and seconded by members of the US Marine Corps that I interviewed.
2. General Giai was aware of the military buildup along the DMZ and had received notification of an impending invasion, yet he still ordered the relief in place and flew to Saigon for the Easter weekend. A relief in place by two regiments is a very difficult military maneuver that requires close monitoring and coordination at the highest level. This was not done. His absence was considered treason in October of 1973 and he was court-martialed and sentenced to five years' hard labor. Wikipedia, s.v. Vũ Văn Giai, last modified August 24, 2022, 18:48, https://en.wikipedia.org/wiki/V%C5%A9_V%C4%83n_Giai.
3. Major Walter Boomer would become the Commanding General, US Marine Forces Central Command and I Marine Expeditionary Force during Operations Desert Shield and Desert Storm. Captain Smith would retire as a major general.
4. A pink team consisted of a command-and-control UH-1H aircraft, an AH-1G gunship and two OH-6 light observation helicopters.

Chapter 9

1. Mike-Mike is military slang for millimeter.

Chapter 10

1. Mike-Mike is military slang for millimeter.
   Seven Days Guest Book, https://thelastsevendays.wordpress.-com/macv-team-155-perspective/.
2. The official call sign for the ANGLICO Team was Custom House. However, at times the call sign Wolfman was used by ground ANGLICO teams. Wolfman was the usual call sign for Marine aerial observers. I have chosen to use the official call sign of Custom House to avoid confusion later on.
3. General Walter E. Boomer, USMC (Ret), interview by Matt Jackson, 24 August 2022.

Chapter 12

1. USMC Oral History Interview: Major Robert Cockell, Senior Advisor, 1st Bn., VNMC, #5092, updated, p. 2.
2. Ngo,

Chapter 16

1. Corporal Worth was initially declared missing in action; later, on 17 December 1976, he was declared killed in action by the Secretary of the Navy under Title 37, Section 5. His remains were never found and his final location never determined.

Chapter 17

1. Captain Raymond Smith retired as a major general from the US Marine Corps. For his actions on 1 April 1972, he was awarded the Navy Cross.

Chapter 18

1. Dai'uy is Vietnamese for captain. It is pronounced die-wee.

Chapter 20

1. Melson, 50.
2. Melson, 50.
3. Sergeant Huynh van Luom was killed in action days later.
4. At the US Marine Corps National Museum at Quantico, Virginia, there is a diorama depicting Captain Ripley's actions.
5. The CAR-15 is a reduced-size M16 with a folding shoulder stock and short barrel. It was not standard-issue but was easily obtained at this time in-country. The 782 gear or LBE (load-bearing equipment as the Army refers to it) consisted of the web belt with ammo pouches, first aid kit, canteen and anything else a soldier could hang on it.

Chapter 21

1. Sandy was the nickname for the A-1 Skyraider aircraft used to support down pilot rescues and provide close-air support.
2. There appears to be a difference of opinion as to the actual crash and end of Blue Ghost 39. I have utilized the events as outlined in POW reports of the crash as I consider them to be an official document. The bodies of Lieutenant Byron Kulland, Specialist Ronald Paschall and Warrant Officer John Frink were identified on April 2, 1994. Specialist Jose Astorga was released from an NVA prison camp in 1973.
3. This Air Force policy had been in effect for most of the previous years but had little effect on ground operations as most were small-scale contacts with the enemy. The previous year in Lam Son 719, however, this same policy cost one firebase being overrun on the north side of QL9 when an Air Force aircraft was lost and all Air Force support went looking for the down crew.

Chapter 22

1. "Surrender at Camp Carroll," http://www.willpete.com/surrender_at_camp_carroll.htm.
2. Not everyone surrendered peacefully. A Vietnamese Marine artillery battery, 105mm, was present on Carroll supporting Mai Loc. When the North Vietnamese entered the main gate, the Vietnamese Marines lowered their tubes loaded with beehive rounds and fired point-blank into the enemy. All the Marines died at their guns. In addition, one battalion commander slipped out with his battalion of three hundred and escaped and evaded in order and discipline with their weapons to Dong Ha. By mid-April, about one thousand solders from Carroll had escaped and made it to safety.

Chapter 23

1. Gerald H. Turley, *The Easter Offensive: The Last American Advisors, Vietnam, 1972* (Annapolis: Naval Institute Press, 1985), 195.
2. Major DeBona indicated that, to the best of his knowledge, not one Vietnamese Marine was left behind. Turley, 199.

Chapter 25

1. Turley, 218.

Chapter 26

1. Turley, 218.
2. Turley, 223.

Chapter 28

1. OPCON stands for Operational Control. An OPCON unit takes orders/missions for one unit while logistical support and administrative actions remain with the parent unit.

Chapter 29

1. Turley, 234.
2. Navigate and Assassin were the call signs for the USS *Bausell* (DD-845) and the USS *Craig* (DD-885). Both were steaming off the coast and providing naval gun fire support.

Chapter 31

1. Vietnamese Marine battalions were moved between the three brigades frequently. The 7th Marine Battalion had been with the 147th Brigade during the retreat from Mai Loc and went to Hue for refit. It was then transferred to the 369th Brigade and then back to the 147th Brigade at Ai Tu.

Chapter 32

1. The Quang Tri River flows north of the city. West of QL1, it was known as the Thach Han River. East of QL1, it was known as the Quang Tri River.
2. Melson, 82.
3. Melson, 83.

Chapter 34

1. General Giai was arrested, tried and sentenced to five years in prison. He remained there until Saigon fell to the NVA in 1975. Many felt his arrest and trial were unjustified.
2. It was reported in one interview that there was an attempt by the NVA to capture one TOW jeep outside of Da Nang that was in a position to block any attempt by tanks. I was told that three Russian advisors were killed in this attempt. I could not corroborate this story.

Chapter 39

1. The UH-60 Blackhawk helicopter was selected to replace the UH-1H in 1976 and has the features outlined.

Chapter 42

1. A red team was one UH-1H aircraft serving as the command-and-control aircraft, two OH-6 observation helicopters in the scout role, and two AH-1G Cobra gunships providing cover for the scout aircraft.

Chapter 43

1. The next day, the wreckage of Blue Star Six was found in a rice paddy field. All indications were that an SA-7 missile had hit the aircraft and severed the tail boom. All aboard were pronounced KIA.

Chapter 45

1. The OV-10 Bronco served throughout the 1970s and 1980s. The Air Force felt the aircraft was too slow and vulnerable for the battlefield during Operation Desert Storm and therefore didn't deploy them. In

1991, the last squadron of OV-10s were deactivated. A specially equipped OV-10 with classified material on board was used by SOCOM against the Taliban and ISIS in Afghanistan.

2. Captain Mike Brown, USMC, ANGLICO, should not be confused with Major Joseph Brown, advisor.

3. Pilots were issued g-suits, which limited their chance of passing out in high-g maneuvers. The occasional rear-seat observers were not, and passing out was expected, but the observers were seldom told this, especially if it was a first-time ride.

4. Captain Stephen Bennett was posthumously awarded the Medal of Honor for his heroic actions. He knew full well that he could not eject from the crippled aircraft and leave Captain Brown behind. He chose instead to attempt to save them both, knowing that no one had ever survived a water landing in an OV-10.

Chapter 46

1. In World War II, Eisenhower's HQ went to the Vatican and sought permission to bomb Monte Cassino in Italy, which dominated the approach to Rome. Permission was granted. Today the US military avoids damaging religious sites, as has been demonstrated in the past thirty years, even at the expense of the safety of our own troops.

Chapter 47

1. "Ring knockers" is a derogatory reference to graduates of the service academies because of the larger rings they wear as a symbol of their graduation.

2. Melson, Charles D. and Curtis G. Arnold. *US Marines in Vietnam: The War That Would Not End, 1971–1973.* Washington, D.C.: History and Museum Division, Headquarters, US Marine Corps, 1991.

Chapter 48

1. Corporal Crody's words with his mom the last time they spoke. See "KIA Incident: 19720711 HMM-165 Vietnam." https://popasmoke.com/kia/conflicts/vietnam/incidents/19720711.

Chapter 53

1. To look at an aerial view of Quang Tri today, the area from the Citadel to the Vinh Dinh River and beyond is all urban. In 1972, the urban sprawl only extended one thousand meters from the Citadel, and only along Route 560.

Epilogue

1. The last official combat casualty killed in the Vietnam War died on 27 January 1973 at An Loc in MR-3. He was LTC William Nolde, US Army. He was killed by artillery fire eleven hours before the ceasefire went into affect.

ACKNOWLEDGMENTS

Writing any historical novel that attempts to put accuracy into the story requires research. Fortunately, there are still some around who lived through these days and were kind enough to put up with my endless stream of questions. General Walter Boomer, USMC, (Ret) provided some great insight into the fighting at Sarge and the retreat from Quang Tri. Colonel Mike Williams, USMC, then an Army warrant officer Cobra pilot, put me in touch with many of those that flew helicopters in that time frame. Major Anthony Shepard provided great details about Marine jargon that I would have missed completely as they were little facts that an Army grunt like me would not know. He also provided insights into the role of the ARVN Airborne units in this portion of the Easter Offensive, which I had found very little information about. To others that I interviewed, I thank you for providing me an hour or so of your life to discuss the events of those days: Roger Nelson, Don Manlove, Ken Mick, Neal Thompson, Steve Jackson, Tim Sprouse, Dwaine Shirley, Michael O'Byrne, Donnie Purvis, Jim Lowe, Charlie Zinger, Joel Eisenstein and Ron Holmes as well as Joe Swift. I thank you all and hope I told your story correctly.

I must thank the United States Marine Corps for their excellent recordkeeping of the events during the course of this action. The preservation of small-unit actions and individuals in documents such as *The War That Would Not End* is central to the preservation of history. The United States Marine Corps does it so well.

I would be remiss to not thank my editor, Ms. Eliza Dee of Clio Editing, for putting up with me, and Infidium.net for some of my maps. As always, give Momir Borocki an idea and within an hour he presents you with a great cover. Rukia Publishing US for formatting my attempts into a proper order. The one person that deserves a major thanks is my wife of fifty-two years, who has put up with my constant time on the computer.

Thank you, readers, for your support.

ABOUT THE AUTHOR
MATT JACKSON

The author enlisted in the US Army in 1968 and served on active duty until 1993, when he retired as a colonel. In the course of his career, he commanded two infantry companies, one being an airborne company in Alaska, and commanded an air assault infantry battalion during Operation Desert Shield/Storm. When not with troop assignments, he was generally found teaching tactics at the United States Army Infantry Center or the United States Army Command and General Staff College, with a follow-on assignment as an exchange instructor at the German Army Tactics Center. His last assignment was Director, Readiness and Mobilization, J-5, Forces Command, and Special Advisor, Vice President of the United States. Upon retiring from the US Army, he went into private business. He and his wife have been married for the past fifty-two years and have two sons, both Army officers.

Matt Jackson Books

Sign Up For Book Updates
https://frontlinepublishinginc.eo.page/mattjacksonbooks

ALSO BY MATT JACKSON

Undaunted Valor Series: Follow a young man from the time he joins the military in 1968 after two worthless years in college and watch his progression from a private to an accomplished combat instructor pilot over the course of two years. All events are true, and most of the characters are people he flew with.

Undaunted Valor, An Assault Helicopter Unit in Vietnam 1969-1970

Undaunted Valor, Medal of Honor

Undaunted Valor, Lam Son 1971

Crisis in the Desert Series (coauthored with James Rosone): How much different would Desert Shield and Storm have been if Saddam had carried his attack through Saudi Arabia and into the UAE? This series examines the difficulties and challenges that would have faced the allied forces if Saddam had carried the attack as well as received assistance from the crumbling Soviet Union at the time.

Project 19

Desert Shield

Desert Storm

Visit Matt Jackson's website: www.MattJacksonBooks.com

Contact: info@mattjacksonbooks.com

Sign Up For Book Updates Via Email

https://frontlinepublishinginc.eo.page/mattjacksonbooks

COPYRIGHT

ISBN-13: 978-1-960249-00-5
Printed in Ruskin, Florida, United States of America
Library of Congress Control Number: 2022915731

Made in the USA
Las Vegas, NV
12 July 2023

74628668R00302